A VILE JUSTICE

A young woman burst through the door. "Oh, Governor Djehuty!" she wailed. "It's terrible! Oh, sir!"

Bak leaped toward the young woman, confused by her words, her demeanor. Could another individual have been murdered? One that did not fit the patterns he had so carefully developed?

Amonhotep, a step ahead, caught her by the shoulders. "What is it, Nefer? What's happened?"

Tears flowed as if from a river and she began to tremble. "It's mistress Hatnofer," the girl sobbed. "She's dead. Her head smashed. So much blood! Oh, so much blood!"

Hatnofer? Bak thought. *Djehuty's housekeeper?* He spat out an oath, and another, and another. From what little the governor had said about the woman earlier in the day, she had been as important to him as were the five men standing before the dais. Yet he, Bak, had failed to think of her, to summon her, and now she lay dead. If her life had been taken while he stood here warning the others, he would blame himself through eternity.

"A wonderful new Egyptian historical
MLB News

"Serious fun!"
The Rue Morgue

Other Mysteries of Ancient Egypt by
Lauren Haney
from Avon Twilight

THE RIGHT HAND OF AMON
A FACE TURNED BACKWARD

LAUREN HANEY

A VILE JUSTICE

A MYSTERY OF ANCIENT EGYPT

AVON
TWILIGHT

This is a work of fiction. Names, characters, places, and incidents either are the product of the author's imagination or are used fictitiously. Any resemblance to actual events, locales, organizations, or persons, living or dead, is entirely coincidental and beyond the intent of either the author or the publisher.

AVON BOOKS, INC.
1350 Avenue of the Americas
New York, New York 10019

Copyright © 1999 by Betty J. Winkelman
Inside cover author photo by Stephen Tang
Published by arrangement with the author
Library of Congress Catalog Card Number: 99-94813
ISBN: 0-380-79265-6
www.avonbooks.com/twilight

First Avon Twilight Printing: October 1999

AVON TWILIGHT TRADEMARK REG. U.S. PAT. OFF. AND IN OTHER COUN-TRIES, MARCA REGISTRADA, HECHO EN U.S.A.

Printed in the U.S.A.

WCD   10   9   8   7   6   5   4   3   2   1

Acknowledgments

I wish to thank Dennis Forbes, editorial director of *KMT: A Modern Journal of Ancient Egypt*, for giving so generously of his time and knowledge. If I asked a question and he didn't know the answer, he knew where to find it. If I'd never trod the sands of a particular locale in the story, he had.

Thanks are also due to Tavo Serina, who read the finished manuscript with his usual critical eye and logical mind, and for his commonsense suggestions for improvement.

While writing this novel, I searched for information in an infinite number of books about ancient Egypt. Though the authors are too numerous to name, they all have a share in my gratitude.

CAST OF CHARACTERS

At the Fortress of Buhen

Lieutenant Bak	Egyptian officer in charge of a company of Medjay police
Sergeant Imsiba	Bak's second-in-command, a Medjay
Hori	Youthful police scribe
Commandant Thuty	Officer in charge of the garrison of Buhen
Troop Captain Nebwa	Thuty's second-in-command
Nofery	Proprietress of a house of pleasure in Buhen, serves as Bak's spy
Psuro and Kasaya	Medjay policemen
Suemnut, Neny, and Dadu	Men caught up in a minor drama in the Belly of Stones

At the city of Abu

Governor Djehuty	Governor of the southernmost province of Kemet, with his seat of power in the city of Abu
Lieutenant Amonhotep	Djehuty's aide
Troop Captain Antef	Head of the garrison at Abu
Amethu	Chief steward of the governor's villa and the province

Simut	Chief scribe of the governor's villa and the province
Ineni	Djehuty's son and manager of his estate at Nubt, north of Abu
Khawet	Djehuty's daughter and Ineni's wife
Nakht	A child, servant in the governor's villa, who meets with a most unfortunate accident
Montu	A guard at the governor's villa, an old soldier, another who has an unfortunate—and incredible—accident
Senmut	Sergeant of the governor's villa guard, whose death was definitely cold-blooded murder
Lieutenant Dedi	A young and green officer, the fourth to die; could his death possibly be an accident?
Hatnofer	Housekeeper of the governor's villa
Sergeant Min	A soldier posted long ago to a far-off fortress
Nebmose	Former owner of the villa next door; deceased
User	Once a spearman in the garrison, now a farmer on an island south of Abu
Kames and Nenu	Guards at the governor's villa
Pahared	An old acquaintance of Bak; a trader, whose wife runs a house of pleasure in the town of Swenet on the east bank of the river
Viceroy Inebny	Viceroy of Kush and Wawat

Plus various and sundry soldiers, guards, servants, and townspeople.

Those who walk the corridors of power in Kemet

Maatkare Hatshepsut	Sovereign of the land of Kemet
Menkheperre Thutmose	The queen's nephew and stepson; ostensibly shares the throne with his aunt

The Gods and Goddesses

Amon	The primary god during much of ancient Egyptian history, especially the early 18th Dynasty, the time of this story; takes the form of a human being
Horus of Buhen	A local version of the falcon god Horus
Maat	Goddess of truth and order; represented by a feather
Khnum	Guardian of the source of the Nile, thought to be near Abu at the first cataract; depicted with the head of a ram
Satet	Guardian of the southern frontier of Kemet, wife of Khnum
Anket	Goddess of the first cataract, daughter of Khnum
Hapi	Personification of the Nile
Osiris	God of the netherworld, depicted as a man swathed in bandages like a mummy
Re	The sun god
Khepre	The rising sun

Set   An ambivalent god generally
                  representing   violence,   a
                  mythical   creature   usually
                  shown with the body of a
                  man and a dog-like head

Apep   A serpent demon of the neth-
                  erworld, representing chaos
                  and evil

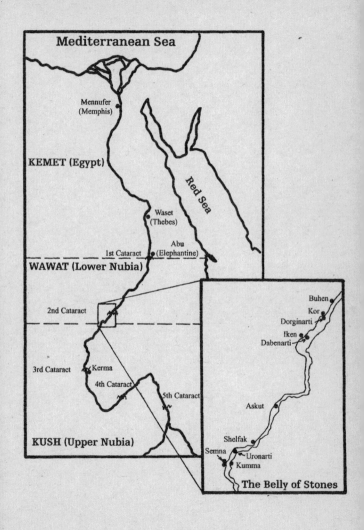

Chapter One

"I'll slay him!" The short, stocky ship's master, his face aflame with rage, glared at the tall, rangy villager standing before him. "I vow to the lord Hapi, I'll take his life with my bare hands!"

Hapi was the god who personified the river flowing below them, for much of its length broad and sedate, predictable. Here, however, its waters were split into a labyrinth of narrow, swift channels forcing their way around black granite boulders and islets, with just a few supporting sparse green growth.

The Medjay sergeant Imsiba took a firmer grip on the seaman's upper arm. Tall and sleek, with dark, glowing skin and the grace of a leopard, he towered over the man he held. "You'll take no man's life today, Captain Suemnut."

"He wrecked my ship!"

"Through no fault but his own, that I swear." The villager Neny, a man burned dusty brown by sun and wind, spouted the words with contempt.

Lieutenant Bak, Imsiba's commanding officer and head of the Medjay police at the fortress of Buhen, a two-hour trek downstream to the north, scowled at the pair. Buhen, the largest of eleven fortresses along this rugged and desolate segment of the river called the Belly of Stones, served as administrative headquarters for the area. Thus, his involvement in their squabble.

Their enmity was long-standing, he had been told, a sore

1

that festered each time Suemnut had his ship hauled upstream through the rapids or eased back down on his homebound journey. Unfortunate, since each needed the other in equal measure. This stretch of rapids could be navigated only when the river was swollen and only with the help of the local men, who, using stout ropes, pulled the ships upstream or guided their passage downstream. Neny was the most influential and skilled headman in the area, able to collect sufficient men from neighboring villages and use his vast knowledge of the rapids to see a ship safely through the rocks. The land on which his and the other villages stood was the most barren along the Belly of Stones, and without the products merchants such as Suemnut exchanged for their aid, the people would have starved.

Certain he would get nothing useful from either man, nothing uncolored by anger and dislike, Bak walked a dozen or so paces to the end of the sandswept promontory on which they stood. The lord Re, well on his way to the western horizon and his descent into the netherworld, glowed bright yellow in a pallid sky. Bak's shadow was elongated, the head and shoulders falling over the edge of the low cliff. A stiff, north breeze dried the sweat on his broad, deeply tanned chest, ruffled his short-cropped dark hair, lifted the hem of his thigh-length white kilt. He licked his lips, tasting salt, and waved off a fly buzzing so close to his head he could hear its song above the roar of the rapids at the base of the promontory. The distant honking of geese drew his eyes downriver, where a flock was settling into a reedy backwater, a safe haven for the coming night.

Beyond the broad stretch of rapids, the brownish, frothing water rushed down a narrow, steeply sloping channel clutched between a multitude of black granite crags, bleak and bare, glistening wet. Other than the swiftness of the flow, the passage looked as safe as a stone-paved street leading to the mansion of a god. Its appearance was deceiving. Obstacles lay beneath the surface, concealed by silt and froth: rocks and falls and eddies that could send a ship careening to certain destruction against the boulders. Unless its journey was controlled by men, men like those standing or kneeling on the boulders and islets at either side of the channel.

What, then, had happened to the vessel lying broken and helpless near the lower end of the passage? The modest traveling ship, roughly sixty paces long, lay smashed against a cluster of three craggy boulders rising at the near side of the channel. Water surged through an impressive hole torn in the vessel's hull. The deck tilted at an impossible angle, yet a surprising amount of cargo remained on board. Bundled cowhides lashed in place, soaked by the turbulent waters. What had gone wrong? Bak found it difficult to believe Neny would deliberately destroy a ship, even a vessel belonging to a man he hated. Other ships' masters would be sure to retaliate, finding a headman who pleased them more, leaving Neny's village to starve.

His eyes raked the rocky outcrops and islets along the channel, where fifty or more nearly naked villagers idled away the hours, awaiting Neny's signal to set to work. Coils of thick rope lay on the rocks at their feet. Other ropes, lifelines attached to the broken vessel, were wound around boulders or heavy poles jammed into crevices, holding the ship in place until the men could swim out and salvage the cargo.

"My beautiful ship," Suemnut wailed, coming up behind Bak. "Why, oh, why did I wait so long to sail north? Why didn't I sail at the highest flood stage, as I should've?"

Bak looked at a man truly distraught. "You were on board when your vessel broke loose?"

The captain nodded. "Only the gods kept me from drowning. Me and my crew."

"Tell me what happened."

"I was standing on deck, as always, but with the fate of my vessel in other men's hands. I don't like Neny, but never once have I had reason to doubt his skill, nor did I this time. I was watching his men laboring to pass us down the channel, taking care not to tangle the ropes. They were working in teams, singing. All seemed well. And then something . . ." He shook his head, as if denying a fact impossible to refute.

Bak bit back the urge to prompt, preferring the seaman tell the tale at his own pace and in his own way.

Suemnut frowned, swallowed hard. "I . . . I don't know what happened. A noise, I remember, and a rope whipped across the deck. Men went flying overboard, and the brazier and a cage of ducks. The cage broke apart, I recall, and birds flew in every direction." A distracted smile touched his lips and fled. "As you can see, the ship was laden with hides, bundles and bundles of them, all securely tied on deck. The rope struck those at the stern. I felt a mighty jerk and suddenly we rammed into the boulders. The vessel shuddered and I heard the moaning and snapping of wood. The next thing I knew, we were swimming for our lives."

"Where'd the rope come from?" Imsiba asked.

"Our hawsers were stowed securely on deck. It had to be one used for the tow." Suemnut glowered at the headman; his tone grew accusatory. "I can't say how it came aboard my ship, but Neny was standing on a boulder close by, shouting orders."

"I'd wager your ballast shifted, Captain." Neny spat out the title as he would a sour fruit.

Bak studied the wreck and the men positioned along the channel to hold the ship in place, their ropes rigid with tension. He had a good idea what had happened. An experienced captain like Suemnut probably did, too, and surely Neny did. But both had closed their hearts to the truth, preferring instead to fan the fire of enmity. He glanced at Imsiba, who nodded agreement. They had no need to air the thought; they had been friends too long.

Bak stared again at the torn and broken ship, squinting to temper the glare on the water. A vessel no different from most traveling ships, it had an enclosed deckhouse painted in a black, white, and green chevron pattern; an open forecastle and aftercastle; a long rudder hanging from the stern of a hull weathered a deep, rich brown; and an intertwined green and white lotus design painted on its high prow. A good, reliable ship, it must have been, but no longer.

"I must go to the wreck and see it for myself," he said.

Neny gave him a doubtful look. "You would risk at best a good dunking, at worst your life?"

Bak's mouth hardened. "I see fifty or more men occupying the boulders on both sides of the channel. Has not each and every man taken a dunking this day?"

"Most have, yes, but . . ."

"Do you think me any less a swimmer than they are?"

"They know the river well—and its hazards."

Bak scowled. "Call one of your men and tell him to guide me across the rocks to the ship. I'll also need a stout lightweight rope."

Neny's eyes flashed resentment at so peremptory a tone, but he bowed his head in acquiescence.

Bak's wait was brief. The young man summoned, fourteen or so years of age, was slim as a reed and seemed always to wear a shy grin. Neny spoke to him in a dialect Bak could not understand, but Imsiba tilted his head, listening closely to words he had known as a child. In the end, he seemed satisfied with the headman's instructions.

Setting off, Bak carried the rope coiled around his left shoulder and the youth, an inflated goatskin used by local people to provide buoyancy in the water. Rather than work their way across the chaos of cracked and broken rock at the base of the promontory, they took a roundabout but less treacherous route, walking ankle-deep through windblown sand, leaping from rock to rock across a swift channel, wading through knee-high weeds and hip-deep water. Beyond a row of islets, craggy and barren of life, flowed the channel through which the ships were pulled. A well-beaten path requiring a modest amount of wading carried them north along the open stretch of swift-flowing water. Bak merely nodded to the men he and the boy passed, certain they would reveal nothing until he had seen the wreck for himself and could question them with the authority of knowledge.

They halted on a high mound of weathered rock adorned with a single tamarisk and dotted with tough, spiky grass. The islet lay slightly upstream, overlooking the wrecked ship. A pole made shiny by the slippage of ropes was wedged between two boulders. The islet was unoccupied, the pole bare of rope. Directly across the channel, a villager sat on his haunches, raising something to his mouth—dates most likely—and chewing with vigor. Close beside him, a taut rope was wrapped several times around a boulder, its far end attached securely to the wreck.

Bak studied the mound on which he stood and the bare pole. "This looks to be a critical place from which to ease a ship down the channel. Why is it not manned?"

The boy shrugged. "Dadu was here. He swam out to the ship with a rope, which he'd made fast to this pole. When last I saw him, he'd come back and was waiting for his team to come help. Then the ship wrecked, and I never thought to look again. Where he's gone now, I don't know."

Bak scanned the channel, the men perched on the rocks overlooking the narrow chute of water, and the calm and safe cove not fifteen paces downstream of the wreck. "Where was Neny when the ship struck the rocks?"

"There."

The youth pointed upstream toward a tall granite monolith rising above the surrounding landscape, an ideal place from which to watch the activity all along the channel and to issue orders. A flatter rock beside the monolith was occupied by a balding man who had snugged his rope around a protruding mass of stone. The far end of the rope was attached to the ship.

Resting his backside against the pole, Bak stared across a short span of swift, tumultuous water, a dozen paces at most, toward the broken ship. The vessel looked no different at so close a distance than from afar. Rather like a lamb savaged by a jackal. Too badly injured to save.

He focused on the cargo, a hundred or more bundles, probably a thousand cowhides total, lashed to the deck in front of the deckhouse and behind it. Those washed by the river were well soaked, but he assumed they could be recovered and dried with no loss in value. No wonder Neny's men were staying close. To salvage so much would earn them ample reward.

Chiding himself for wasting the last precious moments of daylight, Bak knelt beside the water and looked out at the foaming surface. If he were to learn the truth, he must enter the river. He shuddered at the thought. In the not too distant past, he had come close to drowning; now he feared the rapids mightily.

The boy voiced no objection, but watched with dismay as Bak looped one end of the rope around the pole and carried the remainder of the coil to the water's edge. Trying not to see his own fears mirrored in the youth's face, he shouldered the rope and stepped into the river. Taking a deep breath, shutting down the dread, he dove beneath the surface.

Swimming against the current's tug, he examined in light filtered by silt-laden water the liquid world around him. The rock lining the bottom was an extension of the mound he had just left, a tumble of rough, broken boulders that reached out toward the open channel. During low water, they and the boulders on which the ship lay would form a single barren island. A school of fingerlings—carp, Bak thought—swam among the naked limbs of a drowned bush. He imagined he could taste the fish, the silt, the mustiness of the ages.

Spotting a taller outcrop at what he judged to be midway between him and the wrecked ship, he rose to the surface for air and swam toward the projection. The current pulled at him, trying to carry him downriver. The rope got in his way, hampering the use of his left arm and at the same time breaking his speed as he slowly played it out. Nearing the outcrop, which reached to within a hand's length of the water's surface but was hidden beneath the foam, he lunged toward it.

Without warning, an arm broke the surface. A hand beckoned.

He jerked away, so startled he sucked in water. The current caught him, tore him from the outcrop, and carried him downstream. Froth warned of a maelstrom ahead and he came close to panic. The rope pulled him up short.

Swimming with all his strength, trying not to cough, he regained the outcrop, held on tight, and surfaced for air. The hand—if he had indeed seen a hand—had vanished. He coughed water and at the same time tried to give the boy a reassuring smile. When his breath came easily again, he worked his way around and down the outcrop, taking care not to cut himself on knife-sharp edges of splintered rock. On the far side, he found the hand. And more.

The body of a man, pale in death, wide-eyed with fear, bobbed up and down in the current. A stout rope, snarled and tangled in a crevice, was wound around his legs, holding him underwater. Bak noted the rope's frayed end and a long burn-like injury down the man's right thigh and leg where he had been dragged across the rocks. This, he thought, must be Dadu. The tale he read was clear, but only half a story. To find the rest, he must swim out to the wreck. Sensing the passage of time, he resurfaced, took in air, glanced at the sky. The sun would soon disappear, leaving Wawat in darkness. He must leave Dadu submerged and hurry on.

He swam straight to the wrecked ship, noting as he did the taut ropes rising from the broken vessel to the islets lining the channel, holding the wreck in place. The three boulders on which the ship lay were cracked and pitted, weathered by time. Diving down, he saw the rough-cut sandstone blocks used for ballast spilling around the boulders from the ragged hole in the hull. A school of tiny fish swarmed around the hides. A large perch swam among them, feasting on his smaller brethren, sending them darting in all directions. The frayed end of a thick rope waved from among the blocks, the same rope, he felt sure, as the one around Dadu's legs.

Surfacing for air, he swam around the cargo to the rudder. The hides looked secure on the steeply sloping deck, but for how long? He played out the rope he carried around his shoulder and tied the end to the aftercastle, forming a bridge of sorts between the ship and the islet on which the boy sat. A trio of crows scolded him from the surrounding boulders.

He flung a rock their way, sending them squawking into the air, and dove again. In moments, he found attached to the hull the heavy rope he assumed Dadu had carried out to the ship before his death. Rather than rising toward the islet

where the boy stood—as it should have—it curved around
the trio of boulders and back toward the ship to disappear in
the pile of hides. By prodding and poking, he traced its path
through the cargo and back into the water, where all but the
frayed end had been entombed beneath the sandstone blocks.
It looked, he thought, as if a mighty being, a god perhaps,
had torn the rope free and flung it, sending it around the
boulders and in among the hides, dooming the ship.

Bak stood with Imsiba, Suemnut, and Neny on the promontory. The sky was afire with color. The breeze had waned,
allowing the soft evening sunlight to draw the chill from his
bones and dry his kilt and loincloth. Swallows flitted through
the air, catching on the wing insects invisible to the human
eye. The smell of braised onions drifted in the air from a
village nestled among the rocks farther downstream.

In the narrow channel where the wreck lay, a dozen men
were cutting the bundled hides free and letting them fall into
the water. Others were towing the bundles to the rope Bak
had tied to the aftercastle, while a third team attached them
to the line and pushed them across the current to the islet.
Still more men were mounding the salvaged hides well out
of reach of the water, where they would remain for the night.
The work was frenzied, a race against the dark.

"You can't see from here . . ." Bak pointed toward the
river. ". . . but the rocky outcrop where I found Dadu's body
has edges sharper than a flint knife." He raised his hand,
showing a cut he had not realized he had until he left the
water. "It cut partway through the rope and the weight of
the vessel did the rest, snapping it apart."

"So the wreck was an accident," Imsiba said, looking
pointedly at Suemnut.

The captain sniffed. "That a sharp-edged rock might cut
one rope, I can understand, but what of the other ropes that
were supposed to hold my ship in place? Secured on every
side, how could it slew around the way it did, striking the
boulders?"

"We've knocked the edges off that outcrop—and others

like it—more than once," Neny said, his voice defensive.

"The rope was under tension, stretched to the limit," Bak said. "When it snapped, the upper portion snaked back. It jerked free of the post, wrapped around Dadu's legs, and dragged him across the rocks into the river. It then became entangled in a crack in a boulder. He either struck his head and lost his senses or panicked. Either way, he drowned."

"What of my ship?" Suemnut demanded.

Neny glared. "Do you care nothing for the man who died? A husband and a father many times over? A hard-working man of honor and integrity?"

Bak longed to grab them both by the neck and knock their heads together. He had hoped that by finding an innocent reason for the wreck he might put an end to their enmity. Unfortunately, they enjoyed their mutual dislike too much.

"The lower portion of the rope whipped back toward the ship. It wrapped around the boulders, flew across the deck—knocking men, brazier, and duck cage into the water—and buried a good, long segment in the bundled hides, pulling the ship up short and jerking it against the rocks."

"Look!" Imsiba shouted, pointing at the wreck.

The ship, relieved of much of its load and with most of its ballast scattered on the riverbed, had floated free of the boulders. It began to swing across the channel.

"Cut it loose!" Neny yelled. His voice, deep and dark, carried through the still air, reaching the men lining the channel.

"No!" Suemnut wailed. "My ship! My life! No!"

The men slashing the ropes holding the few remaining hides on deck abandoned their task, dropped into the water, and swam at high speed alongside the vessel. Bollards were jerked free, releasing the stout lines holding the ship in the channel. Where the bollards could not be reached, the ropes, too valuable to lose, were axed as close to the hull as possible.

The ship floated downstream, ponderous with the weight of the water it had taken on. Bak feared it would swing farther around, blocking the channel and putting an end to travel down the Belly of Stones, at least for the remainder of the year. But Neny knew what he was doing. The vessel held its course—floundering, to be sure—until a final steep slope of bubbling water carried it into the cove. Becalmed, the stern dropped ever deeper and the prow reared skyward, raising high the intertwined lily design. The men on the promontory held their breath, waiting. The vessel tilted backward, expelling air, and slid beneath the water's surface.

"Sir!" The police scribe Hori raced along the stone quay, his eyes locked on Bak and Imsiba, whose skiff was closing on a mooring post. "The commandant wishes to see you, sir! Right away!"

Bak muttered an oath. "Can I not change into clean clothing?"

"I wouldn't, sir." The chubby youth caught the rope Imsiba threw, made a loop, and settled it around the post. "A sentry reported seeing your skiff from afar. The commandant's expecting you."

"You'd best go, my friend," Imsiba said, with a good-humored smile. "I'll tend to the skiff and that morning meal we thought to share."

Bak rolled his eyes skyward and grimaced. "What Commandant Thuty wants, Commandant Thuty gets."

"He has another man with him, sir, a lieutenant from Abu." Hori's expression remained serious. "And Troop Captain Nebwa as well."

"An officer from the land of Kemet?" Bak frowned. "An inspector, do you think?"

"He looks to be a man with a weight on his shoulders. One seeking aid, not trouble."

With a farewell nod to Imsiba, Bak walked with the boy up the central of three quays, passing a traveling ship similar to that of Suemnut and a broad-beamed cargo ship riding high in the water, its shallow hull rolling on the gentle swells. A sailor bent over its rail to spit in the water. Another hunkered down beside a brazier, stirring the contents of a bowl nestled among the coals. The odor of onions and fish set Bak's stomach to growling.

Moored at the southern quay, he saw a long and slender traveling ship, built for speed and pleasure rather than to ply the waters laden with merchandise as so many ships did in Wawat. A red-and-white-checked deckhouse and fore- and aftercastles surrounded by delicate railings of papyrus-shaped posts belied a sturdy frame and construction. The prow carried the ram-headed image of the lord Khnum, the god favored by the residents of Abu. Bak was impressed. The officer now speaking with Commandant Thuty had arrived in style.

Ahead, the tall mudbrick walls of Buhen rose stark white in the early morning sun. Towers projecting from the face of the riverside wall rose to the crenelated battlements from two stone terraces lining the water's edge. A sentry stood at the base of the twin-towered gate they approached, passing the time with three small boys. A similar gate to the north was busier. A long line of men trudged down the quay, carrying heavy copper ingots from a warehouse inside the fortress to a ship bound for the land of Kemet. They sang a workman's song, out of tune and of scant musical merit, but if volume was any indication, the words were heart-felt. An elderly, wizened priest, his head shaved bald, sat at the base of the southernmost pylon gate. He sat there often, warming himself in the sun after performing the morning ablutions in the dark chill of the mansion of the local god, Horus of Buhen. Bak saluted the soldier, ruffled the hair of one of the boys, and waved to the priest.

He stepped into the dark passage through the gate, and a cool tingle crept up his spine. An omen, he thought, maybe the lord Amon himself warning him to proceed with care. He laughed out loud, driving the thought away, and the chill.

The sentry in the entry hall of the commandant's residence pointed Bak toward a flight of stone stairs leading to the second floor. Bounding up the steps two at a time, he burst into the warm, sunny courtyard. The space was cluttered with

toys, water jars, loom, grindstone, and a deep basin filled
with natron. In the white, salty substance, Thuty's eldest son,
a boy of ten years, was dessicating a dog that had been his
constant companion until its death of old age. The odor of
decay had waned, Bak was glad to note, so the child would
soon be able to wrap for eternity the creature he had loved.

He paused at the door of the commandant's private reception room, where three men sat waiting, no one speaking, as
if all they had to say had already been said. The commandant
sat in his armchair, a stemmed drinking bowl in his hand,
beside a small table laden with bread, beer, cold roast pigeon,
and dates. He spotted Bak and beckoned. Troop Captain
Nebwa, seated on a low three-legged stool in his favored spot
off to the side, glanced toward Bak and nodded. The third
man, a stranger to Buhen, occupied a stool in front of the
commandant. He, too, turned around to look.

"You summoned me, sir?" Bak asked.

"Lieutenant." Thuty raked Bak with his eyes, taking in
his dirt- and sweat-stained kilt, bandaged hand, and assorted
bruises and abrasions. If he was troubled by such an untidy
appearance, he gave no sign. "Have you eaten?" he asked,
motioning toward the food on the table.

"At daybreak in Neny's village." Bak eyed the fare. A
bowl filled with the tiny bones of birds told him the other
men had already consumed their morning meal. "Nothing so
grand, believe me."

"Draw a stool close." Thuty was a short, broad man
whose powerful muscles glistened with the oil he had rubbed
onto his ruddy skin. His brows were heavy, his mouth firm,
his jaw set. A fire burned behind his dark eyes, reflecting the
strength of purpose that had earned him his lofty position.

As Bak selected a pigeon from the bowl and tore a wing
from the body, Thuty nodded toward the stranger. "This man
you see before you is Lieutenant Amonhotep. He's come
from Abu, sent by Djehuty, governor of our southernmost
province in Kemet. He's Djehuty's aide, his right hand."

Savoring the bird, which was braised to perfection, Bak
studied the officer. Amonhotep, a few years younger than

Bak, who had reached twenty-five years, was of medium height and slender, with reddish curly hair and green eyes in a thin, serious face. His frame was slight, but well padded with muscle. His brow was lined with worry.

"I've heard much about you, Lieutenant." Amonhotep gave so brief a smile Bak almost missed it. "The vizier, who's an old friend of Djehuty, praised you highly when he passed through Abu last week."

Bak's eyes darted toward Thuty, seeking an explanation, and on to Nebwa. That the vizier, who had recently toured the fortresses of Wawat, had stopped at Abu on his return voyage to the capital was no surprise, but that a man in so grand a position would speak of a mere lieutenant in charge of the Medjay police at Buhen was astonishing.

"Didn't I tell you the great man would spout your praise?" Nebwa gave his friend a lopsided grin, far short of the generous smile that normally accompanied his teasing. "In no time at all, your fame as a man who stalks human predators will spread throughout the land of Kemet."

The troop captain, next after Thuty in the line of command, was a coarse-featured, untidy man, tall and muscular, thirty years of age. His belt was twisted, bunching his kilt up on one side. His broad, multicolored bead collar had worked its way around so the falcon-headed clasp lay on his left shoulder. His stingy smile, his failure to continue his needling, indicated a distinct lack of enthusiasm for whatever had brought Amonhotep from Abu.

Thuty remained mute, strangely hesitant to explain the officer's mission.

Bak, curious, suspicious, wary of the two officers' reluctance to speak up, dropped a thigh bone into the dish, licked the oil from his fingers, and asked, "You summoned me for a purpose, sir?"

Thuty's eyes slewed toward the officer from Abu. "The tale is best told by one who knows firsthand what happened."

"How should I begin?" Amonhotep ran his fingers through his reddish curls. "Three members of Djehuty's

household have met with an unfortunate death in a single
month, one in the river near the governor's villa, the others
within the compound in which the house stands. The first
two seemed unlikely accidents, but we accepted them as
such. Who wants to believe anything more abhorrent? The
third was murder without question, a man found dead with
a dagger in his breast. To Djehuty's way of thinking—and
mine—that final death makes the first two suspect.''

He stared at Bak as if expecting agreement. Bak let nothing show on his face. He had too few facts to reach any kind
of conclusion.

''The last killing occurred one day before the vizier arrived,'' Amonhotep continued. ''Djehuty, naturally upset by
so recent a death, told the vizier of it and the other two. That
worthy official was as disturbed by the tale as are all of us
who reside in the villa.'' He paused, shook his head as if to
rid himself of a bad dream. ''The vizier thought of you,
Lieutenant Bak. He told Djehuty how clever you are at laying
hands on men who turn their backs on the lady Maat. He
suggested we seek your help.''

How clever I am? Bak thought. Suddenly he understood
the young officer's mission, and his heart sank. The tale was
intriguing, the puzzle it posed a challenge. But only if he
journeyed to Abu could he hope to identify the slayer—and
placate the lady Maat, the goddess of right and order.

''Djehuty is a proud man,'' Amonhotep said, ''one accustomed to depending on his own resources. Yet how could he
turn his back on the suggestion? Without help, we can do
nothing. We've no one to point to, not a shred of proof that
all three lives were taken at the hands of a slayer. So Djehuty
agreed. He ordered his traveling ship provisioned for a voyage, and the day the vizier sailed north to the capital, I sailed
south to Buhen. Now here I am after eight long days on the
river, pleading my case to your garrison officers.'' He leaned
toward Bak; his voice grew hoarse with emotion. ''And to
you. Will you, Lieutenant Bak, return with me to Abu?''

Bak stared at the officer, his thoughts racing. He liked
nothing better than to follow the path of a slayer, searching

out tracks often hidden by time and cunning, closing in on the one he chased, and snaring him. He had done so several times in Buhen, and he had gladly traveled south to the fortress of Iken to investigate the death of an officer. Unlike Iken, which fell within Thuty's command, Abu was a world away, the domain of another man, Djehuty, who had summoned him. Would he be free to move as he liked or would his hands be tied by authority? Would he get help from the garrison should he need it, or would he be forced to stand alone? Would those he spoke with be bound to answer his questions or would they laugh in his face and turn their backs to him?

More important by far: would he be free to return to Buhen after laying hands on the slayer? Would he, could he, lay hands on the one he sought?

He glanced at the commandant, but before he could sort out his questions, his doubts, Thuty stood up, walked to the door, and stared out at the courtyard. After a long silence, he swung around. "This, I feel, is a matter best discussed in private, Lieutenant Amonhotep. Leave us."

"Yes, sir."

Thuty stepped away from the door to let him pass. "I'll summon you within the hour with my answer."

As the young officer's footsteps faded away on the stairs, Bak opened his mouth to speak.

Thuty raised his hand to silence him. "As you well know, Lieutenant, the vizier is not a man to accept refusal. You must go to Abu."

"But, sir . . ."

Thuty slumped into his chair. "I enjoy my rank as commandant and the authority I hold here in Buhen and along the Belly of Stones. I dream some day of rising to the rank of general and standing at the head of a regiment." He picked up his drinking bowl, stared into its depths, set it down again. "Not only might that dream vanish if we ignore the vizier's wishes, but I might well be posted to Kush or Hatti or some other faroff and disagreeable land. It goes without saying that you'll walk beside me, wherever I go. Shall we take the risk?''

"No, sir." Given no other rational choice, what else could Bak say? "All I ask of you is a promise."

Thuty's eyes narrowed. "What might that be?"

"While in Abu, I wish to remain under your command."

Nebwa gave Bak a quick nod of approval, lowered his gaze and, suppressing a smile, stared hard at his outstretched feet. He had guessed Bak's purpose and applauded it.

Thuty, taking care not to look at Nebwa, pursed his mouth in sham disapproval, though his pleasure was evident. "Your reasons, Lieutenant?"

"First, it will set me apart from others within the governor's household, allowing me to remain a free agent. Second, if I should fail in my mission or pose a threat to one who walks the corridors of power, neither Djehuty nor anyone else in Abu will have the authority to punish me for something beyond my control. Finally, I wish to return to Buhen and my Medjays when the task is completed."

Thuty planted his elbows on the arms of his chair and eyed Bak over entwined fingers, stretching the silence as if mulling over the idea. "I see no reason why I can't loan you to Djehuty for a few weeks. Let me summon a scribe and bind you in writing to my command."

Bak, seated on a mudbrick bench, stretched out his legs and leaned back against the white-plastered wall, savoring his last few hours in Buhen. The courtyard was sunny and warm, unusually quiet for so late in the morning, with no customers patronizing Nofery's house of pleasure.

The sound of a broom moving briskly across the floor could be heard in the front, most public room in the house, while a soft snore came through a portal to the rear, where the younger women slept.

"You leave tomorrow?" The query came from a third open door, from which the smell of roast goose drifted. Beneath a lean-to, which shaded half the court, a young lion cub lay sprawled, licking its paws and cleaning its face. Its ears pricked at the sound of its mistress's voice, but it never paused in its ablutions.

"At first light." Bak's eyes began to twinkle. "Too early, I fear, to bid you goodbye—unless you'd prefer I awaken you."

Nofery came out the door, scowling. "The very thought is abhorrent."

Mice scurried unafraid through the straw and the palm-frond roof over the obese old woman's head, competing with sparrows for seeds and nest materials. She transferred her scowl to the movement on the roof, then glanced critically at the lion. Her eyes soon darted around, and she spotted a stool, which she dragged close to Bak. She plopped down, her heavy legs and ample buttocks making the stool almost disappear.

"It pains me deeply to admit it, Bak, but I fear I'll miss you. All the beer you consume, the humor you so often exercise at my expense, the use you make of my knowledge and friendships, the . . ."

Bak reached forward and pinched her fleshy cheek. "Be silent, old woman. Tears will flow from my eyes if you go on with your confession of fondness."

She slapped his hand away. "Fondness, indeed! It's the demands you make that I'll miss. Like I'd miss a toothache."

"How would you ever manage without me?"

"None too well, I'd guess." Nebwa sauntered in from the front room, holding in each hand two pottery beer jars, their plugs already broken away. "If you hadn't made her your spy when first you came to Buhen, she'd still be eking out a living in that hovel in the outer city."

Nofery lifted her head high and sniffed. "Will you never learn tact, Troop Captain? I've no regrets about days gone by, nor do I wish to relive that life in words."

Chuckling, he sat on the floor beside her and handed her a jar of beer. "Drink, my little dove. Drown your sour disposition in the finest brew in Buhen."

Imsiba followed Nebwa into the court, carrying a small basket lined with leaves. "If the beer won't cheer her, per-

haps this gift sent by Sitamon will put a smile on her face.''
Sitamon was Imsiba's beloved, an attractive young woman
he planned soon to take for his wife.

He handed the basket to Nofery and joined Nebwa on the
floor. She folded back the leaves to reveal a dozen or more
small cakes made of crushed dates and nuts, dripping with
honey. Her eyes locked onto them, and she licked her lips.
They were her favorite delicacy, a fact Sitamon knew well.

"So . . ." Nebwa demanded, winking at Bak, ". . . are you
going to eat them all yourself or will you share a few?"

Flashing him a contemptuous look, she handed the basket
over. He took a sweet and passed it on. Bak and Imsiba
refused the offer. Sitamon had meant them for Nofery, and
she should have them.

She helped herself and took a bite, delighting in the taste
and texture. "Would that I could go to Abu, too," she said,
her voice tinged with yearning.

Bak gave her a surprised look. "How many times have
you told me you prefer Buhen to any other place?"

"Can I not sometimes feel a longing for my homeland?"
She frowned, as if unable to believe he could be so obtuse.
"Can I not dream sometimes of returning to a valley of broad
green fields and prosperous villages and cities where men
and women walk the streets clad in fine linen and exquisite
jewelry?"

Bak knew she had long ago been a courtesan in the capital,
a creature of beauty who had lain with the most lofty men
in the land. She seldom mourned the past, but now and again
memories lay heavy within her breast. He asked, "Have you
ever heard of Djehuty, sired in Abu and now governor of the
southernmost province of Kemet?"

Distracted by the question and pleased he had consulted
her, she licked the honey from her fingers. "Djehuty.
Hmmmm." Absentmindedly, she reached for another sweet.
"Yes, son of a nobleman. One who also served as governor
of the province, as did his father before him. And his father's
father, so I heard." She took a bite, chewed. "Djehuty, sent
as a boy to the capital to rub shoulders with the royal chil-

dren. An only son, I seem to remember, spoiled by his mother and father alike. A stubborn youth, who did as he wished, heeding no one's advice, ofttimes taking upon himself authority too great for his age or abilities.''

Nebwa snorted. ''Sounds a true son of the nobility. I hope for your sake, Bak, he's outgrown such childish, headstrong behavior.''

''I'll find out soon enough. We sail at first light tomorrow, and if the gods smile on us, we'll arrive in Abu nine or ten days hence.''

Imsiba eyed him across the top of the beer jar. ''Would that I could go with you, my friend.''

''And I, too,'' Nebwa said, raising his jar to Bak. ''No slayer alive could hide his guilt for long with the three of us . . .'' He glanced at Nofery, read the hurt on her face at being left out, smiled. ''. . . and Nofery hot on his trail.''

Bak shook his head at what he knew was impossible. ''Kasaya and Psuro will go with me. With no rank to get in their way, they can ask questions of all those men and women who might answer me with silence, thinking me a threat to their masters. Besides, I trust both with my life, and so should you.''

Nebwa's eyes darted Bak's way. ''You don't think it'll come to that, do you?''

''I don't know.'' Bak gave him a rueful smile. ''Amonhotep has added nothing to what he told us in the commandant's presence. Djehuty, he claims, has tied his hands, saying he prefers to tell me the tale himself, filling in the details. The reason, Amonhotep refuses to give.''

''How can he blind you to the facts?'' Imsiba asked, indignant.

Nebwa gave the big Medjay a long, thoughtful look. ''I think we must find an excuse to follow Bak to Abu. To walk with a friend along a familiar sunlit street is one thing; to walk alone with strangers down a dark and unknown path is foolhardy.''

Chapter Two

Bak crossed the gangplank and stepped onto the landing-place, a natural stone shelf flattened to suit the needs of man. With Lieutenant Amonhotep in the lead, he traversed the smoothed surface in a half dozen steps and climbed a long flight of stairs cut into the natural stone of the island of Abu. At the top, he turned to look down upon the sleek traveling ship that had carried them north. The long stretch of rapids just upstream of Abu had proven no obstacle to the agile craft. Instead of men letting the vessel down through the rocky channels with ropes, as was necessary in many parts of the Belly of Stones, a pilot had come aboard to sail it among the many small islands and down swift and foaming passageways that, though less hazardous than those near Buhen, were still dangerous.

Bak waved at the two Medjays standing on deck amidst the baskets and bundles of supplies and weapons they had brought from Buhen. Psuro, a man of good sense and courage, close to thirty years of age, was thickset in build, with a face scarred by some childhood disease. The younger of the pair, Kasaya, was the biggest and strongest man in Bak's unit, not greatly gifted with intelligence, but good-natured and likable. They would stay on board until Bak obtained suitable quarters for the three of them.

The journey from Buhen had been pleasant, a lazy time of fishing from the deck, swimming, eating, and sleeping. He and Amonhotep had talked about everything but what lay

21

uppermost in their thoughts: the death of three people in the governor's household. He could not imagine why Djehuty had silenced the young aide. It made no sense.

Curiosity had nagged him throughout the voyage, but now that the time had come to learn exactly what he faced, he hesitated to walk into the villa. Taking a deep breath, shoving aside his apprehension, he strode toward the arched gateway built into a long bare wall, behind which tall palms waved in the breeze and leaves rustled on sycamores and acacias and several other varieties of tree. Very little of the house, which was located near the center of the walled compound, could be seen from where he stood. A second story, much smaller than the first, perched atop the rear rooms. A donkey brayed somewhere in the distance, and two yellow curs snarled at each other across a dirt-encrusted bone. The odors of roasting meat and baking bread wafted through the gate, a siren's bounty beckoning him inside.

"I've nothing to fear." Djehuty stared at Bak, daring him to argue the point. "Why should I? The first two who died were peasants, people I doubt I'd have recognized if I met them on a lane outside these walls. The third was a soldier I respected, admired in many ways, but not a man I invited into my private rooms."

Bak offered a silent prayer of thanks to the lord Amon for the scroll he held in his hand, and another to Commandant Thuty for preparing it. From what little he had seen so far of Governor Djehuty, he would need it. The man thought of no one but himself.

"Sir, as a result of your summons, I've spent nine long days journeying north from Buhen. I've been told three men of this household have died, yet I've been given no details. I know only that two of the victims could as easily have lost their lives as the result of an accident as at the hands of another. Have I come for nothing or for a purpose?"

Djehuty, a tall, white-haired man, angular of face and body, thrust himself forward in his armchair. His eyes glinted; his words came out in a dangerous purr. "Your voyage north was comfortable, Lieutenant?"

"I fished most of every day, sir, and slept." Bak knew if he allowed himself to be intimidated now, this man would never let him go about his task without interference. Djehuty would try at every turn to manipulate him and would then demean him as one too weak to stand up for himself. That he could not permit. "The time would've been better spent if you'd not silenced Lieutenant Amonhotep, if he'd been free to tell me of the dead men and describe the way they died."

Djehuty's mouth tightened. "Impertinent young . . ."

"Sir!" Amonhotep stepped forward, drawing the governor's angry scowl. "Commandant Thuty was very reluctant to lose Lieutenant Bak, even for a few weeks. We must make the most of his time here. Who knows how long he'll be able to stay?"

Picking up on the hint, Bak stepped to the base of the dais on which Djehuty sat and offered the scroll. "I've a document for you, sir, from Commandant Thuty."

The governor glowered at the papyrus roll and the man who held it. Bak could guess his thoughts. In theory, a governor held more power than a commandant, but this particular commandant of Buhen was known to be a personal friend of the viceroy of Wawat and Kush, a man whose responsibility for the movement of trade and tribute gave him the ear of the vizier and, more importantly, of their sovereign, Maatkare Hatshepsut herself.

Djehuty formed a cool smile and leaned back in his chair, hands resting on the arms, thus forcing his aide to take the document, break the seal, untie the string, and pass it on. As the governor unrolled the scroll and began to read, Amonhotep sneaked a cynical glance at Bak.

To hide his contempt for such trifling displays of authority, Bak half turned away from the dais and glanced around the audience hall. Swathes of light from high windows struck four tall palm-shaped columns supporting the high ceiling and fell across the stone-paved floor. Close to empty now, the hall had teemed with life when first he and Amonhotep had entered. Twenty or more people, mostly farmers and craftsmen with a sprinkling of traders, had been milling around the columns, murmuring among themselves, awaiting their turn to make a supplication or air a complaint or ask for a judgment, one man against another. A flock of scribes had whispered together at the rear of the room, while guards stood at rest near all the doors.

Then as now, Djehuty had occupied the spacious armchair, well padded with thick pillows, on the low dais that dominated one end of the room. Beside the chair, a large, wide-mouthed bowl of fragrant blue lily blossoms perfumed the air, shielding the governor from the reek of his subjects' sweat. A scantily clad farmer, on his knees before the dais, had been pleading for lower taxes, while a scribe, seated cross-legged on the floor nearby, recorded the proceedings.

Spotting Amonhotep and Bak, the governor had risen partway out of his chair. The man on his knees had squealed in dismay. Djehuty had dropped back onto the pillows, ordered the scribe to look into the matter further, and announced the end of the day's audience. The petitioners had melted away, angry and resentful at the abrupt dismissal, but resigned to come again another day. The scribes had hesitated to leave, curious about the newcomer at the door. A flick of Djehuty's wrist had sent them scurrying from the hall. All the guards had been dismissed except the man at the double doors, as if Djehuty feared more than anything else that a petitioner might enter unbidden.

An irritated grunt from Djehuty drew Bak's attention back to the dais. The governor, he saw, was staring at the open scroll with distaste, but with a reluctant acceptance of its contents.

In spite of a curiosity honed to the sharpness of a dagger by Amonhotep's silence, Bak hesitated once again to press forward. Partly because he feared Djehuty would never cease to be difficult. Mostly because he had stepped into an unknown world, where the chance of failure was great. Yet he dared not fail, for the vizier would be sure to hear if his mission went awry. Pushing aside so loathsome a thought, he asked, "Now will you tell me, sir, of the three deaths you summoned me to resolve?"

Djehuty shifted in his seat, glanced at his aide, cleared his throat. "The first to die was the servant Nakht, a mere boy, so they tell me."

"He was eleven years of age," Amonhotep explained, "small for his years, quiet, a child who toiled from dawn to dusk with no complaint."

"I didn't know him." Djehuty scowled, impatient with such petty details. "His place was by the river, where the fishermen bring in their catch day after day, and in the kitchen. He cleaned the many fish required to feed so large a household as this one." He rose slightly in his seat, adjusted a pillow. "Early one morning he went down to the river, and he never returned. My housekeeper, mistress Hatnofer, grew impatient and sent a servant out to look for him. Three fishermen remembered seeing him at daybreak, walking along the shore north of the landingplace. The servant found a child's footprints in the mud, but nothing more. Later in the day, a farmer pulled the boy's body out of the river some distance downstream from Abu, where the current had carried him. We all believed he fell into the water, cracked his head on a rock, and drowned."

"Could he swim?" Bak asked.

"Like an eel," Amonhotep said. "And according to the fishermen, he knew the river far too well to drown—better than they, in fact." He gave Bak a wry smile. "They're a superstitious lot. They're convinced a spirit from deep within the river pulled him into the depths. They say only a creature not of this world could've robbed him of the ability to swim."

Djehuty dismissed the fishermen with a wave of his hand. "The second to die was the guard Montu. He was an older man, I was told. A spearman brought from the garrison, long past the age of facing an enemy on the field of battle. He was assigned to patrol the gardens, to fend off the town children who ofttimes climb over the compound wall to take for themselves a succulent melon or an armload of fruit. Hat-nofer had told me he wasn't much good at the task, and she was thinking of replacing him.''

"The children liked him." Ignoring Djehuty's thin-lipped frown, Amonhotep explained, "They came into the gardens, not to pilfer, but to listen to his tales of warfare and courage, stories of the past when our sovereigns marched off to war, leading our armies to victory."

"For some reason," Djehuty said, raising his voice to override his aide, "probably to eat his evening meal undisturbed, he climbed onto the roof of the cattle shed."

"He often spent time there," Amonhotep said. "He could look down upon the garden, and when his joints ached, he had no need to walk the paths."

With a loud clearing of his throat, Djehuty stared pointedly at his aide. Amonhotep lowered eyes Bak could have sworn were twinkling at a jest the governor failed to see. How often, he wondered, did the aide tease his master, and how far dared he go?

"He was seen alive on the roof at dusk," the governor said, "and the following morning he was found dead at the base of the stairway he would've descended, the shaft of his spear broken, the point in his breast. The stairs are steep, and the sergeant of the guard found a smear of oil near the top, spilled from Montu's evening meal, he assumed."

"So you believed he slipped, breaking the shaft as he fell." Bak raised a skeptical eyebrow. "Did he reach the ground first and the spearpoint fall on him, driving itself deep into his breast? Or did the stub of the shaft bury itself in the ground, allowing him to fall on the point?"

Djehuty shifted on the pillows; his eyes sought Amonhotep, looking for an answer that would blunt the point of Bak's sarcasm.

The aide shrugged. "As I said when first we met, Lieutenant, who wants to believe in the abhorrent?"

Bak had known many men who had mastered the art of self-deception. He disliked admitting it, but at times he stood among them, as eager to believe what he wanted to believe as the most adept. But in time the truth had to be faced no matter how hard to swallow. "Tell me of the man who was stabbed, the one whose death convinced you a murderer walked among you."

"His name was Senmut," Djehuty said. "He was sergeant of the guard, the man who found Montu dead. A man in the prime of life, close to me in age. One who worked and played with the vigor of a youth, the strength of a bull."

Of the three who had died, Bak noticed, this was the first the governor had praised. "You knew him well, sir?"

"He grew to manhood in Abu, and so did I. We played together as children, soldiered together as men. We wagered over anything and everything, we shared the same beer jars, we lay with the same women in houses of pleasure both here and in faroff lands." Djehuty's voice strengthened, took on a note of pride. "He was a man among men."

Could Senmut have been chosen for death, Bak wondered, because of his friendship with Djehuty? Or was the slayer unaware they were close? "How did he die?"

Djehuty's voice grew taut. "One morning, inside the rear gate, he was found with a dagger in his breast."

"The dagger was his own," Amonhotep said, noting his superior's distress. "We longed to believe he was slain by someone from outside the wall—from the city of Abu, which abuts these grounds—but the gate was latched on the inside. The thrust to his breast was true, giving him no time to secure the latch. He was last seen after darkness fell the previous evening, checking the guards assigned to night duty. The guard at the front gate reported no one leaving after Senmut made his rounds, and with the rear gate latched . . ." The officer spread his hands wide, accenting the obvious. "Whoever slew him spent the night inside this compound."

Bak whistled. No wonder Djehuty had taken fright! No wonder he had asked the vizier's advice—and acted on it!

Bak paced the gravel path beside the shallow pool, his thoughts flitting in every direction, probing possibilities, seeking a reason that would account for the three deaths, anything that might give him a path to follow.

Djehuty, who had tired of the audience hall, had suggested they adjourn to the garden, where a gentle breeze rustled the leaves of a small, tidy grove of pomegranate, date, and sycamore trees. He and Amonhotep faced each other on two wooden benches shaded by a bower of lush grapevines. The musty scent of fresh-turned earth wafted across the pool from several newly planted garden plots. Other small plots outlined by irrigation ditches and low mud walls contained maturing lettuce, onions, and radishes, beans and chickpeas, and a long, narrow stand of melons. Cornflowers, poppies, and daisies grew among the trees, while the blossoms of the blue lily floated on the surface of the pool, perfuming the air.

"How long ago was the youth Nakht slain?" Bak asked, pausing before the arbor.

Djehuty glanced at Amonhotep, passing on the question.

"I remember thinking when I arose this morning that Montu was slain a month ago today, exactly thirty days. As for the boy . . ." The aide stared at the pool, trying to recall. "Yes, he died ten days before the guard did, a week to the day." A sudden thought brought his head around and he gave Bak an odd look. "They both were slain on the final day of the week, and so was Senmut, ten days after Montu's demise."

Bak stood quite still. "Today is the final day of this week."

"You don't think . . . ?" Amonhotep stared, appalled. He had been absent from Abu for eighteen days, almost two weeks.

Bak swung toward the governor. "Did anyone die on the grounds of this villa ten days ago?"

Djehuty automatically shook his head, then his face drained of color and he moaned. "It was an accident. It had to be. No man or woman was near the animal."

"What are you saying?" Amonhotep looked ready to shake his superior. "Did someone meet a violent end while I was gone?"

"Lieutenant Dedi." Djehuty's shoulders slumped, and he

spoke barely above a whisper. "It happened in the stable here in the compound. He was found in a stall, trampled to death by a horse gone mad."

"What exactly happened?" Bak demanded, his voice so harsh he frightened an approaching duck and her brood, sending them fluttering toward the nearest ditch. "Horses don't go mad without cause. And men don't walk into a stall containing an animal whose spirit is troubled." As a former charioteer, Bak could speak with authority.

"This horse went mad, I tell you." Djehuty rubbed his face as if to wipe away the problem. "Maybe the creature ate tainted food. Maybe a mouse or rat frightened him. Maybe he took a dislike to Lieutenant Dedi's smell." He shook his head, unable to come up with a satisfactory reason. "Maybe the signs of madness were there all along and Dedi failed to see them. He was young and green, new to horses."

"I doubt his death was an accident," Bak said. "It fits too neatly into the pattern."

"Pattern!" Djehuty sneered. "Coincidence, more likely."

Bak felt like strangling him. Each time Djehuty had to face a new horror, he retreated farther from the truth. "You must see, sir, that if Lieutenant Dedi was slain exactly ten days ago, and the sergeant ten days before him, and the spearman ten days earlier, and the servant . . ." A new realization struck and his voice faltered. "By the beard of Amon!"

"What is it?" Amonhotep asked. "What's wrong?"

"A second pattern." Bak saw the perplexity on both men's faces and hastened to explain. "Think of the rank of each man who was slain. First a lowly servant, next a common guard, third a sergeant, and . . ."

"And finally a lieutenant." Amonhotep's eyes slewed toward the governor. "Each man more lofty than the next."

"No." Djehuty buried his face in his hands. "It's impossible! Another coincidence!"

Amonhotep's eyes met Bak's and he shook his head in dismay. "I've known men to slay in the heat of anger or to take an enemy's life on the field of battle. But this? I fear I don't understand.''

"Nor do I." The question the aide had posed was important, Bak knew, but he had a more immediate problem. "Today is the tenth day of the week. If the pattern holds, someone will die today, someone of a rank higher than Lieutenant and not necessarily a soldier."

Amonhotep's voice grew weary. "You speak of all those men closest to the governor, all who toil solely at his behest. The loftiest men in the province."

"They must be warned." Bak glanced skyward. The sun, a burning yellow ball in a vivid blue sky, had risen to within an hour of midday. He prayed they were not already too late.

Djehuty's armchair stood empty on the dais in the audience hall. Filing into the room one after another were the men he had summoned at Bak's request. These were the highest officials on the governor's staff, men he depended upon for the smooth running of the province, his personal estate, and the small garrison situated on the island of Abu. Four men were standing before the dais, talking among themselves, speculating as to the purpose of the summons. Amonhotep, who stood with Bak just outside a door near the dais, had identified them as they entered: Troop Captain Antef, the chief steward Amethu, the chief scribe Simut, and Djehuty's son Ineni.

"I thank the lord Khnum they've all come," Amonhotep said. "I feared one among them would be unable to appear." Khnum was the god who guarded the sources of the river, the inundation. He was the principal god of Abu.

Bak noted the way the young officer skirted around the mention of death. He had surely realized his own situation. Or had he? "Have you thought, Amonhotep, that you're Djehuty's right hand, as essential to the smooth running of this province as any of the four we see before us?"

Amonhotep gave Bak a tight smile. "I'm not my master, Bak. I'm fully aware that I must count myself among those who might next face death."

Djehuty rushed out of a back room, swooped past the two officers without a word, and hurried to the dais. He sat on the mound of pillows padding his chair, his body stiff, his face pale and tight, and spoke with a forced composure. His staff formed a ragged line in front of him, silent, curious.

"You know as well as I of the unfortunate deaths we've suffered here in my household," the governor said. "And you know the vizier suggested I summon an officer from the fortress of Buhen, a Lieutenant Bak." He paused to clear his throat, hurried on. "He's come, we've spoken at length, and he's reached a conclusion I hesitate to endorse."

Bak muttered an oath. The governor had vowed to support him with no reservations. Now here he was, retreating from a positive stance.

"I'll let the lieutenant speak for himself," Djehuty added, "so each of you may judge the worth of his words."

Stifling his irritation, Bak stepped through the door to stand beside the dais. After a few introductory words to identify himself, he briefly discussed the four deaths and went on to the conclusions he had reached. "I believe . . . No! I'm convinced an attempt will be made before the day ends to slay one man among you."

"Bah!" This from a short, portly man with a fringe of curly white hair. Simut, the chief scribe. "I'm sorry, Lieutenant, but I'm a busy man. I can't run away and hide simply because you've arranged the facts to fit a theory you've created in haste. A week from now, two weeks—after you've come to know this place and its people—you might have sufficient knowledge to come up with a convincing argument. But now? Too soon. Much too soon."

Could he be right? Bak wondered. *Could my past successes have made me overconfident?* Hiding self-doubt in a humorless smile, he said, "Sir, if I were to walk on tiptoe and clutch caution to my breast, as you suggest, I doubt your governor will be among the living beyond a week from today."

Djehuty sucked in his breath like a man struck in the stomach. Bak was hard put to sympathize. If the governor had

not yet admitted to himself that his name probably lay at the
top of the slayer's list, he had no one to blame but himself.

"I know of no man who would wish to slay my father."
The speaker was tall like his sire, but harder muscled and
lacking in angularity. His hair was short, dark, and glistening
with good health, his skin burnished by the sun. He was close
to Bak's twenty-five years.

"You must be Ineni," Bak said. "Lieutenant Amonhotep
told me you oversee your father's estate."

"Where the lieutenant is my father's right hand," Ineni
said, bowing his head in mock acknowledgment, "you must
think of me as his left hand."

Bak commended the quip with a fleeting smile. "You
don't take seriously the possibility of another murder, this
one closer to you and yours?"

"Three of the dead out of four were soldiers. Would that
not make Troop Captain Antef the next most likely man to
die?"

"I may be wrong, but . . ."

Simut snorted at the admission.

". . . but I believe the youth Nakht was slain not only because of his lowly status, but to pass on the message that a
civilian is as likely to die as a soldier."

"What kind of swine would slay a child?" The speaker,
Antef, was a large, heavy man in his early thirties. He wore
the short white kilt of a soldier and the belt and sheathed
dagger of an officer. "And for no better reason than to deliver a message."

"You think I err?" Bak asked.

"I pray you do." Antef's mouth tightened. "If you've
read the signs right, the one you seek is no ordinary man.
He does what he wants, giving no thought to the laws of
men or the wishes of the gods."

"Few men walk the earth so fearless." Djehuty's chief
steward, Amethu, was a man of middle years. He had the
broad shoulders and narrow hips of youth, but his stomach
bulged and he was as bald as a melon. He wore the ankle-
length kilt of a scribe and a bronze chain around his neck,

from which hung a dozen or more small colored stone amulets of the ram-headed god Khnum.

Antef gave the steward a scornful look. "Some men don't share your awe of the gods, Amethu. They hold themselves above all creatures, mortal and immortal alike."

"Should I feel shame because I revere the gods?" Amethu asked, raising his chin high. "It certainly wouldn't hurt you to bend your knee before a shrine or in the forecourt of a god's mansion."

"I served my turn less than a month ago as web priest in the mansion of . . ."

"Enough!" Bak raised his hands for silence and spoke to them all as one. "You each have duties, I know. They can't be laid aside because I believe the slayer intends next to slay one of you. Go on with what you must do, but stay always in the company of other men. Don't ever walk alone. Don't . . ."

"Sir!" A young woman, a servant if her rough linen sheath told true, burst through the rear door. Her roundish face was whiter than her dress, her eyes wide open, horrified. "Oh, Governor Djehuty!" she wailed. "It's terrible! Oh, sir!"

Bak leaped toward the young woman, confused by her words, by her demeanor, very much aware of the men before him, all alive and well. Could another individual have been murdered? One that did not fit the patterns he had so carefully developed?

Amonhotep, a step ahead, caught her by the shoulders. "What is it, Nefer? What's happened?"

Tears flowed as if from a river and she began to tremble. "Oh, sir! Oh!"

"Speak up, woman!" Amonhotep shook her none too gently. "Tell us what's happened."

"It's mistress Hatnofer," the girl sobbed. "She's dead. Her head smashed. So much blood! Oh, so much blood!"

Hatnofer? Bak thought. *Djehuty's housekeeper?* He spat out an oath, and another and another. From what little the governor had said about the woman earlier in the day, she had been as important to him as were the five men standing before the dais. Yet he, Bak, had failed to think of her, to summon her, and now she lay dead. If her life had been taken while he stood here warning the others, he would blame himself through eternity.

Chapter Three

Djehuty sat as if turned to stone by the gods, his face pasty white, his hands clutching the arms of his chair.

"No!" Someone—Ineni, Bak thought—breathed the denial.

The portly chief scribe Simut stared at the servant, blinking like a man unable to comprehend. Troop Captain Antef muttered a curse, calling the lord Khnum for strength, and groped for the handle of his dagger as if seeking its protection. The chief steward Amethu's lips began to move, but no words came out—a prayer of some kind, most likely.

"I must see her," Bak said, his voice sharp above the girl's sobs.

Amonhotep, still grasping her shoulders, shook his head as if waking from a dream—or a nightmare. "Where is she, Nefer? You must take us to her."

"I can't look at her again!" Sobbing, shaking her head, she tried to back away, to free herself. "Oh, sir, please don't ask it of me!"

Bak laid a hand on her arm. His touch was gentle, his demeanor kind, yet he felt her cringe. "We ask only that you show us where you found her, Nefer. Nothing more."

She gave him the look a drowning man would give one who had thrown out a lifesaving rope, but the tears continued to pour, the sobs to break the flow of words. "We went into the master's quarters in Nebmose's villa. We thought to pre-

35

pare the rooms for you, sir. That's where we came upon her. Mistress Khawet and I.''

"Nebmose's villa?" Bak threw Amonhotep a puzzled glance. "She wasn't slain within this compound, as the others were?"

"Our walls surround both houses." The aide kept his eyes on Nefer, spoke to her, calming her with facts she surely knew well. "This has long been the governor's villa, occupied by Djehuty's family for many generations, since a long-dead ancestor was made governor of the south by Kheperkare Senwosret. The other house and its outbuildings belonged to a family as old as Djehuty's, probably descended from the same ancestor. When the last of the line, Nebmose, lost his life and no man or woman remained to inherit, Djehuty took the property in the name of our sovereign, Maatkare Hatshepsut, and made it a part of his own. The rooms once occupied by the master of the house we now use to shelter visiting dignitaries, the remainder for storage."

Normally, property that reverted to the royal house was handed over to a god's mansion to be used for income or was given to a private individual as a reward for services. Had Djehuty simply taken the villa as his due? Or had he performed some worthy act?

"Hatnofer lies where we found her," Nefer sobbed, "in the master's bath. I dared not touch her, but mistress Khawet knelt by her side and sought the pulse of life in her neck."

"Mistress Khawet?" Bak asked.

"My daughter," Djehuty croaked.

"My wife," Ineni said at the same time. His eyes flitted toward Djehuty and he added in a caustic voice, "She serves as mistress of this household for her father."

Bak gave him a sharp look, but Ineni's expression gave nothing away. Any message he had meant to convey had been for Djehuty's benefit, not for an outsider, a police officer.

Bak turned to the servant, smiled. "We must go, Nefer." He waited for her nod, then glanced at Amonhotep. "I'll need you, too, Lieutenant."

"Of course." Amonhotep released the young woman's shoulders and stepped back, but not so far that he could not stop her should she attempt to flee.

"What of the rest of us, Lieutenant?" Simut demanded. "The wretched woman was a housekeeper, important to this household but of no appreciable worth to the affairs of the province. On the surface, her death appears to verify your theory, but does it?"

Was the scribe always so irascible? Bak wondered. Or was he using irritability to shield himself from grief—or fear? Simut undoubtedly knew the power a housekeeper could wield, as did he. Bak's father, a physician highly regarded for his skills, had been unable to save his mother, who had died in childbirth. He had grown from a babe to manhood in the care of a woman who had ruled the servants with an iron hand—and himself and his father with the tact and skill of a royal envoy.

"In a large establishment such as this, the mistress of the house ofttimes serves as a hostess, leaving the housekeeper to oversee the servants and see that no task is forgotten and all are done well. Was that true here?"

"It was." Amethu, who had ceased his prayer, stepped forward. "But now and again, when Hatnofer complained of drowning in a flood of duties, mistress Khawet eased her path by helping."

"I have a feeling," Bak said, turning again to Simut, "that the slayer wishes to damage Djehuty, not the province. In that respect, Hatnofer stood among you as an equal and you no longer have to fear for your lives."

"And if you err?" Simut shot back.

Taking care not to show how annoyed he was, praying a second death would not occur before the sun dropped below the western horizon, Bak's eyes traveled along the row of men. "Go on about your business, all of you. But go with care, extreme care, surrounding yourselves at all times with other men, giving the slayer no chance to draw near."

*   *   *

They hurried out of the audience hall, Amonhotep in the
lead, Nefer whimpering a step or two behind, and Bak close
on her heels. They strode through a series of chambers, all
comfortably furnished with low wooden tables, stools, and
chests. Rush mats covered the floors and floral paintings decorated many walls. In the larger rooms, flowers of every
color imaginable were massed in pottery jars, perfuming the
air. Deeper in the dwelling, a series of corridors took them
past smaller, plainer chambers containing sleeping pallets
and storage chests.

Leaving the building through a rear door, they hastened
across a bare patch of sand, passing a row of four tall, conical
granaries built alongside the house. A gate through a waist-
high wall took them into another sandy yard, which fronted
the long, low building housing the kitchen and servants'
quarters. The yeasty scent of fresh bread vied with the aroma
of roasting meat, reminding Bak of the midday meal he had
missed. The tangy odor of manure drifted from a building
hidden behind a wall; the whinny of a horse identified its
occupants.

Within another, smaller enclosed yard, he saw the well, a
wide-mouthed round hole surrounded by a low wall, with a
flight of steps leading downward. Beyond a higher wall, date
palms whispered in the breeze and birds fluttered among the
leaves of a sycamore: the garden he had seen earlier in the
day.

As they passed through yet another gate, this in a wall
much too tall to see over, Nefer's feet began to drag, telling
Bak they had entered the grounds of the neighboring villa.
The passage had been opened between the two properties—
whether at Djehuty's command or sometime in the past he
had no way of knowing—to provide a shorter path between
the two dwellings, eliminating the need to walk around to
the formal entrance at the front. The house, he saw, was
about half the size of Djehuty's but palatial compared to most
of the dwellings in a provincial city such as Abu.

After passing four granaries and an empty stable, they
stepped through a door Nefer had left open in her haste to

get help. Beyond three small rooms filled with sealed storage jars, they entered a hall whose high ceiling was supported by two papyrus-shaped columns. The room was bright and cheerful, a place designed to please visitors of lofty rank. The musty smell of an empty dwelling underlay the odor of fresh paint.

Another door led to a spacious room furnished with wooden chests, stools, and even a chair. Thick rush mats covered the floor. The walls were white, with a simple lily motif running around the room near the ceiling. This had once been the private reception room in the master's suite. The quarters were far too grand for Bak's purpose and taste, far too sumptuous for himself and his Medjays, and with the governor's villa so close, far less private than he liked. A problem Hatnofer's death had solved for him.

A slender woman with hair curling around her shoulders sat in the chair, staring at nothing. An untidy pile of sheets lay on the floor nearby, bedding she or Nefer must have dropped, now forgotten. In her early to mid-twenties, she had the same prominent cheekbones and jaw as Djehuty, the same long and slim body, but the whole softened by femininity. No man would call her beautiful, nor could she be called plain.

When Amonhotep and Bak stepped into the room, she started as if awakened from a nap. "You've come at last." She rose to her feet and walked toward them, her eyes on the newcomer. "You must be the officer from Buhen."

"Lieutenant Bak," he said, nodding. "And you're mistress Khawet?"

"You couldn't have come at a more opportune time." She formed a smile, but her voice trembled, making a lie of the attempt at humor. "I'm sorry. I fear I'm not myself."

Bak took a quick look around the room. Two open doors revealed small chambers containing folded sleeping pallets, a few stools, and woven reed chests. A third led to a far more spacious chamber containing a bed made up with fresh linen, wooden chests, and several stools standing on a carpet of woven reed mats.

He stood in the doorway, eyeing an opening in the wall
at the far end. "You found mistress Hatnofer in the bath,
Nefer said."

She gave the open portal a haunted look, nodded. Bak
could see she was as horrified by what she had found as was
the servant.

Not sure he wanted to share the experience but knowing
he must, he strode across the bedchamber and slipped
through the opening. Passing the toilet, a pottery seat on a
mudbrick box of sand, he stepped through a second opening,
offset from the first to form an alcove. Inside, a woman lay
sprawled across the floor and atop a limestone slab with a
slight depression to contain water. Forty or so years of age,
she was small and wiry, her skin pale, her hair coarse and
unnaturally black. Disheveled tendrils had burst from a bag-
like linen headdress, torn partway off when she fell—or
when she was struck. Her features were sharp, like those of
a bird and even in death looked cunning.

The shallow stone basin had been built into a corner whose
walls were lined with two other slabs to protect the mudbrick
walls. One slab was heavily splotched with blood, the second
barely dotted. The woman's head, the right temple smashed
and bloody, lay close beside a slim, elongated pottery jar,
broken at the base, set through the wall to drain water to the
outside. While still she breathed—judging by the massive
wound, not long, he thought—a thin stream of blood had
trickled into the jar. The odor of a heavy, sweet-scented perfume hung in the air, as if her body had already been prepared for eternity.

"May the lord Osiris take her unto himself," Amonhotep
murmured. He stood beside Bak, staring at the great, ugly
wound, his face pale, appalled.

Swallowing to rid himself of the sour taste rising in his
throat, Bak knelt beside the body to feel for the pulse of life.
None, nor had he expected to find one. No man or woman
could have survived such a ghastly wound. Her wrist was
cool to the touch, as was her bare shoulder. She had lost her
life some hours ago—not long after dawn, he suspected—

long before he had called together the members of Djehuty's staff. Though unseemly, he offered a quick prayer of thanks to the lord Amon that she had not died because he had failed to consider her as a victim.

He stood up and glanced around. Linen towels lay neatly folded on a mudbrick shelf built into the wall. Three alabaster perfume jars and a dark blue faience container for eye paint sat beside a bowl of natron for cleansing the skin. Four large pottery jars, all filled with tepid water, stood in a row below the shelf. She had come, he had no doubt, to prepare these rooms for use. After making up the bed, she had entered the bath, a small and enclosed space well suited for attacking and slaying a slightly built woman like her.

Bak saw no object that might have been used to bludgeon her, nor did he see any sign that she had fought to protect herself. She had known her assailant and held no fear in her heart—just as the previous victims had allowed their slayer to come close.

When he turned away, prepared to leave, he found Amonhotep outside the door by the toilet.

The aide looked unwell, uneasy. "I can't help seeing myself in her place, my head crushed, the breath of life torn from my body for no good reason."

Bak laid a hand on his back and gave him a gentle push toward the bedchamber. "The slayer could as easily have chosen Antef. Or Ineni or Amethu or Simut."

Amonhotep seemed not to have heard. "I know I shouldn't be glad she's dead . . ." He gave Bak a grim smile. ". . . and I'm not, but . . . but I feel . . ." He shook his head, unable to air what lay in his heart.

Relief, Bak thought, *relief that Hatnofer is lying lifeless on the floor while he remains alive and well. And who can blame him?*

"It's my fault! My fault alone!" Khawet stared out across the river, rubbing her arms as if chilled. "If I'd only gone earlier, as I said I would!"

"You've no need to blame yourself." Bak had suggested

Amonhotep report to Djehuty, more to escape the aide's un-
warranted guilt than because he thought the need pressing,
and now here he was, listening to another who wished to
shoulder the blame for Hatnofer's death. "The slayer
would've struck somewhere else if not in the guest quarters."

"She raised me from a babe! She was a mother to me!"

Bak walked to the edge of the high natural terrace that
followed the course of the river, a strip of land covered with
patchy grass and wild shrubs ablaze with blossoms. A sandy
path bisected the terrace, beginning at the stairway that rose
from the landingplace, passing a deep, well-like water gauge,
where the yearly flood was measured, and farther along, a
large public well, and ending near the pylon gate of the mansion of the lord Khnum. Willow trees shaded those who
walked the path or came for water or to speak with the god.
A stately sycamore towered over the water gauge and an
ancient grapevine clung to the wall around the deep structure.
A monkey chattered in the tree, too shy to allow itself to be
seen.

Below, the river surged down the broad channel between
the island of Abu and the east bank. Massive black boulders
rose from the depths on both sides of the channel, mighty
buttresses glistening in the sun, impervious to the continual
assault of the water flowing between them. To men with a
strong imagination, they resembled elephants, huge ungainly
animals living far to the south, creatures that seemed more
mythical than real to men who had never seen them. Creatures from which much of the ivory was taken that had given
Abu its name.

The loud calls of men at work drew Bak's gaze downstream, where four fishing boats were pulling in the day's
catch. Silvery arcs flashed in the distance as fish leaped out
of the water, trying to escape the closing net. Farther downstream, a small transport ship rode low in the water beneath
a heavy cargo of reddish pottery jars, making slow progress
against the current. Its patched red sail stood at an angle to
the breeze, sacrificing speed to reach the trading village of
Swenet on the opposite shore. A smaller, sleeker vessel, its

sail full to bursting, swept past the transport and veered in a westerly direction toward the island and the more substantial city of Abu.

The sound of laughter drew his eyes to Djehuty's traveling ship, still moored at the landingplace below the villa. Kasaya had left the vessel, he saw, and was sitting on a projecting boulder a short distance downstream, chatting with several women kneeling on the mudbank, washing clothes. He had to smile. The young Medjay, tall, hard-muscled, and good-natured, had a way with women few other men could claim. The older among them sought to mother him, the younger to gain a caress—if not more. Information flowed from their lips like water from an overturned bowl.

Psuro, more mature and practical, stood at the base of the stairway, haggling with an old woman holding a plucked duck and a basket overflowing with fruits and vegetables. The Medjay was planning a feast. The very thought made Bak's mouth water.

He turned back to Khawet, who had stopped pacing to sit on a mudbrick bench in the dappled shade of a willow. "When did you last see Hatnofer, mistress?"

"This morning. Soon after daybreak. In the room where we store linens. She was counting sheets." She bit her lip. "With so many so recently dead in this household, our supply has dropped far below the numbers we normally keep on hand. And now . . ." She swallowed hard, turned away so he could not see her face. Her voice trembled. "Now we must send more to the house of death. For her!"

Bak resisted the urge to go to her, to offer sympathy, fearing too gentle a demeanor might set the tears flowing in earnest. "What did you speak of?"

"You." She raised her hand to her eyes, most likely to wipe away tears, and turned around. "We spoke of your arrival. Today, we thought, if the gods had smiled on Amonhotep and he'd journeyed to Buhen and back as swiftly as he'd hoped."

"Was it she who decided to quarter me in the guest villa? Or did you think to place me there?"

"That was my father's decision."

Bak was surprised, and he let it show. "The rooms are more befitting a vizier than a police officer fresh from the frontier. I'd have thought Djehuty would have preferred I stay in the barracks."

She gave him a tremulous smile. "He wanted you close in case of need, but not so close you'd remind him every moment of the deaths he yearned to forget."

"I see," he said, his voice dry. "You spoke with Hatnofer of my arrival and then . . . ?"

Khawet stared at her feet, which were protected by leather sandals little more than a sole and a couple of narrow straps. "She set aside several sheets, saying she'd take them to Neb-mose's villa and prepare the rooms for your use. She was ready to leave, her arms laden with bedding, when Amethu sent a message, saying he was toiling over the household accounts and he needed her assistance right away." She plucked a flower from a nearby bush and twisted the stem between her fingers, making the fragile reddish petals shiver and dance. "She seemed so distracted, so overburdened with tasks that I took the linens from her, saying I'd prepare the rooms."

"But you didn't."

"No." She spoke to the flower, not to him, and her voice was tight, almost brittle with strain. "My father summoned me. He was displeased with his fan bearer and wanted him whipped. It wasn't easy to convince him the boy was too small by far to hold so long and heavy a handle high in the air. By the time I had done so, I had forgotten my promise to Hatnofer. Later . . . Much later, I remembered. I summoned Nefer and we . . ." Her voice broke and she turned away. "I feel ill. Will you leave me now?"

Bak yearned to probe further, but he could not in all conscience do so. He was too new on the trail of the slayer to limit his questions only to those that were necessary, for he had no idea which were essential. And she was too upset to tolerate questions that had no obvious purpose.

*   *   *

" 'How will I explain to Djehuty?' " Bak said, imitating as best he could Amethu's harried expression and voice. " 'He wanted you close—within the walls of this compound, not in some empty house in the city.' "

Psuro gave the duck a quarter turn on the makeshift spit he had erected over the mudbrick hearth. Grease dripped into the fire, filling the air with smoke. The cloud billowed upward, passing through the light roof of branches and straw, leaving in its wake a tantalizing aroma. "How'd you convince him you wanted none of it, sir?"

Fanning away a tattered ribbon of smoke, Bak grinned. "I told him you Medjays are a superstitious lot and you'd get no rest in a place so recently defiled by murder."

Psuro gave him a doubtful look. "He believed that?"

"I don't know," Bak admitted. "He was so startled by my wish to keep you by my side, he could do nothing but sputter."

"I thank the lord Amon you held out, sir." Kasaya, carrying a folded sleeping pallet over his shoulder, peered through the door of the tiny house the steward had found for them on a narrow lane a few streets away from the governor's compound. Over the rear wall, they could hear the laughter of neighborhood children. "It's one thing to walk into a house, eyes wide open, in search of a murderer, and another to sleep there."

"I doubt we'd be in any danger," Bak said. "Not yet, at any rate. If I've read the signs right, the slayer has set his sights higher than us."

"Governor Djehuty." Psuro picked up a stick and stirred a steaming bowl of lentils and onions cooking at the edge of the coals. "From what you've said of him, sir, he seems a weak man, one too preoccupied with the small world around himself to step hard on another man's toes."

"He'd have to step very hard to anger a man so much he'd slay time after time to make his point," Kasaya said.

"He would indeed." Eyes smarting, Bak stood up and joined the younger Medjay at the door. "But maybe Djehuty's not what he seems. We know too little of him. Nor do we know enough about those who've died thus far. We must look for a tie that binds them. Something more than the mere fact that they all earned their bread in the governor's villa.''

''Where shall we begin, sir?'' Kasaya asked.

Psuro scowled at his younger companion. ''You can start by laying out our sleeping pallets and unpacking the rest of our gear. Unless we hear tonight of another death, I, for one, mean to eat my fill and sleep like a babe held close to its mother's breast.''

Bak drew Kasaya into the front part of the house, a single room with an open stairway to the roof, where a spindly wooden frame was all that remained of a lean-to. Two stools, a small table, and a reed chest, all provided by Amethu, stood near a door that opened onto the lane. Scattered around were the baskets and bundles they had brought from Buhen and jars of grain and other foodstuffs the Medjays had drawn from the garrison stores at Abu. Spears, shields, bows and arrows, and smaller hand weapons had been stacked against the wall. One side of the room held a mudbrick sleeping platform on which lay bedding the steward had provided. A wall niche, empty of the image of the household god it once had held, broke the starkness of the opposite wall.

Bak lifted one of four large, heavy water jars, carried it out to the kitchen, and leaned it against the wall beside a round oven, long unused from the look of it. Going back inside, he said, ''Tomorrow, Kasaya, you must go to the governor's villa, familiarize yourself with the grounds and buildings, and make yourself useful to the servants. The sooner they accept you as one of them, the sooner they'll feel free to speak with an open and frank tongue.''

''Yes, sir.'' Kasaya pulled the sleeping pallet off his shoulder, shook it out, and laid it on the floor. ''Would it suit your purpose, sir, if I took special pains to befriend the guards? We may need men we can trust.''

''Good idea.'' Bak clapped him on the shoulder and crossed the room for another jar, which he carried outside to stand with its mate.

"What am I to do, sir?" Psuro asked, looking up from his cooking.

"I know of no better measure of the man than the way his people think of him. Walk first around Abu, getting to know the city and befriending its residents, both military and civilian. When you feel you've gleaned all you can—by the end of the day tomorrow, I hope—take the skiff Amethu loaned us and sail across the channel to Swenet. There, too, you must learn the streets and lanes and get to know the people."

Psuro gave him a dubious look. "This city is small, I know, and Swenet smaller yet, but to befriend everyone would take months. Can you not narrow the task to the possible?"

"Do what you can, Psuro, that's all I ask. If Hatnofer was meant to die today, as I think she was, we've only a week before the slayer strikes again."

"Yes, sir."

Bak resisted the urge to smile at the Medjay's gloomy countenance. "As you go about your task, you must seek out a man named Pahared. He once was a merchant in Wawat, one who traveled from village to village, trading the small objects needed by men and women who have close to nothing. I met him once in Nofery's house of pleasure. He'd just wed a woman of Kush and was giving up the life of a wanderer to return to Kemet. I last heard they'd settled here, but whether in Abu or Swenet, I don't know."

"He's a man we can trust?" Psuro asked, a flicker of hope shining through the gloom.

"We talked and drank long into the night. He seemed a man of good sense and honor."

Looking none too pleased with so vague an answer, the Medjay nodded. "If he's here, I'll find him."

Bak walked inside for the third jar of water.

Kasaya, immobilized by thought, knelt beside a second sleeping pallet he had just spread out on the floor, a folded sheet in his hand. "I know we're not far from the governor's villa, sir, but do you think it wise to spend the night here?

What if someone else is slain? From what you say of Djehuty, he'll be the first to lay blame—if he's not the one to die.''

Bak gave the young Medjay a quick smile. "As soon as we eat our evening meal, I plan to return to Djehuty's house. I see no need to open the door to disaster.''

Chapter Four

Bak, stifling a yawn, stood in front of Nebmose's house, letting the chill morning breeze awaken him. He had gotten some sleep, thanks to Psuro and Kasaya, but not enough. The night had passed without incident; the occupants of the governor's villa had slept in peace. He doubted the police presence had made a difference. Hatnofer had died because she had been close in importance to Djehuty.

He eyed the small, neat garden that surrounded the family shrine inside the main entrance to the property. Venerable trees, thick bushes, and lush flowering plants filled the space with color. Birds chattered from on high, while tiny, fuzzy ducklings swam with their mother on a small, shallow pool and frogs sat on lily pads, soaking up the sun. Bees waded in pollen, humming an ancient tune while they harvested the sweet juices hidden inside the flowers. Bak could well imagine how impressed a distinguished visitor might be, striding through the gate after a long, wearisome voyage. The garden was like the Field of Reeds, where the justified dead spent eternity.

He followed the path to the shrine, a small, white-plastered structure with a cornice painted red and green. A narrow flight of four steps carried him to an entrance flanked by red columns. He had expected the building to be empty. Instead he found an ancestor bust on a limestone plinth. A fresh offering of flowers lay at the base of the red-painted, summarily formed figure with the head of a man. The last of the family might be gone, but someone remained to care.

Leaving the shrine, he crossed the garden to the gate, which was almost as high as the wall around the compound and securely barred on the inside. He opened it and looked out onto one of the many lanes that ran through Abu. Two neighbors' gates, both on the opposite side of the lane, had been cut through walls equally tall and solid. The few windows he saw there were narrow and very high, admitting light and air, but allowing no view of the world outside. The far end of the lane vanished in a jumble of small, sometimes squalid dwellings. As was usually the case in Kemet, the poor touched elbows with the wealthy, but seldom met face-to-face.

Returning to Nebmose's compound, he barred the gate behind him and hurried around the house. Beyond the empty stables and the granaries, he found a dusty yard in which a cluster of palms were being smothered by tamarisks. The mouth of a well gaped open in front of a squarish building containing four long, narrow storage magazines with a portico in front. Three of the chambers were empty; the fourth contained a chariot with a broken axle. He strode to a narrow gate shaded by the warring trees, lifted the pole that barred entry, and pulled it open. The lane outside was narrow, meant solely for foot traffic. Toward the south, it disappeared in a huddle of small houses. In the opposite direction, it passed the governor's villa and dwindled to nothing among a patchwork of fields that covered the northern end of the island.

Disappointed in spite of low expectations, he swung the gate shut, dropped the bar in place, and walked back to the house. Hatnofer's slayer could have come and gone unseen through the front entrance or the back, or from Djehuty's villa. Other than the audience hall and the visitors' quarters, the rooms were all used for storage. The house had been empty of life, the woman alone—or so she had thought. Anyone could have slain her.

"It seems a terrible waste, doesn't it?"

Bak, standing in the doorway of the stable, eyeing a long

row of empty stalls, started and swung around. The governor's son Ineni stood behind him, looking past him into the shadowy building.

"In days gone by, when I served as a charioteer with the regiment of Amon, I dreamed of a stable like this each time I had leave to go home." Bak gave the young nobleman a wry smile. "My horses, a worthy team but creatures of no discernment whatsoever, were content with the lean-to where my father housed his donkey."

A brief smile lit Ineni's face. He stepped around Bak and led the way down the dimly lit corridor. Each stall, built of mudbrick with an arched ceiling, would have held two horses. Now the wooden gates were gone, as were the leather trappings that had hung from the walls and the chariots that had stood in the yard outside. The building had been swept clean and nothing remained but a few bits of straw, traces of grain, and dark stains on the hard-packed earthen floor, which still gave off a faint odor of manure. A waste it was, agreed Bak, an abomination to allow so useful a building to lie idle.

"I came here often as a child," Ineni said. "The horses were some of the finest in Kemet, the stallion from the faroff land of Hatti. They were beautiful, spirited, the stuff of dreams. I longed to become a charioteer." He stooped, picked up a straw, and stuck it in the corner of his mouth. "But the gods stepped in, and now I'm a farmer." He laughed—at himself, Bak felt sure. "Don't misunderstand. The life of a farmer suits me. I manage my father's fields with a skill not many men can claim."

Bak was surprised. Not because Ineni's family had an estate, perhaps more than one, at a distance from Abu. Most noblemen lived off the labor of those who toiled on land far from the cities where they spent most of their days. Not one in a thousand would call himself a farmer.

"What happened to the horses?" he asked.

"When my father took this villa as his own, he had me move them to our estate in Nubt, a half day's sail north of here. They're there yet, as are their descendants."

Bak paused in front of an empty stall and asked with reluctance, fearing the answer, "What happened to the horse that took Lieutenant Dedi's life?"

"I . . ." Ineni hesitated, then evaded the question. "My father ordered me to have it slain."

Bak eyed the young farmer closely. "Did you obey?" Getting no answer, glimpsing defiance in Ineni's downcast eyes, he said, "Horses were my life for more than eight years, Ineni. I cherished my team, and if anyone had suggested I slay them, I'd've cut off my hand first, the hand I use to thrust my spear."

Ineni's eyes darted to Bak's face, searching for a lie. Evidently satisfied, he glanced toward the open doorway and lowered his voice lest anyone hear. "As soon as I took the poor, terrified beast out of the stall, away from the scent of death, he quieted. My father had insisted he was mad, but I could see he'd simply been consumed by fear. I had him taken that night to our estate in Nubt, and there he will remain, alive and well. My father need never know."

Bak nodded approval. "He'll not hear the tale from me."

They reached the end of the corridor and turned back, sharing the silence and a vision of the stable as once it had been. Somewhere in the dark, a cat growled. A half-grown rat shot out of a stall and down the passageway a pace ahead of a huge orange tomcat. As the rodent raced into the sunlight outside the door, the cat leaped with a ferocious snarl. Clamping its teeth into its kicking and squeaking prey, it trotted off.

"Why, do you believe, was Hatnofer slain?" Bak asked.

Ineni gave a short bark-like laugh, rending their brief camaraderie. "You surprise me, Lieutenant. You told us yesterday, did you not, that the next to die would be one who walked close to my father. Have you since decided you erred?"

Bak chose to ignore the sarcasm. "She died because of her importance in this household, of that I've no doubt, but you are equally important. As are Amonhotep, Antef, Simut, and Amethu. Why was she chosen over the rest of you?"

"I see no mystery there. She was small and no longer young. And she walked alone into an empty building, easy prey."

Bak opened the gate to the governor's compound and glanced into the yard containing the well. Two young women, servants he had seen in the kitchen at daybreak, stood chatting near the top of the steps leading down to the water. One balanced a large, heavy jar on her head, the second held an empty container by the neck. Glimpsing Ineni, the former hurried toward the kitchen and the latter hastened down the steps to fetch water.

Bak made no comment until he and Ineni were midway along the row of granaries, when the servants were too far away to hear. "Was the sergeant who died, Senmut, small and no longer young?"

"He was as tall as you," Ineni admitted with a crooked smile, "and he prided himself on his strength."

"Yet there was no sign of a struggle."

"None."

Bak stopped in the shade near the rear door of the house, and gave his companion a curious look. "You seem unmoved by Hatnofer's death. Wasn't she a mother to you, as she was to Khawet?"

Ineni's laugh was harsh, derisive. "My mother was a servant, Lieutenant. She was young and beautiful, I've been told, and he took her as his own the day she walked into this villa. Hatnofer hated her from that time forward, and she had no more use for me. When my mother died giving birth to a stillborn daughter, I was sent to our estate at Nubt. There I was raised by a houseful of servants, all of whom I think of as parents."

The tale was not unusual, but moved Bak nonetheless. "Do you go often to Nubt?"

"I'd be there now if my father hadn't summoned me." Ineni snorted. "Sometimes I think he fears his own shadow."

Bak eyed him curiously. "Aren't you yet convinced he has reason to fear? Five people have died thus far."

Ineni walked to the door and lifted the latch. "If I'd been so inclined, I'd have slain Hatnofer many years ago. Sergeant Senmut was a braggart, a man who believed himself above all others in any endeavor he chose to pursue. The guard Montu . . . Well, he seemed a nice enough fellow, but he drank to excess and he loved to talk. He could say more about less than any man I ever met."

"What of Lieutenant Dedi? And the boy Nakht?"

"Dedi was young and full of himself, not one to take too seriously, I'd have thought. But who knows? Maybe someone resented his . . . His enthusiasm." Ineni lifted the latch and shoved the door open. "Nakht is a puzzle. The child was small and slight, gentle. An innocent. Why he had to die, I can't begin to guess."

Nor could Bak. If Hatnofer had been slain because she was small and vulnerable, the child's death could be explained in the same way. However, neither Senmut nor Montu had been small men, and both had been stabbed without a struggle. Five deaths, with not a man or woman or child offering resistance to the assailant. Bak could think of no way to accomplish such a feat unless the man who slew them had blinded them with magic. Or, more likely, with familiarity.

"I must admit my relief when I learned another had been slain and I could rest easy." Amethu hiked up his long white kilt, bunching the fabric over his bulging stomach, and dropped onto a portable stool. "Does that sound heartless, Lieutenant?"

"You're not the first to voice the thought," Bak said, "and I doubt you'll be the last."

The steward gave him a fleeting smile, his thoughts on the task before him: the weekly distribution of grain to those who toiled in the governor's kitchen.

Bak knelt beside him in a strip of shade cast by Nebmose's villa—how quickly he had come to accept the local name for the dwelling—watching servants empty one of the granaries. One man knelt before an opening twice the size of a man's head located at the base of the tall conical tower. Another man, who had climbed down an interior ladder, swept the remaining wheat into a basket and poured a golden stream through the hole, gradually filling the larger basket his companion held. Dust billowed from the cascading grain, making the man outside cough. Amethu noted the amount on a bit of broken pottery. Later, Bak knew, he would total the various quantities and record them on a scroll.

"I'll miss Hatnofer," the steward said. "She was one of the few people in this household to know the value of keeping accurate accounts. The rest of them . . ." He gave a long-suffering sigh. "They just don't seem to care. They take an item from a storage room, don't bother to note its removal or to tell anyone, and then complain when they go in search of another like item and find none."

"Was she as diligent in managing the household and its many servants?"

"To a fault, some would say." Amethu frowned. "I don't mean to be critical, but you'll find out soon enough. She was not well liked. Too stern and unforgiving. Too demanding. But she kept the household running as smooth as a well-oiled chariot wheel. She'll be greatly missed."

"What of mistress Khawet? Can she not oversee the servants?"

"Enough!" Amethu scrambled to his feet and hurried to the man kneeling at the base of the granary. He reached into the basket, withdrew a handful of wheat, and let it trickle from one hand to the other. His mouth pursed in disapproval. "We can't distribute this. It's full of sand. We'd have a rebellion on our hands."

He flung the grain to the ground and took a fresh handful. Sifting it through his fingers, he shook his head. "Unacceptable. Set this basket aside and move on to the next granary. After you've gathered enough wheat for today's needs, come back here, sweep this one out, and pour all this dirty grain into the storage chamber where we're saving the seed for planting."

"Yes, sir," said the man outside, his voice echoed from within.

Amethu returned to his stool and bowed his head in what Bak took to be a prayer. When at last the steward raised his eyes, he again shook his head, this time in vexation. "They never learn. Never. A foreman should sit out here, not me, but the last time I entrusted this task to another man, we had sand in our bread for a week."

Bak held his tongue. Gritty bread was endemic to the army. "We were speaking of mistress Khawet, of her ability to take over Hatnofer's duties."

"Khawet is a nice woman. I've known her from a babe. The question is: can she oversee a large and busy household in addition to satisfying her father's many demands? Not to mention the demands of a husband."

"She has no children."

"A pity." Amethu paused to watch the servant climb out of the granary and drop onto a shoulder-high platform that joined the empty structure to the one beside it. Hurrying down a stairway that descended to the ground, he knelt beside his partner, who had broken the seal that attested to the integrity of the full granary. "I've long been of the opinion that Hatnofer's problem was her failure to conceive. She was a woman of good humor and sweetness in her youth. A few years ago, as life began to pass her by, her disposition soured. Now I see Khawet traveling the same path, and I fear for her."

From what Bak had seen of Djehuty, he was more than enough child for any woman. Or perhaps he was being unfair. "You've been with Djehuty for many years, I see."

"My father was his father's steward. I grew to manhood in this province, learned to read and write in the governor's villa. When my father left this worldly realm, Djehuty's father appointed me to his place, as was right and proper."

"Can you think of a reason anyone would want him dead? Would kill and kill again to plant fear in his heart?"

Amethu looked distinctly uncomfortable. "He's stepped on toes What man hasn't?"

"Has he come down so hard he'd merit death?"

"He's basically a good man, Lieutenant." Amethu cleared his throat, as if the next words were caught there. "Oh, he can be thoughtless at times. Selfish and petty. Altogether a most aggravating individual. But as he intends no ill, all who know him forgive him."

Especially those who walk the corridors of the governor's villa, Bak thought. *Men who wield a moderate amount of power and live in far greater comfort and style than their neighbors. Those who owe their lofty positions to Djehuty and dare not speak out lest he replace them with others more agreeable.*

"If you truly believe a murderer walks these corridors, why are you not living within these walls?" Simut's voice pulsed with frustration as he tried to balance vehemence and the need to speak softly so his students would not hear his words. "Why do you not send for Medjays—not from Buhen, for the journey would take too long, but from the capital? Men with dogs who'll patrol the rooms night and day?"

"If I were to summon additional men, Djehuty might well be slain long before they arrive." Bak spoke softly, as reluctant to draw the boys from their studies as the chief scribe was. "Have you never watched a cornered animal, forced to strike rather than bide its time?"

A chunky boy of ten or so years looked up from a pottery fragment on which he had been writing and sneaked a peek in their direction. He and a dozen or so other youths ranging in age from ten to fourteen sat cross-legged on the floor of the open courtyard, scribal pallets beside them, pieces of broken pottery or slabs of limestone in their laps. A boy of about twelve sat before them, dictating from a scroll the maxims of a long-dead sage. A younger group of boys sat beneath a shallow portico, copying words from a list of household objects. A slick-haired black dog lay in a shady corner, nursing four spotted puppies.

"Not so loud!" Simut's hiss traveled across the courtyard,

drawing the eyes of all his students. "Now look what you've done."

"Boys are born to be curious," Bak said, forcing himself to exercise patience. "If you don't want them disturbed, come away with me. There's an unoccupied room not a dozen paces from here."

Simut gave him a horrified look. "Do you have any idea what would happen if I left these children alone? They'd run amok, that's what they'd do."

Remembering his own youth, Bak had to agree. Boys forced to study day after day, copying dry texts from times gone by, had far too much energy to sit still and quiet when left unattended. "I'll be brief then."

"Do so."

The scribe's attitude grated, bringing forth a question Bak normally would have approached slowly, the one that had set Amethu on the defensive. "Do you know of any reason anyone would want Djehuty dead?"

Simut gave him a sharp look. "Why ask that question of me?"

"How long have you served as a scribe in Abu?" The question was rhetorical, meant to point out Simut's long tenure in the governor's villa.

The scribe chose to take the query at face value. "I learned my profession in this very courtyard. That's why you see me here now. I feel no end of fulfillment in teaching other boys as I once was taught. When their regular tutor ails, or has another task he must do, I freely give of my time." He paused, nodded his satisfaction—with himself, Bak assumed. "I've toiled in this building ever since. I began as a lowly apprentice writing letters for farmers, as the boys you see before you will most likely do, and my life has been filled to the brim from that time until now. I can climb no higher."

"Far more lofty positions are available to scribes in the capital," Bak pointed out.

Simut raised his head high so he could look down his nose at one so lacking in understanding. "Abu is my home, the home of my wife and my children and their children. The home of my father and his father before him.''

The scribe, Bak noted, had begun to speak with greater ease. Talk of himself suited him. ''With so many years in the governor's villa, you must've heard complaints about Djehuty, some serious enough to be called transgressions.''

Simut sat quite still, then sniffed. ''If you're interested in gossip, young man, I suggest you visit a few of the local houses of pleasure.''

''I want the truth, not the ramblings of men besotted by beer.'' Bak adopted his most serious demeanor. ''Need I remind you that I'm here at the vizier's request?''

''I was told he suggested Djehuty send for you.'' The scribe raised his voice in triumph. ''That's quite a different matter.''

''When a man as lofty as the vizier . . .'' Realizing he, too, was speaking too loud, Bak glanced toward the students. All were staring, including the boy supposed to be dictating. Bak grabbed the scribe's arm and towed him through the nearest door into a short hallway. ''Simut! In nine days' time the slayer will strike again, his next victim Djehuty. Do you want the governor's death forever on your conscience?''

''I've every confidence you'll soon learn what you need to know, Lieutenant, but you won't hear it from me.'' Simut shook his arm free and stalked back to the courtyard.

Bak passed through the unimpressive mudbrick pylon gate of the mansion of the lord Khnum and walked along a rough path that carried him toward the river. At the end, he came upon thirty or so nearly naked men, reeking of sweat, toiling on a small, dilapidated shrine that overlooked the water. Half the crew struggled with slabs of stone, laying new pavement over the old. Others were erecting sturdy stone columns in place of rotting wooden supports, while the remainder repaired crumbling walls. Good-natured banter, a man whistling a lively tune, the rhythmic beat of a mallet on stone could not silence a multitude of sparrows in the trees.

Bak walked to the edge of the steep, rocky slope. Below, several small boats skimmed the water, their sails spread wide like the wings of birds free to fly where they wished. He longed to be down there with them, to feel the breeze stirring his hair and to hear water whispering against the hull. Shaking off temptation, he forced his thoughts back to the puzzle he had traveled so far to solve.

Djehuty had committed an offense—that much Simut had implied—and sooner or later someone would reveal its secret. What the secret was, Bak could not begin to guess, but its grievous nature was apparent. Few men would look into the face of death rather than admit a wrongdoing.

Bak had left the scribe to his students, determined to learn what Djehuty had done. Only then could he establish whether or not that particular offense could have led to five deaths, with a sixth looming. If so, he could go on from there. If not, he must search for another reason for murder. He had to smile. It sounded so easy. However, experience had taught him that a course of action that on the surface appeared smooth and direct more often than not was filled with obstacles.

After a hasty midday meal, he had hurried to the garrison, a jumble of barracks buildings and houses located near the southern edge of Abu. The old, much-repaired, and oft-altered structures blended into the city. Unlike Buhen, no high, fortified wall surrounded them. Evidently the river had been thought, in days long past, to offer sufficient protection from the enemy.

Troop Captain Antef, the sergeant on duty had told him, had gone to the granite quarries. When he would return, no one could say.

Bak had hastened back through the narrow, crowded streets to the mansion of the lord Khnum, thinking the chief priest might—like Amethu and Simut—be a long-time resident in Abu, but unlike them a man bound to speak the truth, leaving no secrets buried in silence. He had again been faced with disappointment. The priest who had greeted him was young, new to the mansion and the town. His elderly predecessor had, not six months before, departed his worldly life and gone off to the Field of Reeds. The younger man could offer nothing of value.

A skiff speeding northward caught Bak's attention. The sail was down and two men were rowing, adding thrust to the current's downstream pull. Troop Captain Antef was one of the pair. Just the man Bak wished to see—and he appeared to be heading for the landingplace.

Bak had no idea how long Antef had dwelt in Abu, but few professional soldiers remained in one place for long. The queen's nephew and stepson Menkheperre Thutmose, who shared the throne but not the power, had begun to rebuild an army long neglected by the royal house. Ranking officers of proven incompetence were being removed, and men could no longer inherit positions of authority from their fathers. Newly reorganized regiments were led by men who moved from place to place, proving themselves proficient and versatile.

He also assumed that, although required to report to Djehuty, Antef's real master resided elsewhere, probably in the capital. With little or nothing to lose, he might well divulge Djehuty's secret—if he knew it.

Bak trotted along the path above the river, praying the officer could—and would—help. Several women who had gathered at the well to gossip eyed him with curiosity, as did a pair of lovers lying deep in the shadows of a willow tree. He reached the stairway at the landingplace as Antef's skiff bumped stone. The troop captain leaped ashore and shoved the boat back into the current. His companion rowed on downstream.

Spotting Bak at the top of the stairs, Antef raced upward. "Lieutenant!" He clapped Bak hard on the back. "Have you come to greet me in friendship? Or to shackle my wrists and carry me off to the desert mines?"

Slipping out of arm's reach, Bak forced a smile. "Have you committed an offense deserving of so drastic a punishment?"

The troop captain's good humor evaporated, his eyes flashed anger. "I've kept my men so long at the granite quarries they no longer know how to soldier. If they'd ever have to stand on the field of battle, they'd not last a half hour. That's not an offense; it's an outrage.''

They passed through the gate, nodded to the guard standing before the gatehouse, his spear raised in salute, and strode up the path toward the governor's villa. Antef walked fast, his anger driving him forward.

''You deserve no punishment for that,'' Bak said. ''Unless I'm mistaken, mining the stone is Djehuty's responsibility.''

''As is the well-being of the garrison.'' Antef expelled a cynical snort. ''The granite travels north on a barge, bound for the capital, while our troops stay here. Which is the most likely, Lieutenant, to gain the attention of those who walk the corridors of power?''

Bak well understood the problem. Their sovereign, Maat-kare Hatshepsut, cared for nothing but the smooth flow of products traveling downriver to the royal house. Like Antef's soldiers, the men who manned the fortresses on the frontier, making sure trade objects continued to move north, were of no importance. Only when the flow was disrupted did they attract attention—and angry messages from the capital.

''You don't like Djehuty,'' he said.

''He has no more common sense than the granite we ship north.'' Antef shoved open the door of the governor's villa and strode into the anteroom, a light and bright chamber with two lotus-shaped columns supporting a high ceiling. ''Unfortunately, for this enforced labor at the quarry I can blame no one but myself. If I'd had sufficient wit when first I came to Abu . . .'' He paused, gave a low, bitter laugh. ''Amonhotep can usually talk him around, but not in this case. I pushed too hard, spoke when I should've remained silent. The swine'll never forgive. More important, he won't forget. And my men are made to suffer.''

Could this be Djehuty's offense, Bak wondered, the reason so many people had been slain? Surely not. Ordering the army to continuous service at the quarries was a decision the governor could justify, for the stone would be shipped to the most important building projects in Kemet, the mansions of the gods, in most cases. Bak sympathized with Antef and his troops, as would any soldier, but he could offer no way out. "Five people have died and the next, I feel sure, will be Djehuty. Do you know of any tie that might've bound the victims together? Anything Djehuty might've done to warrant their deaths as well as his own?"

Antef hesitated a long time and finally said, "You'd best ask Amonhotep."

Bak gave him a long, thoughtful look. His answer was more forthright than those of Amethu and Simut but came down to the same thing: he had an idea what might have brought about the murders, but he would not be the first to step forward with the information. "If he won't tell me what I need to know, Troop Captain, I'll come back to you. And I'll expect the truth."

"I've been told you and your Medjays have moved into a house outside the walls of this villa." Antef's tone turned derisive. "Do you feel safer there, Lieutenant?"

"A suggestion has been made that I summon a unit of Medjays from the capital to patrol this compound. What do you think, sir?" Bak kept his voice level, pleasant, as if unaware of the lack of trust the proposal implied.

Antef's expression hardened. "If it's men you need, come to me. I've more than enough. Good, trustworthy men who long to be soldiers, not beasts of burden in the quarry. I can have them armed and on duty within the hour. A man in every room and every hallway, if need be."

Bak was tempted to accept the offer, at least in part, but before he could begin to negotiate terms, Ineni's voice whipped across the room.

"I won't have my home overrun by soldiers!" The young nobleman, who had been standing unseen in a doorway at the back of the anteroom, listening, strode toward the two officers. "We've plenty of guards, men who've been in our service for years. I'd trust them with my life."

As Hatnofer must have relied on them, Bak thought, *and the other four who were slain*. He resolved to speak with Amonhotep, under whose command they served, to make sure the guards stayed alert, their vigilance never faltering.

"They're nothing but farm boys," Antef sneered, "trained to use a plow, not a spear."

Ineni's mouth tightened. "Set ten of our men against ten of yours, and we'll see who's most apt to win a battle."

"Why put our men to the test? Why don't you face me man-to-man? Weapon of your choice."

"Silence!" Bak stepped between the two. "Haven't you seen enough death over the past few weeks?"

"The man's a fool," Antef muttered.

Ineni glared.

Bak had sensed animosity between the two when first he had met them. He could not begin to guess its source, but he had a feeling their mutual dislike was long-standing. "I suggest you each go your separate way, staying well clear of the other. How can I lay hands on a slayer if I'm forever distracted by you?"

"I have to report to Djehuty," Antef grumbled, swinging away and hastening to the portal through which Ineni had come. Khawet shoved the door fully open. He took a quick step back, barely saving his nose.

"Oh, Troop Captain Antef, I'm so sorry." She reached out to touch his arm, then quickly withdrew her hand. "Are you alright?"

"Of course." His voice was gruff; a flush spread across his face. A blind man could have seen the admiration he held for her. He seemed not to know what more to say, so he gave her a quick nod. "I must go."

After he disappeared, she glanced across the room. Her gaze settled on Bak and Ineni, and she hurried between the columns to stand before her husband. "Father's been looking for you." Her voice had turned chilly, the warmth it had held for Antef lost. "He's seeking an explanation as to why you haven't brought another young steer to Abu for slaughter."

"I told him . . ." Ineni glanced at Bak, grimaced. "My father knows nothing of farming."

Khawet gave her husband a too-sweet smile. "You know

something of plowing and planting, I grant you, but my father has ten times ten more worldly experience and knowledge.''

Flushed with anger, Ineni pivoted on his heel and stalked to the rear door, aping Antef in every way though he probably had no idea he did so. Khawet watched him go, her expression almost wistful. Did she in fact love him? Bak wondered, or was she merely wishing she had someone else, the troop captain, maybe?

The smile she turned on Bak was soft, gentle, friendly rather than flirtatious. ''Yesterday I was too upset to thank you properly for coming, Lieutenant, but today . . . Well, I can't tell you how relieved I am that you're here. My father has told me of the pattern you saw in the slayings. That you, a stranger to Abu, should notice what no one else could see gives me a confidence I thought never to feel. I'm certain you'll lay hands on the slayer before he can . . .'' She hesitated, added, ''. . . before he can go on with whatever he plans.''

Bak liked her smile, her pleasant manner, but cautioned himself to be wary. Whether she had noticed her husband in the room initially he had no idea, but she had certainly shown Antef more warmth and consideration. If her behavior had been intentional, if she made a habit of using one man to anger the other, no wonder the pair could not get along.

Bak remained in the anteroom, waiting for Djehuty to finish with the daily reports of the men on his staff and to hear the last of the petitioners. If he was to pry the truth from the governor, he could not do it with an audience hall full of onlookers.

To speed the passage of time, he reviewed the day thus far, ending with the confrontation between Antef and Ineni, two strong men who disliked each other enough to fight yet were very much alike. Both greatly resented Djehuty for disrupting the tasks to which they had devoted their lives. He had been thinking of them, as with all who stood close to the governor, as potential victims, men who might have died if Hatnofer had not been selected by the slayer. Should he be thinking of them instead as men who might harbor so great a hatred in their hearts they would slay Djehuty?

Chapter Five

Djehuty sat on the dais, hands resting on the arms of his chair, posture erect. He looked down at the man on his knees before him. "Speak up, Ipy. What favor do you want this time?"

The petitioner, a man of medium height with broad shoulders and muscular arms, shiny with sweat smudged by smoke or ashes, scuttled forward half a pace. He reeked of sweat, filling the audience hall with his sour odor.

"Oh, please, most kind sir, if you deem it right and proper to give me a favorable judgment, I'll honor you more than I honor our sovereign, that I swear to the lord Khnum."

"I'm sure you will," Djehuty murmured, more to Lieutenant Amonhotep, standing beside his chair, than to the craftsman.

Bak stood near the massive double doors through which supplicants entered the audience hall, amused yet sympathetic. Men like Ipy abounded along the Belly of Stones, and from long experience he knew that dealing with them required infinite patience as well as a firm hand.

Few people remained in the hall. Most of those who had come seeking judgment or wise counsel had gone. The scribes who were no longer needed had returned to Simut's lair to document the day's proceedings. Antef had made a perfunctory report and left some time ago, as had several other members of the governor's staff. The guard standing nearby in front of the doors, impatient to be on his way,

67

constantly patted his bare leg, as if keeping time to a tune
he alone could hear.

Ipy inched forward. "I'll go each day to the shrine of
the hearing ear behind the mansion of the lord Khnum, sir,
and I'll pray on bended knee for your well-being for
ever and ever. I'll make offerings of food and drink, of
flowers and incense. Then I'll go to the other shrines of Abu,
each and everyone, seeking for you and yours all the good
things of life. Health, wealth, happiness . . ."

"We know, Ipy." Amonhotep glanced toward Bak but
made no sign of greeting. "You've vowed to pray for the
governor each time you've approached this dais. You've no
need to repeat the promise."

Scooting forward again, Ipy bowed his head. "I sometimes backslide, sir, forgetting to pray as I've said I would."
His head shot up, his voice rang with sincerity. "But this
time, I'll not break my word. I'll throw down my tools and
leave my workshop, letting my customers wait for the pots
I've promised. I'll let my wife wear rags and my little children suffer hunger. All so I can spend half of each day on
my knees. So I can . . ."

Djehuty's eyes darted around the room, as if seeking relief.
He noticed Bak, grimaced, looked back at the petitioner, and
his voice turned testy. "What is it you want, man?"

"You're wise and noble beyond your years, sir. I trust
you always to make a right and proper judgment, to aid all
who need help, to . . ."

Amonhotep stepped forward. "That's enough, Ipy. Either
make your petition or leave us."

"But, sir, I was just trying to . . ."

"Guard!" Djehuty stood up and pointed. "Take this man
away," he commanded. "I've no time to listen to foolish-
ness." He gave Ipy a venomous look. "A few days' impris-
onment should teach him the value of short and concise
speech."

A guard hurried up, grabbed Ipy by the arm, and jerked
him to his feet. The craftsman's sly smile faded. His eyes

darted from Djehuty to Amonhotep to the guard, registering confusion and fear.

"Sir," Amonhotep said, "Ipy's been here before—more than once. You know he meant no harm. If you let me speak with him, I'm certain he'll tell me the reason he's come again, and he'll do so with no further nonsense. Why lock him up if there's no need?"

Djehuty, his mouth tight and determined, waved his hand, signaling the guard to take the craftsman away. The guard stood where he was, looking from the governor to his aide as if unsure what he should do. Bak guessed from his failure to respond immediately that Djehuty's quick anger and Amonhotep's attempt to moderate were not new to those who stood in the audience hall day after day, watching the proceedings.

Djehuty glared at the officer, the guard, and finally the craftsman. Not until Ipy began to whimper did he drop back into his chair. "Alright, Lieutenant, if you want to waste your time with this spawn of a dog, you may do so."

The guard released Ipy's arm and pivoted. As he did so, he winked at his colleague standing before the double doors, verifying Bak's guess that Amonhotep often tempered the governor's hasty decisions.

"They try my patience, Lieutenant." Djehuty closed his eyes and rubbed the lids, a man utterly exhausted by the pressure of duty. "If I could sit on this dais and judge matters of importance brought before me each day by men of substance, I'd feel my task of some use. But all too often, a week will go by—a month even—and no one comes before me with any petition more weighty than that of that dolt Ipy."

"Yes, sir." *Does the man believe justice thrives solely for those of lofty birth and position?* Bak wondered.

"My father sat in this chair, as did his father before him and his before him. I often wonder if they had some special way of maintaining patience."

Bak shifted his weight from one foot to the other, unable

to think of an appropriate response. In fact, he was not sure the governor expected one.

As if roused by the silence, Djehuty's eyes popped open and he looked at the younger man as a schoolmaster would a pupil he suspected of whispering behind his back. "Are you aware that my family goes back all the way to Sarenput, who was governor of the south and hereditary prince during the reign of Kheperkare Senwosret many generations ago?" He stared at Bak as if daring him to doubt. "Yes, young man, I have royal blood coursing through my body. The blood of those brave and noble men whose houses of eternity look down upon Abu from the hillside on the west bank of the river."

"I've seen them from afar, sir." Bak longed to get on with his pursuit of the slayer, but too abrupt a dismissal of Djehuty's heritage might seal the man's lips forever. He regretted Amonhotep's hasty departure with Ipy. The aide appeared quite adept at manipulating his master.

"Sarenput had his eternal resting place excavated among other, far older sepulchers, those of men who governed this province when the land of Kemet was young and Abu stood on its southern frontier." Djehuty clutched his long baton of office, leaning against the chair beside his leg, and his expression grew wishful. "Maybe they, too, were my ancestors. Would he have chosen to dwell forever among strangers?"

"Sir . . ."

Djehuty sat back in his chair and smiled, cheered by the possibility, unlikely as it was, of so long a regal lineage. "Fortunately, my distinguished heritage has given me a strength of character few men can claim and the fortitude to do what I must, no matter how distasteful. Take that man Ipy, for example . . ."

"That's why I've come to you now, sir," Bak said, leaping through the door the governor had unwittingly opened.

Djehuty's eyes narrowed. "Oh?"

"If I'm to find the man who's slain five people, you must help me." Remembering Antef's admission that he had pushed Djehuty too hard, thereby sentencing his troops to

unending duty at the quarries, he spoke with the honeyed
tongue of a nobleman who has spent all his days in the royal
house. "I realize you've a multitude of tasks, all far more
weighty than you're willing to acknowledge, but if you could
spare me some time and the benefit of your experience and
knowledge, your insight, you might set me on a path I've up
to now failed to find."

Djehuty stared at the man standing before him. Bak feared
he had gone too far.

"When first I saw you at the back of the hall, Lieutenant,
I looked also for a man in shackles, thinking an officer so
fast to find a pattern in these crimes would be equally quick
to lay hands on the slayer." Adopting a fatherly manner,
Djehuty chuckled. "Now, with no prisoner in tow, your in-
itial confidence seems to be wanting."

Biting back a sharp reply, nearly choking on it, Bak did
his best to sound like a dutiful officer, not a humble servant.
"I freely admit I know scarcely more now than I did at this
time yesterday, when the servant Nefer came with word of
mistress Hatnofer's death. Sir."

Djehuty's mouth tightened at Bak's near lapse in courtesy.
"I told you all I knew when first we spoke. I've nothing
more to add." He stood up, gripped his baton, and stepped
down off the dais, forcing Bak backward. "Now, as you
yourself have pointed out, I'm a busy man. My daughter
Khawet must already have servants waiting to bathe me."
He strode across the pillared hall with the same air of purpose he might have used to approach a formal dedication.

Bak kept up with him step for step. "Will you tell me,
sir, anything you've done that could've set off this string of
deaths? An incident that may not have seemed significant to
you but was important to someone else? Possibly resulting
in a threat?"

Djehuty's step faltered, but only for an instant. "I've done
nothing wrong. Nothing."

"Men have hinted that you've a secret, one all who know
you are either afraid or ashamed to repeat."

"All lesser men wish to tear down the stronger, Lieutenant, hinting at weaknesses that burden them alone. Surely a man as experienced as you can sort the grain from the chaff.''

Bak stopped, demanded, ''Do you want to die, sir?''

Djehuty, his face flaming, pivoted and raised his baton, ready to strike. Realization came to him, the knowledge that Bak was another man's man, and he whipped the baton down, making it whistle through the air. ''You want to know what secret I harbor in my heart, Lieutenant?'' His lips twisted in a sneer. ''I don't like you. Nor do I like the insinuations you're making. If I hadn't sent a message to the vizier, telling him of your arrival, I'd send you back to Buhen before nightfall.''

Bak's eyes met Djehuty's. The governor tried to hold the stare, but could not. He looked away, seeking escape, and strode rapidly to the door.

No, Bak thought, *you're not worried about the message you sent to the capital. You're afraid to die. And you know of no one but me who has the slightest chance of laying hands on the slayer before he comes for you. The slightest chance? Perhaps no chance at all unless I can soon break down this wall of silence.*

Bak followed Djehuty out the door, but turned left at the first short passage. At the end, he came upon a large room, its ceiling supported by two tall brightly painted lotus-shaped columns, with high windows admitting light. Ten scribes sat cross-legged on the floor, each surrounded by the tools of his trade. The reed pens darting across the regular columns on their scrolls sounded like birds scratching in a pile of spilled grain.

Simut, seated on a thick linen pad in front of the lesser scribes, frowned at Bak. ''May I help you, Lieutenant?''

The soft scraping sound dwindled and ten pairs of eyes turned Bak's way. ''I'm searching for Lieutenant Amonhotep. I've been told he came here after he finished with the craftsman Ipy.''

A look of relief, quickly hidden, flickered across the chief scribe's face. "He's come and gone. There was a problem at the harbor above Swenet, where ships unload their cargo for overland transport around the rapids. A fight between caravan masters, I understand."

Bak longed to ask again what secret Djehuty held in his heart, but knew he would get nothing with so many men listening. "Have you told him of my questions?"

"What the two of you discuss is between him and his master and the gods. It's none of my affair."

The answer was oblique, but Bak gathered Simut had said nothing. In the unlikely event that no one else had warned the young officer, he would be unprepared for the difficult questions Bak meant to ask and the even harder choices he would have to make. However, unprepared did not mean compliant. Bak had learned during the voyage from Buhen to Abu that if Amonhotep deemed he should say nothing, he would remain mute.

"Your Medjay Psuro is at the landingplace, sir." The servant, a boy of about eight years, tried hard to look solemn and trustworthy, but his eyes danced with excitement at being entrusted with a message of such great import. "He has news he says you'll want to hear."

Bak thanked the boy with a smile and hurried outside. He found the Medjay a hundred or more paces downstream of the landingplace, talking to a gap-toothed old woman with spotted hands and the protruding stomach of one who has borne many children. While they spoke, she lifted sheets and clothing from the bushes and boulders across which she had draped them to dry, folded them, and laid them in a basket. Psuro might not have had the gift Kasaya had of attracting women who yearned to mother him, but he had a way with those who eked out a living selling foodstuffs and providing minor but necessary services.

Bak stood off to the side, saying nothing, until she had gone on her way. "She'll wash our linen?"

"She has a taste for pigeon," Psuro grinned. "Though she has far too many customers, so she says, she'll squeeze our meager laundry in among the rest, and she'll mend torn articles as well. Each time, I'll give her a bird."

Bak thought the price too steep, but held his tongue. Every time he had tracked a slayer, he had come away bruised and battered, his kilts torn and filthy. If the slayer in the governor's villa proved equally difficult to lay hands on, he feared the old woman would earn a flock of pigeons.

They headed back upstream, walking close to the river's edge, stepping over rocks and around brush, slipping in patches of mud. The western sky was pale, a sheet of gold diluted with silver. To the east, tiny pinpoints barely visible so early in the evening promised a night brilliant with stars.

"You've news," Bak prompted.

Psuro, looking pleased with himself, nodded. "The trader Pahared sends his regards. He remembers well the afternoon he spent with you and Troop Captain Nebwa in Nofery's house of pleasure." A studied seriousness could not quite hide a smile. "A time of revelry and excessive drunkenness, he says."

Smiling at the memory, pleased with Psuro's success, Bak stepped over a turtle making its slow way toward the water. "I thank the lord Amon you had better luck in Swenet than in Abu."

"You must first thank my tenacity," Psuro laughed. "If I'd not searched with due diligence, I'd never have found him."

"He doesn't dwell in Swenet?"

"His wife has a house of pleasure near the market, and they live in a villa close by. I found him in neither place but at the harbor." Psuro pulled back the branch of a bush and held it while Bak edged by. "Pahared, I suspect, is on his way to becoming a man of wealth. He's the master of a trading ship, as he was when you met him in Buhen, and he shows no outward sign of success. But he buys hay downriver, ships it south to Swenet, and sells it to caravan masters to feed their donkeys. He admits he has no competition."

"I took him to be a resourceful man." Bak climbed onto the stone landingplace, thought what best to do, crossed to the skiff. "I must speak with him, Psuro. Maybe one who dwells in Swenet, a place where men come and go, transients who owe no special loyalty to Djehuty, can unlatch a door I've failed to open."

Pahared was just as Bak remembered him: a large, heavily muscled man with an incipient paunch and a hint of gray at the temples. His knee-length kilt rode low on his belly and wide beaded bracelets accentuated the thickness of his wrists and arms. He was good-natured under normal circumstances, Bak recalled, but formidable when pushed too hard. They had greeted each other like old friends, not men who had spent a single afternoon drinking and playing games of chance.

"There's not a man or woman in this province who hasn't heard of the murders." Pahared, seated on a low stool, watched his wife break the dried mud plugs stoppering two beer jars. She was almost as tall as he, but reed-thin, and she had the dark skin and woolly hair of the peoples living far to the south of Kush. "With so many dying so fast and all in the governor's household, most whisper that a demon of the night has come to lay waste to this province. They're scared, if the truth be told. Afraid the crops will fail, their animals sicken and die, their families starve."

Bak accepted a jar with a quick smile of thanks, toed a stool away from the wall, and sat beside the trader. "If Djehuty is the ultimate goal, as I think he is, the demon resides in a man, and he's out to avenge some unspeakable deed."

"I wouldn't know about that." Pahared eyed five sailors filing in through the door, their unsteady gait and slurred speech pointing to earlier visits to other houses of pleasure. "I'm not sure anybody knows. That's what scares them so. They don't know where to turn, which demon or genie or god to placate."

Having no patience with superstition, Bak scowled at the room in which they sat: a large, open space with a high ceiling supported by one square mudbrick column. Long shafts of the waning light of evening filtered down from high windows. A large, gangly gray monkey searched through the straw covering the floor, hunting insects. Three-legged stools and a few low tables stood around the room, while the walls were lined with beer vats, wine jars, and baskets filled with drinking bowls. The room smelled of beer and vomit; the sailors reeked of sweat and fish and garlic.

This place of business reminded him of Nofery, though it resembled neither the old hovel where she had once toiled nor her new, much grander house of pleasure. *It must be the smell,* he thought, *the ever-present stench of the brew and overindulgence.* "You've heard no tales that discredit Djehuty?" he asked.

"I've known of more popular governors, no doubt about it, but nothing that would bring the wrath of the gods upon his head."

Bak gave the trader a wry smile. "You disappoint me, my friend. When I saw this place of business, located on the main thoroughfare running through Swenet, close to the market and within easy walking distance of the encampment where the merchants unload their caravans, I thought to myself: how ideally situated to attract patrons from all walks of life—men who ofttimes drink to excess and speak with loose and frank tongues. When I saw your wife . . ." He nodded toward the woman, who stood with her shoulder against the doorjamb, keeping a close eye on customers and servants alike. ". . . she reinforced my confidence in you. I never thought superstition would reign."

Pahared chuckled. "I hear many tales, I'm bound to admit, some less fanciful than others. Among them, complaints about Djehuty. But none unique to him, I suspect."

"Tell me. I've nowhere else to turn."

Pahared laughed again, not taking him seriously. "They say he's indolent, a man who lives a life of luxury and ease. One who, in his youth, loved to hunt and fish and fowl, but now prefers to loll away the hours in his villa, eating sweets and drinking wine. A man responsible for meting out the law, yet one who has scant knowledge of the laws of the land. A man who, thanks to the gods, is surrounded by men of talent and knowledge who tend to the needs of this province in his stead.''

Bak suspected the assessment was fair. The brief time he had spent in the audience hall had divulged no brighter side to the man. "What of the men close to him? Have any of them committed an offense that might be laid at Djehuty's feet?''

Pahared drank from his beer jar, licked his lips, shrugged. "Not that I've heard—and I would've. Most have lived here since they were babes, and their lives are as open to view as the orb of Re traveling across the sky day after day.''

Bak expelled a quick, frustrated sigh. "When I press Djehuty for help, he acts like a man with guilt in his heart but denies all wrongdoing. Three men on his staff have hinted he has a guilty secret, and none will enlighten me.''

Pahared frowned. "Well, whatever he's done, it wasn't here.'' He watched two men of middle years, merchants from the look of them, wander in from the street and pass through the room to the courtyard beyond. His wife hastened out to serve them. "He was in the army, you know. In fact, as a young officer, he spent a couple years on the eastern frontier. I wonder how he conducted himself there?''

Bak knew garrison duty could sometimes bring out the worst in a man, but the assignment seemed too long ago, the eastern frontier too distant. Especially when trying to account for the death of five other people, two of whom—mistress Hatnofer and the child Nakht—he knew for a fact had never set foot out of Abu.

A new thought struck and his eyes narrowed. Djehuty had succeeded his father as provincial governor. During the older man's tenure, a seasoned officer had probably led the garrison, keeping the troops alert and trained, but the governor had in effect been in command—as Djehuty now commanded Antef. "After he served out his time on the frontier, did he remain in the army?''

"He did.'' Pahared glanced at his wife, who returned to her spot in the doorway. If he noticed the tension in Bak's voice, he gave no sign. "First he served as an aide to a royal envoy, traveling north to the land of Amurru. Then, when the commander of the garrison of Abu was recalled to Kemet, his father appealed to our sovereign, Maatkare Hatshepsut, asking that Djehuty be given the post. That was ten or so years ago, when she was new to the throne and anxious to win the loyalty of powerful provincial governors. So she agreed.''

Bak smiled, satisfied with a guess proven right: Djehuty had come back to Abu as a ranking officer, one in a position to step on many toes. ''Was the garrison peopled mostly with local men? Soldiers born and reared in this province?''

''It was, but no longer. Menkheperre Thutmose, when he took command of the army, assigned men from throughout the land of Kemet.''

Bak, nodding his understanding, watched without seeing a three-legged white dog trot into the room and lie down at Pahared's feet. Not only had Menkheperre Thutmose, the young man who shared the throne in name only, letting the queen have her way, cleared away incompetent officers and forced new men to prove their worth, but he had made radical changes throughout the regiments and garrisons, moving men of all ranks from one post to another so their loyalties lay with him rather than with provincial noblemen or governors.

''After Djehuty came back, did anything—anything at all—happen for which blame might be laid at his feet?'' Bak heard the doggedness in his voice, the refusal to let go.

Pahared shook his head, regret filling his eyes. ''I'd like to help, my young friend, but I can think of nothing.''

His wife stepped forward and spoke a few words in her own tongue. Pahared snapped his fingers, nodded, listened further, and smiled his thanks. She returned to the door, obviously content with herself and his response.

''My wife understands the tongue of Kemet but hesitates to use it, fearing ridicule.'' The merchant gave the woman a fond smile. ''She has a better memory than I do. She reminded me of the storm. The storm that took so many young lives.'' His eyes darted toward Bak. ''But that was long ago.

It may have nothing to do with the here and now."

"Tell me about it."

"A raging tempest out in the desert." Pahared looked surprised at Bak's ignorance. "Have you never heard of it? Five
years ago, it was. Over a hundred men lost in the wind and
sand, never to be seen again."

Bak forced his thoughts back. He had been assigned to the
garrison at Mennufer at that time, newly appointed to head
a company of charioteers, full of his own importance and
barely listening to rumors of an army vanished in a desert
storm.

"I heard tales of an entire company of spearmen lost
and . . ." He stiffened, gave the merchant a sharp look. "And
a commander who returned alive. That was Djehuty?"

"He came back, yes." Pahared stared at the large, cal-
loused hands clasped in his lap, saddened by the tale, by the
loss of so many. "He and a handful of other men."

Bak nodded slowly, dwelling on the news. "I take it Djehuty, as commanding officer, was responsible for so grave a
loss."

"In the year I've lived in Swenet, I've heard no man lay
blame at his feet." Pahared snorted, derisive. "How can you
fault a mere mortal faced with the might and fury of the
gods?

"You can't expect Djehuty to speak of that day!" Lieutenant Amonhotep ran his fingers around the upper inside
edge of his broad beaded collar, as if it lay too tight around
his neck. "Even now he feels the weight of responsibility,
though no man alive could've guessed a storm would strike
so late in the year."

The aide had been brought by Psuro to Pahared's house
of pleasure, expecting a companionable evening with Bak.
Instead, he had been ushered out to the courtyard, which was
lighted by a torch mounted in a bracket by the door, and
pressed for information. Now he sat on a stool, drinking bowl
in hand, offering nothing, admitting a bare minimum.

Bak leaned over to pet the three-legged dog, now curled

up at his feet. Merry laughter and the clatter of knucklebones reminded him of the good time to be had beyond the door, doubling his regret that he must probe and poke. "I was told he was so filled with shame he stepped down from his post as garrison commander, turning his back on the army forever." Pahared had said no such thing, but exaggeration might free Amonhotep's power of speech.

"I suppose to some it looked that way." The aide's voice was as stiff as his spine. "In reality, he left the army to take his father's place as provincial governor—his right as sole heir."

"Did you serve with him while still he was an officer?"

"Since my thirteenth birthday." Amonhotep did not look reassured by the change of subject.

"You, like so many others who toil in the governor's villa, must've been born and reared in Abu."

"I grew to manhood in Nubt, on Djehuty's estate."

"And he took you into this garrison ten years ago . . ." Bak queried the aide with a glance, received a nod. ". . . when he came back to the province."

"He made me his herald, yes."

No wonder Amonhotep was loyal to a fault, Bak thought. He had Djehuty to thank for his rank and position. And possibly his life. Whether herald or aide, the young officer would have accompanied Djehuty on that fateful journey into the desert.

"What was he when he returned? A troop captain like Antef?" Bak's voice took on an edge of cynicism. "Or was he handed the lofty rank of commander?"

Amonhotep's eyes flashed indignation. "Djehuty may have his faults, Lieutenant, but he's always been an honorable man. This garrison is small, warranting no more than a troop captain at its head, and so he was when his father died and he took his seat as governor. While still he served in the army, I pointed out more than once that some men travel to the capital, seeking advantage. He refused to do so."

A refusal to seek preferment did not sound like the Djehuty who had summoned Bak from Buhen but refused to help him, nor the Djehuty he sensed behind the compliments and complaints of the men on the governor's staff. "He had no black marks against him as an officer?"

"None."

Bak raised an eyebrow. "No blame was laid when he lost more than a hundred men in a sandstorm?"

"His record is clean, I tell you."

Again Bak veered away from the point, hoping to unsettle the aide. "Why would a garrison commander lead a company of men out onto the desert? Would that not be a task for an officer of lower rank? A lieutenant like you or me?"

"Normally, yes. But Djehuty was no laggard. He wanted to stand tall and proud at the head of his men."

"Instead . . ." Bak made his voice cool, deliberate. ". . . a storm struck, decimating the column and leaving few survivors."

Amonhotep, eyes flashing with anger, gulped down the last of his beer, set the bowl on the floor, and stood up. A mouse flitted into the shadows behind several pottery storage containers. "The storm was unfortunate. No, worse. It was catastrophic. A cruel whim of the gods."

Bak rose, blocking the aide's path to the door. "Nine days from now, Lieutenant, Djehuty may well be dead. Slain by a man I've failed to lay hands on because no one close to him will speak with a frank and open tongue."

"The storm, those many deaths, can't be laid at his feet! He came close to losing his own life!"

"Convince me!" Bak sensed men at the door, attracted by the raised voices. He waved them away, urging them to mind their own business, and spoke more softly. "Tell me what happened, Amonhotep."

The aide dropped onto his stool, fumbled for his drinking bowl, found it empty. Bak strode to the door, signaled to Pahared's wife for two more jars, and returned to his seat. The dog, its attention focused on the shadows between the pottery jars, rested its chin on his sandaled foot.

Amonhotep lowered his head and rubbed his eyes. He spoke in a tired, defeated voice. "I don't enjoy talking about that storm, or remembering. No man does who lived through it."

Bak nodded, offering no words of sympathy, his understanding limited by a lack of experience he in no way wished to gain.

The aide looked up, his mouth tight and resolute. "Desert tribesmen—thirty, maybe forty men from the western oasis of Uahtrest—had been raiding caravans carrying trade goods past the rapids and attacking outlying farms in the province. The garrison was short-manned. To send sufficient troops to protect the caravans strained us beyond our limit; to guard the farms was impossible."

"Did you not send word to the police at Uahtrest?"

Amonhotep gave a short, bitter laugh. "Twice we did, and neither messenger ever returned. Either they were waylaid in the desert or those men assigned to uphold the law in Uahtrest handed them over to the raiders." He glanced toward the door, where Pahared's wife stood, a beer jar in each hand. Not until she had delivered the brew and gone back to her other customers did he continue. "Djehuty and his officers agreed: the raiders must be stopped and we must do it. The best way, they decided, was to march to Uahtrest, taking all available spearmen, and ambush them. Decimate them."

Bak nodded his understanding. "By making an example of them, they hoped to discourage other tribesmen from future raids."

"Yes." Amonhotep filled his drinking bowl and took several deep swallows, bolstering his will to go on. "A company of spearmen—a hundred strong—set out, as did their officers and a half dozen scouts who knew the desert well. Each man led a donkey, some burdened with food, some laden with water, all carrying weapons. Djehuty marched at their head."

"And you with him," Bak guessed.

Amonhotep gave an odd, strangled laugh, nodded. "We were four days out when the breeze stiffened and the air grew thick with dust. The world turned black. I could see nothing. Not Djehuty before me or the donkey whose rope I held." He paused, swallowed hard. "Over the roar of the wind, I heard shouts, contradictory orders, donkeys braying. Sand clogged my nose, crept beneath my eyelids and under my clothing, abraded my flesh. I tied the rope around my wrist, caught hold of the bridle, and held on as if my very life depended upon the donkey I led. And it did.''

The aide took another deep drink. Bak could see how hard it was for him to go on, how dreadful the memory. He wished he could put an end to the tale, ease the officer's pain, but to do so would be foolhardy, might even cost Djehuty his life.

"The creature turned its back to the wind," Amonhotep said, "letting the storm blow us where it would, and I stumbled along beside him. It was I who fell, not him, and I pulled him down with me. He struggled to rise, but I clung to him, burying my face in his neck, burying his head in my lap. The sand built up around us and I . . .'' He paused; a faint, humorless smile touched his lips. "I felt sure we would die, the donkey and I together.''

Another pause, a soft laugh. "The wind stopped blowing. In a world as silent as a tomb, I stood up and so did my four-legged companion. His back was bare, I saw; he no longer carried the water jars we had set out with that morning. We shook off the sand and looked around, thinking other men and animals would show themselves. None did.''

Amonhotep's breathing had grown heavy, labored, revealing the torment of memory. "I panicked, running first in one direction and then another, digging into every small mound of sand until my hands bled, desperate to find other survivors. At last, exhausted and thirsty, I faced the truth: we—my donkey and I—were alone. We spent the rest of the day hiding from the burning sun in the shade of a low ridge. As darkness fell, we set out, using the stars to guide us. It was cold; our stomachs were empty and our mouths dry. So very dry.''

He swallowed hard again. "As dawn broke, my donkey brayed. In the distance, we heard another and a second one, both somewhere beyond a stony ridge. When finally I realized the sound was real, not an illusion born of thirst, we hurried toward them, I thinking we'd find the rest of our troops." His laugh this time was short, cynical. "We found instead a dozen or so donkeys. Most, like my own, had lost their loads, but two carried water and another food. After that, we had only to ration our supplies, stay out of the sun as best we could, and travel eastward at night, using the stars to point the way. We found other donkeys scattered across the desert, none carrying food or water. We came upon no men."

Bak could well imagine the hot, burning sands, donkeys left to make their lonely way back to the river or to die, the utter absence of men. A dry and desolate land, eerie in its emptiness and silence.

"By doling out water in ever smaller portions," Amonhotep went on, "I managed to get myself and the donkeys—twenty-eight at the end—to the black land of Kemet. I thought never to see so beautiful a sight: fertile green fields, the life-giving river, and men who took us in, fed us, doctored our injuries. Other survivors straggled off the desert a day or two later, sick from too much sun, weak from little or no food and drink. Djehuty, I learned later, had arrived ahead of me. Like me, he'd found a donkey laden with water."

The dog at Bak's feet moaned in its sleep. He reached down to scratch the creature's ears. Pahared was right; Djehuty could not be blamed for the onset of the storm. Why then, he wondered, did his instincts tell him there was more to this incident than the obvious? Amonhotep had clearly told the truth as far as he knew it, but how much of the truth could he know? He had been separated from Djehuty and everyone else from the onset of the storm.

Bak stumbled down the dark, narrow lane, not as sure as he would have liked that the unfamiliar route would take him to his temporary quarters. His torch, which Pahared's wife had urged him to borrow from her courtyard, sputtered and flickered, threatening to go out, its fuel nearly burned away. Each time he lowered it to examine a suspicious shadow or raised it high to illuminate the lane farther ahead, the sudden movement threatened to extinguish the flame. He muttered an oath, directing it at himself. He should have sought out a member of the night patrol and asked for a better light, but he had not wanted to tarry after half carrying the besotted Amonhotep home to the governor's villa.

He turned a corner; the torch spat sparks. A cat, yowling fear, shot down the lane and vanished in the dark. He followed, counting doors as he walked, praying he was in the right street. Like all older cities in Kemet, Abu had grown at the whim of those who lived there, with villas built and smaller houses built in between, one against another. Now the old single-story dwellings, like the one he and his men had been assigned, were being enlarged upward, many two or even three stories high, to make the best possible use of the confined space. Every lane, every house was different, yet each looked much like the rest to a stranger. Especially in the dark.

Approaching the sixth door and a corner, he heard Kasaya's deep-voiced curse on the rooftop above and Psuro's laugh. He relaxed, smiled. With luck, the odors he smelled of braised lamb and onions came from their roof, not that of a neighboring household, and they had saved some for him. He had had plenty of beer through the evening, but nothing solid since midday.

He brushed aside the mat covering the door and stepped into the house, holding the torch low and to his right, well away from the dry, flammable woven reeds. As he let the mat drop and raised the flame higher, a shower of sparks fell from the torch. He glimpsed a long, fish-like object on the floor beyond his foot, and the torch sputtered out.

"Where's a lamp?" he called, edging sideways, trying to avoid the object he had seen.

"Up here." Psuro looked down from the top of the stairway leading to the roof, a black silhouette outlined by stars. "I'll light it from the brazier."

He disappeared from view, but soon returned. Carrying the lamp in one hand, shielding the flame with the other, he plunged down the stairs. Bak stood where he was, trying to see through the blackness beyond his feet.

Kasaya looked down from above. "We saved some lamb for you, sir, and stewed vegetables. I hope you're hungry."

Psuro dropped to the floor with a thud and drew his hand away from the blaze. The flame rose tall and straight, free of smoke, illuminating the floor, the few pieces of furniture, and the baskets of supplies, casting shadows against the walls and into the corners. A large fish, its head pointed toward the door, its scales vaguely iridescent in the uncertain light, lay a couple of paces inside the door, outlined by its own shadow. A perch, Bak saw, an arm's length from nose to tail. That the creature was dead there could be no doubt. Its head was crushed. The weapon, a chunk of black granite sized to fit in the hand, with bits of scale clinging to its rough edges, lay beside it.

"What in the name of the lord Amon . . . ?" Psuro's voice tailed off; puzzlement clouded his features.

"Must be a joke," Kasaya said, staring down.

Bak was as perplexed as they were, as dumbfounded. "Who came to this house tonight? Did you see anyone approach?"

"It is a joke, isn't it, sir?" Kasaya asked, seeking reassurance.

Psuro shook his head. "We've been on the roof since nightfall, eating, playing senet, talking. We paid no heed to the lane."

Bak knelt beside the perch, forcing himself to think. A lack of blood on the floor told him the creature had been slain elsewhere, probably pulled from the water and bludgeoned before it suffocated. If the fish had been intended as a gift of food, the donor surely would have brought it gutted and cleaned, and would have placed it out of reach of scavenging cats and dogs. Since that was not the case, why had it been left? Could it have something to do with his mission in Abu? With the murders in the governor's villa?

A thought surfaced; a chill ran up his spine. This could well be a reminder of the first victim. The child Nakht, who could swim like a fish. His head had been crushed. Was the slayer teasing him? Challenging him? Or could the fish be a warning?

"We'll say nothing of this to anyone," he said. "Not Djehuty, Amonhotep, or anyone else in the governor's household. With luck, curiosity will eat at the one who left it, and he'll give himself away."

Chapter Six

"Nakht was all I had left." The woman grabbed the feet of the duck whose neck she had wrung and dropped onto a low stool to dunk the bird into a large gray bowl of boiling water. The stench of wet feathers filled the air. "Now I'm alone, with no husband to share my old age and no sons or daughters to ease my journey to the netherworld."

She was of medium height and bony, a woman who looked long past her middle years but was probably ten years younger. A life of toil and deprivation, disappointment and anguish, had bent her back, wrinkled her face and arms, and given her a thin-lipped, bitter demeanor.

"Was he your only child?" Bak asked.

"I lost a girl a few days after childbirth, two before they reached full term, and two older boys to a fever that swept through this city before Nakht was born." She pulled the duck out of the water and, letting it drip into the bowl, plucked a handful of grayish feathers. They fell to the ground in a sodden clump, intensifying the stench. "He came late in life, a gift of the gods, and I could have no more."

Bak stood outside the rough lean-to beneath which she sat, letting the early morning sun warm his back. The roof, palm fronds spread across long reeds, was attached to the end of a shed that sheltered seven donkeys with their wobbly newborns and three others big-bellied and ready to give birth. The straw beneath the animals was clean, the smell of manure faint. He hoped the merchant who had taken in the woman in exchange for labor cared as well for his servants as he did for his animals.

"Did he speak of his life in the governor's household?"

"Often." The bitterness vanished from her smile and pride filled her eyes. "Mistress Hatnofer worked him hard and had a tongue as sharp as a scythe, but the rest more than made amends. He slept on a soft pallet and ate food left over from the master's table—all he could hold and more, he told me. He thought the house, its many rooms and rich furnishings, more beautiful than the Field of Reeds, and he looked at mistress Khawet as a goddess."

"And the governor?"

She flicked her hand, sending damp feathers flying, and gave him a scornful look. "What would a boy of the kitchens know of a man so lofty?"

He nodded, pretending he agreed the question was ridiculous. He had in fact gotten what he sought, verification of Djehuty's offhand remark that he had not known the boy.

Bak had lain awake half the night, searching in vain for a more satisfactory explanation for the fish left in his quarters. Finding none, he had turned his attention to the child, seeking a reason for what seemed a senseless death. Nakht had been eleven years of age when slain, six at the time of the deadly sandstorm—assuming the storm lay behind the murders. At that time, he had been too young to have traveled into the desert with the soldiers, too young to have provided the smallest of services to the garrison. But other possibilities existed, other connections, that needed exploring. Thus Bak had come to the child's mother.

"How did your husband earn his daily bread?" he asked.

She turned the duck to pluck the soft white feathers from its breast. "He served our sovereign, Maatkare Hatshepsut, as a scout for the garrison of Abu."

Her voice conveyed pride, but something else. Defensiveness, he thought. Several scouts had accompanied that ill-fated trek into the desert. Her husband must have been among those who failed to return. "How long ago did he die?"

"Four years."

"He didn't vanish in the . . . ?" Realizing his error, he bit off the words. Nakht's father had not marched off to his death, as had the others—or had he come back a survivor?

She looked up from the fowl, her expression dark, her voice fierce. "You don't understand, do you? How a man can come back near death, broken in body and spirit. A shell of the man he was before." She flung away a handful of feathers. Most lay where they fell in a soppy mess, but a few, dry and delicate, were whisked away by the breeze. "You think because he returned alive, because he was a scout, you can point a finger at him, making him responsible for all those many deaths. Well, let me tell you, Lieutenant! Their loss was no fault of his!"

He gave her a surprised look, perplexed by the outburst. He had made no accusation, nor had he thought to. Why was she so quick to take offense, to deny?

"First my husband and now my son." She lowered the duck into the water and swirled it around, washing off the loose feathers. Bitterness again settled on her face, and the frustration of the powerless. "This city of Abu, this province, is cursed. The day those men marched into the desert, the gods ceased to smile on all who dwell here."

She clamped her mouth shut and refused to speak further, whether from superstitious fear or some more down-to-earth reason Bak could not begin to guess. He returned to the governor's villa, his thoughts awhirl. Close-mouthed though she had been, she had laid the foundation for a new idea, one that fitted in well with all he had learned thus far.

"Sure I knew Montu." The guard Kames, a wiry man of thirty or so years, propped his spear against the high mud-brick wall that separated the garden from the well and hunkered down beside the weapon. "He talked too much, told the same tales over and over again until he put you to sleep, but I liked him."

"He was a witless old fool." The second guard, called Nenu, hefty of build, barely seventeen years of age, stood his spear with the other weapon and leaned a shoulder against the wall. He made a contemptuous face. "He acted no older than the children he allowed inside these walls. Against the specific orders of mistress Hatnofer, mind you. Talk about asking for trouble!" He shook his head, laughed cynically.

"I heard she wanted him replaced," Bak said, hoisting himself onto the low wall that curved around the well.

"So goes the rumor," Kames said, "but he managed to hang on in spite of her. Or to spite her, more likely."

Nenu snorted derision. "It was the governor who kept him on."

"Djehuty?" Bak asked, hiding his interest, feigning skepticism.

"I've befriended a servant in the kitchen, a girl. We . . ." Nenu smirked. "Well, let's say I know her well. Very well. She once overheard mistress Hatnofer quarreling with the governor. The housekeeper wanted to get rid of the old man; he refused."

Djehuty had implied, Bak recalled, that he had not known Montu. "Did he give a reason?"

"Who knows?" Nenu shrugged. "My friend was afraid mistress Hatnofer would catch her eavesdropping, so she slipped away."

His older companion grinned. "Maybe the governor wanted to show her who was master. I would've if I'd had sufficient nerve—and the power to go with it."

"You were afraid of her?" Nenu barked out a disdainful laugh. "She seldom had occasion to so much as notice me, but I'd have stood up to her if she ever talked to me like she did most everyone else around here." He looked at Kames as if daring him to challenge the claim. "A woman like her . . . Well, she talked big, threw her weight around, but she bowed low to a show of strength."

The older man winked at Bak, deriding the young man's braggadocio. "Some men like doing battle with women; I don't."

Nenu gave him a searching look, as if he suspected a slur on his manhood.

A flock of pigeons wheeled overhead, wings whirring. They swooped down all at once, dropping onto the walls, the granaries in the next yard, the roof of the servant's quarters.

"I've heard Sergeant Senmut stood up to mistress Hatnofer more than once." Bak had heard no such thing, but from the way Djehuty had praised his old friend, the assumption seemed logical. Hopefully the charge, true or not, would distract the pair from the superstitious nonsense Nakht's mother had used to evade his questions.

"Now where'd you hear a thing like that?" Kames asked. "It's what you'd expect, I grant you, but . . ."

"Senmut had no time for her!" Nenu curled his lip, disgusted. "He could get a smile and an arch look from any woman he wanted. Why would he bother with a dried-up old cat who approached all who came near with bared fangs and extended claws?"

Kames rolled his eyes skyward. "Two of a kind, they were. Each time I saw them talking, I expected a storm, the likes of which I've seen only as a youth, sailing aboard a warship on the great green sea." He frowned, as if disappointed. "But they never fought, just looked at each other like two wrestlers ready for a match, both unwilling, maybe afraid, to strike the first blow."

Nenu shoved himself away from the wall and glared down at the older, smaller man. "You never liked him, did you?"

Kames stood up slowly, warily, and backed off a couple of steps, startling the pigeons on the ground, setting them to flight. "You're too easily impressed by bluster, Nenu. By a man's words, not his deeds."

An argument suited Bak's purpose, for it would loosen tongues, but he was well aware of how fast men could come to blows in a garrison untroubled by warfare. He pulled his legs close and shifted his weight forward, ready to leap between the pair should the need arise.

Nenu, his chin thrust out, took a step toward the older guard. "What do you mean by that?"

Keeping a wary eye on the younger man, Kames edged toward his spear. Bak hissed a warning. The guard flinched, startled, and stepped back a pace. "Senmut was a good, reliable soldier, that I grant you, but he wasn't to be trusted in a game of chance or with another man's woman."

"How would you know?" Nenu scoffed. "How long's it been since a woman's shared your sleeping pallet?"

A flush of anger spread across Kames's face, banishing caution. He took a quick step forward, fists balled, and swung on Nenu. The younger man, caught by surprise, ducked backward. Snarling a curse, he dropped his head low, ready to ram the man who had dared attack him.

"Enough!" Bak lunged toward the pair, glaring at them, daring them to disobey.

They stared defiance, forgetting for an instant who and what he was. Then comprehension flitted across their faces; they backed off, formed forced, half-embarrassed smiles.

"At the time of his death, Senmut was in charge of the household guards." Bak spoke in a cold and harsh voice, emphasizing his authority. "He was assigned to the garrison before he came here, was he not?"

Nenu shifted from one foot to the other, cleared his throat. "He was—until the governor had him reassigned."

"Senmut never failed to remind all who would listen that they were long-time friends." Kames stared straight ahead, taking care not to look at Bak or the younger guard. "Troop Captain Antef, when first he came to Abu, was unimpressed by the claim. He assigned him to quarry duty along with everybody else. Senmut thought himself above standing out in the sun all day, ordering men to toil like beasts of burden, so he outflanked Antef and got himself the softer task."

Bak scowled at the men before him, letting them know they had yet to satisfy him. "You've both lived in Abu for some time, and you know of the desert storm that stole the lives of many men in the garrison, leaving only a few survivors. Was Senmut one of those men? One who came back alive?''

The guards stood as stiff as posts, and as silent.

''Well?'' Bak demanded. ''Was he?''

''Yes, sir!'' Nenu said. ''At least I've heard he was.''

''Was Montu also a survivor?''

''So they say,'' Kames answered.

Bak gave the pair a long, speculative glance. ''That storm was surely the most important event in the history of Abu. The names of those who came back alive must be carved into the hearts of all who live here. Why do you feign ignorance?''

The guards looked at each other as if seeking help—or support.

Kames, the first to look away, shuffled his feet, seemed not to know what to do with his hands. ''I never once heard Montu mention the storm, nor do I know anyone else who has. As much as he talked, as many tales as he told, he never uttered a word about a time you'd think he'd brag about through eternity.''

''Nor did Sergeant Senmut.'' Nenu gave his fellow guard a furtive glance. ''I was told when first I came to Abu never to mention the storm. The men in the barracks said none who came back ever spoke of it, as if it were an awful nightmare they wanted to forget forever more.''

''Or were ordered to forget,'' Kames mumbled beneath his breath.

Bak left the guards outside the villa, well satisfied with what they had told him. The direction in which Nakht's mother had pointed, the idea she had given him, looked considerably more appealing than before. Of the five people slain, two had survived the storm and a third individual's parent had survived. Would the same prove true of Lieutenant Dedi and mistress Hatnofer?

He turned down the corridor leading to the scribal office. Barely eighteen years of age, Dedi had, according to Kames, never set foot in Abu until three months ago. He could not have marched into the desert with that ill-fated caravan. But perhaps his father had served in Abu, as had Nakht's, and had been among those who survived the storm. Making a wager with himself that such was the case, adding a prayer to the lord Amon to ensure success, Bak stepped through the doorway, drawing the eyes of the ten scribes who toiled there and of Simut, seated on a thick pallet before them.

The chief scribe pursed his lips in disapproval. "Here again, Lieutenant? I fear we'll have to make new seating arrangements, adding a permanent space for you."

A youthful scribe tittered. The older, more experienced men dropped their eyes to the scrolls spread across their laps and set their pens to scratching, hiding smiles or smothering laughter.

Eager to prove his theory, Bak ignored the jibe. "I'm in need of a personal record, that of Lieutenant Dedi."

"We're not in the habit of letting anyone and everyone borrow our records. You must go first to Governor Djehuty and if he deems you worthy, he'll see you have clearance to take the scroll."

Swallowing a sharp reply, Bak strode between the two rows of seated men and stopped before the chief scribe. "I've not come to borrow, only to read, a task I prefer to do here."

"Well . . ." Simut hesitated, frowned. "Well, I'm not sure . . ."

Through an open portal off to the right, Bak spotted in a dimly lit room several wooden frames filled with large pottery storage jars lying on their sides, row upon row, their mouths facing outward for convenience. He could see scrolls within the containers closest to the door, while the vessels farther away, barely visible in the gloom, had been plugged with dried mud and sealed, their contents protected from destruction by mice and men alike.

"If you haven't the time to help me," he said, taking a couple of steps toward the records room, "you need only tell me where to look." He assumed Simut would be as appalled by the idea of having a stranger pawing around in his files as was the chief scribe at Buhen, a fussy old man who stood guard over his domain like a mother goose defending her brood of goslings.

"Wait!" Simut scrambled to his feet and hastened to the door. "Stay right where you are. I'll get it." Not bothering with a lamp, he walked into the dusky room.

Bak bowed his head to hide a smile. He did not especially like the chief scribe, but he saw no reason to laugh aloud, to make him look the fool before his subordinates.

Within moments, Simut returned, a good-sized greenish-gray jar in the crook of his arm, scrolls jutting out of its wide mouth like the emerging petals of a huge, stiff blossom. He sat down on his pallet, supported the vessel between his knees, and searched through the documents, reading notes inked on the outside of each scroll. "Ah, yes. Lieutenant Dedi." He eyed the thin cylinder, shook his head. "Poor soul. His life snuffed out at such a tender age."

Adopting an officious attitude to conceal his distress, he handed the scroll to Bak, set the container on the floor beside him, and returned to the document on which he had been writing. Standing close by, Bak untied the string binding Dedi's record and unrolled it. The information provided was as brief as the young man's life had been. About midway through, he found what he was looking for, or at least he hoped so. Dedi's father had been an officer, a lieutenant seriously injured in the line of duty, one whose meritorious career had opened the door to his son when he, too, wished to enter the army as an officer. The location and specifics of the injury were not given.

"Do you recall if a Lieutenant Ptahmose was assigned to this garrison a few years ago?" Bak asked.

Simut gave a long-suffering sigh. "Ptahmose? We had an infantry officer by that name. Why do you ask?"

The chief scribe was irascible, not easy to get along with, the kind of man who brought out the worst in Bak, making him stubbornly resistant to revealing any information demanded. But Simut had been the first to hint at the secret Djehuty harbored, a secret he had implied Bak should learn.

Bak lowered his voice so the other men in the room would not hear. "I know of the sandstorm, Simut, of the many deaths and the few survivors, and I believe I've found the link among those who've been slain during the past few weeks." He went on to explain, then asked, "Could the Ptahmose you remember have been Dedi's father?"

Without a word, Simut laid his scroll aside and stood up. Lines of worry etched his brow. He lit the wick in a reddish pottery lamp and carried it into the records room. Bak longed to follow, but knew an offer of help would be spurned. He remained outside, watching the play of light and shadow fall across the tall wooden frames, the scroll-filled jars, and the short, plump scribe reading labels scratched on the mud plugs.

Ptahmose's file, older and harder to find than that of Dedi, was located out of the way at the far end of the room, but in no time at all Simut returned with a buff-colored jar long ago plugged and sealed. Dropping to his knees, he struck the plug with a stone, shattering the hard, dry mud, and sorted hastily through the contents. Finding the scroll he wanted, he broke the seal with a thumbnail, untied the string, and unrolled the papyrus. Bak knelt beside him, too impatient to wait for an answer, and together they began to read.

"Ptahmose came from the provincial capital of Imet," Simut said, "and there he planned to return when he left the army and Abu."

". . . after recovering from severe wind- and sunburn received during a sandstorm," Bak said, reading on ahead.

Simut ran a finger down the next column of symbols, stopped near the bottom. "Five years ago, that was, as you thought."

Bak unrolled the much thinner cylinder of the younger officer and glanced through its contents. "Dedi, too, came from Imet, and there his father no doubt remains." Imet was a town north of Mennufer, many days' travel downriver from Abu. Ptahmose lived much too far away for the slayer to touch. His son's arrival in Abu must have seemed a gift of the gods.

Simut noticed how slowly the pens were scratching across the scrolls, the curious looks of his minions. He stuffed the two documents into their respective containers, handed the lamp to Bak, and, carrying a jar in each hand, led the way into the file room. He did not speak until they reached the back wall, well out of hearing distance of the men outside.

"You obviously believe someone—a close relative or friend of one who died in that storm—is slaying the survivors."

"I think so, yes." The idea, which had seemed so right in the privacy of his own thoughts, sounded fantastic when aired.

"Why now, after so long a time?"

Bak waved away a wisp of smoke. "Perhaps some incident, maybe only a word or two, ignited a fire in the slayer's heart."

Simut set the gray vessel on the floor and lifted the buff jar high, meaning to slip it into the space from which he had taken it. Noticing its gaping mouth, he made an impatient sound with his tongue and set it down beside the other.

"My nephew vanished in that storm, you know, a youth as close to me as a son."

"I didn't know." Bak eyed him with interest. "Do you resent those who returned, Djehuty among them?"

"No longer, but at the time I did. To lose so fine a young man, one beloved by all who knew him. So brave, so . . ." Simut's voice faltered and he gave a cheerless little laugh. "Djehuty was always one who knew better than anyone else, even when we played together as children, but in this case? No, no man can be blamed for the fury of the gods."

"I remember the men returning from the storm," Khawet said, pity clouding her face. "I'd gone to Nubt for a few days, to my father's estate. Most who survived wandered out of the desert near there—or farther north. Close to death, they were. Burned by the sun, thirsty, starving, so worn they could barely put one foot in front of another."

"Your father among them," Bak said.

"He survived, yes, and each day that's since gone by, I've thanked the lord Khnum."

She stood at the side of a small, square courtyard, watching four young women bent over limestone mortars sunk into the floor, pounding grain with stone pestles. Lengths of newly washed linen stretched across a dozen or so heavy rope lines shaded them from the merciless midafternoon sun but provided no relief from the heat. Sweat beaded on their foreheads and stained their dresses. The heavy odor of crushed grain failed to mask the smell of their bodies.

"Far more men died than lived," Bak said. "In a small, tight world like Abu, where most who manned the garrison at that time came from families who've lived in this province for generations, there must still exist many friends and relatives of those who were lost."

"I was most impressed when I heard of the patterns you saw in the slayings, but in this case?" She touched him lightly on the arm, then quickly withdrew her hand. "A man would have to be terribly bitter to seek revenge after so long a time."

He no longer mistook the gesture as a sign of intimacy, as he had been inclined to do before. She must habitually touch others, he thought, or in this case was merely displaying regret that her opinion differed from his. "I've found no other tie binding Nakht and the three men."

The sound of male and female laughter drew her eyes toward a wooden gate standing ajar at the rear of the court. "I must get on with my duties. The bakers and brewers toiling beyond that wall await direction." She remained where she stood, letting him know she preferred he leave so she could carry out the remainder of her tasks alone. "What of Hatnofer? How was she linked to those who survived the storm?"

"I'd hoped you could answer that question. I've been told you knew her better than anyone."

"I knew her, yes, but she never confided in me."

"Did you not tell me she was a mother to you?"

Her voice grew sharp, annoyed. "She never ceased to treat me as a child, Lieutenant."

He suspected her anger was directed at the dead woman, not him. Lest he err, he attempted a smile, hoping to disarm her, but a whiff of crushed grain made him sneeze. "What of her family?" he managed, and a second sneeze overwhelmed him.

A fleeting smile acknowledged his discomfort. "She was a foundling, a babe left on my father's doorstep in Nubt. If she had a family in Abu or Swenet—or anywhere else, for that matter—she never knew them." Glancing at the gate, she edged away from him. "I must go. With Hatnofer no longer here, I've no time to linger."

"One more question," he said, stopping her flight with an upraised hand. "Of all those who have the freedom to walk through this compound, who had close friends or relatives that vanished in the desert?"

"Most of the servants lost men near and dear, as did the guards. I know Amethu, Simut, and Ineni lost someone close, and I believe Antef did. I, too, cared for men who never returned: lieutenants Amonemhab, Nebmose, Minnakht, and Neferhotep. I miss them even now, all in the prime of life, lost forever to the wind and the sand."

Again she briefly touched his arm. Turning away, she hastened across the court and out the gate, which she swung closed behind her. Bak watched her go, sympathizing with her plight. No wonder she was irritable, he thought; she had every right to be. She had, only two days before, found the body of a woman as close to her as a mother, and she was now burdened with that woman's duties in addition to her own. She was mistress of a household ruled by a man who appeared to Bak impossible to please and was wed to a husband she seemed not to love.

"Kasaya's fallen in love?" Bak chuckled. "Not again!"

"This time he'll be lucky to escape a free man," Psuro said, grinning. "The girl toils in the governor's kitchen, where she's student to the chief cook—her mother. The old woman's the best I've come upon in many a year, and she's stuffing Kasaya like a goose being force-fed for slaughter.''

Walking side-by-side, laughing, they turned a corner into the lane that would take them to their quarters. Failing sunshine lighted the upper edges of the taller buildings, while the deep shadow of dusk filled the narrow walkway. The odors of fish and onions, of herbs and cooking oil, wafted down from the rooftops, as did the soft voices of families enjoying their evening meal.

"Does he realize how dangerous his position is?" Bak managed.

Psuro shook his head. "He's too busy shoving food into his mouth to think of the consequences."

Stifling laughter as best he could, Bak stopped in front of their quarters and shoved aside the mat hanging over the door. The room lay in deep shadow, the objects inside losing color and definition. "Djehuty has an estate at Nubt. If you see a crisis on the horizon, I'll send Kasaya downriver, out of harm's way."

"Yes, sir," Psuro said, wiping his eyes with the palm of his hand.

"Where'd you put the lamp?"

"Inside the door, to the right."

Bak spotted three palm-sized baked clay dishes on the floor, fresh wicks rising from puddles of oil. He scooped one up and handed it to the Medjay. "I saw light in a house halfway down the block."

The Medjay nodded and hurried down the lane. Rather than take the time to start a fire using a small drill and kindling, he would borrow the neighbor's lamp to light his own. Bak rolled the mat up, letting air and the meager natural light into the house, and tied it with a sturdy cord. As soon as he stepped over the threshold, he sensed that someone had entered the house during their absence. He stopped dead still, thinking of the fish he had found the night before, the warning he suspected it conveyed. The last thing he had expected was another such gift.

Psuro came up behind him, lamp flaming. "Our evening

meal,'' he said, looking over Bak's shoulder, his eyes on the
two stools Amethu had furnished, one stacked upside-down
on top of the other, with a large covered basket perched atop
the three legs. ''I hope the old woman included some meat
or fowl. I'm starving.'' Not overly fond of cooking, he had
persuaded an elderly widow he had met at the public well to
provide their meals.

Bak eyed the basket, towering above the other furnishings,
safe from mice and rats, insects, and whatever else might be
tempted. Its presence failed to suppress a strong feeling of
unease. His eyes darted around the room, skipping over
patches of light, probing shadows, coming to rest on the
lower steps of the stairway leading to the roof and an object
impossible to see clearly from where he stood. With the fish
foremost in his thoughts, he bounded across the room.

''Spawn of Apep!'' he snarled.

A clay doll hung head-down off the lowest step, an arrow
with the shaft broken off protruding from its breast. The image, he had no doubt, represented Montu, the spearman who
supposedly fell down the stairs and onto his own weapon.

Psuro came up beside him and held the light close. He
muttered something in his own tongue, too long to be a simple oath, more likely an incantation against whatever malign
force had caused the doll to be brought into their quarters.

Bak preferred a more common sense approach. He picked
up the image to examine it. The eyes were mere slits, probably made with a fingernail; the nose a bit of clay pinched
to stand out from the otherwise featureless face. The body
was cylindrical, its stick-like arms and legs held in place with
straw. The arrowhead was flint, with nothing remaining of
the shaft but a jagged stub of wood. The image was so recently molded it felt cool and damp to the touch, though no
longer soft.

''I wish I knew what message this was meant to deliver,
Psuro.''

''It can only be a threat,'' the Medjay said, eyeing the doll
with distaste.

Bak's voice turned wry. "Would not a note be more direct?"

"I doubt the man who brought it knows how to write."

Bak stared at the figure, unconvinced. The fish with the stone was simple but direct, and so was the doll. The delivery of such items required imagination, not the plodding thought processes of the poor and uneducated. As before, he felt he was being teased, the slayer toying with him to prove . . . what? To prove himself superior in thought and deed? Probably, but something else, too: this blatant intrusion into his quarters was meant to intimidate, to frighten.

One thing was clear: he would have to post one of his men here each evening. The thought grated. He had not sufficient manpower to waste on a task that might prove futile. If only he had more men, more Medjays from Buhen, men he trusted.

Chapter Seven

"I'm fairly certain the storm is the key to the murders, but you mustn't allow my belief to blind you to other possibilities."

"Yes, sir," Psuro and Kasaya said in unison.

Bak fastened his belt clasp over the small, neat knot holding his kilt in place and stepped into woven-reed sandals. "More than anything else, I'd like to talk to someone who came back alive, one who saw more of his fellows during the tempest than did Lieutenant Amonhotep."

"When I wandered around the caravan encampment yesterday, I talked to more than a dozen traders." Psuro, long ago up and dressed, sat down on the stairway and lifted several leaves covering a tightly woven basket brought by the old woman he had hired to cook for them. The yeasty aroma of fresh bread wafted across the room. "A few had heard of a company of soldiers lost in the desert, but in a vague sort of way. None connected the tale to Abu."

"Not surprising," Bak said, tugging down the hem of his kilt, making it even all around. "Most are outsiders, men who remain only long enough to pass on to a ship the trade goods they've brought from far to the north or south." He reached for an intricate bronze chain from which hung several faience amulets, the most prominent among them the lord Horus of Buhen and the lady Maat. "No, you must query men and women who've lived in this province for many years. Not an easy task, I warn you. Half the people I spoke with yesterday resorted to talk of the gods or demons or some other malign force when I mentioned the storm. And the two guards, Kames and Nenu, hinted that the men in the garrison may've been ordered to remain silent.''

Psuro offered a round, crusty roll to Bak and threw a second to Kasaya, sitting cross-legged on his sleeping pallet.

The young Medjay caught it with a grin. "If I'd come back from that storm alive and suddenly I saw my fellow survivors falling to the earth like overripe fruit, I'd turn my back on Abu and walk as fast and far as I could.''

"Nakht and Lieutenant Dedi weren't survivors," Psuro scoffed. "They weren't even here then. They were both too young to march off to battle. So who would think to connect them to Montu and Senmut?''

Kasaya, not in the least miffed, shot the roll back to Psuro. "Lieutenant Bak did.''

Psuro raised his arm, preparing to return the missile. Bak gave him a long, hard look. With a sheepish smile, the stocky Medjay lowered the roll, broke it apart, and took a bite.

"Go see the chief scribe, Psuro. I asked him yesterday to prepare a list of all who survived the storm. He should have their names ready and waiting." Bak glanced around, searching for the document Commandant Thuty had prepared, giving him authority in Abu. He intended to visit the garrison records center and take a look at scrolls unavailable to the average officer. If Troop Captain Antef was not there, or if he refused to give permission, Thuty's message should open the door. "Mark off those who're no longer among the living and find out what happened to the remainder.''

"And pray to the lord Amon that at least one man still lives," Kasaya said.

"And that he lives close by," Psuro added.

Garrison headquarters was located in a row of interconnected houses across a narrow lane from the two-story barracks building. The dwellings had been altered over the years by the addition or removal of walls, and doors had been cut to allow free movement throughout the block. The sole struc-

ture that remained relatively unchanged was the commander's residence, an unadorned two-story house with
offices on the ground floor and living quarters above.

After spending over a year within the high, fortified walls
of Buhen, Bak had trouble reconciling himself to the idea of
a garrison without walls, one surrounded by places of business and crowded residential blocks. Especially since Abu
had once been the southernmost city in the land of Kemet,
a frontier city from which armies set off for what were then
wild and untamed lands farther south, paving the way for
trading expeditions led by the stout-hearted governors of the
province. Men Djehuty wanted very much to claim as ancestors.

A guard posted in the entryway of the commander's residence directed him through the columned audience hall to
a rectangular chamber in which a half dozen scribes toiled.
There he introduced himself to the chief scribe, who sat on
the floor facing the others. The lesser scribes studied him
furtively, any stranger a welcome distraction.

"I understand Troop Captain Antef has gone to the
quarry," Bak said.

"That's right, sir. He left soon after daybreak. There was
an accident. A heavy section of stone fell on a man's leg."
The chief scribe, a slight man of medium height with a small
birthmark on his neck, scowled in a vain effort to conceal
his distress. "If the tale the messenger told was accurate, the
limb is crushed and he'll lose it."

And probably his life, Bak thought with a shudder. Such
injuries were almost impossible for a physician to treat. Only
the gods could intervene. "I'll speak with Antef later, then.
In the meantime, I'd like to look at several documents you're
sure to have filed away among your records."

The scribe shook off his distraction over the injured soldier
and frowned. "I'm sorry, sir, but without the troop captain's
approval, you can see nothing."

Bak handed him the scroll prepared by Thuty. The clerk
read the document and read it again a second time. With an

almost imperceptible sigh of resignation, he rolled it up and gave it back. "What do you wish, sir?"

"First, the daybook containing entries about a sandstorm that occurred five years ago, the storm from which most of the men in this garrison failed to return. I'd also like to see the official report of the catastrophe. And I wish to look at the daybooks for the past two months." Those would include the entries made on the days the deaths occurred in the governor's household and any related items of interest.

The scribe allowed himself a brief, curious glance. "If you'll wait in the audience hall, sir, I'll bring them right away."

Bak followed his suggestion, seating himself on a wooden bench built against one wall of the hall. Scribes came and went, sergeants reported to junior officers, the chief armorer came in to complain about the poor quality of spears received from the capital. Most glanced Bak's way and dismissed him, thinking him just another officer passing through Abu.

In a surprisingly short time, the chief scribe presented him with a basket containing several scrolls and hastened back to his flock. Bak thumbed through the documents until he found the official report of the tempest, labeled year five of the reign of Maatkare Hatshepsut, harvest season. Djehuty, as garrison commander, had prepared the scroll more than a week after the storm, after the last of the survivors had returned to Abu. It went into considerable detail, a bland, sometimes officious accounting, giving away nothing that would discredit Djehuty or his troops. No surprises there.

He took up the appropriate daybook and scanned its entries. References to the storm were short and succinct. The loss of over one hundred men and more than sixty donkeys was dealt with in a cursory, almost offhand manner that angered him in its easy dismissal of their lives.

Setting aside the documents related to the storm, he pulled the remaining scrolls out of the basket and sorted them by date. They proved to be disappointing, to say the least. Since none of the victims were assigned to the garrison and none of the murders had occurred there, the incidents were not referred to in any way.

Bak climbed a gradual slope, a rolling stretch of golden sand softened by the passage of many feet and warmed by the morning sun. Ahead, a hump of reddish stone protruded from the barren landscape, breaking the horizon to the left and right for at least two hundred paces. Men reduced to stick-like figures by distance and heat waves toiled on the face of the outcrop, one of several granite quarries located in the desert south of Swenet. A smaller assemblage, stripped down to loincloths, clustered on the sand at the base of the rock face, surrounding a large object impossible to see with so many men shielding it from view. Two stood slightly apart—Troop Captain Antef, Bak assumed, and a scribe.

As he drew near, plodding ankle-deep through the sand, another man, a sergeant most likely, emerged from among the workmen—troops from the garrison pressed to do duty at the quarry. Striding toward Antef, the man spotted Bak and pointed. The troop captain swung around, placed his hands on his hips, and shook his head. Bak could not see his features, but disgust was apparent in his stance.

He was surprised Antef would show disregard for a fellow officer in front of his men. He felt sure the aversion was not directed at him but at the task he must perform, the questions he must ask. Nonetheless, he resented being the recipient of such a display. Feigning indifference, he narrowed the gap between them. The men on the outcrop paid no heed to his approach; those close by sneaked glances his way, curious.

"Troop Captain Antef," he said. "May I have a word?"

"Lieutenant Bak," Antef said, aping the police officer's tone. "A word, yes. I've no time for a lengthy discourse."

Bak looked pointedly at the men on the outcrop, all going about their business under the expert direction of a half dozen chief quarrymen, and the men standing nearby, idling around what looked like a greater than lifesize, unfinished statue of the lord Osiris or, more likely, Maatkare Hatshepsut as one with Osiris. Details of face and figure had not yet been carved and it lacked the final polish, both of which would be done when it reached its final destination in faroff Waset.

Antef's mouth twitched, as if he realized how pompous he had sounded, but he maintained his cool and serious demeanor. "Djehuty has promised this accursed statue will sail today. I'm here to see that it does."

"One of your men suffered an accident, I was told. I assume it wasn't as serious as I was led to believe."

Antef glowered at the statue. "This wretched image rolled onto him. Thanks to the lord Khnum, the sand beneath him was soft and he suffered only a blow to his pride and a bruise big enough to earn him softer duty in Abu for a few days."

Relieved the man was unhurt, Bak said, "My questions may distract you now and again, but they'll not keep you from your duty."

Again Antef's mouth hinted at a smile. Bak had a feeling he would enjoy this man's company under different circumstances.

"Ask what you like." Antef's eyes darted toward two men hurrying up the slope, carrying wooden shovels on their shoulders. "If I find you in the way, you'll leave, like it or not."

"As the man responsible for this garrison, would it not be to your advantage to see the scales of justice balanced as soon as possible?"

Without a word, Antef strode away. He slipped through the line of men encircling the statue and walked around the rough-cut head to meet the pair who had brought the shovels. Bak followed at a distance, staying outside the ring of men. A sledge, two low runners connected by sturdy crosspieces, lay on the far side of the statue. The fresh-worked granite had taken on the pinkish-red hue especially desired by the royal house of Kemet. Clear crystals embedded among the colored granite glittered in the sunlight.

"You know what you must do. You've done it often enough." Antef looked around the circle. "Move that thing out of the way . . ." He pointed at the sledge. ". . . and dig a long, shallow trench alongside the statue. Bury the sledge up to the crosspieces, and we'll drag the image onto it.'' He strode through the circle and drew Bak away, where they could speak without being heard. ''Yes, Lieutenant, I am responsible for this garrison. I, not you, should've been entrusted with finding the slayer.''

''I've no doubt you're a worthy officer,'' Bak said, trying to balance tact and honesty, ''but you've had no experience looking into the hearts of men who turn away from the lady Maat, taking what they will, including other men's lives.''

Antef eyed him with scorn. ''I've served in the army since I was a youth of fifteen years. I've spent my nights in the barracks and my days on the practice field. If ever we should march off to war, I'd dwell in a tent on the field of battle. I know men, Lieutenant.''

''Ordinary, god-fearing men have little in common with the vile criminals I've tracked and snared.''

Antef's mouth tightened. ''Men are men, I tell you.''

Bak could see that no amount of persuasion would convince him otherwise. ''Did you give any thought to the ten-day intervals between deaths?'' he demanded. ''Or the progressively higher rank of those who were slain?''

''No,'' Antef growled. ''Too many of the deaths appeared accidental to add up details.''

''Did it ever occur to you that two of those who died were survivors of the sandstorm that decimated the garrison five years ago, and two others were the sons of survivors?''

''I knew Montu and Senmut lived through the storm.'' Antef's expression grew thoughtful. ''And Nakht's father . . . Well, yes, I knew he did, too.'' His eyes darted toward Bak. ''Dedi's father as well?''

''He was a lieutenant here in Abu.'' Bak went on to relate what he had learned from Simut's records.

''Troop Captain Antef!'' the sergeant called.

Antef shook his head as if to clear it of all he had just learned and strode toward the men gathered around the statue. Bak stayed well back, out of the way of those who would shift the heavy stone figure.

A couple of men got down on hands and knees to clear sand from beneath the statue. They bared five wooden blocks that had been placed under the image as it was freed from the parent stone, leaving a gap through which they slipped four heavy ropes. These were tied around the statue and laid parallel to each other across the sledge and the sand.

The sergeant barked an order. The circle broke up and the men formed lines along the ropes, ten to each team, facing away from the statue. After checking to make sure no line would snarl, the sergeant called out another order.

The men pressed forward, muscles bulging, sweat pouring from bodies and faces. The ropes grew taut, the statue moved slowly across the blocks toward the sledge. A man slipped and fell, tripping those around him. Three ropes grew slack, while the fourth remained taut. The image began to twist on its axis. Antef snapped out an order to release the last line. The men let go as if their fingers burned. The rope, no longer under tension, writhed in the sand, sending men scuttling out of its path. The statue lay still, flat on its back on four of the five blocks of wood.

Antef gave Bak a quick smile of relief, muttered a hasty prayer of thanks to the lord Khnum that no damage had been done, and gave the men time to rest. A few dropped where they stood; the remainder trudged across the sand, heading toward a group of donkeys laden with goatskin water bags.

The troop captain leaned back against an irregular wall of granite, bruised by the dolorite mallets used to widen the space between it and the block of stone that had become the statue. "I've heard tales of men who lived through sand-storms or were lost in the desert for days on end without food or water. Journeys through the belly of Apep, they were, marking them for life. Why would anyone wish to slay men who suffered so much?" Apep was a serpent demon of the netherworld, representing the forces of chaos and evil.

"Why would anyone slay their sons, youths who had nothing to do with the storm or its outcome?" Bak asked, sitting down on the statue's legs.

Antef stared at his clasped hands, unable to find an answer. Then he looked up with narrowing eyes. "You've said nothing of Hatnofer, I notice."

"As yet, I've found no tie binding her to any who survived."

"Not surprising. She could be warm enough when she wanted, friendly even, but she held all who knew her at a distance." Antef gave Bak a wry smile. "If I were you, I'd not cling too tight to that theory of yours. She may well prove its undoing—and yours."

The thought rankled and so did Antef's smirk. "I know you were a stranger to Abu until you replaced Djehuty as commander of this garrison. I also know," Bak added, stretching the truth, "that you lost someone close in that storm."

Antef gave him a long, measuring look. "I wasn't aware that information so personal could be found in garrison or provincial records."

"I've the basic facts, but I need the details." Bak was not about to betray Khawet to this man he felt sure loved her.

"Ah, yes. I begin to understand. You've gone a step beyond identifying the victims as men who survived the storm. Now you're out to lay blame on men close to those who died."

"I'm seeking the truth."

Antef gave a sardonic laugh and stood up. "You'll find many forms of truth here in Abu, Lieutenant."

"So I've noticed." Bak rose to face him. "Would you prefer I hear of your loss from someone else? Or from you?"

Antef stared expressionless at the younger officer, betraying no hint of his thoughts, letting the silence grow between them. The muffled thud of mallets carried through the air, background to a chattering flock of swallows raiding an anthill built in the crack of a weathered boulder. A few of the troops had begun to straggle back, but most looked in no hurry to return to their task.

"Come," Antef said. "I've something to show you."

He struck off through the sand, staying close to the granite outcrop. Where they were going Bak could not imagine.

"I lost an uncle in the storm." Antef glanced down, watching where he placed his feet. "How much shall I tell you? Shall I assume you know nothing and give you every detail?"

Bak could have sworn the officer was hiding another smile, teasing. "I'll leave that to your good judgment."

A man uttered a string of oaths. They glanced around, saw a short, muscular individual kneeling on a nearby ledge, holding a mallet in one hand, sucking a finger on the other. A soldier, Bak assumed, impressed to do duty as a stonemason, clumsy with the tools of a trade he surely resented.

The troop captain walked on, untroubled by so common an occurrence. "As a boy, I lived on a small estate near the provincial capital of Zawty. My father plowed and planted for our master; my mother served our mistress. I had no future beyond the land. Until my uncle, who long before had entered the army, took me into his household in Mennufer. He was an officer, an infantry lieutenant, and so he desired me to be. Close on twenty years ago, when I reached an age to enter the army, he was posted here in Abu. He brought me with him. Djehuty was here at the time, a lieutenant temporarily assigned to the garrison while he awaited a more desirable post. He refused to have me, saying he had enough young and green spearmen from Abu without taking on one from afar. My uncle had no choice: he sent me back to Zawty and the life I thought I'd left behind forever."

"No wonder you dislike Djehuty!"

"Fortunately, the gods chose to smile on me." Antef veered around a slick-haired white dog sniffing a pile of oily leaves that must earlier have held a workman's morning meal. "A friend of my uncle, a lieutenant in Mennufer, offered me a place in his unit. With his guidance and a natural aptitude for the art of war, I rose rapidly through the ranks. My uncle returned to Mennufer and life went on. I'd already attained the rank of troop captain when he was posted again to Abu. You know what happened: he vanished in the storm."

"Did Djehuty remember you when you came back?"

"No, nor would he care if he had." Antef gave a hard, cynical laugh. "In his eyes, I was—and may still be—of no greater value than a donkey or an ox, to him no different from the men you see there." He swung his hand in an arc encompassing the quarry from one end to the other.

Bak eyed four men down on their knees on a rock surface flattened by some previous removal, a square column, perhaps, or an obelisk. Using as a guide a cord stretched across the stone, pounding chisels with heavy mallets, they were cutting a row of slits in the granite. Wooden wedges protruded from finished slits farther along the cord. After this back side of the block was fully notched, water would be poured on the wedges, making them swell to fracture the stone.

"These men are soldiers, too?" he asked, surprised. "This is the work of craftsmen!"

"Oh?" Antef's voice dripped sarcasm. "Why would Djehuty summon experienced quarrymen? Men he'd have to feed and house in addition to my troops?"

Expecting no answer, he strode on, his anger propelling him forward so fast Bak had to walk double time. They rounded a high, stubby finger of granite and came upon a circular bay excavated from the parent outcrop. A ridge sheltered the spot from the rest of the quarry, isolating it. If not for the distant thud of mallets, Bak would have thought himself far away and alone.

Antef ushered him toward a large red granite block, rectangular in form, with rounded corners at one end and the other end squared off. Even before he saw the partially hollowed interior, he recognized the object as an outer coffin. Only royalty could command the use of hard stone for an eternal resting place. This had to be for one of Kemet's joint rulers, either Maatkare Hatshepsut or Menkheperre Thutmose. The queen, most likely, since construction of her memorial temple was well on its way to completion.

He walked closer, wondering where the men were who should have been hollowing it out and preparing it for shipment north to the capital. A ragged crack midway along the length of the box gave him the answer. The break ran through both walls and what remained of the core, dividing it into two pieces. The coffin had been abandoned for good reason.

Resting his hands on the edge, he eyed the fault. "Maatkare Hatshepsut must not have been pleased when she learned she'd never rest in this."

"This magnificent folly was ordered by and for Senenmut, her most trusted advisor. She knows nothing about it, and I pray to the lord Khnum she never will."

Bak whistled. He had heard tales of the steward's arrogance, but not one came close to this.

Antef's voice turned contemptuous. "Djehuty agreed, all smiles and bows, that we'd do the work and remain mute. A fool paying homage to one who could fall from the lofty heights in an instant, taking all in his wake with him."

Bak better understood the troop captain's anger. The load he had to bear was heavy indeed. "From what I've heard of Senenmut, when he sets his sights on a thing, he doesn't easily give up."

Antef nodded, understanding him perfectly. "Even now, a new coffin is being cut at a quarry north of Abu. Quartzite it is. Not as spectacular as the one before us, but more than adequate. A coffin fit for royalty."

Bak eyed the officer thoughtfully. "Why do you tell me this? You've made no secret of the fact that you don't trust me. Are you hoping I'll pass word of this outrage to the capital?"

"You apparently believe I could, without a qualm, slay five innocent people to repay Djehuty for an incident from the past. Now tell me, Lieutenant, why would I slay them for a long-past offense, and plan to slay Djehuty as well, when each day that goes by the swine gives me greater reason to wish him alone a victim of his own transgressions?"

So great was the officer's anger, Bak could feel it in the air. Antef had made a point, he thought, a good point.

* * *

Bak and Psuro shoved the skiff across the strip of rich black earth. The flat-bottomed hull tore away the dry and cracking surface, revealing soil still damp from the fallen floodwaters. The slope steepened. The vessel got away from them and slid out of control down the slick bank. Its stern struck the water with a splash, showering them. They leaped after it and waded into the river to scramble on board. Psuro took up the oars while Bak sat in the stern with the rudder.

"User, you say he's called?" Bak asked.

"Yes, sir." The Medjay eased the skiff into deeper water, added, "He was a spearman back then."

"I thank the lord Amon you found him." Bak drew close a basket smelling of bread and braised meat and removed the lid. "You've done well, Psuro. I feared all who survived the storm were gone, either living in a faraway place or in the Field of Reeds."

Psuro rowed around a tiny island crowned with a single acacia. Other islands large and small abounded as far as the eye could see. The swift-flowing channels separating them, as often as not foaming over rocks hidden beneath the surface, would shrink or vanish as the water level dropped through the following months. The Medjay located a wide and smooth passage that promised to carry them north with a minimum of effort, shipped one oar, and held onto the other in case of need.

"User lives on an island near the upstream end of the rapids," he said. "He doesn't often come to Abu. I was lucky to find him at the market."

"He's a farmer now?" Bak took an elongated loaf of bread from the basket, broke off a chunk, added a slab of beef, and handed it to his companion.

"Yes, sir. He raises geese and sells the eggs, mostly to the crews of ships either readying their vessels for the voyage upriver or unloading products from faraway Kush for overland transport north around the rapids."

"Sounds an enterprising sort." Bak recalled the unwanted gifts, the threat they implied. His voice sharpened. "I hope you didn't tell him to meet us at our quarters."

The Medjay, his mouth full, shook his head emphatically. "I suggested Pahared's wife's house of pleasure."

Barely able to understand, Bak dug two jars of beer out of the basket and handed one over. "When?"

Psuro swallowed hard, clearing his mouth, and tipped the jar to his lips. "He turned me down flat. I explained at first why you wanted to talk to him, telling him of the murders. He saw right away how unhealthy Abu and Swenet have been for those who survived the storm, so he thought it best he not tarry. As soon as he traded his eggs for whatever necessities he came for, he set sail for home."

Bak applauded the man's common sense and understood his caution, but the delay was frustrating—and annoying. Just six days remained before Djehuty faced death. "How long must I wait to talk to him?"

"We're to meet in the morning on neutral ground. On an island south of Abu, a place where men have, for many generations, left inscriptions on the boulders so no one will forget their passage across the frontier. He wants us nowhere near his home, fearing the slayer will follow us and add him to the list of dead."

Does he think us so careless with other men's lives? Bak wondered. He quickly tamped down his irritation. After all, who could blame the man for an excess of caution?

Bak climbed out of the skiff and sent Psuro on to Swenet to find suitable objects they could exchange for User's knowledge. He stood briefly on the landingplace below the governor's villa, deciding where to go next, who to talk with, then plodded up the stairs. A small brown snake darted into a crack between rocks. A sparrow fluttered in an overhanging acacia, chirping. About a third of the way up, a sound . . . a whisper . . . something . . . nudged his senses and silenced the bird. He stopped, looked around, saw nothing. If not for the sparrow's continuing hush, he would have thought his imagination overactive.

He climbed on, faster, more alert. Another whisper and an arrow sped by, passing through the gap between his arm and torso, narrowly missing his ribs. He leaped off the stairway, flinging himself into the brush. The sparrow darted away.

A third arrow struck the nearest step. The point snapped off; the shaft skidded across the stone and struck a spindly limb close to Bak's leg. The archer was reasonably skilled, he thought, but no expert would aim so low. Deciding a glimpse of the man worth the risk, he felt for his dagger, making sure he had it, and scrambled up the steep, rocky incline, shoulders hunched, head down, shielded by leaves that showered around him. Thin branches grabbed his hair and tore at his arms and legs. Another arrow sped by, striking the slender trunk of a tree. He thought he heard yet another, speeding through the branches whipping the air behind him.

Breathing hard, scratched and dirty, he peered through a screen of brush at the top of the slope. The arrows had come from the left, he thought, from Nebmose's villa or one of the houses in the town beyond its walls. Out of necessity, the angle had been steep, which placed the man on a high wall or the roof of a tall building.

Not a creature stirred. Not surprising. Men who attacked from ambush seldom remained in place for long. Whether their mission failed or succeeded, they dared not linger. As a result, they often left behind telltale signs of their presence.

Lest this assailant prove more foolhardy than most, Bak hunched over, darted out from among the bushes, and raced in zigzag fashion toward the governor's compound. He burst through the entryway. The guard, seated on the steps of the small gatehouse inside the wall, jerked his head up from his knees and blinked in confusion. He had been asleep. Bak doubted anyone could have passed through the gate without waking him, but he would not have been roused by an archer on the nearby walls or rooftops.

Wasting no time on questions, he scanned likely spots for ambush. He saw neither man nor bird. Hurrying outside the portal, he trotted along the wall and turned into the lane that took him to the front gate of Nebmose's villa. The entryway was closed and barred, as he had left it several days earlier.

He backed up a half dozen paces and took a running leap

at the barrier, smooth-faced on the outside. The fingers of his right hand cleared the edge. He clung there for a moment, his digits cramping. Before he could fall, he thrust his body upward and caught hold with the other hand. Scrambling higher, he cleared the gate with his head and shoulders. He examined the visible structures, paying particular attention to the roofs of the taller buildings. When he was reasonably sure he was alone and safe, he heaved himself up the rest of the way, threw his legs over the edge, and dropped to the path inside, raising an impressive puff of dust.

"Hey!" someone shouted. "Stop right where you are!"

Bak started, swung around. He saw no one in the shrine or the garden.

"Spread your hands and legs!" The command came from around the corner of the house.

Praying the voice was that of a guard, praying he had not unwittingly walked into the archer's grasp, Bak obeyed. A man stepped into view, spear poised. The youthful guard Nenu. His face registered recognition, his mouth dropped open, and the spearpoint tipped toward the earth.

Bak breathed a long, deep sigh of relief.

Chapter Eight

"You're lucky he didn't shoot you, sir," Kasaya said.

Bak gave the hulking young Medjay a wry smile. "I can't tell you how fervently I thanked the lord Amon that he was a guard who knew me."

"I'm surprised he didn't fire first and look later." Kasaya fussed with the sail, adjusting the braces for what must have been the hundredth time in less than an hour. No sooner did he settle down to relax than the breeze came from another quarter, emptying the heavy linen and setting it aflutter. As good-natured as the Medjay was and as even tempered, this short voyage downriver was beginning to try his patience. "None of the governor's guards have much training, I've noticed, especially newer men like Nenu. And with so many deaths you can barely count them on the fingers of one hand, they're all as skittish as gazelles being stalked by a pack of hunting dogs."

"That must be the island where we'll find Ineni." Bak, seated in the stern, pointed at a low mound of vegetation in the river ahead. From a distance, it looked like a wayward expanse of fertility broken loose from the narrow strip of farmland between the water's edge and the barren sands of the adjacent desert.

"I thank the lord Amon!" Kasaya muttered, letting the sail drop. Ignoring the fabric crumpled between the upper and lower yards, he took up the oars and began to row. He aimed the vessel toward the narrow channel between the island and the west bank.

"You'd think fear would keep those guards alert and aware of all who come too close, yet Nenu swore he saw no one." Bak still seethed each time he thought of the big, dumb guard, seeing nothing, hearing nothing, plodding around as witless as the unfinished statue Antef's men had loaded onto a barge. The dolt had in fact seemed skeptical about the whole affair, merely going through the motions as if the archer had been a figment of Bak's imagination.

"He was probably sleeping, like the man at the gatehouse."

"He faithfully patrolled the grounds of that villa all morning—so he claims." Bak's voice exuded disbelief.

Kasaya's face registered a similar skepticism.

"After I gave up looking for the archer," Bak said, "I searched out Amonhotep. He agreed the guards are getting careless, and he promised to impress upon them the need to remain alert."

"Somebody better stay awake behind those walls. Even I, each time I set foot inside, take care to guard my back."

Bak gave him a sharp look. His own fear, born of the shooting, had quickly turned to anger. And a strong awareness of the need for caution. "If the guards are afraid and if you, a stranger, also feel threatened, the servants must be terrified."

"They scurry from room to room like mice fearful of a prowling cat." Spotting a couple of skiffs drawn up on the shore, Kasaya lifted the tips of the oars from the water and let the small craft drift toward them. "Only mistress Khawet's firm hand is holding them together."

"They should thank the gods she's there." Bak recalled the last time he had seen her and smiled. "For one who allowed another woman to rule the household, she's taken command in an admirable fashion."

Kasaya grinned. "She'd make a more satisfactory governor than her father, I'd wager."

Bak sat quite still, the words driving home a new thought,

one that should have occurred to him sooner. "You must look after her, Kasaya. I've thought always that Djehuty will be the next to die, but what if I err? What if the slayer takes the life of the one most dear to him? His only daughter."

Bak scrambled out of the skiff and sent Kasaya rushing back to the governor's villa. He clung to his belief that the slayer would not strike until ten days separated Hatnofer's death from the next, but he deemed it best to take precautions. He could return to Abu with Ineni—or walk back, if he had to.

As he watched the Medjay raise the sail, he realized he had neglected to tell either of his men to lie in wait for the bearer of the unwanted gifts. He raised his hands to his mouth, thinking to call out to Kasaya, but decided not to. With the intrusions escalated to ambush, they surely had seen the last of the more subtle threats.

He followed an overgrown path through knee-high grass and brush so tall he could not see over it. As often as not, he splashed through water, puddles glimpsed among the thick foliage, residue of the recent flood. Birds filled the air with song. An ichneumon—mongoose—darted across his path so fast he almost missed it, and some unseen creature set the grass to waving off to his left. Sweat, drawn from him by the moist heat, trickled down his breast. The island, he guessed, was an immense sandbar saved by the lush growth from destruction by floodwaters and swift currents. The river had deposited this transitory haven and would one day carry it away. The lord Hapi at his best and worst.

Somewhere ahead, he heard the whinny of a horse. His heart skipped a beat and his pace quickened. The years he had spent as a charioteer had given him a deep love of the large and graceful creatures, a sense of comradeship with them. For an instant he wished . . . No, his task as a police officer suited him better, challenged his wits in addition to his body. He could not, would not go back.

He burst through a thicket of brush and vines. Ahead lay a pasture covered with grass so tall it brushed the bellies of fifty or more red-and-white-spotted, short-horned cattle. Two small boys sat on a mound of earth, watching the herd. A pack of curly-haired black dogs lay in the grass around them.

The boys glanced at Bak, who waved a greeting. One youth scrambled to his feet, put his fingers to his mouth, and gave a long, trilling whistle, signaling the arrival of a stranger. Warning their father, he thought, and Ineni and possibly others as well, men who would come running if needed. He walked in among the grazing cattle, animals as plump and healthy as any he had ever seen. Small brown birds clung to their necks and backs, harvesting insects, while egrets pecked the soggy earth around their hooves. Ineni had talked of having a skill for farming. If these animals were representative, the claim was no exaggeration.

As he cleared the herd, the governor's son and a tough-looking man with a bent nose waded out of the river. Both carried stout wooden clubs they looked prepared to use. Bak strode toward them across a patch of scruffy grass heavily trodden by animals.

Beyond, a herd of thirty or more horses stood shoulder-deep in the river, blowing, whinnying, throwing up their heads for the sheer joy of life, shaking water from their long manes. About half were a rich golden-brown, the rest white, gray, or black. A boy of twelve or so years sat astride a thick-necked black animal Bak guessed was the stallion from the land of Hatti that Ineni had mentioned a few days before. Three men half swam, half walked among the herd, controlling the animals with gentle hands and kindly voices and at the same time keeping a wary eye on Bak. A second boy stood close to shore, minding a dozen foals.

"So it's you." Ineni's voice was cool, unwelcoming.

"Do you always greet visitors in this friendly manner?" Bak asked, nodding toward the weapons, "or do you reserve so warm a welcome for police officers?"

Ineni's eyes flashed anger. "If you've come at Djehuty's behest, Lieutenant, you've wasted your time."

"I answer to no man but Commandant Thuty—and he's in faroff Buhen."

Bak was puzzled by the clubs, by the defensive posture. The herd was large and impressive, true, and extremely valuable, but the punishment for stealing horses was so harsh few men would take the risk. Even wild desert tribesmen were seldom tempted, with fear of impalement to dissuade them.

Ineni glared, too tied to his own purpose to pay heed. "I'll manage the Nubt estate as I see fit, not trade away its assets in response to a whim."

Bak scowled at the pair before him, not understanding. "I've come in search of information, that's all. Now will you drop those clubs and let me get on with my task?"

"You've not come to . . . ?" Ineni's voice faltered. He lowered his weapon and stared at Bak in confusion. "Djehuty didn't send you? You're not here to see these horses delivered to the animal market in Swenet?"

Bak's eyes darted toward the magnificent animals. "You're not selling them!"

"Djehuty ordered me to." Ineni's voice pulsed with anger—and defiance.

"You've decided to oppose him?"

"I have." Ineni half turned around to look at the herd. "A desert chieftain, head of a tribe of nomads, men who travel the burning sands through all the months of the year, has come to Djehuty time and time again, pleading for horses. Two days ago he came again, and my father agreed to trade away the herd, each and every animal, even the stallion from Hatti."

Bak muttered a curse, stunned by so rash an action. "Why?"

"I know what those tribesmen are. They're wild and unruly, men of great passion but no common sense. If the horses don't die from lack of care and the proper food and water, they'll run them until they drop, then they'll hack them to pieces for food. I won't let that happen."

"Where will you take them?" Abruptly, Bak raised his hands, signaling silence. "No, don't tell me. I was ordered to Abu to track down a slayer, not stand between a man and his father.''

Ineni's laugh was soft, containing no humor whatsoever, but broke the tension between them. "I thank the lord Khnum, Lieutenant, that you care as I do for horses."

Bak squeezed his shoulder, smiled. "If ever I return to the regiment of Amon, I'll need a young team. Now I know where to find them."

Turning away, clearing his throat, trying to rid himself of unmanly emotion, Ineni called to the men in the river, "Bring them out now and dry them off. We must soon get them on their way."

They looked at him, at Bak, and at the man with the crooked nose, confused by the sudden order.

"Move, you laggards!" Ineni shouted. "We've a herd to save."

The boy, breaking into a grin, swung the black horse around and rode the beast out of the water. With their human guardians urging them on—amid sudden laughter and back-slapping—the other horses followed. The foals scrambled to dry land, eager to rejoin their mothers. Bak had seldom seen such fine animals. All were sleek and fit, spirited yet well-behaved. He longed to separate out a fine matched pair, to harness them to a chariot, to feel the reins in his hands and the speed of the moving vehicle.

The men caught the animals one by one and tied them to stakes sunk deep in the ground. Someone passed out rags, and they set to work rubbing down their charges.

Ineni picked up a rag, walked to the black stallion, and began to dry his neck. "Now, Lieutenant, what can I do for you?" He noticed Bak's bemused expression, laughed. "You think we're wasting time and effort? We're not. There's a shallow passage between the island and the west bank. They'll get their hooves wet, little more." He looked a new man and acted like one: bright and cheerful, resolute.

Smiling, Bak grabbed a length of frayed cloth and slipped into the space between the stallion and a long-legged white mare with a dark mane tethered to the same stake. He caught hold of her bridle and set to work. "I've a slayer to find, Ineni, and you owe me some answers."

"I doubt I can help you much." Ineni looked across the stallion's back, his good humor banished by the reminder of murder. "Simut told me you think the deaths were prompted by the sandstorm that came close to destroying the garrison a few years ago. I've never been in the army. Until I wed Khawet, I spent most of my days on our estate in Nubt, well north of the province my father governs and far from the garrison. I take no interest whatsoever in Abu."

Though weary of repeating himself, Bak explained, "Other than Hatnofer, I've learned that all who've died so far were either survivors of the storm or the sons of survivors. I'm now looking for men who lost loved ones, men who might blame their loss on Djehuty and the others who came back unscathed."

Ineni snorted. "I thought your goal was to narrow the field of suspects, not widen it."

"Whoever took those lives has an intimate knowledge of your father's household and complete freedom within the surrounding walls," Bak reminded him. "That fact alone keeps the number manageable."

Ineni eyed Bak, torn by indecision. The stallion nuzzled him, reminding him of his task and of the debt he owed the police officer. He smiled at the animal, rubbed its muzzle. "I could blame Djehuty—and I have—many times. My father was among those who vanished."

Bak's head snapped around. "Your . . . Your what?"

"My father. The man who lay with my mother and sired me."

"Djehuty isn't . . . ?"

Ineni gave a sharp, humorless laugh, startling the stallion, making him jerk the rope holding him in place. "My father—my natural father—was a soldier in the garrison when Djehuty was a young man, staying in Abu until he could find a suitable position in the army. I was still taking sustenance from my mother's breast when suddenly my father was posted to a faraway land. She couldn't travel with him, and she had no family to go to. In three days time, Djehuty took her into the governor's villa and that very night he claimed her as his own.'' His mouth tightened and he rubbed the horse so vigorously it sidestepped, narrowing the gap Bak occupied. ''I'll always believe he coveted her from afar and finally whispered in his father's ear, seeking my father's distant posting. I've no way of learning the truth.''

Bak slapped the stallion's flank, making more room. He could literally feel the young farmer's anger, hear it in the surge of words dammed up for years. Or had he confided in Khawet? His hatred of her father might account for the discord between them.

''My father was gone ten years. When he returned, his wife dwelt in the netherworld and his son in Nubt. He dared not say a word.'' Ineni's face registered a bitter anger; his hands moved swiftly over the stallion's legs. ''He came sometimes to see me, and in a way we drew close. But Djehuty always stood between us. He seduced me just as he had my mother. He saw how much I loved the land, saw how skilled I was with men and animals. He gave me ever greater responsibilities and, at the age of seventeen, made me manager of his estate. The land became my mistress.''

Bak stood erect to wring the water from his rag. ''The land, not Khawet?''

''We were of a marriageable age and I cared for her, but no.'' Ineni gave another of his harsh laughs. ''I was a servant, in no way worthy of the great man's only child.''

Bak nodded understanding. Djehuty claimed descent from a long line of provincial governors. Would he not wish his daughter to wed nobility?

Ineni continued: ''That storm you're interested in altered many lives, mine most of all. I was twenty years of age when the desert swallowed up my father. My mother was long dead, and I was alone in the world. Djehuty was a man with no sons, and Khawet his sole daughter. His estate was thriving, thanks to my good sense.'' He squeezed out his rag, came around the stallion's rump, and continued his task, sharing Bak's space. "One day he came to me—four months, it was, after the storm. He wanted to adopt me as his son, he told me, and in return, I must wed Khawet. He wanted his estate to remain whole, and I wanted the land. As for Khawet . . . Well, he'd made the decision and she had no say in the matter. And so it happened. The contract was drawn up and witnessed, and she came into my bed." He gave a strained little laugh. "All in all, the arrangement worked out as well as could be expected."

"I've noticed a certain distance between you and Khawet." Bak spoke with care, trying to be tactful when tact was impossible.

"Why should I deny what all the world knows?" Ineni's smile was fierce. "I've done everything in my power to earn her affection, but she clings to the memory of a past beloved, one who long ago entered the netherworld. Even that I might overcome, but her father holds her by his side in Abu, while I must spend much of my time on our estate in Nubt."

Bak recalled Amethu's comments about women who had no children. "How old is she? Twenty-four, twenty-five?" He raised a questioning eyebrow, received a nod. "I know that's well beyond the age when most women first bear a child, but it's surely not too late to give her one."

"I seldom touch her, and so it's always been," Ineni admitted in a gruff voice. "She . . . Well, when I go to her, she tolerates me, barely."

Bak eyed him thoughtfully. Through his life, he had known several men whose wives held them at a distance. They all had one thing in common. "You've a concubine?"

"Another secret known to all the world." Ineni tried to make his voice gruff, but pride forbade him to do so. He noticed Bak's hint of a smile and laughed. "Yes, I freely admit I share my bed in Nubt. She's the loveliest young woman in the province, the joy of my life. Last month, she gave me a son. My firstborn. A treasure to behold."

Later, Bak stood alone at the river's edge, watching the long line of horses and men plod through the shallow water to the west bank. He had to admit he was biased in Ineni's favor, preferring to believe that anyone who loved horses as he did would have to be driven hard against a wall to slay a man. On the other hand, the young farmer had more than enough reason to want Djehuty dead. Not only had his true father died in the storm, but all Djehuty's property would someday belong to him and Khawet.

Bak borrowed a skiff from Ineni and spent the remainder of the afternoon sailing back to Abu, the voyage made long and tedious by the fitful breeze. By the time he got his first glimpse of the ancient tombs that overlooked the island from the west bank, tiny spots of light glowed in a darkening sky, and the odor of burning fuel drifted through the air from a multitude of braziers.

As he neared the landingplace below the governor's villa, he had second thoughts about beaching the skiff among several drawn out of the water a few paces upstream, including the vessel Kasaya had left there. The patch of shoreline was too visible from above, as were the stairs he would have to climb. The archer might once again be lying in wait, prepared to slay him. Why take the risk? He sailed on until he found a dozen or more small boats pulled up on shore and a group of men hunkered down nearby, encircling a game of throwsticks.

Although he doubted the archer had the faintest idea where he was, he took no chances. He beached his skiff as close to the game as he could, hastily pulled the vessel out of the water, and darted into the nearest lane. Keeping to the shadows, moving fast and silently, he sped along the unfamiliar streets of Abu. The faint afterglow vanished from the sky, the stars brightened, and the narrow thoroughfares were blanketed in ever-deepening gloom. Voices sounded on the rooftops above, families sharing their evening meal. A lone goat wandered down a lane, bleating. Dogs howled in first one sector of the city and then another, urging each other to greater voice.

As he hurried along, he thought of the unwanted gifts that had been left each evening in his quarters, followed by the blatant attempt to slay him with bow and arrows. Why the threats? Why the more forthright attempt to take his life? He had learned a lot since coming to Abu, but felt himself no closer to the slayer than when he had arrived. He was a long way from the truth. Much too far away.

One thing he did know: if the archer and the slayer were one and the same, Ineni could not be the guilty man. He had been far from Abu all day, on the island with the horses.

Bak saw ahead the mouth of the lane leading to his quarters. He slowed his pace and approached with care, scanning rooftops and pitch-black doorways for any sign of the archer, thinking of the herd, wondering where Ineni would take them. Not far from Nubt, he suspected. Someplace where people knew and liked him. So great a number of horses would be impossible to hide. Ineni would need the help—and the silence—of men and women he could trust.

Finding nothing suspicious, Bak slipped into the narrow lane. The way ahead was cloaked in darkness, a black tunnel with a faint wedge of light at the far end. A figure appeared there, vaguely illuminated and hard to see, a patch of white. His heart leaped into his throat. He dodged sideways and flattened himself against the wall, making less of a target. The figure vanished, probably around the far corner. A neighbor, most likely, going about the business of living.

Laughing at himself but taking care nonetheless, he hurried on. As he neared the end of the lane, he realized the light came from his own quarters. Murmuring voices on the roof and the odors of stewed fish and onions told him Psuro and Kasaya were there. They must have lit the lamp so neither he nor they would be accosted by an uninvited guest hiding in the dark. He smiled, pleased by the reassuring glow, the thought of warm food and friendly faces.

He walked up to the door, stopped in his tracks, sucked in his breath. A stool stood just inside the threshold, barring the way. A bright puddle adorned its upper surface. Fresh blood. He ducked aside, out of the light and the line of fire. Fearing he knew not what, he stood silent and still, every sense alert. He heard no movement inside, felt no human presence. He peered around the doorjamb. A small baked clay lamp cast a feeble light from the stairway, enough to see the room much as he and his Medjays had left it, cluttered with their possessions but empty of life.

Yet the blood made clear that something was wrong.

Puzzled, curious, unsure what to expect and strangely reluctant to find out, he slipped past the stool and ducked off to the right, out of the lighted doorway. He scanned the room a second time, finding nothing altered and no one inside. He half swung around to look again at the stool. His eyes were drawn upward to the woven reed mat, tightly rolled and tied out of the way above the door. Hard against the mat, pinned upside-down with a short, sharp dagger, was a full-grown gray-brown rat, so fresh-killed a final drop of blood clung to its neck. The stool had been carefully aligned below to catch the creature's blood, to draw attention to its murder.

Snapping out an oath, Bak crossed the room in three quick strides, scooped up the lamp and, shielding the flame with a hand, carried it back to the door for a closer look. The dagger was bronze, a plain, unmarked weapon common to the army. The rat's neck had been cut before it had been pinned to the mat. The creature, he knew without doubt, symbolized the slain sergeant Senmut, from all reports a rat in his own right.

The message could not have been more clear, yet Bak was confused. He had been so sure the slayer would leave no more unwanted gifts. Why this now? Why this kind of message when the bow was more direct?

He backed off and stared. The rodent so recently slain, the fresh blood on the stool, sent a chill up his spine. This gift was disgusting, sinister, its delivery demonstrating contempt for himself and his men. The intruder could not have been gone more than a few moments. He had taken the rat's life and left his ugly message, with Psuro and Kasaya on the rooftop only a few paces away.

And Bak himself had missed him by a hair.

Chapter Nine

"Why would a man use a bow and arrow at midday and go back to a more insidious threat that same evening?" Bak, his forearms resting on either side of the prow, scanned the unfamiliar waters ahead of the skiff, searching for rocks lying beneath the surface, awaiting a lapse of attention. "I don't understand."

Psuro sat farther back, manning the sail. "Are you sure he meant to slay you, sir? His arrows never once came close, you said."

"I'm not certain of anything," Bak grumbled. He was firmly convinced someone had set out to slay him, but to argue the matter with Psuro was futile. The stocky Medjay was a good man, but he was not Imsiba. Bak needed the sergeant's ear, his common sense arguments that sent Bak's thoughts down untraveled paths.

"There's the island where we're to meet User," Psuro said, pointing. "The place of inscriptions."

Bak eyed the patch of land rising from the river some distance ahead, an outcrop of granite larger than Abu and as stubbornly resistant to erosion. Acacias and tamarisks lined the water's edge, while mounded boulders, their surfaces blackened by time, rose above a blanket of yellow sand too sterile to support much life. He was not impressed.

Rising to his feet, he turned around to study the river behind them, as he often had since their departure from Abu. Among the many islands through which they had threaded their way, bits and pieces of ships darted into and out of sight, as if playing the child's game of hide-and-seek. He glimpsed mastheads, portions of sails, sometimes a fully rigged craft that vanished in the blink of an eye behind islands crowned with vegetation or massive clumps of boulders devoid of foliage. Distance shrunk the vessels, light and heat waves distorted them, preventing him from identifying any one boat that might have remained behind them all along. He did not think anyone was following, but he could not be sure.

"According to Pahared," Psuro said, "we'll find a multitude of writings left on the rocks from ancient times."

"Rapids to the right," Bak warned, spotting a stretch of foaming water.

A minute adjustment of the braces eased the vessel left. The stiff breeze sped them southward, making light of the northbound current. With their sail fully ballooned, the water whispering beneath the hull, they sped past the eddy and through an irregular row of islets guarding their approach to the island: a channel separating the rocky barrier from the east bank of the river. Patches of froth warned of hidden hazards. The chill of night had passed, and the warm breath of the lord Khepre, the morning sun, had lifted the mist from the water. Birds wheeled overhead, riding the air currents in lazy circles, ready to dive at any fish foolhardy enough to rise to the surface.

"The patterns I spotted the day we arrived in Abu point to a solitary slayer having a single reason for his actions," Bak said, thinking aloud. "If I weren't so sure of that, I'd suspect a second man fired those arrows yesterday."

"Anything's possible, I suppose," Psuro said doubtfully.

Bak scowled at the channel ahead. Imsiba, too, would have doubts, he thought, but he would have alternate suggestions as well.

They raced up the channel, following a small, stout cargo vessel riding low beneath a heavy load of plump sacks he assumed were filled with grain. To their right, a tall, steep ridge strewn with boulders rose from the island. On the east bank, a mudbrick village nestled beside a small bay edged with sycamores, palms, and acacias. Spindly lean-tos shaded a thriving market along the shore. The vessel ahead swung into the bay to merge with a fleet of skiffs whose masters had brought produce for trade. Psuro adjusted the sail, veering in the opposite direction toward the island.

"What rank did User hold when his unit was besieged by the storm?" Bak asked, his eyes on the approaching shore.

"Spearman." Psuro spilled air from the sail, cutting their speed. "He was a raw recruit, a youth not long off the farm, having no experience in warfare."

"That looks a good place to land." Bak pointed toward a stretch of sandy beach near the southern end of the ridge.

"We're to meet him at the shrine of the lady Anket." The goddess, along with the lord Khnum and the lady Satet, served as a guardian of the source of the great river on which they sailed. "He came close to walking with the gods, he told me. He was the last to come back from the desert, and if he hadn't been found by a boy searching for a stray goat, he'd have died less than an hour's walk from the river."

They neared the shore and Psuro let the upper yard fall. Bak leaped overboard before the current could drag them backward and towed the vessel into shallow water. Psuro scrambled out, and together they pulled the boat onto the beach. The island looked peaceful enough, deserted even, and they both wore sheathed daggers at their waists, but with an intruder leaving threatening gifts in their quarters and an archer lurking about, they opted to arm themselves with the spears and shields they had brought from Abu.

They trudged up a short incline blanketed with sand and walked alongside the ridge, a steep jumble of boulders streaked with bird droppings. Bak's eyes strayed to the inscriptions, and his footsteps slowed. He glimpsed messages of kings returning victorious from battles fought far to the south, reminders of proud noblemen leading caravans laden with exotic and priceless trade goods, and records of accomplishments of a more practical nature, such as the digging of a well on a remote desert track.

"Did User say how he managed to survive the storm?"

"He was in too great a hurry to leave Abu." Psuro glanced around, searching for the man they had come to see. "He did say he was so happy to see the river he wanted forevermore to surround himself with water. Now he lives on an island where he can get a drink or go for a swim at any time, day or night."

"If his island is anything like this, he's made a bargain with the lord Set."

Set was a god representing evil and violence, patron of deserts and foreign lands. The sun was indeed ferocious, beating down unrelieved, making the sand so hot it burned their feet. The breeze did nothing to relieve the heat, merely set their teeth on edge as it passed among the boulders, whispering a soft and lonely refrain.

They plodded around the southern end of the ridge, between it and a second, smaller mound. Near the upstream tip of the island, drawn well out of the water and half hidden in a clump of wispy tamarisks, they spotted an empty skiff. User's vessel, they assumed. Walking on, they found on the west side of the ridge a modest sandstone shrine surrounded by a decrepit mudbrick wall. The building looked across a swath of sand toward a fairly broad channel down which a canal had been cut through the rapids many generations earlier, a great feat for its time but now blocked with boulders and impossible to use.

Thinking to find User inside the shrine, they walked through the open gate and crossed the sand to the building. The door stood open, admitting light to a transverse chamber with three small, dark rooms at the back. Except for the one in the center, which contained a red granite pedestal which would support the wooden shrine of the lady Anket when she traveled upstream from Abu to greet the rising flood-waters, the building was empty.

Leaving the sacred precinct, they looked around, seeking User, a priest, some sign of life in this lifeless place.

A short, sharp whistle broke the silence.

"Up there." Bak pointed toward the top of the ridge,

where a man stood among the boulders, his head shaded by what looked from a distance like an overturned basket. "Is that User?"

"He's been watching us all along," the Medjay grumbled. "Why couldn't he show himself sooner?"

User remained where he was, well shielded by boulders, looking out at the water, examining the landscape on the far side of the ridge. *A cautious man,* Bak thought. *A man either afraid of his own shadow or fearful for good reason. A reason not to be found in Abu, but here.*

"Something's wrong," he said, darting toward the mound.

Still the man they had come to see hesitated. After a final long look at the channel beyond the ridge, where their skiff lay, he began to move. As agile as a cat, he worked his way down to meet them, sidling between boulders, climbing around broken chunks of granite, swinging across spaces separating one from another. Never did he show himself fully.

"I'm Lieutenant Bak," Bak called. "What troubles you?"

User stopped not far above and hunkered down in the shelter of an overhanging chunk of rock. He was a stocky man of medium height, wearing a white tunic with loose sleeves that covered his arms and a kilt that fell below his knees. The fabric was heavy and coarse, the garb unusual, restricting freedom of movement for working in the fields or sailing a skiff. What had looked like an upside-down basket from a distance was, in fact, an odd woven reed headdress with a wide brim that kept his face in shadow.

"Do you know you were followed to this place?" he demanded. "A man alone in a skiff, carrying a bow and a quiver full of arrows."

Bak snarled a curse. "Where is he now?"

"Not far upstream from where you beached your vessel. He's in his boat, waiting. I feared this would happen. With so many who survived the storm already dead . . ." User let out a harsh laugh, leaving the rest to the imagination.

"I doubt he's come for you. It's me he wants to slay."

"You?" User asked, skeptical.

Psuro hefted his spear. "Shall I go after him, sir?"

"I wouldn't," User cut in before Bak could answer. "He's sheltered within a clump of trees and surrounded by open space. No man can get close without being seen."

"Did you get a good look at him?" Bak asked.

"He's too far away."

Bak stood, hands on hips, thinking. He had taken every precaution he could and still he had been followed. Maybe the lord Amon had handed him a gift in spite of himself. "Show me where he is. We must decide how best to lay hands on him."

"I'm glad you agreed to help," Bak said.

User, who had had no choice in the matter, gave him a rueful grin. "As you pointed out, Lieutenant, it's my neck, too."

Bak poled the skiff into deeper water, then settled down in the stern. He wished they were sailing his own swift vessel instead of the blocky, work-a-day craft of the island farmer. And he wished for a weapon with a longer range than a spear. He shook off the thought. The beached skiff was unreachable, useful as bait and nothing more, the object that held the archer where he was, the sole reason he had not stalked Bak and Psuro across the island as soon as he arrived.

User dipped the oars deep, sending the vessel across a patch of bubbling water and down a cascade that took Bak's breath away. "The currents are in our favor, so it shouldn't take long to get to him. The problem, as I see it, will be that last stretch of open water."

"With luck and the help of the gods, Psuro will distract him." Bak prayed he was right. The Medjay had a strong arm, but could he hurl rocks far enough and fast enough to hold the archer's attention? "You met us on this island to speak of the sandstorm. I can think of no better time than now."

"I'll be frank with you, Lieutenant. I don't like to talk about it or even think about it. The storm. Those many days in the desert . . ." User raised a shoulder and wiped his sweaty face on his tunic. His voice dropped to a low croak. "I'll never know what kept me alive."

Bak felt compassion, sympathy, but he had to know what drove the slayer on. "I'd like nothing more than to walk away and leave you in peace, but I can't."

"The man you seek will be within our grasp in less than an hour. Let him speak for himself."

Bak eyed him long and hard. "How many men survived that storm, User?" Getting nothing in return but a stubborn scowl, he snapped, "Surely you can answer so simple a question!"

User veered closer to shore, avoiding the stronger current farther out. "Eleven," he muttered.

"Eleven men who've remained mute for five long years." Bak kept his voice hard, cold. "Why? Why hold a time of mutual suffering so close within the heart? Would it not be natural to talk, to share so horrible an experience with all who wish to listen? To lessen the load through repetition?"

"You don't understand!"

"I suspect Djehuty ordered all who survived to remain quiet, but I, too, have lived in a garrison. I know a commander's orders won't silence whispers."

User stared at him, his face wracked with pain. Without warning, he leaned hard on an oar, turning the skiff, and rammed its prow into a stand of thick, spiky grass. Bak, taken unawares, slid off the wooden brace he occupied and landed hard on the centerboard amid a clutter of fishing poles and farm tools.

"We're ashamed!" User cried. "Some of us for one reason, I suspect, and some for another. But we all have reason for shame."

Bak rocked forward, brushed off the back of his kilt, and sat again on the brace. He eyed the former spearman with a mix of sympathy, tolerance, and blame. User read the look and a flush spread across his face. He clutched the oars and, pushing hard against the grass, freed the skiff.

Back on course, he said, "With so many of us so recently slain . . ." He paused, rubbed his forehead as if to ease the pain. "The tale must be told, I know."

"The wind came up and the skies blackened," Bak said, thinking to lead him into his story.

User's expression lightened; he grabbed at the words like a drowning man grabbing at a lifeline. "You know the tale already?"

"I've seen an approaching storm, that's all."

Deflated, User eased the skiff between two boulders. The task seemed to calm him, to resign him. "With the storm upon us, blinding us, the men did what any sensible men would do. They started to bunch up and huddle down with the donkeys. Commander Djehuty ordered us to stay in line and march on." He gave a harsh, cynical snort. "As if any man could keep going in such a tempest!"

Bak recalled Lieutenant Amonhotep saying he had heard contradictory orders. Had the young aide told the truth as he remembered it? Or had he thought it best to show Djehuty in a better light?

"Even I, as green as I was, knew the order was foolish," User said. "With no one able to see his hand in front of his face, the line broke apart and most men lost their way, I among them. By chance, I stumbled upon my sergeant, Senmut, a lieutenant named Ptahmose, and a few other men and donkeys, all crowded together, trying to save themselves."

"Was Montu among them? Or the child Nakht's father?"

"I don't know. I was new to the garrison. Most of the men were strangers to me."

Staying close to the island, User let the current carry the skiff over a stepped series of falls that jarred the spine each time it dropped.

"The storm was fierce," the farmer went on. "The lieutenant ordered us to hold hands, saying all who let go would die, and he told us to hang onto our donkeys' lead ropes. It wasn't easy, let me tell you. The wind blew with such force, we stumbled along before it, all of us together. My donkey soon jerked free, and I guess others did, too."

User shipped his oars, letting the skiff drift around the bend. Bak saw in the distance the small bay on the east bank and the village beside it. He prayed the archer was a patient man, still awaiting them in his skiff. He had no fear for Psuro; the Medjay had the patience of a log.

"How long we staggered on, I don't know." User, well into his tale, needed no further prompting. "Made senseless by the battering we were getting, we fell into a long-dry watercourse. There we lost several men and all that remained of our donkeys except one. Lieutenant Ptahmose, wiser than the rest, had tied its lead rope to his arm. The wind pinned us against the wadi wall, and I was sure we would die there. We didn't. The donkey turned his back on the gale and let it blow him along the wall, taking us with him. And then, thanks to all the gods in the ennead, the creature found shelter—a small cave."

Raising his arm, he wiped his troubled face on his sleeve. "We crowded inside and—may the gods forgive us all—we pushed the poor dumb beast back out into the storm. To keep him out, we shoved a boulder, long ago fallen from the ceiling, in front of the opening. It broke the wind and we had more room. The donkey stood there for a long time, head down, tail between its legs. At last, it drifted off, taking a half-full jar of water with it. We were too afraid for ourselves to notice—until too late."

User rowed the skiff close under the trees lining the water's edge, where he and Bak had to duck the lower limbs. "The rest is a dream I try nightly to forget. The wind, the heat, the air filled with sand and dust. The thirst, the stench of fear."

Bak gave him a thoughtful look. "Other than the donkey, I see no reason for shame thus far."

"You don't understand." User's mouth twisted into a parody of a smile. "We not only pushed the donkey out to die—the creature that saved our lives—but men came to our cave, men who begged us to let them inside. Men who shared our quarters in the garrison, our good times and bad. We turned them all away."

"But didn't you say . . . ?" Bak stared, jolted by what he was thinking. "You said you pushed the donkey out to make more room."

User bowed his head, letting the skiff drift. "We had space for four or five more men, yet we turned away all who begged for refuge."

Appalled, Bak caught an overhead branch to stop the vessel's downstream flight. The tale was incredible. No wonder someone harbored a grudge against the survivors! But how had the slayer learned the truth? One of those who came back alive must have been unable to keep quiet. "You made no mention of Djehuty. Was he among you?"

User shook his head. "He was somewhere else, his life saved, I was told, by a sergeant named Min." He frowned, thinking back. "After the storm ended, I wandered up the wadi, looking for the donkey and anyone who might've survived. A witless thing to do, I know. The other men, anxious to save themselves, left without me." He paused, drew in a ragged breath. "I was the last to reach the river, crazed from so many days of wandering alone, burned by the sun, thirsty, starving. When finally I was able to listen and talk, Min had already sailed north, reassigned to another garrison, I heard. As far as I know, he never came back to Abu."

"And Djehuty left the army for good, as did you."

"I'd had enough, yes, and what remained of the garrison had had enough of me. As long as I stayed, not a man or woman in Abu could forget the many good men lost in the storm." Noticing Bak's puzzled look, he gave him another of his twisted grins. "The lord Re made me pay dearly for my survival."

With both hands, he tore off the headdress, caught his tunic by the hem, and pulled it over his head, stripping it from his body. His near-bald head, forehead, and cheeks, his shoulders, back, and arms were mottled red, white, and brown, scars left by a terrible burn. Sunburn.

"Row us into the current so we can cut him off if he starts to flee. I'll tend to the sail should we need it." Bak selected a fishing pole from among several lying in the hull, unwound the line a few cubits, and dropped the weight into the water. He prepared a second pole for User. "If I hunch over, he shouldn't recognize me. With luck, he'll think we're two local farmers, come out in search of our evening meal.''

"And if he's as wary as he should be?'' User asked.

"He'd be wise to set sail, and we'd be wise to keep our heads down. He's sure to use the bow.''

"And us with only a spear.''

Bak smiled. He liked this man, who went straight to the heart of a problem. "Ready?''

User, fully clad once again to protect his sensitive skin, paddled the skiff out from beneath the trees, setting a diagonal course into the current. Bak shoved aside the clutter in the hull and sat down, back bent and fishing pole in hand. When User deemed them far enough from shore, he let the current carry them northward.

Bak eyed the clump of trees concealing the archer. The situation looked as bleak from here as it had from the mound. Tidy beaches lay to the north and south and an open stretch of sand separated the grove from the mound where Psuro waited. An ideal position for an archer to defend; a terrible place to attack—armed or unarmed.

He gave a series of quick, sharp whistles, imitating a bird, a signal to Psuro. A long, bloodcurdling yell followed, and the Medjay's dark figure popped up from behind a rock at the lower edge of the mound. He raised his arm, snapped it forward. A sharp crack sounded, a rock striking something solid. The skiff? The sturdy trunk of a tree? A boulder hidden by leaves? Bak had no way of knowing. The Medjay vanished from sight. If the archer fired off an arrow, it was too far away to see.

User swung the prow toward the archer's lair, dipped the oars deep, and shoved the vessel forward with skill and speed. Another yell and Psuro sprang up in a new position to hurl a second stone. Light glinted for a moment on the bronze tip of an arrow speeding his way, but he had already ducked behind his granite shield. No sound betrayed the rock's landingplace.

User paddled like a madman. The closer they came to the trees, the lower he and Bak crouched. A third and fourth yell, each louder and longer and more fearsome than the one before, carried across the river, frightening off a flock of ducks in flight. User thought he heard a rock splash into the water; Bak imagined he saw another arrow flying toward Psuro. How much longer, he wondered, before the man hidden among the trees realized he should watch his back?

As if the archer had read his thoughts, a spot of white showed through the trees and an arrow sped across the water. The missile struck the prow of their skiff with a thud; the shaft shattered and dropped into the river. Muttering a curse, User ducked so low Bak doubted he could see over the rail, but he continued to paddle, his course as straight as before. Another arrow followed and a second in quick succession, both flying over the vessel to fall in its wake.

Abruptly, a skiff shot out from among the trees. It was long and slender, similar to those used for sport by the officers at Buhen. Bak's heart sank. User knew his vessel and he knew the river, but could he cut off a boat so easy to maneuver and so fast?

"We have the advantage," the farmer said, his teeth clenched tight with determination and effort. "We're in the current; he's too close to shore."

"Can you keep him there?"

"I can try."

Bak glimpsed Psuro racing across the sand toward their own skiff. Doubting the Medjay would catch up in time to help, he focused on the vessel they chased, at least seventy paces to their left but not far ahead. The man inside, too indistinct to identify, had abandoned his weapon to take up the oars, propelling his boat toward deeper water. User altered course to intercept him. They swept down the channel, not quite side-by-side, toward the end of the island and the turbulent waters guarding the northern approach.

Sweat poured down User's face and his soaked tunic stuck to his back. Bak longed to raise the sail, but knew it would do no good as long as they remained in the channel. Forcing himself to be patient, he pulled in the fishing lines, dangling useless in the water, and laid the poles in the hull where he had found them. Spear and shield close to hand, he knelt on the centerboard, ready to leap into action the instant they caught up with their quarry. He refused to admit the wider channel and more generous breeze would give a distinct advantage to the sleeker vessel, speeding the archer on his way, leaving them far behind lolling in his wake.

The channel ahead began to broaden, revealing a wide swath of rippling silver, water washing over boulders not far beneath the surface after flowing around both sides of the island. The archer, whose view was obstructed by proximity, failed to spot the hazard until he was almost upon it. He swung his skiff hard around, trying to keep out of harm's way. User pressed his vessel closer.

The archer hesitated, then turned back toward the turbulence. The skiff sliced through the ripples, flinging water to right and left. The river ahead turned violent, white with roiling foam. Suddenly the prow rose into the air, the man inside was flung out, and the lovely little boat fell on its side and burst apart on the rocks.

"I can't believe it's over. It happened so fast and now . . ." Bak, standing on the quay at Swenet, spread his hands wide and shook his head. "No slayer. No answers. Nothing."

"I thank the lord Amon he's gone! Now we can go home to Buhen." Psuro, delighted by the abrupt turn of events, tossed the mooring rope to Bak. "When will you tell Governor Djehuty?"

Bak snugged the skiff tight against the stonework and glanced at the sky, where a deep golden sun hovered above the western horizon. They had thought the archer drowned— few men could survive those raging waters—but they could not be sure. Bak had been swept through a worse maelstrom in the not too distant past. So they had spent several hours in a fruitless search of the many islands below the point where the man had vanished. Their failure to find him was not conclusive, but pointed strongly to his death.

"Tomorrow will be soon enough. Another anxious night won't hurt him."

"He deserves far worse, if you ask me. If he'd let his troops settle down among the donkeys, he mightn't have lost a single man or beast. Why was he never called to account, I wonder?"

"I'm convinced he coerced the survivors into remaining mute." Bak scowled his disgust. "And he has friends in high places. We wouldn't be here if the vizier hadn't interceded."

Psuro joined him on the quay and they climbed the short slope to the village of Swenet. Huge old trees towered over the water's edge, and birdsong filled the air. Women chatted in a small square, awaiting their turn at the public well or sitting in the shade on mudbrick benches, enjoying the breeze and an end-of-day chat. A yellow dog lapped water from a puddle, while her three puppies chased grasshoppers across a patch of newly sprouted clover.

"Someone didn't keep his mouth locked tight," Psuro said. "That's why those who survived are now being slain. But why wait five years? And why Djehuty? He wasn't in that cave."

Bak turned down the lane leading to Pahared's wife's house of pleasure. A bowl or two of beer would be in order, maybe more. Enough to chase away the feeling of a task unfinished. "We'll never know now, will we?"

"I guess you no longer care about Hatnofer." Kasaya, seated on the floor on a pillow stuffed with straw, gave Bak a bleary-eyed look. "After all, our task is done and we'll soon sail south, this ugly place forgotten."

Psuro, not half as unsteady as the man beside him, broke the plug from a fresh jar of beer, flung the pieces into a basket used for the purpose, and splashed the pungent golden liquid into their bowls. "This town is alright. It's the governor who's ugly."

Kasaya bumped his elbow, spilling beer on the floor. "And the man who died in the rapids today."

Bak, not at all drunk, beckoned a skinny, scraggly-haired

female servant to clean up the mess. He had come to this house of pleasure to celebrate, yet had found himself in no mood to do so. Too many questions remained, questions Djehuty would never answer, and he had no one else to query. User had rattled off the names of the survivors, which matched the list Simut had provided. Other than him, Amonhotep, and the governor, all were dead or had gone far away from Abu.

A scuffle broke out in the corner, a disagreement over a game of knucklebones. One man cursed another. Stools skidded across the floor. Pottery crashed. Pahared's wife strode across the room, carrying a baton Bak suspected she had taken from some visiting official—perhaps by force. She held it firmly, her expression making clear that she was prepared to smash a head or two. The men slunk back, thoroughly cowed.

Bak had to give credit where credit was due: Pahared had wed quite a woman. "Tell me of Hatnofer," he said to Kasaya. "Did you discover her connection to the sandstorm?"

The young Medjay scooted sideways, making room for the servant to pour dry sand on the wet floor. Beer sloshed from his bowl, spilling down her leg. The girl's mouth tightened; her eyes flashed anger. He turned to Bak, unaware. "When she was a babe, a guard found her on the doorstep, and Djehuty's father took her in. She grew to womanhood as a servant. Arguments abound among the household staff as to whether or not Djehuty took her to bed. Half say her jealousy knew no bounds, so he must've. The others swear no man would touch a woman so sour."

Psuro snorted. "What kind of woman would crawl in with a man so small in his every thought and deed?"

"They were close to each other in age," Kasaya said, as if that explained everything. "A couple of the servants, both men, hinted that Djehuty wasn't a youth to overlook any tender young morsel, especially one who earned her daily bread in his own household."

"Admirable," Psuro said, looking scornful.

Kasaya's eyes drifted to a slim young dancer who had red

ribbons woven into the long black braid hanging down her naked back. The servant, finished with her task, dribbled sand onto his pillow, across his leg, and down his spine. He yelped, swung around, glared. She turned away, triumph lighting her face.

Bak bit back a smile. "Get on with your tale, Kasaya!"

The young Medjay threw a pained look at Psuro, whose face was stiff with smothered laughter. "When Hatnofer reached an age to wed, another servant, one who toiled in the gardens, took her as his wife. She had two stillborn children, the second near the time mistress Khawet was born, thus she became her wet nurse. Her husband died, and she conceived no more."

"A convenient marriage," Bak said.

"Djehuty's father arranged the match, so I was told." Kasaya grinned. "About the time Djehuty wed Khawet's mother, I suspect."

"He may've set her aside for a noblewoman," Psuro said grudgingly, "but he did well enough by her in the end. Not many foundlings rise to the lofty position of housekeeper in a governor's villa."

"So she must've thought." Kasaya drank from his bowl, licked the foam from his lips. "They seldom quarreled, though from what I've been told, he often gave her reason to burn with anger."

Bak raised an eyebrow. "Someone—I don't recall who—mentioned an argument not long ago."

"Oh, they sometimes argued. Not often; she wouldn't let him bait her. But you're right: a couple of months ago, they had a good one."

"Tell me," Bak said.

Psuro gave him a surprised look. "You don't think Djehuty slew her, do you, sir?"

Bak waved off the suggestion as unlikely. "Well, Kasaya?"

"Let's see. Around two months ago, it was. In Nebmose's villa." The young Medjay gave his drinking bowl an exaggerated frown, as if forcing himself to think. "The door was closed and no one could hear what they said, but their voices were heated and Djehuty came away with the red mark of Hatnofer's hand on his cheek.''

"Good for her!" Psuro chuckled. "Can't think of a man more deserving."

"That's it?" Bak demanded, deflated. "Words led to a blow, and you can tell me no more?"

Kasaya shook his head. "No, sir."

"She didn't confide in anyone, telling what happened or giving a reason for the quarrel?"

"She was so angry no one dared ask—ever."

Bak scowled at the young Medjay. He had a good idea how a fish felt when a man dangled a worm in front of it and then jerked it away. No wonder the poor creature grabbed the hook the moment the man let it drop again. "What of the storm? Did you find any connection between her and the tempest?"

"No, sir." Kasaya wiggled around, twisting his torso, and ran his fingers under the waistband at the back of his kilt. Evidently sand had trickled inside. "Oh, she knew some of the men who died. After all, she toiled in the governor's villa for a long time, and he headed the garrison. And Abu's not all that big. But . . . Well, if she was close to one, no one will speak out."

Bak set his drinking bowl on the floor, leaned back against the wall, and closed his eyes. In this, too, the gods had failed him.

Bak stumbled on a rough spot in the lane, lurching forward. Kasaya swayed toward him, resting much of his weight on Bak's shoulder. "We should've left you in Swenet," he growled at the besotted Medjay.

Psuro, who had dunked his head in a water trough to clear away the haze, tugged at the arm across his shoulders, trying to shift some of Kasaya's weight onto himself. "I doubt he can hear you, sir."

They maneuvered their shuffling, stumbling load around the corner and into the lane leading to their quarters. Bak peered into the blackness, imagining he could see a darker rectangle near the far end. Their door seemed a long way off.

"I fear I'm getting old, Psuro. This is the second man I've half carried to his quarters in less than a week. Both times I've reached my sleeping pallet as sober as a priest, a feat unheard of in my younger days."

"I shouldn't have reminded him of Djehuty's cook's daughter. That's what set him off." Psuro hesitated, added, "You may have to hustle him onto a ship, sir, and smuggle him out of town."

"I know nothing about this latest fling, nor do I want to. It's time he solved his own problems."

"You, sir, are a hard man," Kasaya mumbled.

Bak would have kicked the young drunk if he had thought the effort worthwhile, but the punishment, he suspected, would fade from Kasaya's memory faster than a flame from a lamp burned empty of oil.

"Here we are," Psuro said, pausing before the gaping doorway.

"I thank the lord Amon!" Bak helped maneuver their burden across the threshold and into their quarters. The room was as black as a scribe's ink, blinding him. "Where's his sleeping pallet?"

"Does it matter? We could leave him in the lane, and he wouldn't know the difference."

"How right you are," Bak laughed.

They let their besotted companion crumple and stretched him out as best they could. Bak went outside to search for a house showing a light, while Psuro fumbled around near the door for the lamp he had left there. Not a creature stirred all along the lane, and every fire had been extinguished. The Medjay came out, lamp in hand, and went off to find a night patrol with a torch. Bak's wait was probably not long, but it seemed so.

When Psuro returned, he held the lamp in the doorway so his superior officer could enter first. As Bak stepped across the threshold, Kasaya let out a yell that must have awakened the dead. He rolled, crashed into the woven reed storage chest, and scrambled to his knees. He gave Bak and Psuro a wild-eyed look, tried to talk, could not, and pointed. The light was dim, the flame unstable, making the shadows deep and impenetrable, setting them aquiver like wraiths from the netherworld. A fitting habitat for the object they saw.

Propped against a folded sleeping pallet close to where Kasaya's head had been, the first thing he must have seen when he opened his eyes, was an egg-shaped green-and-white striped melon about the size of a human head. Drawn in black ink were huge eyes, a long nose, and a mouth twisted as if in agony. The top and one side of the obscene head were crushed, showing the reddish interior. Sticking out of the wound was the foreleg of an animal, a goat, Bak thought.

Another unwanted gift, this representing the fourth death, that of Lieutenant Dedi trampled by a horse.

He hurried to Kasaya, squeezed his shoulder to calm him, and knelt beside the disgusting object. The foreleg was dry and bloodless, the creature from which it had come long dead. The meat inside the melon had begun to dry on the surface, but was glistening wet beneath. The ghastly thing had been left some time after midday, he guessed, after the archer had disappeared in the rapids. Even if the man had somehow managed to survive, he could not have left this awful gift.

Chapter Ten

"Will you see the governor today?" Psuro asked.

Bak knew what the Medjay really wanted to know: whether or not they were soon going home to Buhen. "I think it best we go on as before, making no reports until we've something substantial to say."

Psuro gave him a pained look. "But sir!"

Bak took the basket from the old woman and handed her a plastered wood token for the garrison quartermaster so she could collect the grain due her. As she shuffled away, he grabbed the uppermost of the two stools Psuro had stacked, one upside-down on top of the other, on which to place the food if by chance they had already gone when she delivered it. Swinging the seat upright, he sat down and lifted the lid from the basket. The aroma of fresh-baked bread wafted out, competing with the smell of braised fish, which she had wrapped in leaves and placed atop the bread.

A low moan drew his eyes to Kasaya, who was lying on his sleeping pallet, face to the wall, suffering from the previous evening's overindulgence.

"The instant I tell Djehuty about the archer, he'll send us packing. How will we account to the vizier if later, ten days from the day of Hatnofer's death, when we're well on our way to Buhen, a courier delivers a message that the governor's been slain?"

"He'd not be pleased," Psuro answered ruefully.

Bak spread open the leaves, took a flattish loaf still warm

from the oven from beneath them, and laid a fish, equally warm, across the bread. Passing the basket to Psuro, he said, "We don't know for a fact that the archer's dead. I lived through worse rapids, thanks to the lord Amon. I know few men do, but . . ."

"Unless they know the waters well," Psuro cut in.

"If he knew the river, would he have allowed himself to be pressed so close to the island that he had nowhere to go but into the maelstrom?"

"No, sir."

Psuro took a loaf and a couple of fish from the basket. Winking at Bak, he knelt beside Kasaya and held the food close, giving the younger man a good, strong whiff. Kasaya moaned louder and shoved the offending hand away.

"Too much celebration," Psuro grinned. He walked to the stairs, sat down, and the smile faded. "And now you say we had no reason to make merry."

"The more I think about it, the more convinced I am that the gifts we've found here, the threat they imply, have nothing to do with the archer. The goal was probably the same— to get us out of Abu one way or another—but the means of reaching it was entirely different."

"Which of the two is the slayer?"

Bak took a bite of fish, thought over his answer while he chewed, swallowed. "I think the gift-giver the more likely. He has sufficient imagination to work out the patterns I spotted when first we came to Abu. I've seen no sign that the archer is that creative."

Psuro shivered. "I don't know which was worse: the rat or the melon."

"If the slayer still walks the halls of the governor's villa, as I believe, a day or two more might bring forth the truth. If I err, and he died yesterday among the rapids, the worst we can do is to rouse some dormant tempers."

Psuro looked up from his meal, frowned. "I dread to think of what we'll find on our doorstep tonight."

"So far, the gift-giver has never thrown caution aside to enter the house in the full light of day. I think it safe to let you go about your business until an hour or so before darkness falls. Then I want you on the rooftop across the lane, your eyes locked on this house.''

''You've only five more days, Lieutenant, and then—if your guess is correct—Djehuty will die.'' Amethu, seated on a low stool in the shade of a portico, glanced over the edge of the scroll open between his hands, giving Bak a quizzical look. ''Are you closing on the slayer, or aren't you?''

''Perhaps.'' Bak stood before the steward, resting a shoulder against a slim wooden column. A yellow cat paced the floor around him, rubbing against his legs.

''Humph!'' Amethu rolled the document tight and dropped it into one of three baskets lined up beside his stool. ''You sound like a man who knows no more now than when these distressing events began.''

''Like the granite in the quarries south of Abu, sir, this problem I must solve is made of many tiny granules, some transparent, others opaque, all squeezed so tight together they're difficult to pry apart.''

The steward gave him a sharp look, as if he suspected he was being made light of. ''Have you thought to bend a knee before the lord Khnum? A plump goose or a tender young kid would make a worthy offering.''

Bak vaguely recalled someone needling Amethu about religious fervor. ''I fear he'll pay no heed without diligent effort on my part.''

''Have you seen the shrine at the back of the god's mansion? The shrine of the hearing ear? I often go there. It's a quick way to seek the god's aid, convenient, providing solace in times of travail.'' Amethu's bright eyes darted toward Bak. ''You, as a police officer, would find it of special comfort and worth. An image of the lady Maat is carved high on the wall, wings outspread to encompass all the world.''

If the steward had not been such a staid individual, Bak would have suspected him of using talk of the gods to retaliate for his own comparison of granite with the problem of murder.

"Sir!" An earnest-faced young scribe hurried across the patch of bare earth outside the colonnade, ducked into the shaded portico, and presented a large chunk of broken pottery to the steward. "Here's the inventory of linens, as you requested."

"So soon?" Amethu took the shard, glanced at the numbers, and scowled. "Are you certain you counted all the uncut lengths, the sheets, the . . ."

"Our supply is very low, sir." The young man appeared untroubled by the implied criticism. "Over the past few weeks, we've sent a large quantity to the house of death. With so many people dying within these walls . . ."

"Yes, yes, yes." Amethu waved his hand, signaling silence. "The subject is one I prefer to forget. You've no need to remind me." He pursed his lips, thinking. "Go now to the men counting jars and dishes. They're certain to need your help. We've given no pottery away."

Puzzled, Bak watched the scribe hurry off. From the moment he had entered the compound, he had seen men scurrying hither and yon, writing pallets and water jars suspended by cords over their shoulders, carrying rolls of papyrus or baskets filled with limestone and pottery shards. Here, beneath the portico where Amethu sat, located at the end of three long, narrow warehouses, the activity was magnified tenfold.

"I've never before heard of anyone taking an inventory during the season of planting," he said. "Aren't your scribes needed elsewhere? Setting boundary lines, for example, or counting baskets of grain to send out to the fields as seed?"

Amethu's mouth tightened. "This was Djehuty's idea, not mine. All this work. All this interference in tasks for which he has no aptitude. The man should be taken into the fields and . . ." His mouth tightened, cutting off whatever punishment he longed to mete out.

Drowning in an irrigation ditch, Bak suspected. "From what I've seen and heard, he doesn't usually concern himself with the running of his household."

Amethu glanced around, assuring himself that no one

would overhear. "Ineni," he said, lowering his voice. "It's his fault, his alone. He disobeyed his father, refusing to rid the estate of horses. Now Djehuty plans to disinherit him."

Bak, raising an eyebrow, knelt to scratch the cat's head, making it purr. "I thought he made an agreement at the time Ineni wed Khawet."

"He did, but he vows to have it set aside."

Bak's voice turned cynical. "What does the governor mean to do? Plead his case before the vizier?" *A man he's known for years,* he thought, *one he counts among his friends.* Bak's heart went out to Ineni, who stood little chance of retaining his due.

"I see you understand." Amethu eyed the shard in his hand, sighed, and dropped it into a basket. "I've known Djehuty since childhood, and I seldom question his actions. But at times he goes too far." His eyes darted toward Bak and his mouth snapped shut, as if he suddenly realized his anger had carried him into the opposing camp. "Stress. That's what's bothering him now. The reason he's being so contrary, so irrational. Must you come to this villa day after day, poking and prodding and prying as if we were all vile criminals? Must that Medjay of yours always hang around, asking impertinent questions of the household staff and guards?"

Bak took a seat on a mudbrick bench that ran along the wall. He doubted the questions were rhetorical, but he chose to take them as such. "You must've heard by now of my interest in the soldiers who vanished in the sandstorm five years ago."

"I've heard you seek to blame Djehuty for their loss." The steward scratched his prominent belly, frowned. "Well, let me tell you, young man, he came as close to death as any man can and still survive. He owes his life to the gods, to the lord Khnum. They alone saved him. Those of us who stayed behind in Abu knew not what was happening out on the desert or how greatly our prayers were needed."

"I was told you lost someone in that storm."

Laughter sounded through a door leading into the rightmost storage magazine, scribes finding humor in the most mundane of tasks. The cat jumped into a basket of scrolls and curled up for a nap.

Amethu failed to notice. "You probably don't realize, Lieutenant, but the residents of this household talk to me. They confide in me as they would a respected uncle. I know you suspect one of us closest to Djehuty of slaying all who've died thus far, and I've been told you're aware that we each lost someone dear in the storm. You yourself have made it clear you think Djehuty's death the ultimate goal." He paused to get his breath.

Bak bowed his head in acknowledgment. "Go on."

"From what I've been told, you've caught several of us at a time when our shoulders were bowed beneath the weight of anger or resentment. As a result, you've unearthed a multitude of personal reasons for wishing Djehuty dead."

"None of which would've resulted in the death of five innocent people," Bak pointed out.

"Exactly!" the steward said, smiling triumphantly.

"Unless the one who slew them believed the storm a path that would lead me astray. Or unless the dead are bound by some other tie I've failed to discover. Or unless the slayer's wits are so addled he's developed a taste for murder."

Amethu's smile faded. He opened his mouth as if to disagree, but could think of no opposing argument.

"Did you lose someone close in the storm?" Bak repeated.

"My only brother perished in the desert. He was much younger than I, but a man I held in high esteem. To this day, I miss him." Amethu hastened to add, "Let me assure you, I don't blame Djehuty. If I thought blame was due, I'd be the first to accuse. But I know him. I know him well." His eyes probed the area outside the colonnade, searching again for an eavesdropper, and he lowered his voice to a murmur. "Djehuty is usually a man of strong will, but he can sometimes be manipulated. I'm convinced someone offered poor advice and he, rattled by the tempest, heeded words he should've rejected."

Bak could see he was getting nowhere. Amethu either sin-

cerely liked Djehuty and could find no wrong or feared for
his lofty position—or he was an accomplished liar. "Because
your tasks meshed with those of Hatnofer, you must've been
as close to her as anyone. Other than mistress Khawet, of
course."

"Me?" Amethu shook his head. "I'd not use the word
'close.' Nor, I suspect, would Khawet. The woman ran this
household in an admirable fashion, but she was as cold as a
night can get on the desert."

"As the confidant of all who toil in this villa day after
day . . ." Bak could not help smiling. ". . . you've surely
heard that I'm seeking a connection between her and those
who died in the storm, or those who survived."

"She was a foundling—as I believe you already know—
and her husband died many years ago, leaving her child-
less."

Bak allowed impatience to enter his voice. "Few men or
women exist alone, Amethu, and Hatnofer was no exception.
She was mistress Khawet's wet nurse, which would've
drawn them together as close as mother and daughter, at least
when Khawet was a child. And I've heard rumors that many
years ago Djehuty took the woman into his bed."

"He did, yes. As did I." Noting Bak's surprise, Amethu
gave a wry smile. "It's difficult to imagine, I know, but I
had hair then . . ." He patted his bald pate and his paunch.
". . . and the lithe body of one who spends his days at sports
and hunting."

Bak tried to picture a well-built and handsome Amethu;
the task was formidable.

"She was cold even then." Amethu surprised Bak with
another smile, this filled with humor. "I thank the lord
Khnum she held no warmth. I was young and ardent at the
time, tempted by lust and a dream of home and family. If
she'd offered the slightest encouragement . . ." He shuddered. "It was my good fortune that she remained aloof. I
soon wed another, a good-hearted, gentle woman who
showed me the true meaning of love and marriage. She filled
my life to the brim, and she's with me yet."

Bak had to give credit where credit was due. Not many men would admit so freely to their youthful delusions, nor confess their gratitude for so narrow an escape. "I've heard Hatnofer harbored jealousy in her heart for Djehuty. Was that as true the day she died as when she was young?"

"You've been talking to Ineni, I see. He's told you of his mother." Amethu noticed the cat sleeping in the basket, scowled. "No, she hadn't shown him any special affection for some years, not since . . ." His voice tailed off and a new thought registered on his face, a memory come to life.

"Tell me, Amethu, what've you recalled?"

"Something I once heard . . ." The steward's eyes darted toward Bak and he hesitated. "A rumor. But even whispers in the wind ofttimes contain some truth."

"Tell me."

"I heard . . ." Amethu paused again, shrugged. "Exactly how long ago I don't remember, but I was told by a man I knew at the time, the garrison quartermaster, that one of the survivors of the sandstorm was whispered to be her lover. A man named Min, a sergeant. He sailed north soon after the incident, which made me doubt the tale. Would he not have taken her with him if they were close? Or did the lord Khnum smile on him, as he did me, and allow him to escape a free man?"

"You will pay for your transgression!" Djehuty's voice thundered across the audience hall. "You've taken four men from my fields north of Abu, men whose task it was to clean the irrigation channels and rebuild the dikes, and you've set them to work on your own fields. You must free them today and send them back to me, and you must reimburse me for the time they've been within your power."

"But sir!" The man on his knees before the governor's dais, his body bent until his head touched the floor, was so frightened he trembled from head to foot. Bak, standing at the back of the columned hall beyond the reach of long shafts of midafternoon sunlight, could clearly see his fear.

"Silence!" the guard commanded, stepping forward to prod the offender with his foot.

Djehuty glared down at the prisoner, his expression dark and unforgiving. "In addition, you'll receive two hundred blows and five open wounds."

Someone gasped, then quiet descended upon those in attendance, thirty or so men scattered throughout the hall. The judgment far exceeded the norm. The kneeling man whimpered. As if released by his cries, shocked murmurs traveled through the room, rising in volume until Djehuty could not help but hear. His mouth set in a thin, hard line. Bak was as stunned as the rest. If the offense had been committed against the estate of a god, the punishment might be fitting, but this was a private matter.

"So be it," Djehuty said, rising from his chair, signaling the end of his audience.

The murmurs dwindled, the men standing among the columns stared. Djehuty stepped down off the dais and strode from the room. Lieutenant Amonhotep, looking unhappy but at a loss as to what he could do, hurried after him. The guard collected his wits, jerked the sobbing prisoner to his feet, and hustled him from the hall. The men who remained looked at one another, surprised, shocked. Voices rose in consternation.

"This is the third day in a row I've come in search of justice," Bak heard someone complain. "Each day the governor has left early, ignoring six or eight of us whose pleas have yet to be heard. We've no choice but to leave, our business unfinished, and come again another time."

"Justice?" someone asked. "I'd not call his judgment of Ahmose justice."

"Who does he think he is anyway?" someone else muttered.

"Not half the man his father was, let me tell you."

Bak stared at the door through which the prisoner had been taken. Amonhotep had had no opportunity to intercede before Djehuty's judgment, and the governor was too stubborn to alter his decision after the fact. By punishing the man far beyond his due, Djehuty was poisoning the hearts of the people of Abu.

He hurried from the hall, leaving through the same door the governor and his aide had taken. He hoped he would find Amonhotep alone. If so, maybe he could lure him away from the villa. Freed of Djehuty and the weight of responsibility, freed of the many tasks that fell on his shoulders, the young officer might let down his guard and be more forthcoming.

He found himself in a short, windowless corridor lit by a narrow strip of light reaching in from the room beyond. A guard stood midway, looking in the direction the governor had gone, rubbing an elbow. He heard Bak's step and swung around. Though difficult to see in the dimly lit passage, Bak recognized Nenu, the none-too-bright young man who had helped him search for the archer after the first attack.

"Lieutenant Bak. Sir!"

"What're you doing here? Don't you usually guard Nebmose's villa?"

"My sergeant sent me with a message for Lieutenant Amonhotep. I tried to deliver it just now, but didn't get the chance." Nenu, sounding aggrieved, walked with Bak up the corridor, rubbing his elbow all the while. "The governor brushed me out of his way as he would a fly, shoving me hard against the wall."

In the brightly lit room beyond, Bak got a better look at the young guard. His right temple was skinned, his eye black, his lip swollen and cracked. An ugly and no doubt painful abrasion ran down his arm from shoulder to hand, and the knuckles of both hands were swollen and red. The strong scent of fleabane emanated from a cloth covering some type of injury to his leg.

Bak stared. "By the lord Amon, Nenu! What happened to you!"

The guard shuffled from one foot to the other, gave a half-hearted smile. "A fight, sir."

"Dare I ask who won?"

"I would've, sir, except . . ." Nenu refused to meet Bak's eyes. "Well, he hit me in the stomach and knocked me down. My head struck a rock. I must've lost my wits for a while, and when I came to my senses, I had these." He gingerly touched his arm and motioned toward his leg. "I guess he kicked me when I couldn't fight back and dragged me along the ground. Only the lord Set knows what else he did."

Noting how reluctant the guard was to speak of his defeat, how embarrassed, Bak promised to tell Amonhotep of the message, should he find him, and walked on.

With the help of a shy and very skittish female servant, Bak found the young aide in Djehuty's private reception room, located on the second floor. High windows admitted light and air, making the space bright and at the same time pleasantly cool. Yet instead of offering comfort and ease, the room was a disaster. It was cluttered with tables and stools, baskets brimming with scrolls, chests with lids askew, and drawers standing open. A line of ants marched across the floormats, carrying off bread crumbs. Scrolls were strewn around the dais on which the governor's armchair stood as if, of no importance, they had been flung aside. The bright, spotted skin of a leopard lay crumpled beside the chair, partially covering an elaborately embroidered pillow stained with wine. The sweetish smell emanating from a bowl of perfumed oil failed to smother the odors of stale beer and dog.

Amonhotep, his face pale and strained, knelt beside a pile of clothing and jewelry that had been thrown into a corner. He glanced up, gave Bak a forced smile. "Lieutenant. I saw you in the audience hall and wondered who you might seek out next."

"You surely guessed I'd come here. What was Djehuty thinking of? Is he trying to alienate every man and woman in the province?"

Amonhotep let out a bitter laugh. "I tried to get him to change his judgment and I failed. All I managed to do was anger him further. Ahmose will be beaten until he's a broken man, and I can do nothing to stop it."

Bak could see how upset the aide was, how greatly he blamed himself for his failure. Further talk would not console him, but a distraction might help. "I thought I might persuade you to go sailing with me."

"I can think of nothing I'd like better, but . . ." The aide glanced around the room, shook his head.

"I've beer in my skiff, fishing poles, and harpoons. If you've not had your midday meal, we can stop in the kitchen on our way to the landingplace."

Amonhotep, giving the matter more thought than Bak felt it warranted, sorted through the pile, removing a broad multicolored bead collar, bracelets, armlets, and anklets, and laid them on a nearby table. He took a fringed robe from the clothing that remained, stood up to shake it out, and began to fold it. "Tempting. Very tempting. Perhaps when I finish with this room."

Bak eyed him critically. "Is this not a task for servants?"

"Normally, yes, but . . . Well, Djehuty no longer allows them to come and go as they used to. He's banned them from his rooms."

"He's afraid."

"Wouldn't you be?" Amonhotep scooped a handful of green and white playing pieces off the top of a legged game board, dropped them into the open drawer, and shut it with a thud. He laid the folded garment where the pieces had been and picked up a white linen tunic. "You yourself have seen to that."

"I doubt the slayer is a servant."

Amonhotep gave him a tight-lipped parody of a smile. "If you can convince him of that, I'll be eternally grateful."

"Turn your back on this mess and come sailing with me. We both deserve a few hours' respite."

Bak saw the longing on Amonhotep's face, the desire to escape, and the decision to abandon his duty forming in his heart.

"Amonhotep will go nowhere." Djehuty burst into the room, his face ruddy with anger. "I need him here, and here he'll remain."

"But, sir . . ." Bak and the younger officer spoke together.

"No!" Djehuty strode across the room, eyes blazing, and glared at Bak. "You and your Medjays come into my home, prying into the lives of all who dwell here, asking impertinent questions no man or woman should have to answer. I won't allow you to take my aide from his duties, drawing him away so you can question him as you've queried others who owe their loyalty to me."

"Is this his duty?" Bak demanded, eyeing the messy room with distaste.

"Who else can I trust to care for me?"

"You've lived here a lifetime. You must have at least one trustworthy servant."

"You were in the audience hall. Not a man in attendance was a stranger, but they all turned against me when I judged that wretched Ahmose. I was fair, generous even, yet murmurs of resentment flowed from men's lips like water from a shattered bowl. How can I trust servants if I can't depend on men of greater status to stand beside me when I need them?"

The man's irrational, Bak thought. *Forced to see what he wants to overlook, filled with fear and tension, his normal obstinacy has turned to a dim-witted, arrogant defensiveness.*

Bak stood at the rear door of the governor's house, looking across the stretch of sand lined with conical silos. The servants who had inventoried the grain had spilled wheat and barley on the ground. Birds, domestic and wild, and a half dozen young goats stood among the golden kernels, gorging themselves. A black dog, stretched out in the shade between two silos, raised its head to sniff the air, heavy with the scent of roasting beef smothered in onions.

Where, he wondered, was Khawet? He had stalked out of her father's reception room, seething with anger. After a half hour's swim had cooled his temper, he had gone in search of Simut. The chief scribe had told him in no uncertain terms that he was busy with the inventory and had no time to answer questions. Antef was at the granite quarry, he had learned, and Ineni had not returned from Nubt.

Bak walked along the row of silos, a thought born of his conversation with Amethu nagging. He had assumed Hatnofer had been slain because she stood close to Djehuty in importance, but maybe he erred. Her life might well have been taken because she knew too much about the past. If the steward's rumor was true, if she and Min had been lovers, the sergeant could have told her about the storm before he sailed north, leaving Abu forever. With luck, Khawet would know of their relationship.

He passed through the gate and headed toward the kitchen. The smell of beef and onions grew stronger. Raised voices issued from the structure. Women arguing.

Khawet came through the far gate. She saw Bak and, smiling, hurried toward him. "Lieutenant! How nice to see you! Amethu told me you were here and said you might wish to speak with me."

Warmed by a welcome rare in this household, Bak grinned. "I wasn't sure you'd have the time. Everyone else is either tied up with the inventory or hiding out to avoid it."

She laughed. "How long ago did you arrive in Abu? Only six days? Yet already you've seen through us."

"I fervently wish that were true."

"All households are much alike. Have you never wed?"

Few households were victim to a five-time slayer, he thought. "I've never been so fortunate."

A hint of a smile touched her lips and her voice softened. "To share your life with one you love must be close to perfection. To be wed to another . . ." Her tone hardened, as did her expression. ". . . one who's a lesser man in every way, can be a burden difficult to bear."

Ineni had said his wife had loved another, a man who had died far in the past. Bak could see the loss in her eyes, a grief she should long ago have pushed aside. "I met a woman when first I went to Buhen. She was as lovely as a gazelle, gentle, kind, and generous, yet she had a strength of will that few men or women can claim. She . . ." He broke off, laughed softly at himself, at the warmth that never ceased to enter his heart when he thought of her. "The time was wrong and I lost her."

She smiled, her voice regained its softness. "Do you think of her always?"

"I go on with my life. As I must."

A young woman burst through the kitchen door, shrieking. A second girl followed, screaming curses, brandishing the long tongs used to stir burning charcoal.

Khawet's smile faded. "Oh, no! Not again!"

The young woman in the lead spotted Khawet and ran toward her. "Oh, mistress! Help me! Help!"

The girl with the tongs raced after her, shrieking. "You! You bride of Set! You took away my beloved! You stole him!" Her body shook with fury, her face was a mask of hatred.

She swung the tongs back and, leaping forward, slashed them hard across the other woman's shoulders. Blood gushed from the broken flesh. The injured girl screeched.

Bak lunged at the assailant, grabbed the tongs, and tore them from her grasp. Gripping her upper arm, he shoved her roughly to the bare earth. Khawet rushed to the other young woman, helped her to the mudbrick bench against the wall a few cubits away, and went to the kitchen door to call for cloth for bandages. Several women hurried out, more to look than assist, Bak suspected. A short, barrel-shaped woman he took to be the cook brought a bowl of steaming water and strips of linen.

Khawet turned to him and smiled an apology. "You must forgive me, Lieutenant, but this wound can't wait."

Bak walked slowly down the lane, passing through shadows cast by the taller houses and broad strips of sunlight that reached over the lower buildings. A breeze stirred the hot, dry air and lifted dust from the hard-packed earth. He smelled oil heating over charcoal braziers, but the hour was too early for the odors of cooked food to drift down from the rooftops. Children's laughter and the rhythmic click of wood on wood told of boys playing with make-believe spears somewhere nearby.

He wondered if he would find an unwanted gift in his quarters. He had never before approached the house so early in the evening, nor had the gift-giver ever come before dusk, when shadows filled the lane and neighbors, preoccupied with their evening meal, were unlikely to be about. He glanced at the roof across the lane, but it was even too early for Psuro to have taken up his post.

He stopped before the doorway and peered inside. The room, illuminated by a lone shaft of light coming through the opening at the top of the stairs, was dim and shadowy but not dark. A round red pot three hand-widths across sat a pace or so inside the door. A white cloth, held tightly in place with string, covered the top. His first thought was food; the old woman had brought their evening meal. Then his eyes darted toward the stools he had restacked in the center of the room before leaving the house early in the day. They stood as he had left them, one upside-down on top of the other. No basket sat atop the three legs. The old woman would never have left their evening meal on the floor, where mice or rats could get to it.

This had to be another gift left by . . . By whom?

His next thought was not so rational; the pot might contain a human head, crushed as Hatnofer's had been. A chill crept up his spine and at the same time he rejected the idea. The neck of the container was too small.

Chiding himself for too vivid an imagination, he stepped over the threshold and knelt before the jar. The linen cover bothered him. The fabric would admit air, where the more usual mud plug would not, leading him to believe the container held a living creature. Hearing nothing inside, he examined it for signs of cracks, thinking it might break in his hands, releasing a viper or something equally dreadful. The container looked solid enough, undamaged.

Sucking in his breath, he reached out with both hands and lifted it. Nothing happened. He brought it closer to his face, his ear, and shook it gently. Again nothing. He thought of untying the string, but common sense prevailed; such a precipitous move would be foolhardy. He shook the pot again, much harder. Inside he heard a soft but frenzied rattling sound. His mouth tightened and he nodded, fairly sure he knew what was inside.

Carrying the container with outstretched arms, he hurried outdoors and around the nearby corner. A short, dead-end lane took him to a low mudbrick wall. Beyond lay an open field. The broken walls of houses built and abandoned many generations before protruded from a heavy blanket of windswept sand littered with garbage, items of no value whatsoever, unwanted by the most impoverished of Abu's residents.

Bak set the container on the wall. Glancing around, he spotted a rock that would fit nicely in his hand and he picked it up. He slipped his dagger from its sheath and held it at arm's length, point down, over the linen.

"Sir!" Psuro hurried up behind him. "What're you doing?"

"The gift-giver arrived ahead of us, leaving this. I suspect it's lethal."

Psuro's eyes widened. He spat out a curse and stepped back a pace. "Do you wish me to open it, sir?" he asked with no enthusiasm whatsoever.

Bak drove the dagger into the fabric and slashed to right and left, enlarging the hole. The soft rattling sound erupted. Psuro muttered a quick incantation designed to hold at bay poisonous reptiles and insects. Bak sheathed his dagger, shoved the pot over the wall, and threw the rock with a mighty heave, smashing the baked clay into a dozen or more rough-edged pieces. Yellow scorpions, their tails raised in fury, darted in all directions.

Bak stared at the creatures, his face grim. A single scorpion's sting would be painful but not deadly. Could a man live if stung by so many? "I think it best we spend the night in the barracks, Psuro. And tomorrow we must find new quarters."

Chapter Eleven

"This should suit you, sir." Pahared eyed the empty room, a proprietary smile on his face. "It's the safest place in the province, that I guarantee."

Glancing around a chamber he had already examined for vulnerable points, Bak nodded approval. "I couldn't have asked for better quarters."

"Not a man or woman in Swenet can come up here without being seen. My wife never closes her place of business, and when she's not in attendance, her steward is. And you've seen how many servants she has."

The room was large, providing ample space for Bak and his men. Diffused light fell through high windows protected by wooden grills. Above mudbrick stairs leading to the roof, a north-facing airshaft caught the breeze and channeled it downward. Hints of leather, oil, spices, and wine scented the air, elusive smells betraying the room's frequent use for storage. Through an opening in the floor, muted laughter and a faint smell of beer filtered up another stairway, this rising from a storage room at the rear of the house of pleasure.

Passing through an open door, he walked onto the first-floor roof, which was walled by a knee-high parapet. From there, he looked over the rooftops of a block of single-story interconnected buildings and across the river toward Abu. No structures stood close enough to provide easy access. To the north, beyond a patch of young clover, he spotted Kasaya standing on the quay, keeping an eye on their fully laden skiff.

"Good. Very good," he said, coming back inside.

Psuro, seated in the opening above the descending stairway, dangling his legs, looked as pleased as Bak with their new quarters. "Can I now go to the quay and get our belongings, sir?"

"Before you bring them here, you and Kasaya must go through them once again, searching for unwanted creatures."

"Yes, sir." The Medjay dropped onto the stairs and, whistling a light-hearted tune, hurried away.

"I, too, must go," Pahared said. "I've a load to deliver before nightfall. A caravan's been sighted coming in from the west, and the donkeys will need fresh fodder and grain. Only the lord Set knows how many days they've been on the desert trail." He took several steps down the stairs, paused, looked back up. "I've given orders that no one be allowed up these stairs and nothing be delivered. If you need anything—food, drink, a game of chance, or a woman—speak to my wife. She'll see you get it, but you or your men must bring it up."

Bak laid a hand on the trader's shoulder, smiled. "You've thought of everything, Pahared. You're a good man."

The big trader grinned. "I've been called sly, greedy, and a multitude of other names, none so pleasing to my ears." Laughing, he hastened down the stairs.

Left alone, Bak examined the contents of the two rear chambers, windowless rooms he had earlier given no more than a cursory glance. One was piled high with bundles of cowhides, stacks of rough linen, baskets of glazed beads, and piles of ordinary cooking pottery. The second held baked clay jars large and small whose contents were scratched on the mud plugs or scrawled on their shoulders: unguents, oils, wine, and honey. Except for the hides, a trading staple which came from Kush far upriver, all were common trade goods regularly shipped south from the land of Kemet to exchange for the more exotic products of Wawat and Kush. Pahared's business enterprises were clearly more far-reaching than shipping hay to the donkey paddocks below and above the rapids.

Walking back to the main room, Bak's thoughts returned to the previous evening's gift. He had taken the scorpions as a direct threat, an intent to inflict pain and maybe even death on him or whichever of his men might have opened the pot. An escalation of the previous gifts, more fearsome in nature. A good night's sleep had not altered the assumption. As for its relationship to Hatnofer, from what he had learned of the housekeeper, she had had the temperament of a scorpion, a creature that goes peaceably about its business when left alone but attacks with a vengeance when disturbed.

"Lieutenant!" Kasaya came racing up the stairs, his arms loaded with folded bedding. "Governor Djehuty has summoned you, sir. He wishes to see you right away."

Bak hastened into the audience hall, thinking it the most logical place in which to find Djehuty so early in the morning. Though logic, he knew, had scant influence on the governor's behavior. Nor did common sense. Which made him wary of this summons, suspicious of what Djehuty might want. For him to break his silence seemed too much to hope for.

Guards stood at attention at all the doors. Twenty or so men and three women clustered around the columns, talking among themselves. Most were easy enough to identify: farmers, scribes, a couple of craftsmen, and a merchant. Standing out in bold relief was a bearded man wearing a long, colorful robe, a trader from the land of Retenu far to the north.

Anger darkened the visages of several men, petitioners Bak remembered seeing the previous day, men forced to return because their pleas had remained unheard. Other, more optimistic individuals threw frequent expectant looks at the empty chair on the dais and the doorway nearby through which the governor would make his entrance.

Bak paused, not quite sure what to do next. Should he wait here or go in search of Djehuty? Had the governor forgotten he summoned him? Had he summoned him to charge him with some unspeakable offense? Or did he simply not care that Bak would have to wait while he held his audience?

"Where is he?" asked a young farmer. "Does he not take his place on the dais each and every morning?"

"He should, yes." The scribe who answered, one whose duty it was to present the petitioners to the governor, looked decidedly uncomfortable.

"I waited all morning yesterday," a grizzled farmer grumbled. "As my time to be heard came close, he got up from his chair and walked out. Now here I am again when I should be toiling in my fields, plowing the earth and planting new crops."

"I was here, too," a plump scribe said. "And I also waited for no good reason."

"And I," a couple of men spoke up together.

Why am I worried about me? Bak chided himself. *These are the people who have waited before and may have to wait again, while Djehuty goes on with whatever he wishes to do, indifferent to their needs.*

"His father was a good man, as honest and fair as they come," an elderly craftsman said. "But this one . . ." He spat on the spotless white-plastered floor, showing his contempt. "He surely didn't come from the old man's loins. He must've been spawned by some sailor passing through Abu on a cargo ship."

Hiding a smile, Bak hurried across the room and out the door near the dais. If Djehuty had heard that last remark, he would be furious. He took great pride in the long, unbroken line of men from which he was descended, those men who, during the long-ago reign of Kheperkare Senwosret, had excavated tombs overlooking Abu from the high escarpment west of the river. He probably laid claim in his dreams to an even older and grander heritage.

Bak found Amonhotep in Djehuty's private reception room. The young officer sat on a stool at the foot of the governor's empty chair, sorting scrolls and placing them in baskets marked according to content. They would ultimately go to Simut, who would have the documents filed away in the records storage room.

He looked around, smiled his approval. Every chest, table, and stool stood in its proper place. The woven mats covering the floor were no longer strewn with crumbs or clothing or any other objects. The pillows on the armchair had been fluffed up and the leopard skin draped over its back. White lilies floated in a large, low bowl of water, their strong, sweet scent freshening the air.

The aide gave him a wry smile. "If ever you need a servant, would you take me into your household?"

Bak grinned. "Should I become a man of wealth—an unlikely occurrence, I warn you—I'd compete for your services with spear or bow or fists, if need be."

"I'll take that as a compliment."

"Few men are as devoted to their masters as you are."

Amonhotep gave an odd little snort. Bak suspected cynicism, bitterness, a helplessness to alter the situation, but as always the aide would commit himself no further.

"The governor wishes to see me, I understand."

Amonhotep laid down the scroll he had been reading and rose to his feet. Bak had heard the expression "he girded his loins," but had never been sure of its meaning. Now he was. The aide visibly braced himself, as if about to face a foe on the field of battle.

Taking the act as forewarning, Bak followed him out of the room with leaden feet. What new manner of mischief could Djehuty have thought up?

A short corridor took them to a spacious bedchamber, where the governor lay in a mass of rumpled sheets on a fine cedar bed decorated with inlaid ivory images of the ram-headed god Khnum. His head and shoulders were propped up on several folded sleeping pallets and pillows. Beer jars, a basket of bread, and a bowl half full of coagulating stew sat on a nearby table. The room smelled strongly of sweat and the thick-bodied brindle dog curled up on a pillow atop a reed chest.

Bak, thinking of all those people standing in the audience

hall, awaiting this man, had trouble concealing his disgust.

The governor pulled himself higher on the pallets and his lip curled into a sneer. "So nice of you, Lieutenant, to respond at last to my summons."

Bak feigned indifference to the taunt. "I came as soon as I received your message, sir."

"I've been told you've moved out of your quarters in Abu."

Amonhotep gave him a surprised look. As close as he was to the governor and as important to the smooth functioning of the province, Djehuty apparently failed to keep him as informed as he should.

"That's right." If the swine wants an explanation, Bak thought, let him ask for it.

Djehuty stared at him, waiting. When Bak failed to oblige, he raised his chin high. His smile, meant to display triumph, betrayed defiance instead. "I, too, have decided to leave Abu. I plan today to sail north, to travel to my estate in Nubt, where I'll have no further need to live in fear."

Bak silently cursed the man—and himself. He should have guessed the urge to flee would sooner or later be irresistible. "Do you plan to take your staff with you? Your steward, chief scribe, and all those men closest to you?"

"Of course." Djehuty flashed him a contemptuous look, a man of noble birth looking with scorn upon a peasant. "I'll need servants, too, and guards. That accursed Ineni has let the household staff dwindle to only seven men and women. Not enough. Not nearly enough."

"You'll be no safer there than here." Bak kept his voice hard, matter-of-fact. "The man we seek knows every square cubit within this compound. He has to be a member of your household. If you take even a portion of them, you've as great a chance of taking the slayer as you have of leaving him behind."

"I trust the men closest to me, and I need them." Djehuty's chin jutted. "You're just trying to frighten me, to justify your presence in my home."

"If you trust them so much, why won't you let anyone

but your daughter and Lieutenant Amonhotep enter your rooms?''

"Someone—a townsman who's lost his wits maybe, or a wandering desert tribesman—has found a way to get inside our walls, to trespass on my property. He's the slayer, the man you should be looking for.''

Bak's head spun. Djehuty's thought processes defied comprehension. "If you go to Nubt, I'll have to go with you.''

"No!'' Djehuty's voice rose. "I'll not have you there!''

The dog raised its head, disturbed by its master's strident voice, but made no move to come to his aid. Reassured that it would not attack, Bak stepped forward to tower over the reclining man. "Are you ordering me back to Buhen, sir?''

"Go away! Get out of my sight!''

Amonhotep moved up beside Bak. "What of the vizier, sir? How will you explain to him your lack of faith in the man he suggested you summon?''

Djehuty gave his aide a sullen look. "Lieutenant Bak is like a fly, buzzing around, asking endless questions, making vile insinuations. No man would tolerate such behavior, least of all the vizier.''

"If you wish me to go, I will,'' Bak said. "But first you must prepare a document explaining to one and all that I've tried to convince you the slayer will strike again four days from now, and you're the most likely target. You must make clear that you've refused to listen and I should in no way be blamed should you die.''

"I can write it up now, sir,'' Amonhotep said, "and have witnesses acknowledge it before midday.''

Djehuty stared at first one officer and then the other. Defiance melted away and the shock of realization took its place. His trusted aide had allied himself with Bak. More important, he had no alternative but to place himself in Bak's hands. Suddenly he pulled a sheet up to his chin and huddled down in the bed, a man shrunk within himself.

"You'll stay in Abu?'' Bak demanded.

Djehuty nodded.

Bak stared down at an individual who looked utterly defeated. If he wanted the truth, this was the time to get it. "You hold a secret within your heart, one you've thus far failed to divulge. If you wish me to lay hands on the slayer before he lays hands on you, you must tell me."

"No." Djehuty shook his head in an exaggerated fashion. He squirmed beneath the sheet. "I have no secret."

"Governor Djehuty. You must speak up."

"I have no secret!" he cried.

"What have you done that you'd rather die than admit?"

"Nothing!" Djehuty gripped the sheet so tight his knuckles lost their color. "I've never committed an unspeakable deed! Never!"

Unspeakable deed, Bak thought. The words were an admission, but of what? "Need I remind you that five people have been slain?"

Djehuty closed his eyes and clamped his mouth tight, armoring himself in an impenetrable silence. Amonhotep shook his head, signaling how hopeless it was to pelt him with further questions.

Bak glared at Djehuty, contempt filling his heart, leaving no room for pity. He thought again of all those men and women waiting in the audience hall, most of them poor, people who toiled day after day to eke out a meager living. All who believed in right and order. All who expected to stand before their provincial governor, seeking and getting justice.

"Get out of bed and clothe yourself," he commanded. "Petitioners await you in the audience hall."

Amonhotep glanced his way. Surprise that anyone should speak so abruptly to the governor gave way to a tenuous smile. "The lieutenant's right, sir. You mustn't disappoint all those who depend upon you, need you."

"They didn't need me yesterday." Djehuty stopped wiggling, pouted. "They hated me, whispered about me behind my back."

"You're the governor of this province, sir. You must show them how strong you are, how wise."

Strong? Wise? Bak closed his eyes, grimaced. How could the aide stoop so low?

Djehuty clutched the sheet, trying to decide. "They're awaiting me, you say?"

"You'd better get dressed," Bak said in a curt voice. "Most have fields to plow and seed to sow. They can't wait all day."

Djehuty hesitated a long time, threw back the sheet, hesitated again, and finally swung his long, thin legs off the bed. Amonhotep gave Bak a brief but grateful smile. Convinced the aide could bolster Djehuty's pride enough to get him moving, Bak slipped out of the room.

Standing at the rear of the audience hall, Bak spoke with the guard as they awaited Djehuty's appearance. A few of the people he had seen here earlier in the day had given up and left the building, but most remained. Years of waiting had given them tenacity, though not the ability to suffer in silence. They grumbled, whined, complained, made futile threats and demands. He had no idea what he would do if the governor failed to show up. Perhaps he could search out Troop Captain Antef and try to convince him to mete out justice, at least temporarily.

A whispered warning drew his eyes to the door behind the dais. Djehuty strode into the room, silencing the aggrieved. Baton of office in hand, he stared straight ahead, his face set, defying those in attendance to utter a word against him. Amonhotep followed close behind, his grim expression betraying the ordeal he had gone through to prepare his master to do his duty.

Djehuty climbed onto the dais and took his seat. His eyes darted toward Bak and his mouth tightened. "Who will approach me?"

The scribe brought forward the first petitioner. The young farmer Bak recalled seeing earlier in the day dropped to his knees and touched his forehead to the floor.

"This is Sobekhotep," the scribe said, "a farmer of the village of . . ." He went on to give the necessary particulars, beginning with where the young man dwelt, who his parents were and his wife, and added details of his small farm.

Sobekhotep rose to his knees to present his tale, one all too common along the river. A ship had anchored near his farm one dark and moonless night. The next morning, when he and his family awoke, the ship was gone and so were his cow and calf and a dozen or so geese. "The sailors took them in the dark of night, I know for a fact."

"How can you be sure?" Djehuty demanded.

"Who else would take them? Not my family nor my neighbors, and there was no one else about."

Djehuty's mouth tightened at what sounded like impudence but was probably no more than fear. His voice turned mean. "How dare you come before me, expecting justice, when you've given no description of the vessel, leaving us with no way of finding her master and crew?"

The young man's face flamed. The men and women who were watching, listening, exchanged resentful glances. Angry murmurs swept through the room. Again the governor had failed them. Djehuty's mouth snapped shut. Naked fury showed on his face.

With shaking hands, Sobekhotep removed a folded cloth from beneath his belt. He opened the packet, revealing a grayish pottery shard, which he handed to the scribe. "I made a drawing of the symbols on the prow, sir. The vessel is moored at the quay at Swenet even now."

Someone in the audience hall tittered. Someone else sputtered, unable to contain himself. A third individual laughed outright, setting off the rest. Djehuty sat as still as a statue, his body paralyzed by anger. Amonhotep whispered in his ear. Djehuty shook his head. Looking frantic, the aide whispered long and hard. With obvious reluctance, Djehuty nodded.

Amonhotep stepped forward and spoke. "We'll summon the captain of that ship and call him to account. If your animals and fowl still live, you'll have them back. If not, the master of the vessel must repay you three times their worth."

Murmurs filled the audience hall; the people nodded approval. This was the law they believed in, not the cruel whimsical law they had seen before and feared they would see again.

For the remainder of the morning, Djehuty sat stiff and straight in his armchair, his cheeks ruddy in a pale face. Like a man suffering from shock, he merely went through the motions, too distracted to pay attention. Amonhotep listened closely to each petitioner, as his master should have. He whispered in Djehuty's ear, making those who watched believe he consulted him, and pretended he got a response. He then made wise and honest judgments, announcing them in Djehuty's name as if they were the governor's decisions and not his own.

"You're a master of tact," Bak said, "a man any ranking officer would be proud to have on his staff."

Amonhotep flushed. "I did what I had to do, that's all."

Bak, sitting at the edge of the dais in front of the governor's chair, scowled at the aide seated beside him. "You saved Djehuty today, making him look far more worthy than he is, but can you continue to do so?"

"If he lets me, yes."

"For his own good, he'd better." Bak stood up, paced to the nearest column and back. "I've heard tales of men so angered by unfair treatment that they traveled all the way to the capital to stand before the vizier and plead for justice. I doubt the men in this province have been pressed that hard. Not yet, at any rate. I know the vizier is Djehuty's friend, but one who's so desperate he'll go to the capital carries ten times more weight than one who seeks justice in his own province."

"Djehuty hasn't always been this erratic." The aide clasped his hands tight between his knees. He refused to meet Bak's eyes. "Fear has made him worse each day, and you're the man responsible."

"What would you have me do? Tell him he's safe and let him offer himself to the slayer?"

Looking miserable, Amonhotep shook his head.

Bak eyed the officer, wondering how far he could trust

him. He had to tell someone in the governor's villa where he and his men had moved. The aide was the most logical, the man first to know of any incident requiring Bak's presence. He had been in faroff Buhen at the time of Lieutenant Dedi's death, so he could not be the slayer. But his loyalty lay with Djehuty, an unquestioning loyalty that boded ill for anyone who threatened the governor in any way. Bak's one advantage was his desire to keep Djehuty alive.

"Who told Djehuty my men and I have moved to Swenet?"

Amonhotep shook his head. "I don't know. I wasn't by his side every moment—I had tasks to perform, errands to run—and I suppose someone could've entered his rooms, but . . ." He hesitated, frowned. "Khawet? Did you tell her of your move?"

"We told no one." Bak thought it best to reveal the bare minimum. If he mentioned the archer, he would have to admit the man had probably drowned. One word to Djehuty, who seemed chastened now but could quickly go on the offensive, and they might well be sent back to Buhen. "Someone left a deadly gift on our doorstep. I thought it best we move to safer quarters."

Amonhotep stared, appalled. "A gift? What was it?"

"I'd rather not say. With luck, the one who left it will let slip the fact that he did so."

"I see."

From the bemused look on the aide's face, Bak doubted if he did. "I feel you should know where we've gone, but I'd like your sacred vow that you'll keep the location to yourself, not even sharing it with Djehuty."

Amonhotep appeared none too pleased with the last stipulation, but he nodded. "I swear by the lord Khnum I'll tell no one."

Later, as Bak watched the aide leave the audience hall, shoulders bowed beneath the weight of responsibility, he prayed he had trusted the right man. If he had erred, if another attempt was made on his life, he would know in which direction to look first. Or would he? Who had told Djehuty of his move?

Chapter Twelve

"I can't just walk away and leave them," Khawet said.

"Why not?" Bak eyed the five nearly naked men spread across the roof of the cattle shed, cleaning fish and laying them out to dry. "Not a man here is neglecting his duty, and they all know their tasks very well."

"Hatnofer always said that our servants would feel neglected if we didn't watch them closely."

"All men need supervision, but the more accomplished they are in their tasks, the greater distance you must maintain. If you don't trust their judgment, they grow lazy and resentful."

She flashed him a smile. "How profound you are today, Lieutenant!"

He returned the smile but offered no further comment. With a father as erratic as Djehuty and a substitute mother as difficult to please as Hatnofer, he was amazed her instincts were serving her so well. The servants seemed more aware of him than her, and certainly more wary. She was a familiar and comfortable figure, while he was a stranger who reminded them of death and a slayer still free to take another life.

Several times, he had surprised furtive glances from the three men sitting a few paces away surrounded by loosely woven reed baskets from which water leaked. Their task was to gut, bone, and scale the morning's catch. Another man took the cleaned fish and spread them out in the sun to dry.

A fifth crushed bones and scales and heads into a foul-smelling mess that would be worked into the soil in the garden as fertilizer.

"Alright, I'll leave these men in peace." Laughing softly, she led the way across the roof. "Have you had your midday meal? My next stop is the kitchen."

He liked the way she smiled, the delicate curve of her lips and the twinkle in her eyes. "Each time I see you, you're either involved in some task or rushing from one to another. Do you never take time to sit and rest?"

"Not often through the day. I must admit I sleep better at night now than when I spent much of my time in idleness, letting Hatnofer have her way." She walked ahead of him down the stairs, the same flight down which Montu had fallen to his death, and strode around the corner to the open front of the shed. "I find the responsibility of running so large a household taxing and at the same time a wonderful test of my abilities. Why I never demanded my rightful place as mistress of the house, I'll never know." Her expression grew rueful. "Still, I wish she were alive and well."

Bak stayed close, determined not to let her out of his sight until he learned what she knew of the housekeeper. "I'd've thought that tending to your father's needs was a full-time task."

"Only because I allowed him to make it so. Now I feel I serve him best by managing his household. Besides, he's shifted much of the load to Amonhotep's shoulders. Not merely the errands I ran, but the task of keeping him safe as well."

"Your father's afraid, and so he should be."

"I know. I sometimes awake in the night and imagine him in his bedchamber, too fearful to sleep, too frightened to get the rest he needs." She paused to look into the shed, where three milk cows with calves were tethered to stones sunk into the soil. Fresh hay spilled from their mangers and covered the floor of a pen in which a half dozen milk goats lingered. "He told me this morning you've moved out of your quarters in Abu. Too far away, should he need you."

"He has no immediate cause for worry." Bak followed her across the sunny yard. "If I'm right about the slayer's pattern—and I believe I am—he won't strike again for four more days. A lot can happen in so short a time, I know, but for the present, he remains far out of my grasp. I need help, your help."

"My father's very angry with you." She stopped at the gate and turned to face him. "He says you're prying into the past, reopening wounds that long ago healed."

Bak looked into dark, worried eyes, a face as delicate and vulnerable as that of a new-born lamb. "Prying into the past? Yes. Reopening healed wounds? For that, he must blame another man. The slayer."

She bit her lip. "Are you sure the tie that binds all those who've been slain is that dreadful tempest which took so many innocent lives five years ago?"

"I've trod several paths, none as long and convoluted— or as promising—as the one pointing to the storm."

"Since first I talked with you about Hatnofer, I've searched my heart time and time again, trying to recall some connection. I've found none."

She swung away, shoved the gate open, and walked on, heading toward the kitchen. Three naked and very dirty toddlers played outside the door, pushing wooden animals over mounds and ridges they had formed in the sand. Even from a distance, they smelled sour, in dire need of a dunking in the river.

Bak latched the gate and hastened to catch up. "I've been told she was close to a sergeant named Min, the man who saved Djehuty's life."

Khawet gave him a quick, rather surprised look. "Sergeant Min?"

"Surely you remember him."

"As you say, he saved my father's life." She stopped a dozen paces from the children, frowned. "I vaguely recall something . . ." Her brow cleared. "Yes, I did hear a rumor linking Hatnofer to him. I thought it best never to mention it to her. In fact, I wasn't sure the tale was true."

"She never confided in you? Don't women usually share their conquests with those closest to them?"

"She thought me too young and unworldly, I guess." Khawet's smile was wry. "I was close on twenty years then, no longer untouched or innocent, but she kept me forever in her heart as a babe."

"I was told Min sailed north a few days after the storm. If he and Hatnofer were close, why would she not go with him?"

She shrugged. "Perhaps she didn't care enough."

"Few women would throw away the opportunity of having a home and family of her own."

"This was her home." Khawet's voice carried a hint of criticism, as if no other place would serve as well and he should have recognized the fact. "She'd spent all her life on our estate in Nubt or in this villa in Abu. My father was a brother to her and I a daughter. Why would she give up so much to travel far away, maybe never again to see us?"

Bak was surprised Khawet was so insular. As the daughter of a provincial governor, she must have journeyed to Waset and Mennufer. Djehuty would have wanted his daughter to rub shoulders with the children of other nobility, as he had done when he was a youth. Yet here she was, a mature woman with a husband of her own, behaving as if no place but Abu would do, no other form of life but this.

Now that he knew her better, now that he had seen her smile and tease, she seemed much more attractive than she had initially, more appealing by far. But to have such a blind spot was a flaw few men of means or intellect could condone. Ineni perhaps, a man who loved the land above all else, but would he thrive in the governor's villa? Would he want to stand at the head of the province, given the opportunity? Would Khawet like him any better if he occupied the seat of power?

"Do you have any idea what Djehuty has asked of us?" Simut demanded. "He knew I'd sent as many men north to Nubt as I could spare—they're needed in the fields at this time of year, documenting land use, seeds sown, young animals dropped. And still he demands a detailed inventory. Outrageous!''

Bak eyed the two rows of men seated on the floor, shards piled beside them, scrolls spread open on their laps, reed pens scratching across the surface. None sneaked curious glances, as they had the last time he had come into the scribal office. They were too busy turning rough counts into an official report.

He kept his voice low, confidential. "I understand he means to disinherit Ineni."

"Ridiculous! As I pointed out when he told me." The short, stout chief scribe shook his head in disgust. "The estate in Nubt thrives because of that young man. Without him, it would founder."

"Some believed Hatnofer equally indispensable."

"In that case we erred, and I thank the lord Khnum that Khawet has proven us wrong. The estate in Nubt is quite another matter. Djehuty's lost the power of rational thought."

"How much of his wealth is derived from his land?" Bak asked.

Simut flung him a disdainful look. "I'm not at liberty to divulge information of so private a nature, Lieutenant. You should know better than to ask."

If Djehuty was like many provincial governors, his land was his heritage, just as his position was, but the bounty from his fields need not contribute to any great extent to his wealth. He was, first and foremost, entitled to a portion of the taxes collected from all who lived within his domain. The province was far from being the most fertile in Kemet, but its position on the border between Kemet and Wawat more than compensated for the scarcity of arable land: he was also allowed a share of the tolls paid by traders passing through Abu.

Though the estate's contribution to Djehuty's well-being would likely be small when compared to his income from taxes and tolls, to Ineni, the man who worked the land, the drain of produce and animals no doubt seemed exorbitant.

Simut glanced at the scribes toiling before him, pursed his lips, rose to his feet. "You wish to look at a personal record, you said."

Bak had an idea Simut would have given him a hint if they had been alone, but with so many men in the room, so many sharp ears, he would divulge nothing. "Sergeant Min. He served in the garrison here, in what capacity I don't know. He survived the sandstorm but left Abu soon after."

Simut frowned, thinking. "Hmmm. The name's familiar, but I don't know why."

"He was the one who saved Djehuty's life."

"Was he?" The chief scribe shrugged, indicating his failure to remember, and walked into the records room.

Bak followed as far as the door. "I know how proud Djehuty is that he's one of a long line of men who've governed this province. Until now, until he decided to disinherit Ineni, he must've bent a knee daily before the lord Khnum, praying his son would take his seat, and his son's son after him. On through eternity."

Simut chuckled. "He did for a fact."

The decision, then, was serious, one not lightly made. Was Ineni's refusal to get rid of the horses so important to Djehuty that he would end his family's long tenure as provincial governors? Or had he concluded for some reason that his adopted son was the man who wanted him dead? Or did he believe he could convince his daughter to divorce her husband and wed another, a nobleman, perhaps, who might give him a grandson worthy of his ancestors?

Simut pulled a reddish jar from the wooden frame, broke the plug that sealed it shut, and sorted through the documents. "Ah, here it is. Min. Sergeant of a company of spearmen."

Bak hastened to intercept him, to herd him toward the single lamp that burned at chest level atop a tall reed tripod at the back of the room, where privacy reigned. "Should Djehuty die today, would Ineni petition our sovereign, Maatkare Hatshepsut, to take his father's seat as governor?"

"He'd accept the task if she gave it to him. What choice would he have? He wouldn't seek it. He wants nothing more than to walk the fields of that estate in Nubt." Simut chuckled, but with a minimum of humor. "Ironic, isn't it? Djehuty adopted a son to succeed him and carry on the family line, but all the prayers in the world could neither give Khawet a child nor mold Ineni in his own image."

For the latter, all who dwell in the province must be thanking the lord Khnum, Bak thought.

"Unfortunately," Simut went on, "not another man in Abu is well enough known in the capital to get a nod from the queen." His expression turned gloomy, and he shook his head. "No, if Ineni is disinherited, our next governor will be a stranger, one who knows nothing of this province and its needs."

"Does Djehuty?" Bak asked.

Simut gave him a wry smile. "Lieutenant Amonhotep does. As you saw for yourself this morning."

Bak grinned. He had never expected to like this irascible little man, but he found himself warming to him. Then he chided himself for a fool. He had begun to like or respect every man on the governor's staff, men he had to consider as possible slayers. The only one he could not warm up to was the governor himself, the man he must keep alive.

The chief scribe broke the seal with his thumbnail, released the string and unrolled the scroll, and held it close to the lamp. Aloud he said, "Min came as a young man from Wawat, I see, the fortress of Kubban. Son of a soldier." His finger moved slowly down the right-hand edge of the column. "Hmmm. Rose through the ranks. Attained the level of sergeant."

Bak craned his neck, trying without success to read the document for himself. "Does it say anything about his surviving the storm?"

Simut unrolled the scroll a bit farther, adjusted it so he could see better, and his eyes darted to the top of the next column and downward. "Hmmm, here we are. Caught in a sandstorm. Returned from the desert more dead than alive.

Saved his commanding officer's life. Recommended for the gold of honor for . . . Yes, for behaving in an exemplary manner.''

"Where've I heard that before?" Bak asked in a dry voice. The statement was oft used, worn and frayed with age, a way of saying nothing when something needed to be said. "Did he ever get the fly?" The golden fly was a coveted award given to soldiers who distinguished themselves above all others.

"I see nothing here."

"Maybe he received it after he left Abu." Bak tried again to read the document, but Simut held the scroll closer to the lamp, not about to lose the upper hand. "What does it say of his speedy transfer north?"

The chief scribe raised an eyebrow at this fresh information and the added cynicism. He unrolled another segment of scroll, revealing a new and very short column. "Reassigned to the garrison at Mennufer." He glanced at Bak. "There the record ends."

"Mennufer." Bak scowled. "I, too, served there five years ago, but as a charioteer, not an infantryman. We seldom crossed paths. Usually only on the practice field, and in such great numbers we didn't know names or recognize individual faces."

Simut eyed the scroll, thinking back in time. "I vaguely remember a Sergeant Min. Not an especially admirable individual, I seem to recall, but no worse than some I've met." He rolled the document into a tight, neat cylinder and retied the string around it. "If you tell me what you wish to learn . . ."

"I've heard he and Hatnofer were close, and I'm trying to prove the rumor true or false."

"If he was the man I remember, he used to hang around this villa more than his duties in the garrison warranted. Not because of her, I'd've thought. There was another man, one who came often to see Djehuty, a Sergeant Senmut . . ."

"The man who was slain."

Simut nodded. "The pair were close. Too close, if you

ask me. I heard they often caroused together, played throwsticks and knucklebones, won more than they should in
games supposedly honest. However, Senmut was a favorite
of Djehuty—a sentiment well beyond my understanding—
so I said nothing.'' Deep in thought, he tapped the scroll on
a leg of the tripod supporting the lamp. ''If Min came also
to see Hatnofer, I never noticed.''

Bak let out a long, disappointed sigh. Another dead end.
Who could he turn to next? He needed Nofery, a skilled
collector of gossip. But she was ten days' journey to the
south, too far away to summon. Who, of all the people he
had talked with since coming to Abu, would be the most
likely to have his ear to the wind, gathering whispers as a
hearing ear gathered prayers?

Bak found the guard Kames seated in the shade on the
uppermost step of the family shrine in front of Nebmose's
villa, head and shoulders supported by a column, mouth
open, snoring. The wiry guard had been there for some time.
Birds chirped overhead, so accustomed to the raucous noise
he made that they had grown indifferent. Frogs croaked in
the small, shallow pool, trying to compete. His spear lay on
the ground, and a mother duck and her young waddled back
and forth across the shaft, tearing apart the remains of a loaf
of bread he had dropped near his feet.

Bak walked close. Quacking a warning, the duck led her
chicks to the far side of the pool. The frogs grew silent. He
peered inside the small building. As before, a fresh offering
of flowers lay at the base of the ancestor bust. Whoever
tended the shrine was faithful indeed.

He tossed the remains of the bread to the ducks, picked
up the spear, and frowned at the sleeping man. Kames continued to snore. *With guards like this,* he thought, *any number of outsiders could slip within the walls and slay five
people. This one needed a lesson he would not soon forget.*

Bak turned the spear around, point backward, and placed
the butt end of the shaft under Kames's chin. Abruptly he
lifted it, jerking the guard's head up, waking him with a start.

"Wha . . . ?" Kames's eyes focused on the shaft, widened in terror, darted to Bak's face. "Sir!" He pulled his legs close, meaning to scramble to his feet, but dared not rise.

Bak kept his head pinned against the column. "Five people have been slain and this is the way you stand guard? What kind of man are you? One who naps while others die?"

"Sir." Kames tried to swallow, moaned. "I never sleep on duty, sir. Never!"

"Has it not occurred to you that the slayer might find you with your eyes closed and you, too, might forfeit your life?"

"Please, sir. This is the first time. I swear it!"

Bak did not believe him for a moment, but he had come for information, not to see him punished for idleness. He withdrew the shaft from beneath the guard's chin. "When first I met you, Kames, I thought you a man of good sense. I searched you out to talk, not to accuse you of neglecting your duty."

The guard's face paled as the implied threat struck home. He scooted forward, well away from the column. "I've already told you all I know, sir."

"Where's your partner, Nenu?"

"He went to Lieutenant Amonhotep, thinking to gain advantage for himself by complaining about me." Kames stared at his clasped hands, his expression aggrieved. "He told the aide that I amble around like a cow in a pasture, paying no heed to my surroundings, thinking only of food and rest. Now, while I patrol this empty villa, he comes and goes, running errands for those of lofty status who toil for the governor."

"Who told you this?" Bak demanded. "Not Amonhotep, surely!"

"Nenu. He had to brag." Kames looked up at Bak, worry clouding his face. "Do you think I'll be punished on his say-so alone?"

Bak had seen for himself how indolent Kames was, but the truth was not always useful. "I see you as a man who's very much aware, one who watches and listens but keeps to himself all he sees and hears."

The guard's chest swelled at the praise. "Oh, I don't know about that, sir," he said, feigning modesty.

Bak sat down on the step beside him, a friendly companion, not a police officer. "Kames, I'm in need of information about a Sergeant Min. Have you ever heard the name?"

"Not that I recall, sir."

"He was one who survived the storm we spoke of the other day. He saved Governor Djehuty's life."

"Oh, him!" Kames clapped a hand to his forehead, grinned. "Now I know who you mean. Sergeant Min!"

Bak had a feeling he should have brought along a couple jars of beer, one to jog Kames's memory and the other to foster patience within himself. "He's been gone nearly five years, but his memory must live on. What've you heard about him?"

"I never knew him. I toiled in Nubt, guarding the governor's estate, until a year or so after he left. Not until I came to Abu did I hear him mentioned, and then not often. Few men dared speak of anyone connected to the storm when Sergeant Senmut was alive."

"They were friends, I've been told."

"They drank and wagered together, not always to the benefit of those who shared their good time. And I once overheard someone say . . ." The guard glanced around, assuring himself he and Bak were alone. ". . . they shared a secret about the governor."

Bak had trouble keeping his voice casual, his body relaxed. "What kind of secret, Kames?"

"Will you talk to Lieutenant Amonhotep for me, telling him Nenu lied?" The guard stared at his clasped hands, pretending nonchalance.

Bak wanted to take him by the neck and shake him. This was blackmail, plain and simple. "I have a feeling the lieutenant's already suspicious of the tale. Why else has he said nothing to you? If that's the case, it's best I remain apart and you go on with your task in as diligent a manner as you know how."

"But sir!"

Bak raised a hand, demanding silence. "If you find your-self in trouble, send for me. I'll do what I can—but only if you help me here and now."

Trying to look suitably chastened, but with a smirk slip-ping through, Kames leaned close and lowered his voice to a murmur. "The man who spoke, one I'd never seen before and have never seen since, said he knew for a fact that the governor panicked during the storm and Min saved him from himself. I heard later, from men whispering in the barracks, that they came back from the desert far ahead of the other survivors: Min, the governor, and a donkey carrying food and water. They were burned by the sun and tired, but neither man was hungry or thirsty."

"I wonder how great an effort they made to find others who might've survived?" Bak spoke more to himself than to the guard.

Kames gave him a knowing look, a nod of agreement. "They say Min was sent away so he couldn't make trouble in the garrison, but as a man of questionable character, would he not demand wealth or a lofty position in exchange for silence?"

Bak thought of Hatnofer, a woman reputed to be close to Min. Did he leave her behind as unwanted baggage and travel to Mennufer alone? Or did someone slay him to keep him quiet, leaving her to await a summons he could never give?

The wiry guard leaned so close their shoulders touched, and Bak could feel his warm breath on his ear. "Some say Min sailed north to a lofty position in a garrison far away. Others say he never set foot on board that ship. He was slain here, pushed down the water gauge, where the level of the floodwaters is measured."

Bak stared at the barred gate in front of the garden, trying to fit this new information into the old. As he had already concluded, Djehuty held within his heart a secret related to the sandstorm, one so shameful he would rather die than admit to it. Assuming Kames's tale was true, he had behaved in a craven manner. If he would die rather than confess to cowardice, would he not also kill to protect his secret? He might well have taken Min's life or, more likely, have had someone else commit the foul deed for him.

What of the five recent deaths? The patterns of the slayings pointed to Djehuty as the ultimate victim, not the slayer—unless he had become so afraid his secret would be divulged that his wits were addled. Unlikely, but a possibility nonetheless.

Thinking of Kames's nap and the sleeping guard he had surprised at the gatehouse a few days earlier, Bak made a quick tour of the governor's compound. He was forced to conclude that security was irresponsibly lax. One would have expected the violent death of the sergeant of the guard, Senmut, to bring about a strict adherence to good practices, but the reverse had happened. Or, more likely, Senmut had been as negligent as they, demanding nothing more than their present behavior. The problem now lay with Amonhotep, but he was too preoccupied by Djehuty's demands to come down with a firm hand, or even to notice.

Though convinced the slayer had come from within the compound rather than outside the grounds, Bak decided he would be equally lax if he failed to make a quick and, hopefully, intimidating inspection. After warning Amonhotep of his intent, he summoned Psuro and Kasaya. For the remainder of the day, the trio went from one guard to another, demanding cleanliness of individuals and weapons, improving stance, instilling proper procedures. Planting fear in their hearts, not only of the slayer but of the hard-nosed policemen from Buhen.

Finished with the inspection, Bak sent Psuro and Kasaya into Abu to pick up their evening meal from the old woman who cooked for them. They had found the food in Pahared's wife's house of pleasure filling but singularly lacking in taste and appeal, so they had retained her services. While awaiting the pair's return, he would look at the water gauge, the place where Sergeant Min was rumored to have been slain.

After observing the gatehouse from a discreet distance, he strode out the front gate of the governor's compound, confident the guard—wide awake and vigilant—would have spotted anyone occupying the nearby walls or rooftops. If the archer still lived, he would not be lying in ambush close by. He hurried along the terrace overlooking the river. The sun hung low over the western escarpment, sending shafts of gold into a pallid sky, reflected on the smooth surface of the water.

Beyond the willows, whose graceful limbs waved gently in the breeze, he reached the entrance to the thigh-high mud-brick wall built close around the rectangular mouth of the water gauge. An ancient grapevine, its trunk thick and knobby, its vines laden with clusters of ripening grapes shaded by a profusion of leaves, draped over the left-hand wall, covering much of its inner and outer surface. A stately sycamore towered overhead. Its rustling leaves sheltered a tiny black monkey that swung from limb to limb, squeaking.

Bak stepped through the open gateway and knelt at the top of an enclosed, steeply graded, rock-hewn staircase that plunged to the river. The steps served as the gauge by which priests from the nearby mansion of the lady Satet measured annual flood levels. In the gloom below, he could see the last of the year's deluge washing the lower stairs. A pale glimmer shone through the water, either a trick of the light shining from above or the opening to the river through which floodwaters entered and retreated. The hole through which a man would be pulled by the current should he fall—or be thrown—down the steps.

He eyed the well-like structure, trying to imagine a man pushed headlong down the steep stairway, tumbling out of control; head, shoulders, back, arms, and legs pounded by the hard stone steps; broken body swallowed by the waters below. After so long a time, with at least four floods to wash away any sign of violence, he did not expect to find confirmation of Min's death. But his first glance told him how easily a man could be slain here.

He rose to his feet. With his eyes on the water gauge, his

thoughts on Min, he stepped back to the opening in the wall. The monkey's chattering increased in volume and rapidity; leaves rained down as it scrambled higher into the sycamore. Bak glanced up, wondering what had frightened it.

Just as he glimpsed the creature, something struck him hard on the back, forcing the air from his lungs, making him stumble forward. His foot hit the edge of the uppermost step and he lost his balance. He reached out, trying to save himself. His right hand slid over the rim of the open shaft and down the rough stone wall, scraping away a layer of skin. Leaves rushed through the fingers of his left hand, something hard scratched his wrist—the grapevine—and he grabbed. The vine dipped beneath his weight. A long section tore away from the mudbrick wall above and flung him out over the depths of the water gauge. The far end held tight to the bricks, pulling him up short. He slammed face-forward into the rough-cut stone wall.

Shaking his head to clear it, he glanced up at the top of the stairs. He saw no one. He had not been pushed. He had been struck by . . . What? A good-sized rock thrown from a sling, inflicting a stunning blow on his back. A soldier's weapon. A weapon used by most children in Kemet. A skill learned early in life to slay birds or small game. As long as he clung there, hanging in the open shaft high above the stairway, he was no safer than a duck or a hare caught in a hunter's net, awaiting execution.

He shifted his glance to the mass of vines above him, seeking a second secure handhold. Leaves, grape clusters, shadows cluttered his view. He could see wrist-thick stems and tendrils as thin as thread, but not the vine he clung to, or any other close enough to grasp and sturdy enough to support his weight.

Offering a tardy prayer of gratitude to the lord Amon, adding a quick plea for additional help, he shot his right hand upward. Tendrils snapped and the vine he clung to dropped further. His heart leaped upward, clogging his throat. Again the far end held and stopped him with a jolt. Pain flared in his left shoulder, taking his breath away. He gritted his teeth to keep from crying out, stretched his right arm high, and felt around among the leaves and tendrils. His fingertips touched rough bark. He stretched higher, sharpening the pain. A torn muscle, he suspected. He found a good-sized vine. His fingers curled around it, but he could not reach high enough to grasp it. Sweat popped out on his forehead, his upper lip. The agony was intense, his fear of falling worse.

Desperate to relieve the weight on his left arm, his back prickling with vulnerability, he shook off his sandals and probed for a foothold. The added movement kindled the fire in his shoulder, making it blaze. Just as he was certain he could hang on no longer, he located a crack between the rocks. Shifting much of his weight to the one foot, he managed to raise himself high enough to catch the vine with his free right hand.

He held on tight with both hands, swallowed hard, kept as much weight off his left arm and shoulder as possible. He looked up again at the mouth of the water gauge. As before, no one was there. His assailant must believe him dead—or was biding his time.

Aware of how exposed he was to attack, how shaky, how fast pain could further sap his strength, he knew he had to move. He had to shift his body toward the mouth of the water gauge, moving to his left a little at a time. He had to move now.

Praying the vine would continue to support his weight, praying that if it broke he would somehow survive, he loosened his grip, inched his left hand along the rough bark, caught hold. He found a new foothold with no trouble. Shifting the right hand was torture, the burning in his shoulder dreadful with much of his weight hanging from his left hand. When he once again settled into place, both hands firm around the vine, he figured he had moved at least two palm widths closer to safety. How much farther did he have to go? He estimated the distance, considered his height, judged where he had to be before he could drop onto the steps. Slightly more than three cubits, he concluded, twenty-one or -two palm widths. Not far at all, yet an alarming distance.

He forced himself to move on, inching across the rough wall, his shoulder aflame, skinned arm stinging, hands slippery with sweat. His concentration was total. Move one hand, find a fresh toehold, move the other hand. He forgot the man who had assaulted him, the stairs beneath him, the darkening wedge of sky above him. He ignored his weariness and thirst. He tolerated his aching muscles and scraped knuckles. He endured the fire in his shoulder.

After endless torment, his lead foot brushed something cold and hard. He looked down, startled. A step. In his trance-like state, he had gone farther than he had to. With soaring spirits, he planted both feet on the stone and let go of the vine. His arms were so numb he could hardly feel them. Weak from effort and tension, wobbly from exhaustion, he dragged himself on hands and knees up the steep stairway.

At the top, he peered over the edge. The monkey sat on the wall, holding a bunch of grapes, eating the ripe fruit and flinging away the green. It skittered well out of his reach and scolded him, but showed no special terror. Nor did it show any interest in the surrounding landscape. Fairly certain they were alone, Bak hauled himself on up and sat, his back to the wall, inside the enclosure near the opening. He lowered his face into his dirty, scratched hands and offered a silent prayer of thanks to the lord Amon.

Chapter Thirteen

"You were truly blessed by the lord Amon, sir." Psuro, standing at the top of the water gauge, eyed the thick vine draped over the wall and the steep flight of stairs below. "If you'd fallen to the bottom . . ." His voice tailed off and he shook his head in consternation.

Bak turned his back on a place he preferred to forget and walked outside the enclosure. He moved with care, trying not to ignite the dull ache in his shoulder. The bandage the physician in Swenet had wrapped tight around his upper torso helped some, but any wrong move seemed to tear the muscle more. Compared to the shoulder, he barely felt his skinned arm, which was covered from wrist to elbow with a second bandage stained brown by a salve whose odor was overwhelmed by the strong smell of the poultice the physician had daubed on his shoulder.

"I wish we were as close to laying hands on the slayer as he evidently thinks we are," he said. "Another exercise like this, and I might not survive."

"Don't talk like that, sir!" Kasaya, standing at the base of the sycamore tree, trying to lure the black monkey with a chunk of bread, threw him a worried look. "Some malevolent genie might hear and turn your words around, bringing upon you the very misfortune you speak of."

"Oh?" Bak asked, eyebrow raised.

The young Medjay flushed. "I know you wish us to seek common everyday reasons for things that happen before we look to malign spirits as the cause. But here in Abu, with so many people slain . . . Well . . .''

"The man who took those lives has a reason, one that may never make sense to us but is most compelling to him.''

"Who do you think used the sling, sir?'' Psuro asked. "The archer? Did he survive the rapids after all?''

"I don't know.'' Bak leaned back against a boulder. "Its use puzzles me. It's not subtle, like those unwanted gifts, nor is it as direct as a bow and arrows.''

Psuro gave him a wry grin. "I'd not call a bowl of scorpions subtle, sir.''

Bak's laugh was quick, humorless. "Ingenious, then. I wasn't sure the insects were meant to kill, but I'm certain I was supposed to die in the water gauge.'' He stared at nothing, brows drawn together in thought. "If we leave out the archer's attempt to slay me with the bow, what do we have? A steady escalation from a small, harmless message to a serious attempt at murder.''

"Another pattern,'' Psuro said. "What kind of man toys with his victims this way?''

Kasaya, lost by so complicated a thought, tore the soft white center out of the bread and began to press it into a ball. "Maybe the archer broke an arm when his skiff overturned. One arm's enough to use a sling.''

"A possibility, I suppose. Or maybe my death in the water gauge was meant to resemble that of Sergeant Min—if the rumor Kames heard is based on fact.'' Bak watched the monkey working its way along a limb above the young Medjay. "Psuro, you must go again to the garrison. See if you can find anyone who remembers Min. Look to those who would've remained behind, supplying the troops or serving their needs. Quartermaster, armorers, and so on.''

"Yes, sir.''

"In the meantime, I want another look at the garrison daybooks. I glanced through them when first we came to Abu, and nothing struck me as being of importance. Perhaps today, with a more educated eye, I'll have better luck. And it occurred to me that the governor might also keep daybooks.

Djehuty was garrison commander, as was his father before him. As such, both were obliged to make daily entries. A habit once learned is not easy to set aside.''

Kasaya, munching on the bread ball, patted his flat stomach and smiled. ''A few more days in the governor's villa and . . .''

The monkey dropped out of the tree. It landed on his arm and grabbed for the hollow crust. The Medjay yelped, startled, and caught the creature by the neck. It squealed, terrified. Its little hands reached out for the bread, greed taking precedence over freedom. Laughing, Kasaya broke off a bit of crust and offered it. The monkey snatched it away and stuffed it into its mouth.

Psuro gave man and beast a disgusted look, then leaned back against the wall to study the landscape from which the rock must have been slung: the small walled mansion of the lady Satet, the much larger enclosed precinct of the lord Khnum, and houses crammed together in the space between, their walls pierced by a few windows too high and narrow for a sling to be used. Near the mansion of the lord Khnum, a lane opened onto the terrace, offering the women of Abu easy access to the public well.

Bak guessed what the Medjay was thinking. ''The whole time I was hanging from that vine, I expected my assailant to appear and finish what he'd started. If I'd given any thought to this area, I'd've known better. Standing at the lane, where he could see anyone coming and going, he could risk using the sling a time or two, but he dared not approach the water gauge, where he'd draw attention to himself as well as to me.''

''Whoever he is,'' Psuro said, impressed in spite of himself, ''he has the nerve of a god and the luck to go with it.''

Striding through the entry portal, Bak nodded to the neat and alert guard who manned the gatehouse. He was happy to see that the previous day's effort had made enough of an impression to last at least overnight. He walked on toward the governor's house, reluctant to go inside. The morning was pleasant, the intense heat of the inundation season dissipating as the season of planting began. He longed to go hunting in the desert or fowling in the marshes or sailing on the open river. Anything other than facing another day of this seemingly futile search. Seven days had passed since Hatnofer's death. He had to admit he had learned a great deal since then, yet he had no more idea now who the slayer was than he had had at the beginning. With only three days remaining, he needed divine intervention.

Smiling at the thought, at so unlikely an occurrence, he paused before the family shrine to look inside. No fresh flowers here, he noted, only an incense bowl long ago burned out, setting at the base of a red-painted statue similar to the one at Nebmose's villa. If no one bothered here, who was tending the shrine there?

Three men nearing their middle years came out of the governor's house, traders from the look of their sun-darkened skin, practical clothing, and mix of jewelry from Kemet and the lands to the south.

One, taller than his companions, raised a hand in greeting. "If you've come with a petition, sir, your luck's run out. Governor Djehuty's ailing today, unable to conduct an audience."

Not ailing, Bak thought, *but malingering. Too fearful to show himself.* "Did anyone say what the trouble was?"

"He can't leave his bed, we were told. Other than that, nothing. I pray he feels better tomorrow. We've a contract dispute with a man from Swenet and need a decision before we set sail for the Belly of Stones."

"May the gods smile on you," Bak said, moving on.

Twenty or so men straggled out of the house, each displaying hope, patience, dismay, anger, or disappointment according to his temperament. By the time Bak entered the audience hall, the last of the petitioners had gone, as had the scribes who assisted the governor and his aide. Troop Captain Antef and Lieutenant Amonhotep stood at the foot of the empty dais. Their raised voices resonated through the high-ceilinged room. Bak stopped near the door, not wanting to intrude.

Antef glared at Amonhotep. "If he's not available to make decisions, what am I to do? Make them myself and face his wrath later?"

"You're assuming your decisions will differ from his," the aide said.

"They always do."

Amonhotep stood stiff and silent, his face troubled, strained. At last he gave the more senior officer a tight smile. "Alright, I'll speak for him." He closed his eyes, drew in a breath, commanded, "Pull your troops out of the quarry. Give them a few days' rest. I'll send a courier to Waset saying the next Osiris figure will arrive late. I'll give as the reason our shortage of professional stonecutters, and I'll ask for additional experienced men."

Bak guessed this was the first time the aide had made so important a decision without Djehuty's nod of agreement. In this case, a decision Djehuty would not condone.

Antef clapped the young officer on the shoulder. "Your talents are wasted, Lieutenant, on this thankless task you have."

Khawet came through the door near the dais. Smiling, she walked toward the two men. Bak, preferring not to be thought an eavesdropper, strode in among the columns, heading their way.

She spotted him. Her eyes widened and she gasped. "Lieutenant Bak!"

The two officers swung around, stared.

"By the lord Khnum!" Antef exclaimed. "What happened to you?"

Bak considered passing off his injuries as the result of an accident, but decided the time had come to be candid. "I was standing at the top of the water gauge when I was struck in the back by a hard-flung stone. Fortunately, the lord Amon smiled on me, and I managed not to fall down the stairway."

Amonhotep muttered an oath. "Who would do such a thing?"

"The slayer." Antef's eyes narrowed. "Are you so close on his heels?"

Khawet's eyes were wide, horrified. "You didn't see anyone?"

"I assume the slayer struck, yes." Bak's eyes darted from Antef to Khawet. "And I saw no one."

"So you're to be the next to die while Djehuty lives on." Though seeming to joke, Antef looked none too happy at the prospect.

"Would the man you seek disrupt the pattern you found in the other slayings?" Looking chagrined at himself, Amonhotep answered his own question. "Of course he would, if threatened."

Antef gave Bak a cynical smile. "I'd better lend you a few spearmen as personal guards. Think of the impression you'll make. Lieutenant Bak and his retinue, marching through the streets of Abu and Swenet." The door near the dais opened, drawing the officer's eyes to Ineni, who stood on the threshold. For the newcomer's benefit, Antef added, "A dozen or more men marching down the halls of this villa and across the fields of Djehuty's estate in Nubt."

Ineni's eyes flashed anger, but instead of taking the bait, he backed up and let the door close between them. Bak hurried around the dais and followed him through the door. Ineni was some distance ahead, his hands balled into fists, walking rapidly toward the rear of the house.

Bak caught up with him outside, at the gate leading to the kitchen area. "Ineni, we must talk."

The farmer swung around, prepared to lash out in anger, but the bandages subdued him. "What happened to you?" His tone was grudging, like that of a man obliged to be civil.

Bak told him, then blurted, "Are your horses safe and well?"

The question was unexpected—to Bak as well as Ineni. Their eyes met in mutual understanding. They exchanged a conspiratorial smile.

"They are." Ineni glanced toward the house. The windows of the upper story were too high for a man inside to look through, but he grimaced, as if he thought Djehuty was watching. "Let's leave this place. Nebmose's villa should offer privacy."

Bak closed the gate behind them and they walked side-by-side across the barren sand in front of the kitchen. "When I saw you'd returned from Nubt, I thought maybe you and your father had reconciled your differences."

Ineni's voice grew caustic. "I went up to his rooms, but he wouldn't let me near him."

"He's banned everyone: the servants and guards, his staff, all except Amonhotep and Khawet. I saw him yesterday, but would he allow me close today?" Bak shrugged, instantly regretting the sudden movement. "Who knows?"

"He's never behaved well in a crisis, but this time . . ." Ineni snorted. "I ofttimes think we'd all have been better off if you'd never come to Abu, if you'd never pointed out that wretched pattern in the earlier slayings and the obvious goal at the end."

"The slayer's intent was to frighten him before striking in earnest. If I hadn't noticed the pattern, he'd have found another way to make your father see it." *Not an easy task,* Bak thought, *considering Djehuty's proficiency in closing his heart to any truth he would rather not see.*

They passed through the gateway to Nebmose's villa and sat on a mudbrick bench shaded by the stable. A flock of pigeons had settled on the sunny roof. The throaty cooing of mating birds softened the silence of the empty building.

Bak leaned back against the wall and stretched out his legs. "I've heard Djehuty plans to disinherit you—or has he already?"

"He'll let no one near him. Remember?" Ineni's smile dripped irony. "Before they were banned from his rooms, Amethu and Simut repeatedly told him he dared not drive me from the estate in Nubt, for it needs my guiding hand. Amonhotep has denied all knowledge of procedures he knows as well or better than anyone in the province. As for Khawet . . . Well, she's too busy playing mistress of the villa

to concern herself with mundane matters like her husband's
loss of his life's work.''

"The daybooks." Simut pointed to several rows of shelves
on which lay dozens of storage jars, most of them plugged
and sealed. "You've been here before and know your way
around, so I'll leave you to seek out what you want. I must
finish that wretched inventory. My scribes are needed elsewhere.''

Bak felt honored. Never before had a chief scribe trusted
him to go through his precious records alone and unwatched.
"I'll return each document to its proper place, never fear."

"I suggest you do," Simut said, hurrying from the room.

Bak did not know whether to take the words as a threat
or a jest. Best assume both, he thought, lifting the lamp off
the tripod. Holding the light close, he moved along the ranks
of jars, reading labels inked on their shoulders. He soon
found the container he wanted, labeled year five of the reign
of Maatkare Hatshepsut, harvest season. Returning the lamp
to the tripod, he broke the plug on the jar, found the daybook
whose entries should include the deadly storm and, holding
it near the light, began to unroll the scroll and read.

The storm had arisen in the desert, missing Abu and Swenet altogether, so no mention was made until the survivors
began straggling in, first Troop Captain Djehuty and Sergeant
Min and then the rest, one or two at a time. No mention was
made of Sergeant Min leaving Abu. Not surprising. A soldier's departure for a new post would be entered in the garrison daybooks, not necessarily this one.

He read on, day after day, paying particular attention to
the governor's audiences. The entries were clean and neat,
with no one pointing a finger at Djehuty or anyone else for
the loss of so many men. The governor was, of course, Djehuty's father.

Slightly more than a month after the storm, the old man's
death was noted and Djehuty himself sat on the dais. A week
or so later, a brief note referred to the death at some earlier
date of a nobleman named Nebmose. No kin had laid claim

to his property, so Djehuty had confiscated for the royal house the adjoining villa and a good-sized plot of farmland at the north end of the island of Abu. Property of considerable value, Bak realized. Another, later entry mentioned Ineni's adoption contract and the marriage contract between him and Khawet.

Replacing the document in the proper container, he carried the lamp to another shelf and more recent daybooks. The jars here had not yet been sealed, making the scrolls more accessible. "Year ten of the reign of Maatkare Hatshepsut," he murmured, glancing at the dates, seeking first the daybook in which the murder of the child Nakht would be noted. "Here it is: fourth month of the inundation season."

He found mention of the boy's death, which was dismissed as an accident. So was Montu's death the following week. Senmut was slain plain and simple, and so it had been noted, the blame laid at the feet of a wandering band of desert tribesmen out to steal what they could find. Four days later, a tax inspector and several scribes had arrived from the capital. Djehuty had greeted them with appropriate ceremony and had entertained them in his home that evening. Early the following morning, the chief scribe Simut had accompanied the inspector north. Their mission was to estimate the size of the coming year's crop based on the amount of land that could be placed under cultivation after the floodwaters receded.

Bak read on, alert for Simut's return. Lieutenant Dedi's death was noted, another accident, so the daybook said. Two days later, Simut came back alone, his assistance no longer needed as the inspector had moved on to the next province. Hiding a smile, Bak glanced over the edge of the scroll at the short, rotund man sitting before the scribes who toiled at his behest. Unless the slayer was two men instead of one—which he firmly doubted—Simut had slain no one. He had been somewhere north of Abu with the tax inspector when Dedi was slain. Delighted by the discovery, he thanked the lord Amon—not only for the chief scribe's sake, but for his own: he could finally strike one man from his list of suspects.

Bak had found in the past that seeking out people's whereabouts during a crime was time-consuming and as often as not unsatisfactory, but he had clearly been proven wrong in this case. With luck, the garrison daybooks would be equally enlightening. At the very least, they should tell him where Antef had been during the murders.

Bak walked out the rear door of the villa, deep in thought.

"Out!" The voice was Khawet's, loud and angry. "Take that creature and go! And don't come back!"

Wondering what the fuss was, eager to help if he could, Bak ran along the line of granaries. He paused at the gate, seeing no one, and looked across the bare patch of sand toward the kitchen. The woven mat covering the door flew up and Kasaya burst out. He cradled the whimpering monkey close in his arms as if sheltering it from assault. A whitish powder was sprinkled down the Medjay's chest and legs. The animal's black fur was matted with some sticky substance clotted in places with white.

Kasaya spotted Bak, gave him a look of naked relief.

Khawet plunged through the door behind him, holding her skirt high for greater freedom of movement and clutching a long, slim pot as a man would brandish a club. Her cheeks were pink, her hair disheveled, her voice shaking with anger. "You're nothing but trouble, Kasaya, flirting shamelessly, causing dissension among the women of my household. Now you bring that monkey into our kitchen! How could you?"

The Medjay looked wildly over his shoulder at his pursuer. "Sir! I didn't mean any harm! I didn't!"

"Lieutenant!" Khawet slowed, let her skirt fall, and lowered the jar. "For close on a week I've let this . . . This imbecile! . . . spend his days in my household, prying into our affairs, getting underfoot when my servants are busy, stuffing himself with our food. Even using my female servants as a sexual diversion. Now he's gone too far. I want him out. I want him out now!"

"What did he do?" Bak demanded, trying not to look at Kasaya, trying not to laugh.

Kasaya threw him a pleading look. "I was just . . ."

"He brought that creature into my kitchen!" Khawet shook her finger at the monkey and glared. "While he dallied with the women who toil there, he let it gorge itself on honey and melon and sweetcakes. If that wasn't bad enough, he let it play in our fresh-ground flour and our dried beans and peas. We'll never get the mess cleaned up!"

"I tied him to a stool." Kasaya looked at Bak, and his voice turned from defensive to pleading. "How did I know he could untie knots?"

Swallowing laughter, hoping he looked suitably stern, Bak swung the gate open and beckoned him through. "Go to the river and wash yourself." The furry delinquent, he saw, was clinging to Kasaya's thumb like a baby to its mother's finger. He had not the heart to order it back into the sycamore tree. "Clean up the monkey, too. I'll see you both in our quarters later today."

With a look of pure gratitude, Kasaya hurried away.

Bak passed through the gate in the opposite direction, clinging to his serious mien. Khawet clearly could see no humor in the situation. "I'm truly sorry, mistress. After you've both calmed down, I'll send him back to clean up the mess they made."

"You'll do no such thing!" She must have realized how harsh she sounded, for her voice softened to a more reasonable level. "You sent him here for a purpose, that I understand. But I've had enough of him, of his endless prying and continual flirting. More than enough. I won't have him back."

"His greatest value is not to pry, but to protect you and yours."

"No." Her mouth was set in a thin, determined line, the resemblance to her father uncanny. "I know you mean well, Lieutenant, but I've neither the time nor the inclination to look after that overgrown babe and his hairy friend."

He could see she would not reverse her decision. He was certain she would be more reasonable if she had less to think about, but worry for her father, whether really ill or pretend-

ing, and the responsibility for managing so large a household
was enough to distress anyone.

Bak had assumed Antef would have gone directly to the
quarry to relieve his men of their onerous task. Instead, he
found the troop captain at garrison headquarters, seated on a
stool in the room he used as an office, dictating to a scribe
who sat cross-legged on the floor, writing faster than any
man Bak had ever seen. The room was small and sparsely
furnished, with a woven reed chest filled with scrolls shoved
against one wall, weapons and quarry tools stacked against
the rear wall, and two stools near the door. Antef waved him
toward a stool and continued without pause. The document,
Bak realized, was a list of craftsmen and laborers needed in
the quarries to replace the soldiers.

"That should be sufficient," Antef said at the end. "If we
ask for too many men, we might get none."

"Yes, sir." Smiling, the scribe collected his writing im-
plements and left the room.

Bak eyed the officer with interest. "The last I heard,
Amonhotep intended to write that letter."

Antef grinned. "If you want a task done right, do it yourself—and this I wanted done right. Amonhotep has vowed
to send off whatever I give him." Sobering, he added, "I've
no objection to having my men move rough-sculpted works
from the quarry to the river. Soldiers have always helped out
in that way, and the time it takes is slight. I do object to
their doing the work of craftsmen, spending all their days
toiling on the stone when they should be practicing the arts
of war."

"What will Djehuty do when he realizes you've usurped
his authority?"

"He hates to be made to look the fool, especially before
his lofty friends in Waset. He'll let the matter stand." Antef
grinned again. "Of course, I dare not turn my back for a
while. He's certain to retaliate."

They both spoke, Bak noticed, as if Djehuty would live
on into the future, as if no threat clouded his existence.

"Commandant Thuty isn't perfect," he said, "but I thank the lord Amon he's as good a man as he is."

"You've been blessed by the gods." Antef glanced around the room. "What'd I do with my baton of office?" He pivoted on his stool to search through the clutter against the rear wall. Locating the baton among a sheaf of spears, he stood up. "I must deliver the good news to the men at the quarry. Why have you come?"

"I'd like another look at the garrison daybooks."

Antef grabbed a tunic off a small upended sledge that had a broken runner and slipped the garment over his head. "Why?"

While Bak explained, the troop captain pulled his broad collar out from beneath the fabric. When it would not immediately lie flat, he fumbled with the clasp, undid the collar, and tossed it onto a stool. As soon as he had heard enough, he strode to the door without a word, shouted a name, and his scribe came running.

A short time later, Bak sat on the floor of a tiny courtyard shaded by palm fronds spread loosely across two sturdy reed beams. Lying along a mudbrick bench in order of their dates were the dozen or more scrolls the scribe had brought from the records office.

Once again he unrolled the copy of the official report of the sandstorm. This time he knew better what to look for, more specific information based on the additional knowledge he had gained over the past few days. As was to be expected, with Djehuty the author of the document, no mention was made of his irrational order to keep the men moving in the face of disaster, or of men who had found shelter but had turned away their fellows. To be fair, Djehuty might never have been told of the latter offense, but a good commander would have dug the truth from the survivors.

A third, unexpected omission proved far more interesting. The report included no recommendation that Min receive the Gold of Honor, contrary to the statement in the sergeant's personal file. Had Djehuty failed to make the request because he knew Min was no longer among the living?

With nothing further to be gleaned, Bak set the report aside. Picking up the daybook that included entries about the storm, he searched this time for mention of Min. Exactly a week after he and Djehuty returned from the desert, a brief entry indicated that a Sergeant Min had departed from the garrison. No further information was given. Bak glanced back through the daybook and forward. Entries were often slipshod, omitting a detail or two, but they never failed to provide the reason why a man left the garrison, his destination, and usually the name of the ship on which he sailed. Min had never left Abu, Bak felt sure.

He moved on to the more recent daybooks, looking specifically for information about Antef's comings and goings when the first four murders occurred. On the surface, the troop captain's life appeared full to the brim with interesting and challenging tasks. In reality, his days were all much alike, his duties unremarkable. He spent a few hours each day at the quarry and the rest of his time in Abu, overseeing the routine activities of the garrison. Each night he slept in his residence, whether alone or not the daybook made no mention.

Only once in the past six weeks had he ventured away from Abu. A month ago, he had traveled into the desert to inspect patrols, the journey lasting four days. Sergeant Senmut had been slain on the last day of the trip, when Antef and a sergeant, accompanied by ten spearmen, had been far out on the desert, inspecting a six-man patrol. Whether they had returned before Senmut was slain or later in the day was a question the sergeant could answer.

Chapter Fourteen

"Where's Kasaya now?" Psuro asked.

"At the river, trying to wash the monkey." Bak grinned. "The creature hates water. It's all arms and legs, screaming as if caught in the jaws of a lion."

Psuro gave him a sour look. "You don't intend to let him keep it, do you?"

"He may as well. The damage has already been done."

"Pahared's wife won't be happy if it gets into her stores." Psuro looked pointedly toward the door, where the woman in question stood in a shaft of sunlight, haggling with a traveling metalsmith over the price of bronze rings, pendants, and bangles, finery for the young women who toiled in her house of pleasure.

Bak followed his glance. She was as sharp-tongued as she was sharp-eyed and she allowed no transgressions. It took a strong-willed man to live with such an exacting woman—or one who spent his days on his ship, as Pahared did.

"I told him he has to keep it leashed—and tied with a knot it can't undo. The first time it gets loose, it goes back to the sycamore tree." Taking care not to stir up the sediment, he raised his beer jar to his lips. "Now tell me what you learned of Min."

"I went to the garrison offices, stores, armory, anyplace I could find someone who'd talk to me. Not a man in Min's unit survived the storm, and not many support personnel remain in the garrison." Psuro eyed with appreciation a tall,

211

slim young woman from the land of Kush, standing in a rear doorway in a suggestive pose. The girl's dusky cheeks, forehead, and shoulders had been scarified, her hair dyed a coppery orange. "Worse yet, details have blurred after five long years. The truth isn't easy to come by."

"Do those who remain remember him with a smile or a frown?"

"They say he was a hard man to please on the practice field. Experienced in the arts of war, skilled with weapons, proud of his battle scars." Psuro winked at the young woman. "All agreed he was a man to avoid in games of chance, dishonest to the core. But once befriended, a friend for life."

Taking the wink as an invitation, the girl ambled across the room, swaying as if touched by a gentle breeze. The Medjay, enthralled, lost the power of speech.

Scowling his impatience, Bak waved her away. "After we finish here, Psuro, I've another task for you. One you must do right away. Our time is running out."

"Yes, sir." Psuro watched her retreating backside with obvious regret. "One man, an armorer some years past the prime of life, said he thought never to see Min care for a woman. The sergeant was too fond of himself to give freely and too much the man of action to be gentled. When first he expounded the virtues of mistress Hatnofer, all who toiled in the armory thought he was jesting. Until one day the chief armorer took her name too lightly. Min threw him against the wall, furious. He truly loved her, they realized, and never again did they cast aspersions."

Bak nodded, satisfied. Min and Hatnofer had indeed been close. "Why, then, did he leave her behind? Did anyone say?"

"No one could understand." Psuro tore his eyes from the girl, standing again in the doorway. "Rumors abounded that he never set sail, that he was thrown down the water gauge. He never sent word back to friends, saying how happy or discontented he was at his new post, nor was his body ever reported found in the river. Mistress Hatnofer gave nothing away, no angry words or any sign of sorrow. Just a growing bitterness through the years.''

''He's dead. I'm sure he is.'' Bak set his beer jar on the floor and stood up. ''He knew Djehuty's secret, some shameful and abhorrent act, and he had to be silenced.''

Rising to his feet, Psuro gave the young woman a final, lingering look. ''You think Djehuty slew him?''

''I'd bet a year's ration of grain that he did. Or he gave the task to someone else.''

They strode out the door and turned down the narrow lane, which was heated by the midday sun, tempered by a soft breeze. A train of donkeys, their backs loaded high with fresh green fodder, clip-clopped across the intersection ahead. The heavy smell of new-cut clover made Bak sneeze.

While they waited for the animals to pass, he plucked a stalk bright with yellow flowers and nibbled the sweet blossoms. ''You must go to the garrison and seek out a sergeant.'' He went on to explain what he had learned of Antef's whereabouts during the earlier murders and how the sergeant should be able to prove or disprove the officer's innocence at the time Senmut was slain.

''In the meantime,'' he said with a grimace, ''I'll go again to the governor's villa.''

''I won't see him!'' Djehuty's voice, surprisingly strong for a man so sick he had taken to his bed, carried down the narrow hallway. ''Why is he here in Abu? Didn't I order him to leave?''

''He came because the vizier wished it, sir.'' Amonhotep's voice carried an edge of irritation. Obeying the slightest and most whimsical command of a man behaving like a spoiled, fearful child had begun to try even his patience.

''I don't care. Send him away!''

''I can't do that.''

''You can and you will!'' Djehuty spat out the words like one tomcat spitting at another.

''Sir, if anything happens to you . . .''

''Nothing will happen!'' Djehuty snapped. ''As long as

you remain close, no one will dare approach me.'' His voice
took on a querulous note. ''You're the son I never had, the
one individual I trust. With you by my side, I don't need
that wretched Lieutenant Bak or his Medjays. Or Ineni. Or
Antef. Or . . . or anyone!''

''You have mistress Khawet, sir.''

Djehuty dismissed his daughter with a snort.

Bak muttered a quick prayer to the lord Amon, seeking
patience, and marched down the corridor to the bedchamber.
The governor lay amid the usual tangle of sheets, his head
and shoulders raised on folded sleeping pallets and pillows.
The high windows allowed fresh air to circulate, but the cloying scent of an overly sweet perfume vied with the odor of
the unwashed body it was meant to conceal. The brindle dog
was gone, but its smell lingered. *Poor Amonhotep*, Bak
thought.

''Governor Djehuty,'' he said. ''I thank you for seeing me.
I know you're unwell, so I feel greatly favored to be admitted
to your presence.'' The words came out unplanned, an in-
spiration of the lord Amon, no doubt.

The aide gave him a startled look.

Djehuty stared at the bandages around Bak's upper body
and arm. He seemed about to comment, but changed his
mind and glared. ''You . . . You . . . What're you doing in
my bedchamber?''

Bak regretted making life more difficult for Amonhotep,
but his sole hope of breaking the governor's silence was to
shock him. ''I've come to speak of the sandstorm in which
so many men were lost . . .''

''That again. Must you continue to probe an incident all
who live in Abu wish to forget?''

''. . . and to speak of Sergeant Min, the man who saved
your life.''

Djehuty drew his head back as if struck. ''Min? He . . .
He's gone. He sailed away to Mennufer.'' As he went on,
his words came out with growing confidence, a tale well-
practiced, dredged up from memory. ''He asked for a transfer
to the garrison there, thinking to better himself at a larger

post closer to the heart of the army. Close to our northern capital, where he might catch the eye of Menkheperre Thutmose. I recommended him for the gold of honor, thinking to aide his cause.''

Menkheperre Thutmose, rightful heir to the throne and co-ruler in name only, was rebuilding the army to its former glory while, according to rumor, he bided his time, waiting for an opportunity to grasp the reins of power. With Maatkare Hatshepsut preferring to reside in the royal house in Waset close to her priestly power base, the young king had chosen the administrative capital of Mennufer as his home and as the seat of command for the army.

Bak did not believe Djehuty for a moment. Much of the tale made sense, but he had been too quick to explain. As for a golden fly, the official report of the storm proved that untrue.

"Sergeant Min was the tie that bound Hatnofer to the storm,'' he said, his voice cool, crisp. "They were lovers. So close he fought for her honor in the garrison. Did you know that?''

"No, I . . .'' Djehuty's eyes darted around the room, seeking a way out. "Yes, she told me.''

"Min survived the storm, but a short time later he vanished. She was slain because she was close to him and because she was next in line below you, managing your household.''

"Amonhotep fits into your so-called pattern as well if not better than Hatnofer.'' Djehuty's voice challenged. "He actually survived the storm; she never set foot in the desert.''

And he is, in every sense, your right hand, Bak thought, *but you would never acknowledge how much you lean on him, how much you need him.* "He was on a ship returning to Abu from Buhen the morning she was slain.''

"The slayer could have awaited his arrival. Barring an unforeseen delay, the vessel was expected that day.''

In a way, Djehuty had a point. Had Hatnofer been slain merely because circumstances threw her in harm's way? Or had she guessed the slayer's identity and faced him with her knowledge?

Aware that the pause had stolen the momentum from his questions, Bak said, "They say in the barracks that Min never sailed to Mennufer. He was slain before ever setting foot on a ship. Would such a rumor survive if it had no substance?"

The brief silence had bolstered Djehuty's defenses; his chin jutted and he glared. "Go away, Lieutenant. I'm ill, too ill by far to respond to your vile insinuations." He pulled the sheet up beneath his chin and rolled onto his side, his back to the two officers standing by the bed.

"Sir!" Amonhotep, his face set, reached out as if to shake his master. Within a finger's breadth of the governor's shoulder, he pulled his hand back. "If you're to help yourself, you must help Lieutenant Bak."

Djehuty tugged the sheet higher, covering his ears.

Bak walked to the door, thoroughly disgusted. "If you wish to die, sir, you have my blessing." He stopped on the threshold, waiting for a reaction. He got none.

Bak stood at the top of the stairway rising up the slope from the landingplace. Below, Ineni stood on the deck of a small cargo ship from which baskets piled high with fresh produce were being off-loaded. Fruits and vegetables raised on the estate at Nubt had been shipped upstream to fill the governor's belly and that of his household. Sailors and household servants carrying laden baskets on their shoulders trudged up the stairs and through the gate past the sentry.

He was far from alone, yet he felt uneasy. Was the archer yet alive, hidden somewhere behind him, even now seating an arrow in his bow? Swinging around, he studied the walls and rooftops of the governor's villa and that of Nebmose. He saw no one but the guard at the front gate.

Shrugging off his momentary anxiety, he turned away to walk along the terrace. The interview with Djehuty had disheartened him. How could he hope to protect a man who would do nothing to help himself? He strode past four small boys playing tag, their laughter and shouts filling the air with joy. He fervently wished he had as few cares as they. He circled around the water gauge, raised a hand in greeting to the women collected at the public well, and sat on a mud-brick bench shaded by willow trees in front of the mansion of the lord Khnum. Barely aware of the chatter of women drawing water, he tried to make sense of all he had learned thus far.

He had been so quick to see the patterns in the deaths that had occurred. Why could he not identify the slayer? He wanted above all things to succeed in his task, as he always had before. Here he was, however, unable to see the smallest glimmer of light. He had been utterly convinced the sand-storm was the key, and he continued to believe so, but each time he learned a new fact, it led nowhere. If only Djehuty would reveal his secret! But he would not. And if he did, would it help point the way?

The governor was exactly as Nofery had painted him as a young man: spoiled, stubborn, heeding no one's advice, tak-ing on authority too great for his abilities. The first three traits Bak had seen for himself. The disaster of the storm, the loss of so many innocent lives, had undoubtedly been the result of the last.

Three days until week's end, he thought. *Three more days until the slayer strikes again.* Khawet might be his next target but, assuming he meant to continue with the patterns he had established, he then would have to wait yet another week before striking Djehuty. Would he do so? Probably not. The risk of discovery was too great. Still, Bak had to take pre-cautions for her safety as well as that of her father.

Her father. He could think of no more worthy a target than Djehuty, yet he could not let him die.

"I want no more Medjays in my house." Khawet's mouth was set, determined. "Kasaya did nothing but make a nui-sance of himself."

"Psuro is older and more responsible," Bak said. "Unless

he's needed to protect you or yours, you'll be unaware of his presence for much of the time.''

The last thing he wanted was to assign Psuro to the governor's villa day after day. The Medjay was far more valuable gleaning information from the residents of Abu and Swenet or the soldiers assigned to the garrison. But what choice did he have?

"Can you not respect my wishes, Lieutenant, simple as they are?''

Giving him no time to answer, she stepped beneath the lean-to and focused her attention on two men seated on the ground in the shade. Both were making round reddish clay pots on horizontal wheels, deftly building up the walls of the swiftly turning vessels. Twenty or more similar pots stood drying in a corner, waiting to be fired.

"Your father's life is in jeopardy, mistress Khawet. I want someone near when the slayer makes his appearance.''

"Three days from now,'' she pointed out.

"He could strike at any time. Wouldn't you alter your plans if all the world knew you'd established a pattern?''

She gave him a tight smile. "My father refuses to leave his rooms, and he insists that Lieutenant Amonhotep remain by his side at all times. Only Amonhotep. No other man. Under the circumstances, your Medjay would be close to useless.''

"I'm as concerned for you as I am for your father.'' He raised a hand, cutting off her objection. "The slayer enjoys this game he's playing. I'd not be surprised if he decided to draw out Djehuty's agony by slaying the one closest to him.''

A boy of twelve or so years entered the open courtyard, carrying a basket of dried dung and an armload of dead twigs and branches. He knelt before an open hole at the base of a round baked clay furnace half again as tall as a man and began to build a fire.

Her mouth tightened. "I'll have no Medjays here, and that's final!''

Bak wanted to shake her. She was as stubborn as her father, and almost as irrational. "Mistress Khawet . . .''

"No," she said, her eyes on the boy. "I'm in no danger."

Bak watched a potter dip a hand into a bowl of water and smooth the surface of the vessel he had just finished. He could override her decision and force her to accept Psuro, but he had no wish to place the Medjay in such a difficult situation. Treated as a pariah, his worth would be halved— or worse. He needed an alternate, but who? He thought of the men he had met since arriving in Abu, the few he felt he could trust. The best he could come up with was by no means equal in competence to Psuro or Kasaya.

"If I were to find someone else, a man of Abu and not a Medjay, would you allow him to stay close by your side?"

She gave him a sardonic smile. "Not so close he shares my bedchamber, I hope." Noting how serious he was, she sobered. "Who're you thinking of?"

"A guard who's been here for several years and knows both house and grounds. Kames, he's called."

"I don't know him."

Bak was not surprised. Kames was not one to attract notice. "I don't know what other tasks he's had, but now he keeps watch over Nebmose's villa."

"Oh, yes, the husky young man with a rather surly look on his face. The one recently thrown into the river and battered by the rapids."

He pictured Nenu as he had last seen him, recalled the guard's tale of a fight, and opened his mouth to reject her version of the story. Then the truth struck him. A half-formed smile vanished from his lips and he let the statement pass. First things first. "Not him. A smaller, older man. They patrolled the villa together until a few days ago."

Her expression was singularly lacking in enthusiasm. "If I must be watched, he sounds no worse than anyone else. At least he'll respect the rules of this household. Unlike your Medjays."

Bak resented the barb, but let it pass. She was like a fruit tree so heavily burdened its limbs were bowed beneath the weight. He must have a serious talk with Kames. The guard

must stick to her like plaster to a wall, and he must not close
his eyes for an instant.

"They didn't find the patrol until midafternoon." Psuro
shouldered the basket of clean laundry and lifted the jar of
fish stew by the rope handle attached to its neck. "Troop
Captain Antef insisted they go on with their task, keeping to
their schedule, and he and his men stayed with them for close
on two hours."

"They were far out on the burning sands?" Bak asked.

"Almost three hours' march west of the river, searching
for intruding tribesmen."

The old woman handed Bak a basket covered with leaves,
and he gave in exchange the token due her. The yeasty aroma
of fresh bread wafted from the container, along with the
sharp odor of cheese and the tangier, more subtle smell of
boiled eggs.

"According to the sergeant," Psuro said, "he and Antef
and their men didn't return to Abu until an hour or more
after sunset. He had good reason to remember. They couldn't
find their skiff in the dark—someone had taken it—and
while they searched, a man fell into the river. They finally
gave up and spent the night on the west bank."

Smiling her gratitude, the old woman entered her tiny
house. Bak sidled past several homeward-bound archers and
led the way down the narrow lane. A slick-haired black dog
trotting at the soldiers' heels swung around to follow the
food.

"When during the day was Senmut slain?" he asked.

"He was found early in the morning, so sometime the
night before. The men who came for him from the house of
death guessed he had lain there for several hours."

"Good," Bak said, well contented with the news. "Now
two men are freed of guilt: Antef and Simut."

They reached an intersecting street wider than most running through Abu and turned north toward the governor's
villa. A unit of twenty or so spearmen marching four abreast
toward the garrison forced them into the open doorway of a

sandalmaker's shop. The man glanced up from his work and gave them a quick smile, never missing a beat in the steady tap-tap-tap of his mallet. The rank smell of leather tanning in urine assailed their nostrils.

Bak reached down to scratch the dog's head. "Earlier today, mistress Khawet said something in all innocence that set me thinking. These are her words: 'The one who was thrown into the river and battered by the rapids.' Who do you think she meant?"

"You were carried through the rapids, sir. And you were hurt. Upriver at Iken. How did she know about that?" Psuro, noting Bak's censorious expression, paused for further thought. His eyes widened. "The archer? She was speaking of him?"

"She was talking about Nenu, a guard in the governor's compound. And, until a day or two ago, at Nebmose's villa."

"I recall seeing him there when first we came to Abu. A young man who needed a comeuppance, I thought." The Medjay's eyes slewed toward Bak, the look on his face skeptical. "Why would he wish to slay you?"

The last of the spearmen marched by and they strode on down the street, the dog at their heels.

"I bumped into Nenu the day after the archer was thrown into the rapids," Bak said. "He was battered and bruised and, when I asked what happened, he spoke of a fight. He's an ill-natured sort, so I took him at his word." He scowled at the memory. "Never did I think of him as being the archer, but now . . . ? We'd best learn the truth—and soon."

"Was he not the one who helped you search Nebmose's villa when first the archer struck?"

"Don't remind me," Bak groaned. "The perfect defense is offense, and his performance that day proves it. I dropped over the gate in front of the villa and there he was, spear in hand, challenging my presence."

"No wonder you never found the bow and quiver! Each time you came close, he steered you in another direction."

"Laughing all the while, no doubt," Bak said bitterly.

Psuro's expression again turned dubious. "I'd never have taken him as so quick-witted a man."

"I suspect he isn't under normal circumstances, but when his well-being is threatened, he's cunning like a jackal." Bak's mouth tightened. "Maybe we can outsmart him."

"You asked for me, sir?" Nenu stood at attention, his eyes on Bak, his expression wary.

"There you are. Good."

Bak, resting his uninjured shoulder against a column in the audience hall, eyed the guard long and hard, hoping to unsettle him. The young man's appearance had not improved, although his injuries were on the mend. His abrasions had scabbed over, and his bruises were a mottled purple and yellow. His lower lip was dry and swollen, the cut red with recently clotted blood. He stood stiff as a palm, breathing loud through his nose.

Bak had to admire his control. "My Medjay and I . . ." He nodded toward Psuro, standing near the dais. ". . . were on our way to our evening meal when the chief scribe Simut summoned me. As you can see . . ." He nodded toward the baskets of food and laundry and the bowl of stew. Psuro had added a net bag containing a half dozen beer jars and another basket filled with clusters of deep purple grapes and a couple of striped green melons. "We've too much here for one man to carry, so you must help him take them to our quarters in Swenet."

"Yes, sir." Nenu visibly relaxed. "Is that all, sir?"

Bak smiled, further easing his suspicions. "When you finish, you're free to go."

"Shall I reheat the stew?" Psuro asked. "I can borrow a brazier from Pahared's wife and set it on the roof outside our quarters, where the fire will be shielded from the breeze."

"I doubt I'll be long, but . . ." Bak smothered a smile. The Medjay was as artful as the most accomplished performer in an enactment of the sacred drama of the lord Osiris's victory over his rival Set. "Perhaps you'd better. Cold fish stew is an abomination."

"If Nenu is the archer," Psuro said, "he should come soon."

"Before nightfall," Bak said, nodding agreement. "He'll want sufficient light to see his target and at the same time enough darkness to hide his identity and allow him to steal away unseen."

Looking down from the rooftop outside their quarters, he studied the dark and empty doorways in the block of buildings across the lane. The narrow thoroughfare lay deep in shadow as the sun dropped beyond the western horizon. The black dog, which had crossed the river in the skiff with Psuro and Nenu, lay on the threshold of an empty dwelling, looking upward, patiently awaiting a handout. Kasaya was on a roof near the northern end of the lane, hidden from view. Loud and raucous voices issued from an open expanse of sand to the south, where a half dozen or so of Pahared's sailors and a growing crowd of onlookers were betting on a wrestling match soon to begin.

Bak's eyes leveled on the still-lit rooftops across the lane, where several families sat, enjoying the gentle northerly breeze while they consumed their evening meal. With no other buildings close by, the archer would have to strike from there. Bak had thought of sending the people away, but their absence would have proclaimed a trap. With luck, they were not so close they would be endangered.

"I don't like this," Psuro grumbled. "We need more men."

"We have plenty. It's their quality I'm worried about, not their numbers."

When Bak had asked for help, Pahared had volunteered crewmen from his ship. They were the best brawlers along the river, the trader had bragged, but did they have the patience to await the signal to act and, once set in motion, would they do as they were told? Or, preoccupied by the match, caught up in the excitement of the noisy crowd, would they respond at all?

Psuro nested the bowl of stew on the unfired charcoal in the brazier, perfecting a picture of two men readying their evening meal. "We should've waited until tomorrow, after you'd had a chance to talk to Troop Captain Antef. He'd've been glad to lend all the men we need. Good, trustworthy men."

"Must I remind you, Psuro, that our time is running out? I doubt the archer—Nenu, I'm convinced—had anything to do with the five deaths in the governor's household. If we can eliminate him and whatever vile acts he's committed, we're that much closer to the truth. If he used the bow at the orders of another, which I think he did, our path should grow shorter still."

A man yelled a wager, his voice raised above the general clamor. Another bested him and a third went higher yet. Excited laughter rippled through the crowd at stakes higher than expected.

"Who would have him slay you? One who wants the governor dead?"

Bak gave the Medjay a wry smile. "You speak of almost everyone in the province. I hope to shorten our list of suspects, not lengthen it."

A spot of light darted across his chest and the outer wall of their quarters, grabbing his attention. Bak looked toward Kasaya's hidingplace. The Medjay, crouched behind a rooftop parapet, repeated the signal, catching the sun on a bright square of polished bronze. Bak scratched his head, letting him know he had seen. Another signal, a series of short, bright flashes, and Kasaya ducked out of sight.

"Nenu's at the quay and he's armed." Bak walked away from the wall and knelt beside the brazier, facing the lane at an angle. If he made too easy a target, he would rouse Nenu's suspicions. Or be slain. He would never forget the first ambush he had set up soon after his arrival in Buhen. Thanks to his lack of foresight, one of his Medjays had lost his life.

"So now we wait," Psuro said.

"Not for long, I suspect."

They pretended to converse, pretended an offhand interest in the loud exchanges of the bettors, grinned at each other when the voices heated up with excitement. The time dragged. The sun vanished below the horizon, leaving a sky bright in its afterglow. The lord Re, clinging to the world of the living, was reluctant to submit to twelve hours in the netherworld. The glow faded rapidly, leaving behind a darkening sky speckled with stars. Torches were lit at the southern end of the lane, illuminating the sandy arena and the men awaiting the bout. Bats shot through the air, hunting insects drawn to the light. The shrill call of a nightbird—Kasaya's signal—rose above the rumble of the expectant crowd.

"Nenu's come," Bak said.

In the lane below, the dog began to bark. It broke off abruptly in a sharp cry of pain. Muttering a curse, Psuro reached for his spear. Bak slipped his hand through the grip of a shield lying close on the rooftop, and offered a silent prayer to the lord Amon that Nenu's first arrow would fly far from its mark. The guard's skill was modest, he knew, but bad luck could kill as quickly as a well-aimed missile.

"There!" he hissed.

The dark silhouette of a man raced across the roof of the empty house across the lane. He knelt several paces behind the parapet and raised a bow with an arrow already seated. Details of space and body were hidden in the gloom, but the archer was definitely Nenu.

Chapter Fifteen

An arrow sped toward Bak, its bronze tip and white feathers ghost images in the dwindling light. He ducked low and swung his shield up. The sudden movement wrenched the torn muscle in his shoulder, catching him short, slowing him. The shield's heavy wooden frame deflected the missile, saving him from a mortal wound, but the point sliced through the bandage wrapped tightly around his upper torso and tore across his ribcage under his left arm. A hasty glance showed blood beading up along the edge of the slit linen.

Shouts burst out in the open area south of the building block. Whistles. Applause. The wrestlers entering the arena, the match about to begin.

Kasaya burst from his hidingplace and raced across the rooftops, zigzagging around families, leaping over braziers and pets and pottery stacked for cleaning. Raised voices followed in his wake. Adults and children craned their necks, anxious to see what provoked such haste. Nenu, seating another arrow, must have heard the alarm in their voices, the curiosity. He swung around, spotted the large dark figure racing toward him like a creature risen from the netherworld, spearpoint glinting eerily in the failing light. He raised his bow toward the new target, released the missile. A cry rang out and a woman crumpled into her husband's arms. A man yelled, angry voices rose in the air: the family and friends of the injured woman. Nenu froze, evidently realizing what he had done.

Spitting out a curse, Bak grabbed his spear from the rooftop, ran to the parapet, and flung it hard at the archer on the opposite roof. The weapon flew past, missing its target by a hair's breadth. Nenu pivoted, startled by the near miss. He fumbled with an arrow, obviously panicked by the heated voices and Kasaya pounding toward him. Finally seating the missile, he took a wild shot at Bak and dashed for the southern end of the block. There an outside stairway led down to the street and the open space where the wrestlers would compete. Where Pahared's sailors waited.

"Psuro, now!" Bak yelled.

The Medjay was already on the move. Lifting a long board from the shadows, he darted to the edge of the roof, planted a foot on the parapet and leaned forward, and dropped the plank over the span, bridging the lane.

Not sure he could be heard over the shouting spectators, Bak whistled the long, loud signal meant to alert Pahared's sailors. Still carrying his own shield, ignoring the drag of its weight on his sore shoulder, he scooped up Psuro's spear and shield, shoved them at him, and leaped onto the board to race across. As he knelt to retrieve the spear he had thrown, he noticed again his torn and blood-smeared bandage. The cut merely stung, indicating a surface wound, with no harm to the rib. He offered a silent prayer of thanks to the lord Amon.

Psuro leaped off the bridge and Kasaya dashed past. Bak glanced at the woman lying amid a circle of family and neighbors. Confident she would be cared for—if still she lived—he raced with Psuro after Kasaya and the fleeing man. He heard thudding feet behind, a small party of men who knew the fallen woman, seeking vengeance.

Nenu set a straight course for the stairway, making clear his knowledge of the area. He paused on the top step to look down at the wrestlers and their audience, whose shouts had gained in volume and enthusiasm as the match began. A quick glance back at the men in pursuit and he plunged down the stairs. Kasaya raced after him a dozen paces behind. Bak whistled another signal. The yells of the spectators never faltered.

Like Nenu before him, Bak paused atop the stairway to look down. Sailors, soldiers, traders, townsmen, five or six women at most, stood in the fluttery light of four flaming torches mounted high on buildings around the open square. Their attention was focused on two well-oiled and sweating wrestlers locked together in combat; the raised voices goaded them on. A judge hovered close, keeping the pair honest. The spectators formed a loose circle, staying well back and out of the way, filling much of the squarish expanse of sand enclosed by housing blocks whose walls were unbroken by windows or doors. Somewhere down there were Pahared's crewmen. Families who lived within the surrounding dwellings looked down from the rooftops.

Nenu was shouldering his way through a clamorous crowd indifferent to everything but the match, with Kasaya a few strides behind. Stepping aside so Psuro could go on ahead, Bak whistled again. One man looked up, saw the short, stocky Medjay racing down and the officer from Kemet above. He grabbed the shoulder of another man, who shook off the offending hand, made a horn of his own hands, and yelled at the wrestlers, demanding greater effort.

Bak muttered a curse. From where he stood, he could see the mouths of six or eight dark, narrow lanes, any of which Nenu could enter. If the guard knew the rest of Swenet as well as he did this area, he would lose his pursuers with ease. They needed help, men who knew their way around, even in the dark. How could he attract the attention of Pahared's crewmen?

Feeling the weight of the weapon in his hand, he had an idea. He had first hurled a spear as a small boy and, given sufficient time and care, was reasonably skilled in its use. He studied the scene, chose as his target a clear patch of sand near the combatants, and launched the weapon. The blade buried itself deep in the earth. The long shaft stood tall and rigid, vibrating from the force of the thrust.

Silence descended over the crowd. The wrestlers grappled

and grunted and groaned, unaware. The judge stepped back, gave the spear a startled look, hissed a warning. The pair continued to fight.

Bak whistled again, the sound loud and clear, impossible to ignore. To a man, the spectators looked upward, as did Nenu and Kasaya. Psuro leaped off the bottom step, too intent on his goal to be distracted. Six or seven men, Pahared's sailors, headed toward the stairs from several different directions.

"There!" Bak yelled, pointing emphatically at Nenu, who was elbowing his way through the crowd, angering the people he passed and drawing attention to himself. As the seamen altered course, Bak called out to the rest, "Get on with the match!" and raced down the steps.

The wrestlers paused, looked around, saw their audience's attention turned elsewhere. Bewildered, they broke their hold and drew apart. The judge repeated Bak's order. Like everyone else in the makeshift arena, the pair ignored the command and watched with rapt attention the fleeing man and his pursuers.

Nenu burst free of the crowd and slipped into the nearest lane, its mouth dark and forbidding. Kasaya darted into the blackness a few paces behind him. Bak flung his shield aside for better mobility and leaped off the steps. He glimpsed Psuro and Pahared's crewmen shouldering paths through the spectators, trying to catch the younger Medjay and his quarry.

Questions broke the hush of the crowd: What's happening? Who're these men? Why are they chasing the man in the lead?

Bak's identity and word of his quest spread through the crowd. Suddenly the mood changed. Excitement crackled in the air. The spectators turned their backs on the match and, with voices raised in a frenzy of purpose, moved as a single unit in the direction Nenu and Kasaya had gone, lured by the promise of livelier entertainment.

Entangled in the flow of men, helpless to stop them, and

thoroughly disgusted by this unforeseen turn of events, Bak clamped his hands together, forming a battering ram, and thrust his body forward. Those he struck ducked aside, muttering curses and glaring resentment. He caught up with Psuro, who was pushing forward behind spear and shield, opening a path for the few crewmen who had caught up with him. Ahead lay the lane that had swallowed Nenu and Kasaya.

The narrow thoroughfare was as black as a nobleman's tomb closed and sealed for eternity. An invitation to an ambush. The more timid onlookers dropped back, unwilling to face whatever terrors the dark might hold, but most surged forward, caught up in excitement and the flow of humanity. Bak prayed Kasaya was close on Nenu's heels, prayed he would not allow himself to be waylaid in the dark, prayed he would lay hands on the guard before this mob, in its very zeal to witness Nenu's downfall, provided a setting in which the guard could escape.

He pointed toward a torch protruding from the neck of a large pottery jar on the roof of the corner dwelling. "We need that light," he shouted to Psuro.

Sailors in tow, they veered toward the building and forced their way to the wall. With no prompting, Pahared's burly pilot locked his hands together, forming a step, and lifted Bak high. Bak pulled the torch free and dropped back to earth. Several more sailors trickled out of the crowd, the remainder of Pahared's crew taking advantage of the detour to catch up.

Moments later, they merged with the stream of men crowding into the lane, jostling for space, shoulders brushing shoulders, elbows digging ribs, toes prodding heels, voices pulsing with the thrill of the chase. Cursing the crowd beneath his breath, Bak held the torch high and pressed forward through what looked in the flickering light like a river of heads flowing along a curving streambed. Bronze spearpoints glinted among them, carried by soldiers from the garrison who had come across the river to watch the match. Faces

looked down from the rooftops, men, women, and children
drawn by the tumult.

They gained on the leaders slowly, too slowly. When first
Bak had heard of the wrestling match, he had thought it a
gift of the gods, a place where Pahared's men could merge
into the crowd and remain unseen. It had been a gift alright,
a gift handed out by the demons of the night.

A sharp, piercing whistle sounded over the din. Kasaya's
signal. Ahead and to the right. Relief flooded through Bak
that the young Medjay had not fallen in a shower of arrows.

"They're heading upriver," he said unnecessarily.

The men ahead, as quick to interpret the signal, swerved
into a narrow side lane that meandered toward the river. Dust
rose beneath stumbling feet; the smell of donkey manure was
strong. Determined to reach Nenu first, Bak lowered the
flame to just above head level and, using man's fear of fire,
drove a wedge into the crowd before him. Psuro plowed
forward behind his shield, widening the path.

They burst through the leaders of the mob and out of the
lane. Compared to the dark, narrow thoroughfare, the shoreline and river seemed awash with light. The moon and stars
glowed strong and full on the narrow sandy beach. Low
swells on the river glittered with a reflected sheen, carrying
fragments of light north on the current.

Some distance upriver—how far was hard to guess with
night flattening the landscape—two figures ran along the
steep bank above the strip of sand and the water. Farther
south, bank and shore gave way to blackish boulders much
like their counterparts across the river at Abu. To get away,
Nenu must either go into the river or out on the desert. Either
way, he could vanish in the night.

The mob burst from the lane. Seeing Bak and his party at
a standstill, they spread out along the riverbank, momentarily
at a loss as to where to go.

Determined to reach the guard before the crowd could in-
terfere, Bak issued hasty orders. "Take Pahared's men and
cut Nenu off from the desert." Psuro would need all the help
he could get to cover so vast an area. "I'll try to catch

Kasaya. With luck, the two of us can keep him out of the water.''

Psuro gathered up his men and hastened away. Bak headed down the bank, half sliding, half running on earth that tore away beneath his weight. He hit the sand at the bottom and, without breaking stride, raced full-tilt along the shore. The torch he carried sputtered; sparks showered in his wake. He heard pounding feet behind, glanced back. The crowd had begun to move upstream along the bank, those at the rear urging their leaders to greater speed. Three men, one a soldier carrying a spear and shield, raced after Bak along the water's edge. He could have ordered them away, but decided not to. He might need the weapon.

Approaching a small flotilla of skiffs drawn out of the water for the night, he plunged into the shallows. Water splashed around him, cooling his legs and dousing a kilt already damp with sweat. Flying sparks struck the water and sputtered out. Ahead, Nenu slid down the bank to the river, sped along the shore to the first of the boulders, and ducked out of sight in its shadow. Kasaya slowed, wary of an opponent carrying bow and arrows, and pulled back from the edge of the bank to kneel behind a rock not nearly large enough to shelter his bulk. On the riverbank, the flow of men stopped well out of Nenu's range yet near enough to have a good view of the action. The excitement dwindled, sapped by inactivity and speculation. Someone yelled a wager, hoping to revive the fun with bets on the outcome of the chase. Soon the betting grew raucous, loud with fervor.

A speck of white caught Bak's eye, a kilt. Nenu, hunched over to make himself small, slipped farther along the water's edge and disappeared behind another boulder. Bak darted forward, giving him no time to arm his bow, and took shelter behind the first boulder. Kasaya leaped to his feet to race along the riverbank to a stony outcrop above the archer. The trio following Bak held back, unwilling to face a rain of arrows, but the mob surged after the young Medjay, their voices gaining in volume and excitement, each man's frenzy feeding on that of his fellows. Bak's blood ran cold.

Nenu had no choice but to enter the river. Vowing to catch him before he disappeared as he had at the island of inscriptions, Bak rammed the torch into the sand. He disliked giving up the light, but could not manage it in the water. He patted his sheathed dagger, reassuring himself that he had not lost the weapon in the crowd, then waved to catch Kasaya's eye and signaled his intent.

Certain the Medjay understood that he must remain on shore, Bak slipped into the river. Keeping his head low, making as little noise as possible, he swam upstream toward Nenu's hidingplace. Each stroke he took seemed to tear his shoulder muscle further, making the swim a trial as well as a necessity. He offered a silent prayer to the lord Amon, pleading for a hasty end to the chase.

The distance shrank to fifteen paces, ten, five. Someone among the mob spotted him in the water, yelled to urge him on, and pointed so all could see—including Nenu. Others joined in, pointing, yelling, so intent on winning their bets that rational thought fled. Nenu fired off two arrows in rapid succession, both missing by at least an arm's length. The onlookers booed and jeered.

Bak sucked in air, ducked beneath the surface, and lunged toward his quarry. Touching bottom, he clutched his left arm close to relieve the pain and eased his head out of the water. Nenu, standing not five paces away in the shadow of the boulder, was looking straight at him. The guard let out a harsh laugh, flung his bow aside, tore the quiver from his shoulder, and leaped. Bak shoved himself backward, making for deeper water, and rolled sideways. Nenu struck the river's surface hard and flat. Water erupted, showering them both. Bak reached out, meaning to grab the other man, but again his shoulder failed him and he missed.

Nenu, taking advantage of a weakness he clearly did not understand, grabbed Bak by the neck and began to squeeze, at the same time forcing his head underwater. Feeling himself sink, Bak spread his legs wide, caught Nenu's legs between them, and pulled the guard down with him. Nenu held on. Their combined weight dropped them to the riverbottom; the current dragged them across the rocky bed and through the heavy silt. Bak's head began to throb, his lungs felt ready to burst. He tried to pry the guard's fingers from around his neck, but Nenu simply tightened his grip.

They struggled on, a silent desperate battle in the black depths of the river, with neither man able to gain an advantage. Bak weakened fast, his fingers grew numb, his thoughts fuzzy. He had to free himself. Soon. Or he would die.

Then he remembered his dagger. Or perhaps the lord Amon whispered in his ear.

He fumbled for the weapon, pulled it from its sheath, and pressed the point against Nenu's side. Though close to a state of utter desperation, he hesitated. If he took the guard's life, he would leave unanswered a multitude of questions.

He released Nenu's legs, and together they rose through the water, slowly, gradually, a journey that seemed never to end. They broke the surface. Gasping for air, the guard shoved Bak's head back underwater, never for an instant relieving the pressure on his neck. Bak sliced the top of Nenu's left wrist. Blood gushed. The guard tore the hand away, cursed, but continued to hold on with his right hand, his fingers digging deep and cruel. Bak shifted the blade to Nenu's neck and ran it across the flesh, no longer caring how deep the cut. Again blood gushed. Nenu's eyes widened. He jerked back, released Bak's neck to touch the wound, and stared at the stains that came away on his hand, stunned, horrified.

Bak sucked in air, tried to swallow. The sound of yelling, made hollow by ears clogged with water, seeped into his thoughts. The mob, forgotten in the struggle. Ignoring his aching shoulder, the queasy feeling, and a blackness around the edges of his sight, he lunged forward and grabbed Nenu by the upper arm. The guard offered no resistance, apparently convinced he had only moments to live. Bak knew better; the cut could not be much more than skin deep. Shifting the dagger from neck to breast, displaying not the slightest sign of weakness, Bak forced Nenu to swim toward the shore. The crowd on the riverbank roared approval.

Locked together and exhausted, they swam erratically, splashing water, bright gems of liquid color. Along with the moonlight, Bak realized, the waves around them were aglow with light beaming from several torches on the shore. He aimed for them and a large silhouette he hoped was Kasaya.

Not until they neared the shore and Bak's feet touched the bottom did he notice that the river had carried them a couple hundred paces downstream. The onlookers, who had followed, were standing along the bank, looking down upon them, while a dozen or so spearmen stood at the water's edge with Kasaya.

The big Medjay waded out to meet them, the look on his face one of intense relief. Bak, his knees so weak he could barely stand, shoved Nenu roughly through the shallow water. The guard stumbled. To save himself, he grabbed his captor's arm. Bak staggered, came close to falling. A soldier raced forward and plunged his spear deep into Nenu's breast. The guard crumpled to the earth. The crowd gasped.

"No!" Bak croaked.

He signaled Kasaya to snare the soldier and knelt beside Nenu. He spoke fast, aware the guard's life was draining away. "Did you slay mistress Hatnofer and the others in the governor's household?" His throat hurt; his voice sounded raspy.

"No," Nenu whispered.

"Did you leave those gifts in my quarters? The fish, the doll, the scorpions?"

Nenu, looking puzzled, tried to raise his hand. Bak lifted it for him and laid it on his chest. The guard inched it upward to clutch the spear. "Scorpions?"

The confusion on his face verified Bak's guess: someone else had left the unwanted gifts. "Did you strike me with a sling while I stood at the water gauge?"

Nenu licked his lips as if about to speak, but shook his head instead, the effort to talk too great for his failing strength.

"Why did you try to slay me?" The question was too

broad, demanding too much of a man breathing his last.
"Who told you to slay me?"

"I won't . . ." Nenu frowned, trying to think or maybe
just to form the words. "Governor Djehuty. He said . . ." He
coughed. Blood bubbled from his mouth. His head fell to the
side and his body went limp. His ka, his eternal life force,
had fled.

"Is it possible?" Psuro asked. "Would the governor order
slain the man who's trying to save his life?"

"Who knows? He becomes more irrational each day."
Bak tilted the bronze mirror to reflect the early morning sun
and raised his chin to examine his neck. Dark bruises marked
the flesh, fingerprints of the dead guard. "He reeks of fear."

Kasaya swallowed a mouthful of bread spread liberally
with honey. "I'd be afraid, too, if I knew I would die in
only two days' time."

The monkey, perched on the young Medjay's knee, licked
honey from its sticky hands. The black dog lay against
Psuro's thigh, sniffing a chunk of bread the monkey had
thrown aside. A soft breeze drifted across the rooftop, carrying the mingled odors of the river, animal waste, and beer.
In a nearby lane, a woman hummed a love song in a light,
sweet voice.

"No, as witless as he is, I doubt he'd have me slain for
trying to save him." Bak laid the mirror on the rooftop,
broke a chunk from a flat slab of fresh bread, and dunked it
into the fish stew left from the previous evening. The cold
stew was soft and bland, easily swallowed. "More likely, he
wants me gone before I learn the secret he refuses to tell."

Psuro swirled his bread in the stew, stirring it up. "What
could be so important, so shameful he'd take another man's
life rather than speak out?"

"And at the same time risk his own life," Kasaya added.

"No officer wants to be accused of incompetence, especially if men have died at his orders." Psuro frowned, thinking out loud. "Djehuty's poor leadership caused the deaths

of more than one hundred men, but we've known that for some time.''

''No officer—no soldier, for that matter—wishes to be thought a coward,'' Kasaya said, ''yet rumor hints that he behaved in a craven manner during the storm.''

''Look at him now,'' Psuro sneered. ''Hiding away in his bedchamber like a frightened babe.''

Bak swallowed another bite of stew. ''If he took Min's life, especially if he did so with his own hands ... Now there's a secret that if divulged would not only destroy his reputation but might well cost him his life. I doubt even his friend the vizier could turn his back on such a crime.''

''We have no witnesses,'' Psuro said with a slow, thoughtful nod, ''and as long as he doesn't admit to wrongdoing, he knows we can do nothing.''

Bak aired the thought that had kept him awake far into the night. ''A secret too dreadful to reveal, whether the death of Min or some other vile deed, would surely be an abomination to the gods.'' He took a bite and let the stew slide down his throat, cooling, soothing. ''Would he not, then, do all in his power to remain alive, giving himself time to seek absolution so he could enter the netherworld and the hall of judgment with a free conscience? Would he not wish his heart to reveal no trace of deceit or treachery when it's weighed against the feather of truth?''

Psuro and Kasaya stared, both men silenced by the reminder that the stakes reached beyond Djehuty's worldly life. If he had ordered Nenu to slay Bak, the one man who might be able to save his life, the risk he took was awesome, an invitation to spend eternity unjustified, unable to enter the Field of Reeds.

''There must be something else,'' Bak said. ''Some other reason for his mad behavior. Something I've overlooked.''

''My father is very ill, Lieutenant.'' Khawet stood in the hallway outside Djehuty's private reception room, a reddish pottery bowl in her hand. The contents smelled of vomit. ''I can't let you see him.''

"I must speak with him." Bak's voice broke, the vehemence straining his bruised throat. Irritated, he tried again. "If he wishes me to save his life . . . If you wish me to save him, you'll let me see him."

"I can't." Her voice was tense; the flesh stretched tight across her face. "Don't you understand? He's too ill to see anyone."

He was reluctant to add further pressure, but if he was to save Djehuty, he had no choice. "My father, a physician, believes speech can free a man from worry."

"If you have a message, one that will drain my father's heart of fear and anxiety, I'll relay it to him." Her voice turned chilly. "If you've nothing but endless questions, I can't help you. I won't add weight to his burden."

Bak glanced pointedly into the empty reception room, which was as clean and neat as if the governor had never set foot inside. "Where's Lieutenant Amonhotep? Did not Djehuty order him to remain by his side at all times?"

"I needed more herbs. As soon as my father slept, I asked Amonhotep to go to the market for me. He wanted instead to send a servant, but I insisted he go. He was sorely in need of a respite." Her mouth tightened. "You'll not gain admittance through him, Lieutenant. Even he, as exhausted as he is, wouldn't be so foolish as to let you disturb a man so ill."

Bak bit back a sharp reply. At times she was as impossible as Djehuty, as stubborn. "You've surely heard that Nenu, one of the guards here in this household, tried to slay me last night, and he, in turn, was slain."

"I've heard the tale, yes." She gave him a sharp look. "What does that have to do with my father?"

"Nenu told me as he lay dying that Djehuty ordered him to take my life."

She flung up her head, startled. "He wouldn't do such a thing. The guard lied."

"Perhaps." Though his voice was difficult to control, he hit exactly the right note: noncommittal with doubt seeping in.

"Why would he?" she demanded, defensive. "If your the-

ory is correct, if you're his only chance of survival, as Amonhotep believes, it would make no sense.''

"Now you know why I must speak with him.''

She hesitated, glanced down at the bowl, scowled. "I'm
giving him a herbal broth that should relieve his stomach.
When he's able to see you, I'll summon you.''

Bak strode away, cursing the day the vizier had suggested
he come to Abu. Why were people always so unwilling to
do what was best for them?

"He's worked himself into such a state he can keep no
food in his stomach. I didn't want to leave him, but how
could I refuse mistress Khawet? Her days are already too
long and filled to the brim. So I went to the market for her.''
Amonhotep held out a basket from which several bundles of
dried herbs protruded. Beneath lay linen-wrapped packets
containing crushed herbs and potions. "Actually, I didn't
mind. I needed a reprieve, as she said.''

Bak had intercepted the aide at the back gate opening onto
the narrow lane behind the governor's compound. "She told
me he was sick, very sick.''

"He is, but the illness is of his own making, I'm sure.''

"If that's the case, her broth is unlikely to settle his stomach enough for me to speak to him.''

"I'll see that you do.'' The aide's voice was firm, the
words a promise.

"Do you have any idea why he'd order Nenu to slay me?''

"It makes no sense.'' Amonhotep stared down the lane at
a young woman heavy with child, dragging a naked boy of
three or four years along behind her. The child was dirty, his
face tear-stained, his arm stretched as high as it would go.
"I was surprised when he told me to remove the guard from
his post at Nebmose's villa so he could use him to run errands. Until then, I didn't know he knew the man.''

"Nenu admired Senmut, the sergeant who was slain. And
Senmut was close to Djehuty.''

Amonhotep nodded, understanding the tie. "What of the
soldier who slew Nenu?''

"We took him to the garrison." A whine drew Bak's attention to the woman and child, who rounded the corner at the end of the block and walked out of sight. "He thought Nenu was attacking me, trying to escape. An honest mistake, but to use his weapon without thought . . ." Bak shook his head in disgust. "Antef will deal with him."

"I expect soon to see him in the audience hall." Amonhotep gave a cynical snort. "If Djehuty can ever tear himself out of bed. Or if he survives the next two days."

He'll survive, Bak thought grimly, *if I have to sit beside his bed and guard him myself.* "When can I talk to him?"

"After midday." The aide gave Bak a humorless smile. "I think it best not to warn him that you'll be coming, but I'll need time to pacify mistress Khawet."

Chapter Sixteen

Bak sat on the bench at the back of Nebmose's villa, elbows on knees, and buried his face in his hands. His throat was sore and scratchy. A dull pain throbbed in his shoulder. He was tired, discouraged, at a loss as to where to turn next. Nenu alive might have revealed a path to the truth. Nenu dead raised a new set of difficulties.

He could not imagine why Djehuty had ordered the guard to slay him. Could he have misunderstood the dying man's meaning? No. Only a long stretch of the imagination could interpret the words in any other way. The governor wanted him dead. If the past was any indication of the future, he might never reveal the reason. So far, Bak had had no luck in prying the truth from him. How could he believe another interview would be more productive?

He would try again, and again and again if need be, but in the meantime he had to look elsewhere.

Raising his head, he stretched out his legs and leaned back against the wall, letting inactivity heal his battered body and the breeze soothe his troubled soul. He thought of all he had learned about the five deaths: Nakht, Montu, Senmut, Dedi, and Hatnofer. Each had been slain in the light of day and, with the probable exception of Dedi, slain by a horse frenzied by an unknown method, each had been killed at close range while facing the slayer. Which meant he was someone known and trusted by all. Djehuty? No, his fear was real, attesting better to his innocence than witnesses swearing he was elsewhere at every slaying. Who else then? All who held lofty positions in the villa would have been trusted. If Nenu was to be believed, and Bak did believe him, he had had nothing to do with the murders. He had known he was dying, and with his heart so soon to be weighed against the feather of truth, he dared not lie. Amonhotep, Simut, and Antef had each been far away during the time of at least one slaying, but the whereabouts of the others remained unknown. He had been lax in that respect, allowing himself to be distracted when he should have followed through to the end. This he vowed to do.

The tie that had bound the victims together had been the fateful storm five years earlier. Other than Amonhotep, who had wandered the burning sands alone, all the survivors had behaved in a despicable fashion. Bak thought a moment, revised the notion. The survivors who had sheltered in the cave with User had behaved abominably. Djehuty and Min had not been among them. They had been elsewhere, no one knowing where or what they had done to survive. This, Bak felt certain, was the key to the governor's secret.

Sergeant Min was gone, probably slain, his lips sealed forever. He may have confided in his friend Senmut or, more likely, in mistress Hatnofer, his lover. They, too, were dead. Djehuty alone could offer enlightenment, and he refused to speak.

Is that all I've learned in close on a week? Bak asked himself. *Am I no nearer to the slayer today than I was yesterday or the day before or the day before that? How can I hope to save Djehuty in less than two days if I can uncover no new answers?*

A thought reared its ugly head, one so unworthy he squashed it like an insect: the southernmost province of Kemet would be a better place to live if its present governor were dead.

Frustrated, he stood up and strode to the stable. An orange cat lay stretched across the doorway in the sun, washing its face. He stepped over the creature and walked inside. The structure was as devoid of life as when last he had seen it, with a few bits of straw and the faint scent of manure to remind him of its proper function. He envied Nebmose— whoever he had been—and he well understood Ineni's resentment at not being allowed to keep horses here. Djehuty's decision to bar animals from the stable and reserve the house for illustrious guests seemed odd. Why had he not given the property to his married son and daughter?

Bak left the stable and, driven by curiosity more than purpose, entered the house. Passing the rooms used for storage, he walked through the high-ceilinged, bright-painted hall and down the corridor to the master's suite, his footsteps loud in the silence. He glanced around the private reception room with its elegant furnishings, decorative wall hangings, and senet game ready for play. He peered into the two small bedchambers, noting the neatly folded sleeping pallets, and ambled around the larger bedchamber that led to the bath where Hatnofer had been slain. Here, the bed was made and toilet articles laid out. A bowl of dried flowers sat on a wooden chest. Not a speck of dust marred any surface. If not for the silence, he might have thought these rooms inhabited. By rights, Khawet and Ineni should have occupied them, filling them with laughter and children, instead of a series of noted guests who passed through in haste.

He strode to the doorway, intending to leave, but his steps faltered at the threshold. Troubled, not sure why, he turned around to study the room. It looked much as it had when first he had seen it, a guest chamber ready for occupancy. But he, the intended guest, had spurned the room, and no other visitor was expected. Why were the linens still in place when normally they would be stowed away, protected from dust, insects, intruding birds, and small animals? Khawet must have forgotten. She had proven herself a superb mistress of a demanding household. She surely could be forgiven this one lapse.

A new thought came to him, a fresh possibility. One he swept aside as nonsense. Another idea loomed larger, more promising. Vowing to return to the first notion if need be, he left the bedchamber and wandered throughout the house, seeing the building as the hollow shell it was, getting a sense of the comfortable home it once had been.

What had prompted Djehuty to take the life from this dwelling? Had he loved Nebmose like a brother, or had he hated him? Who, in fact, was Nebmose? Other than that he was a descendent of an old and noble family, Bak knew nothing of him. Nothing except the fact that he had left behind a desirable residence on a valuable piece of property and farmland on the north end of the island that was probably of even greater value than this dwelling.

Bak peered inside woven reed chests, pulled drawers out of wooden chests, looked through the few objects kept in a storeroom in the master's suite, mostly bedding and toilet articles. He found no documents anywhere, nothing that revealed in any way the former owner. A rapid search through the rest of the house proved equally fruitless. If any of the deceased nobleman's possessions remained, he could not distinguish them from those of the governor's household.

Unbarring the front door, he walked out onto the porch. Midway along the path to the gate, the family shrine stood among well-tended trees and flower beds offering a riot of color. Like the house, the building and surrounding garden looked a product of constant care and loving attention.

He plunged down the stairs, hurried along the path to the shrine, and climbed the four steps to the columned entryway. Inside stood the ancestor bust, sitting atop the limestone plinth. Like most such images, the inscription down the front contained no name. Before the bust, blue lilies floated in a low, wide-mouthed bronze bowl, their scent delicate, evasive in the light breeze.

Someone—Amonhotep, Bak thought—had told him that Nebmose had died leaving no living relatives and Djehuty had taken the villa in the name of their sovereign Maatkare Hatshepsut. If no one remained, who was tending this shrine with such devotion? A distant relative, one who should have inherited the property upon Nebmose's death? A forgotten concubine or lover? Or merely a faithful servant?

If a relative had surfaced, he would have had every right

to resent Djehuty's grasping the property as his own. The land and the dwelling, located in crowded Abu, would have been a legacy well worth slaying for, as would the farmland north of the city. Amethu would know. As steward of Djehuty's household, he was responsible for all transactions conducted by the governor. As a long-time resident of Abu, he would have been acquainted with Nebmose and his family.

A sudden thought dampened Bak's enthusiasm for the theory. A long-forgotten relative of Nebmose might slay Djehuty to regain his property, but would he slay five innocent people? Also, what were the odds that those five people would all be bound together by a deadly sandstorm?

He muttered an oath. Nothing ever seemed to fit in a nice, neat package. As he had told Psuro and Kasaya that very morning, something was missing, a crucial fact he had yet to discover.

He eyed the bust, wishing it could speak. It stared back, enigmatic. He had to smile. Whatever secrets it held, it fully intended to keep them to itself.

Bak tracked Amethu down at the mansion of the lord Khnum. He found the steward in the outer, colonnade court, kneeling before the blocky stone image of a nobleman seated with his knees beneath his chin, a scroll spread across them, displaying through eternity his ability to read and write. A long-dead official of Abu, Bak assumed, one of many whose statues occupied the court, left in the expectation that the deceased would forever be remembered and honored. Food, drink, and other good things offered to the lord Khnum were reoffered to these lesser images before the priests took possession for their own use.

Fairly certain the prayer would be brief, Bak backed away, allowing privacy, and left the temple to wait in the shade of the willow trees outside the pylon gate.

Amethu must have seen him in the court, for he soon bustled out, looking to his right and left. "Ah, there you are." Reaching the leafy shelter, he eyed the officer's bandaged upper body and arm, his bruised neck. "I must say, Lieutenant, you don't look at all well."

Bak gave him a wry smile. "So I've been told."

"The one you fought is dead, I hear."

"Unfortunate but true."

Amethu gestured toward a mudbrick bench under the drooping branches. "Do you mind if we talk out here? I can't bear to return so soon to the governor's villa. We've done with the inventory—I thank the lord Khnum—but the atmosphere inside those walls is so oppressive it's hard to breathe."

"The privacy suits me, and the quiet."

The steward brushed leaves off the bench, hiked up his ankle-length kilt, and plopped down. "Ahhhh. Good, clean air, with no stench of fear."

Bak sat down beside him. "I've much compassion for Lieutenant Amonhotep and mistress Khawet, but those in the household banned from the governor's private rooms appear to be functioning in a reasonably normal manner."

"You've made it clear you believe Djehuty's the target of this madman, and it's obvious he agrees. The guards are jumpy—as they should be. The servants, while spending an excess of time whispering among themselves and peering over their shoulders, are carrying on quite well, all things considered. They'd feel better with you and your men in the house, but they know of Khawet's ban."

Bak's voice turned flinty. "Ban or not, we'll be there on the crucial tenth day. I'll not let Djehuty die to satisfy the whim of a dictatorial woman."

Amethu chuckled. "Best you don't call her a tyrant to her face. She prides herself on her kind and considerate manner."

"Don't get me wrong. She has every right to be short-tempered. But at times she seems as irrational as her father—and as stubborn."

"I've never known her to be this difficult." The steward brushed a fly off his bald head. "I've urged her to allow a servant to care for Djehuty while he's ill. She refuses, insisting that no one else can satisfy him. And I've selected a capable and responsible woman who could easily step into Hatnofer's sandals, performing the duties of housekeeper. Again Khawet has refused.''

Bak gave him a sympathetic smile. ''Perhaps when I lay hands on the slayer, your load will be lighter and so will hers.''

''I pray you're right.'' Amethu gave him a sharp look. ''Are you closing on him?''

''Sometimes I feel I'm so close I can almost smell him. At other times, I doubt I'll ever lay hands on him.''

''In other words, you haven't the slightest idea who he is.''

Nettled by so bald an assessment, Bak glared at the river flowing along the base of the terrace. Three small boats raced upstream, their sails swollen with the morning breeze. Across the channel, near where Nenu had died, four women knelt at the water's edge, washing linen and spreading the objects over the bushes to dry.

''Four of the five deaths occurred before I came to Abu,'' he said, waving off a yellow butterfly. ''Can you remember where you were at the time those lives were taken?''

The steward's head snapped around. ''I resent the insinuation, Lieutenant!''

Bak formed the most amiable smile he could manage. ''I've more or less admitted I'm desperate. Will you not humor me?''

''Humph!'' Amethu searched his face. Evidently convinced Bak fully intended to get what he sought, he offered a tight smile. ''Oh, all right! I was in the governor's villa, where I spend all my days. I've no special memory of what I was doing or who I was with except . . .'' He hesitated, cleared a throat that did not need clearing. ''Well, except for the time Lieutenant Dedi was slain. But let me assure you: I've taken no lives.''

''If all were slain by a single man, as I believe, the one accounting will do.''

The steward's eyes fell away; he made a pleat in the skirt

of his kilt and another and another, busying himself with minutiae. "This isn't the easiest tale to tell. You see, in a sense I'm responsible for that young officer's death."

"You?" Bak asked, not sure he understood.

"That morning, I summoned the servant who tends the animals. His accounts were chaotic—his mathematical skills are close to nonexistent—and we spent several hours going over them, sorting them out. When he returned to the stable, he found the young man dead. If I'd not kept him so long . . . Well, you can imagine how I felt. How I still feel."

"Lieutenant Dedi was meant to die, Amethu." Bak laid a sympathetic hand on the steward's wrist. "If you hadn't eased the slayer's path, he'd've found another way."

"So I've told myself."

Bak let the matter rest, aware that words alone could heal no open sore. If Amethu was the man he thought he was, time and a will to forget would soothe his conscience. "What can you tell me of Nebmose, the man who dwelt in the villa next to Djehuty's?"

"Nebmose?" Amethu released the pleats in his kilt and glanced up. "You are reaching far afield, aren't you?"

Bak ignored the jibe. "I walked through the house and grounds this morning and was struck by their value. It occurred to me that Nebmose might've had some distant relative, one whose relationship is unknown to all who dwell in Abu, a man seething with resentment at having his birthright confiscated."

"No, no, no." Amethu shook his head vehemently. "Nebmose had no living relatives, close or distant. That I know for a fact."

"How can you be so sure? I've lain with women I've told no one about. Might not he or his father or his father's father have done the same, creating a child at the time?"

"You don't understand." The steward wiggled around on the bench to face Bak, the better to make sure he got his message across. "Nebmose was his father's only child, and his father was his father's only child, and so it had been for at least six generations. That was their curse. Somewhere in the distant past, the gods had willed that each man in that family would have only one child—one boy. No girls were ever born, no second sons.''

Bak frowned, skeptical.

The steward read the look on his face and turned indignant. ''I knew Nebmose's father well, Lieutenant. We studied together in the scribal school at the governor's villa. And my father knew his, studying with him a generation earlier.''

''I can't believe none of Nebmose's ancestors had concubines.''

''None who conceived, but . . .'' Amethu hesitated, scowled. ''I've heard tales . . . Well, who knows how true they are? They're told in the servants' quarters and enter the homes of respectable men and women through the back door. They say that pretty servant girls in Nebmose's villa have, in past generations, given birth to babies born deformed, sad little creatures fortunate to die within an instant of seeing the light of day.''

Bak found the tale difficult to believe, the curse superstitious nonsense. But the steward, he felt sure, was not a man to pass on information containing no grain of truth. *If only my father were in Abu*, Bak thought; *as a physician, he would know if such a thing were possible.*

A new thought struck. ''You grew to manhood with Nebmose's father?''

Amethu nodded. ''A good man, he was, one I valued as a friend. All who knew him loved and respected him. No malformed babies were born to his servants, I can tell you. His one and only son, Nebmose, was as fine a man as his sire.''

Bak stood up and walked to the edge of the shade, giving himself time to absorb the news. Throughout his stay in Abu, he had assumed Nebmose to be Djehuty's age. Never had he thought him a young man. Walking back to the bench, he asked, ''How old was Nebmose when he died?''

''He'd just celebrated his twentieth year.''

''How long ago?''

Amethu drew his head back, surprised. ''Has no one told

you? He was an officer in the garrison. A lieutenant. One of the many fine young men who died in that frightful sandstorm five years ago. The storm in which you've shown so much interest.''

"By the beard of Amon!" Bak was staggered. He had been looking at that house for eight long days, walking its grounds, taking it for granted. Could he, after so much time, have stumbled upon the right path at last? "Was anyone—anyone at all who toils in the governor's household—related in even the most remote fashion to Nebmose?''

"Simut.'' Amethu spoke as if he could hardly credit Bak's lack of knowledge. "He was Nebmose's uncle.''

Bak eyed the steward warily. Simut's name was the last he had expected to hear, the relationship hard to believe. "Did you not just tell me Nebmose had no relatives?''

Amethu waved off the objection as if of no significance. "Simut was no blood relative and had no right to the property. His wife's sister was wed to Nebmose's father, and she died long before her husband. He didn't tell you? I'm astonished. He thought of the boy as one of his own.''

Bak recalled the chief scribe mentioning a nephew lost in the storm, a youth as close to him as a son. Which might explain the offerings left in Nebmose's family shrine. But would it account for the unusual care given the interior of the house and the garden in which the shrine stood? Bak's thoughts leaped back to the possibility that had occurred to him earlier—a notion he had rejected without due consideration. If that idea had any merit at all, and now he was inclined to think it might, the donor was another individual altogether.

For one thing, Simut could not be the slayer. He had been at the farthest end of the province at the time of Lieutenant Dedi's death, accompanying the tax inspector.

Simut lived in Abu, in a housing block a short walk from the governor's villa. His home was similar to dozens of others Bak had seen in the crowded cities of Kemet, revealing nothing of his lofty position in the province. It was a modest single-story dwelling of five rooms laid out in a square, with an open kitchen at the back that contained a hearth, an oven, and a small conical granary.

The chief scribe spoke with Bak in the reception room, which was larger than the other chambers and whose high roof was supported on a single wooden column painted red. Windows close to the ceiling allowed light to enter and air to circulate. The household gods Bes and Taurt stood in niches along one wall, while a small ancestor bust occupied a third niche.

Simut's short kilt and lack of jewelry testified to his intent to spend the day in the comfort of his own home. "Now that that wretched inventory is complete, I thought to escape for a few hours the cares of my daily task," he explained.

His wife, short and round like her husband and as cheerful as a sparrow, hurried in with open jars of beer and a basket of sweetcakes that smelled of yeast, with bits of dates and raisins peeking through a crusty brown surface. She placed the food and drink on a low woven reed chest between the stools on which the men sat, brought out drinking bowls, and hustled away.

Simut, plucking a cake from the basket, examined his guest's bandages and bruises with an open and curious mien. "From what I hear, Lieutenant, you put on quite a show last night. The tale's already reached near-mythical proportions."

"The men of Swenet and Abu are easily amused." Bak made no attempt to hide his irritation. "I caught my man in spite of them, but I couldn't keep him alive."

"My wife just returned from the market." The scribe handed a drinking bowl to his guest and a jar of beer. "She heard Nenu was the one who took all those lives in the governor's household and he was attempting last night, not for the first time, to slay you. Frankly, I find it difficult to credit him with so many vile deeds. He seemed a lackadaisical sort, one without enough purpose to plan so elaborate a scheme."

"He was a tool, nothing more, one used by the governor to . . ."

Simut gave him a startled look. "You're accusing Djehuty

of murder? Surely he's not responsible for all those deaths!''

"Only for Nenu's attempts to slay me."

"Oh, come now, Lieutenant. Why would he want dead the one man who . . .'' Simut noticed the look of conviction on Bak's face and his voice tailed off. He shook his head, utterly mystified.

Pouring beer into his drinking bowl, Bak admitted, "To be quite honest, I don't know. I suspect he wanted to prevent me from learning the secret he's refused all along to divulge."

"A secret born in that fatal sandstorm five years ago."

"So I believe."

"I wish I could help you, but I know almost nothing of that tempest." Simut took a bite of cake, swallowed it, added, "What little I do know I've told you."

"Have you?" Bak's voice carried an edge of cynicism.

Simut frowned. "What are you implying, Lieutenant?"

Bak set bowl and jar on the table, stood up, and strode to the door. Abruptly he swung around. "You told me of a nephew who died in the storm, a young man you loved as a son. Yet you neglected to mention that he was Nebmose, the man who owned the villa Djehuty claimed for the royal house and took as his own."

"I thought . . .'' The scribe blinked, taken aback by Bak's accusing stance and tone. "Well, I . . . I guess I just assumed you knew."

"You told me you once resented Djehuty for returning alive, but you no longer harbor the feeling. What of Nebmose's villa? That lovely house and outbuildings now sitting idle except for an infrequent lodger. And the farmland north of this city. An estate most men would covet."

Simut gave him a pained look. "I'm satisfied with my lot, Lieutenant."

Bak walked to the niche holding the ancestor bust. A bowl for burning incense stood before the image. Someone had dropped a broken needle into the small mound of cold ashes, indicating a lack of reverence he could not imagine in the individual tending Nebmose's shrine. "Forgive my poor manners, Simut. My time is running out and I'm floundering.''

The scribe acknowledged the apology with a stiff smile. ''If Nebmose had lived, he'd've wed and had a son of his own. As it was, he left no one, nor did he ever document his wishes with respect to his property. Djehuty has no more right to it than I, but at least now it'll go to mistress Khawet and not a stranger.''

Bak tore his eyes from the small, red-painted figure and stared at Simut, barely daring to breathe. The scribe's unmistakable belief that Khawet was entitled to Nebmose's property came close to verifying the suspicion that had been growing in his thoughts all morning. An idea he had gone out of his way to deny but must now face.

Like the young man who had lived in the adjoining villa, Khawet would have been about twenty years of age when the sandstorm occurred. Close in age, thrown together by proximity, similar in their noble heritage, they most likely would have developed a strong bond. A marriage would have been logical, a merging of the two estates.

Though certain he now knew the answer, Bak asked, ''Who's leaving offerings in Nebmose's family shrine?''

''She is. Khawet.''

''And she's caring for the house and garden?''

''She's always kept close watch on the servants who toil there, yes.''

Releasing a long pent-up breath, Bak dropped onto his stool. ''The lord Amon preserve me for being so dense!''

Simut blinked, not understanding.

''I knew she wed Ineni at the age of twenty,'' Bak explained, ''much later in life than most, but I assumed Djehuty held her close. I should've realized by the way she treats her husband that he was second best, that another man took pride of place in her heart. Ineni himself told me so, but I let his words pass over my head as a cloud does.'' His eyes leaped toward Simut. ''Were she and Nebmose wed when he died?''

''The marriage contract had yet to be witnessed and sealed.''

"Why wait so long past marriageable age when they dwelt so close together?" Bak could not keep the growing excitement out of his voice.

Simut, sensing the younger man's agitation, answered with alacrity. "As Nebmose approached manhood, his father sent him to the royal house in Waset to rub shoulders with his equals. Khawet now and again accompanied her father to the capital, and there she and the young man consummated their love. Or so I believe. He entered the service of an envoy to faroff Naharin, and she vowed to await his return. I, for one, thanked the lord Amon when he came back with no other wife, but he was as true to her as she was to him.

"Negotiations had been concluded and the marriage contract prepared when Nebmose's father died. They waited to wed until the period of mourning had passed. Before they could do so, Djehuty summoned his troops, and they marched off to Uahtrest to punish the desert tribesmen. Nebmose never returned, and Khawet wed Ineni instead."

"At Djehuty's insistence," Bak said in a grim voice.

"Ineni knew of her love for Nebmose and wanted to wait. Djehuty issued an ultimatum."

The two men stared at each other, the scribe with a dawning awareness, Bak with growing conviction. Many of the answers he had sought for so long fell into place, even Djehuty's attempts to slay him. The governor had a secret, probably one he was hiding from Khawet, and he had feared Bak would reveal it. Perhaps he had contributed more directly to Nebmose's death than mere negligence as a commander. Khawet had learned that secret—or had a good idea what it was—probably from Hatnofer. She had decided to seek revenge. Djehuty, though a master of self-delusion, had at some point come to suspect his daughter of wishing him dead.

No wonder he was ill. No wonder . . .

"By the beard of Amon!" Bak shot to his feet. "She's with her father now! Giving him herbal broth to soothe his stomach!"

"This is only the ninth day!" Simut was clutching at air

and he knew it. "She wouldn't spoil her pattern now! Would she?"

Bak leaped toward the door. "Go summon a physician. Quickly!"

Racing up the stairs to the second story of the governor's villa, Bak spotted Amonhotep seated, head bowed, hands locked between his knees, on a stool in Djehuty's private reception room. The aide, his face drawn and pinched with worry, looked a perfect picture of dejection and exhaustion.

"Where's mistress Khawet?" Bak demanded.

Amonhotep, too tired to think clearly, failed to notice the urgency in his voice. "Amethu came not long ago, wanting to know of Djehuty's health. She spoke with him briefly. I think they talked of you and of Nebmose's villa and of Nebmose himself."

Bak muttered a curse. When he had spoken with the steward, he had seen no reason to urge silence. Now it was too late. "And then?"

"After Amethu left, she had me take a brazier out on the roof. When I had the fire going, she took the herbs I'd brought from the market, added others she already had, and made a fresh broth. She gave some to her father, which soothed his stomach, and he slept. She then went away, saying she had other tasks to perform."

Bak cursed the aide's innocence, and his own belated realization of the truth. "I must see Djehuty."

"When last I looked, he was sleeping."

Bak strode to the door. "We must awaken him."

"Khawet said sleep is the best medicine a man can have."

"Lieutenant!" Bak barked out the word, gaining the young officer's full attention. "Mistress Khawet is the slayer I've been seeking."

"But . . . But she's Djehuty's daughter!"

"Are you going to sit here in this room, immobilized by disbelief, while he lies dying not twenty paces away?"

With doubt plain on his face, Amonhotep led the way to the governor's bedchamber. To his credit he did not tarry.

The room was dark, with most of the windows covered with reed mats, and smelled strongly of sweat and vomit.

Bak tore down the mats, admitting light, and hurried to the bed. Djehuty lay on his back, covered to the waist with a sheet. His right shoulder and the side of his face were bathed in vomit where he had half turned to throw up. His forehead was beaded with sweat, his pallid body hot to the touch and so wet the sheet clung to him. His breathing was loud and hoarse, the pulse of life in his wrist irregular.

Amonhotep sucked in his breath, horrified. "May the lord Khnum forgive me for being so trusting."

"He's thrown up a lot of the broth. He still may live."

Amonhotep swung around to leave. "I must summon a physician!"

Bak grabbed his arm, stopping his flight. "There's no need. I sent Simut for one the moment I saw the truth."

The aide stared down at the prone man. "Why? Why would she slay her own father?"

Bak, too, stared at Djehuty. He thought the governor one of the least worthy men he had ever known. Nonetheless, he dropped to his knees and offered a fervent prayer to the lord Amon that the man's life would be spared.

Chapter Seventeen

"Where did mistress Khawet go?" Bak demanded.

"I don't know, sir." The guard Kames stood as stiff as a tree, trying hard not to be buffeted by the winds of circumstance. First, his former partner Nenu had been proven untrustworthy, now mistress Khawet. "She didn't tell me. Why should she?" His voice came perilously close to a whine. "I'm only a guard, sir, a fixture of the villa. Kind of like a doorjamb with a spear."

Bak did not know whether to laugh or shake the man. "Did you overhear her say anything when she left?"

"You mustn't blame me for the governor's death, sir." Definitely a whine. "How was I to know she was the slayer?"

"Kames! The governor's not yet dead!" Bak's voice, sharp and fierce, carried across the empty audience hall, gaining a hard edge as it slammed against bare, white walls and the high ceiling. The guard snapped his eyes shut as if he feared a blow.

"What did she say when she left?" Bak repeated.

Kames shook his head. "I don't remember."

"Can you at least tell me which direction she took?"

"Sir?" A plump young servant girl stepped through the door near the governor's dais. "I don't know what mistress Khawet said, sir. She talked to the cook, not me. But I saw her go down to the landingplace and sail north in her husband's skiff."

*   *   *

"She told me she wanted to be by herself for a time."
The cook, a shapeless woman with graying hair, swirled her
flour-dusted hands in a large-mouthed reddish bowl filled
with water and shook off the excess. "Why a woman her
age needs time to herself I'll never know. And her with no
children!"

An older man looked up from the brick hearth, where he
was brushing oil on a half-cooked beef haunch suspended
above the hot coals. "If you had to take care of that old
wretch, you'd need to escape, too."

"She has servants, hasn't she?" Her look of disapproval
changed to one of censure. "You'd best take care who you
call a wretch. You never know who'll go running to him to
pass on the tale. You know how often he orders the lash."

"If the slayer strikes tomorrow . . ." The man sneaked a
glance at Bak. ". . . as the Lieutenant thinks he will, he won't
be able to punish me or anyone else."

"You've no sense of respect, that's your problem."

Bak chose not to enlighten them about Djehuty's health
or why he wished to find Khawet. They would learn soon
enough anyway. "Does she go to any special place when she
wishes to be alone?"

"To Nebmose's villa most often," the cook said. "Sometimes to the tombs of her ancestors, those old sepulchers high
above the river on the west bank."

"I pray we find her at the tombs." Bak shoved the skiff
off and jumped from the landingplace into the stern. "If not,
we'd best go on to Nubt. I doubt she'd add Ineni's concubine
and son to her list of victims, but we must take no chances."

Psuro rowed toward deeper water and a faster current.
"We know for a fact that she wasn't in the governor's compound or Nebmose's villa. We searched them both with due
diligence."

"I don't know why we bothered," Kasaya grumbled.
"The girl said she took the skiff."

"It doesn't do to leave one pebble unturned." Psuro gave

the younger Medjay a condescending look. "How many times do I have to tell you?"

"Why would she take the skiff if she wasn't going to use it?"

Bak scowled at the pair, silencing them. Given free rein, the argument could go on through eternity. Psuro turned his attention to his task. Kasaya sorted through the weapons on the floor of the skiff: their spears and shields and the bow and well-armed quiver Nenu had abandoned on the river-bank. Most of the weapons, Bak suspected, would be of little or no use much of the time. Khawet had had a substantial head start. If she had indeed gone to the ancient tombs, she would be high above them when they approached, with a steep, sandy slope between.

"I know mistress Khawet doesn't have any use for me," Kasaya said, "and I don't like her much either, but I find it hard to believe she'd take five innocent lives."

"She's the last person in the household I'd have suspected." Psuro lifted the oars from the water and frowned. "Are you sure, sir?"

"I don't know exactly what set her off, and I've several other unanswered questions, but I'm certain of her guilt."

Noticing they were drifting into the shallows, Psuro went back to rowing. His effort more than doubled the current's speed, and the small vessel raced headlong downstream toward the lower end of the island of Abu. A traveling ship, its sail aloft and swollen, swept south toward a fleet of fishing boats. Angry shouts from the smaller vessels warned of a seining net about to be breached. A dozen or so pelicans, rare so far south this early in the year, flew low over the water, waiting for the laden net to rise, bringing prey to the surface.

"Before Khawet left," Bak said, "she made sure nothing remained of the stew—I thank the lord Amon. At least she doesn't want anyone else in Abu to die."

Kasaya barked out a laugh. "Isn't it a bit late for her to show concern? How many deaths has she brought about so far?"

"We must never forget that in her own heart she believes she's seen justice done. A vile justice, to my way of thinking, but warranted to her."

"She believes the death of the child Nakht justified?" Psuro shook his head in disgust. "She has to be mad."

Bak could not argue the point.

"There's her skiff!"

Kasaya, who had stood up in the prow as they rounded the northern tip of the island, pointed at a small boat drawn up on the shore of the far bank amid a thicket of tamarisks. A narrow oasis of trees and bushes followed the bend of the river around the base of a tall, steep hill cloaked in sand and crowned with rock. Two terraces girdled the mound midway to the top. Along these high promenades, dark rectangles marked the entrances to ancient houses of eternity carved into the rock. Three lengthy stairways, almost buried in windblown sand, rose from the oasis to the tombs. If others existed, they lay out of sight around the curve of the hill. Bak could see no sign of life, but the distance was great and segments of terrace were concealed behind mounds of debris excavated by ancient tunnelers.

Kasaya, eyeing the extensive golden slope, shook his head in wonder. "Funny place for a woman to go."

"A good place to be alone," Psuro said.

Manning the rudder, Bak eased the skiff through a cluster of partially submerged boulders guarding the tip of the island. He wondered why Khawet had chosen the tombs as her destination. She must have realized after talking with Amethu that he and his Medjays would be hot on her trail. Yet rather than run away in search of freedom, she had sought refuge in the dwellings of her ancestors, a place not easy to reach, but reachable.

"I hope that skiff is hers," he said, "and if so, I hope she didn't abandon it at the river's edge to lead us astray."

The words were like water thrown on a fire, quenching his companions' optimism. Psuro rowed grim-faced and with purpose. Kasaya stared at the distant craft as if willing it to keep its promise that Khawet was close by. Clearing the boulders, Bak swung their vessel diagonally across the current, his eyes on the steep, sandy incline and the terraces above. The deserted boat lay midway along the row of visible tombs, giving no clue as to which of the stairways she might have climbed.

The river whispered beneath their speeding hull. The oars sliced through the water with barely a splash. A fish leaped in front of them and landed with a smack. Gentle swells glistened in the sunlight, reflecting the clear blue sky and the golden slope above the far shore. The hill drew closer, its incline looked steeper, its height more impressive. A falcon soared high in the sky above. The lord Horus, watching, waiting.

As they neared the beached skiff, Kasaya shaded his eyes with a hand to take another, better look. "The vessel is Ineni's," he stated. "See that broad scratch on the hull? It's his alright."

Their prow bumped earth under the water, throwing the young Medjay to his knees, and momentum carried them onto the muddy shore. They leaped out and drew the craft up beside Ineni's. Bak distributed the weapons, giving the bow and quiver to Psuro, a more skilled archer than he or Kasaya. A path invited them into the tamarisk grove. Beyond, a patchwork of garden plots arced around the base of the hill, each plot separated from the others by irrigation channels shaded by palms, tamarisks, and acacias. An ox lowed, drawing their eyes to a faroff field. The creature, led by a small boy, was pulling a plow guided by his father, while another child walked behind, sowing seeds. Nothing else stirred, neither man nor beast, not uncommon at this time of day.

Walking on narrow ridges alongside the ditches, they hurried to the base of an ancient staircase rising up the hill. The slope was smooth, the steps blanketed with untrampled sand. From the water, they had seen two other stairways ascending to the southern end of the burial place. They hastened in that direction, walking one moment on the sand and the next on the cultivated land, sometimes with one foot in each. Insects and reptiles, frightened by their passage, darted beneath boulders that had tumbled from above to lie along the edge of the fields. Fallen giants resting.

Kasaya loped on ahead to the closest of the two stairways. "Someone's climbed up here," he called.

Bak and Psuro hurried to join him. The footprints, shapeless indentations, rose up a long and steep flight of steps covered much of the way with sand. Enough remained bare to see that the ancient staircase consisted of two parallel flights of steps separated by a low ramp up which heavy coffins had been drawn many generations earlier. A knee-high wall set the stairway apart from the hillside.

The three men stared upward. Psuro whistled softly between his teeth. Kasaya muttered something in his own tongue, impossible to understand. Bak stood silent and still, awed by the determination that had driven Khawet to the top. If the prints were hers.

Psuro knelt to examine the indentations. "The breeze hasn't worn away the sharp edges. I'd say they're fresh."

Bak studied the terraces above. He did not like the silence, the utter lack of life. Was Khawet standing somewhere out of sight, determined to fend off any man who approached? Or was she on her knees in some ancestor's house of eternity, making a final offering before she gave herself up? Or had she brought along a vial of poison, meaning to take her own life? He turned around to scan the oasis and added another possibility. Was she even now making her way to the two skiffs drawn up at the water's edge?

"Psuro, you must hurry to the river and set sail, towing mistress Khawet's vessel behind ours. Keep a wary eye on shore. Let no one else set out. I'd not like to be stranded here while she makes her escape."

"But, sir!" The Medjay pointed at the terraces, clearly unhappy with what he considered a lesser assignment. "You might need me up there."

"Your task is as necessary as mine. Go!"

"Yes, sir." Psuro swung around, too quick for Bak to catch his expression, and stalked away.

Bak turned to the younger Medjay, the hard look on his face brooking no argument. "You, Kasaya, will remain here, while I climb up to the terraces and look for her there. If I find her and she attempts to flee, I want you here to snare her."

Kasaya's mouth tightened in objection, but he nodded compliance.

Bak eyed his spear and shield, tempted to leave them behind and go armed with only his dagger. The heavy shield aggravated the ache in his shoulder, both it and the spear would be awkward during the climb, and the latter would be close to useless until he reached the terrace. But he had badly underestimated Khawet before, never once considering her a suspect, and he knew better than to do so again. Resigned to the discomfort, he nodded a curt good-bye to the young Medjay and headed up the stairs on the right side of the center ramp.

He was accustomed to long, steep, and arduous stairways, having climbed many in the fortresses of Wawat. Thinking the effort here no different, he started out fast and confident, treading in the footprints of the one who had gone before him and looking up at his ultimate goal more often than at his feet. A mistake, he learned at the sixth step, one that could have had grave consequences. He took a quick step up, but the stair was not there, the stone broken. His foot came down hard, jarring his teeth, pitching him forward onto a knee.

He growled a curse.

"Are you alright, sir?" Kasaya called.

"Fine." Bak brushed the grit from his skinned flesh and climbed on, his pace slower, his eyes on his feet much of the time, paying more heed to where he placed them.

The staircase was old, treacherous, the steps uneven and broken, and at times inconsistent in height. Buried in sand as they were, hidden from view, he stubbed his toes, stumbled on shattered stones that rocked beneath his weight, and stepped into holes of varying depths. The windblown sand was slippery, flowing downhill at the slightest disturbance, threatening to carry him with it. No longer trusting the earlier footprints, he began to probe the steps with the spear, using the butt end to locate irregularities.

The higher he climbed, the more conscious he became of the long way down to the bottom. With the sand as slippery as wet river mud, the gradient steep, and the hill denuded of outcrops, offering nothing to grab hold of, he could imagine himself sliding, falling, tumbling head over heels like a ball, coming to rest at Kasaya's feet, looking the fool. Worse, he might break an arm, a leg, his back.

Shaking off the thought, he plodded on, dogged in his determination. His leg muscles tightened, prelude to a cramp. Pain nagged his shoulder. The sun beat down, heating the sand beneath his feet. Sweat beaded on his forehead and rivulets flowed down his chest. He passed the halfway point, neared the three-quarter mark. Why, he wondered, had he not had the good sense to send Kasaya on this infernal mission?

Without warning, a rumbling sounded above him. His eyes, which had been locked on the next step, snapped upward. A boulder, poised on the upper edge of the stairway, pitched forward. Kasaya yelled, his words meaningless in the instant of shock. The heavy stone landed on a lower step, bounced, struck another step, bounced a second time. Another bounce and it would be upon him.

With no time to think, barely time to react, Bak leaped to the side, hurdling the low stone wall, and landed in the sand beside the staircase. Immediately he began to slide downhill. His feet skidded out from under him, the spear flew from his hand, and he fell on a hip. Khawet, he was sure. She had shoved the boulder off the terrace. She had meant him to die. Anger struck him and with it a rock-hard determination not to give her the satisfaction.

Aware he risked tearing his flesh to shreds, he shifted the shield from left hand to right, held it hard against his side, and flung himself toward the low wall. His sandal skidded along the stones, and the shield bumped the rough surface, making it hard to hold. Digging the heel of his other foot into the sand, using it as both brake and rudder, he brought his downhill plunge under control. Much sooner than he dared hope, he mercifully stopped.

Catching his breath and at the same time scrambling to his knees, he looked upward. Khawet stood at the top of the staircase, watching him. Slowly, deliberately, she raised a sling and lobbed a stone at him. Snarling an oath, he swung the shield up, deflecting the missile. When next he looked, she was gone.

Holding the cowhide barrier before him, he rose to his feet and took a hasty glance around, evaluating his position. He stood about halfway up the stairs, out in the open with no available shelter and the enemy above. The boulder had lodged between two others at the edge of a field of young melon plants. His spear lay at the bottom of the steps, its point glinting in the sun.

"Are you alright, sir?" Kasaya, heading upward as fast as the damaged steps would allow.

"I'm fine. Now get off those stairs! If Khawet descends this hill by another route, I want you in a position to cut her off."

"Yes, sir." The Medjay lowered his head and plodded down, sulking, Bak suspected.

Preferring to keep his dagger hand free, Bak switched the shield back to his left hand, reviving the ache in his shoulder. He stepped over the low wall and, muttering a quick prayer to the lord Amon, headed up the stairway once again. The smudged sand marking the boulder's path impressed upon him how important it was that he keep a wary eye on the terrace as well as watch his feet. In spite of the added caution, his divided attention, he climbed steadily.

He passed the highest point he had reached before. As if she had been monitoring his progress, Khawet appeared above, sling loaded, pouch of rocks slung over her shoulder.

He wondered if she had set that spot as his upper limit and planned not to allow him to advance beyond.

She stood in the open, taunting his inability to get at her, and hurled a rock at him. He swung the shield up. The missile struck hard, jolting his arm, setting his shoulder afire, and dropped into the sand at his feet. He tried to scoop it up, thinking to hurl it back, but the stone rolled away to the next lower step. She shot off another rock and another and another, launching them as fast and hard as she could, casting the missiles with uncommon accuracy and a rare strength for a woman.

Unable to retaliate, refusing to retreat, he trod on up the stairs, parrying the stones with his shield, thinking to unnerve her with a steady pace. The sling could be a deadly weapon in the hands of an experienced warrior. As Khawet was proving herself to be.

Suddenly she turned and darted north along the terrace. He was surprised to see how close he was to the top, with only seven or eight more steps to climb. She must have emptied her pouch of stones. Or had she chosen to run rather than face him, fearing his greater strength and weight? He staved off the temptation to race upward, risking a fall, and continued to climb with as much care as before. Never once did he let down his guard lest she return with another, deadlier weapon. Seeing nothing, hearing no sound, he stepped onto the terrace. There he found the lever she had used to shift the heavy boulder. Other than that, no sign of her remained.

The slope of the hill had been cut away, he saw, providing a vertical surface for the facades of a lengthy row of tombs dug deep into the rock. A broad walkway edged with a knee-high parapet followed the curve of the hill, offering a comfortable approach to these houses of eternity. He eyed the line of entryways, wondering which, if any, sheltered Khawet. Certainly not the two atop the southern staircases, for he had seen her run away from them. He scowled at the gaping portals, black rectangles that warned of the depth of darkness inside. How was he to find her without a torch?

He strode north along the sunlit terrace, peering into tombs whose doors had long ago vanished and whose contents had been desecrated and robbed, passing others whose entrances were blocked by stone or brick walls that looked untouched but had probably been defiled like the rest. On mounds of debris before several entrances, he saw fragments of bone and linen and wood, the residue of ancient robberies. These sepulchers, he assumed, were very old, dating to a time when Abu stood on the threshold of the frontier and Wawat was a place to explore and conquer, not settle and exploit as at present.

If he remembered accurately an early conversation with Djehuty, when the governor had laid claim to a long and esteemed ancestry, he had spoken of a direct line as far back as Kheperkare Senwosret, who had ruled many generations after these early kings. True, the governor had spoken with longing of a more ancient lineage, but even he had not dared press the claim as fact.

Bak had no idea what Khawet's purpose was in coming to this burial place, but if she took her heritage as seriously as Djehuty did, she would waste no time in the older tombs. She would go to the one closest to her heart.

Beyond an entrance half buried in windblown sand, he approached a trio of open portals. The faint odor of incense teased his nostrils, then drifted away. Every sense suddenly alert, he crept to the nearest and peered down a short, narrow passage. A shaft of light, vague and indistinct, reached from the depths of the tomb toward the entry to blend with the faint illumination from outside. The smell of incense was stronger here, wafting out through the portal.

Bak slipped his dagger from its sheath, took a deep but quiet breath, and sidled through the passage, keeping his back to the wall. At the end, he peeked into a rectangular chamber, its ceiling supported by six square columns. Nothing stirred in the near-dark hall. A few silent steps took him to a handsome granite offering table laden with a braised pigeon, onions, cucumbers, and dates, along with a bouquet of white lilies and a pottery bowl holding the burning in-

cense. The perfumed smoke was cloying, overwhelming the
sweeter odor of the flowers and the tantalizing scent of the
bird.

The vague light drew him up a low flight of steps at the
rear of the hall and into a corridor where six niches, three
on either side, framed rock-cut, painted figures of the deceased as one with Osiris, the lord of the netherworld. In the
gloom, deep shadows hovered around the dark, shrouded figures. They and the heavy smell of incense made the corridor
seem a passageway to death. Bak crept along on silent feet,
chilled by the thought.

He paused at the end of the corridor, where the light was
brighter. In the chamber ahead, he heard the faint whisper
of a burning torch and sensed the presence of another individual. Khawet, he felt sure. Dagger in hand, he held the
shield before him and took a cautious step forward. He found
himself in a room too small for the four square columns that
provided surfaces for drawings of the deceased, figures illuminated by the leaping flame of a torch. Khawet stepped
into view at the rear, holding the light aloft, her back to a
niche containing lightly carved paintings of a man and his
family, her ancestors Bak assumed.

"Stay where you are, Lieutenant. I'll not let you lay hands
on me." The long-handled torch, the kind carried by town
guards assigned to night patrol, burned close to the ceiling.
The angle of light turned the planes of her face hard and
unyielding, matching her voice.

"You can't escape, mistress Khawet."

"I've done nothing worthy of condemnation. I've simply
been a tool of the lady Maat, balancing the scales of justice."
Her smile turned smug, irritating. "As you are."

"I've not spent the past days tracking you down only to
let you slip through my fingers."

"You've earned a reward of sorts, that I concede." Her
eyes flashed determination. "But you'll not have it at my
expense."

He stepped forward, between the first pair of columns. She
swung the torch down, pointing the flame along the central

aisle, holding him off. He had to overpower her, but how? The chamber was so small and the columns were so large, there was not much room to maneuver. Even his spear would have been impossible to use in so confined a space.

"Nor will you reach your goal," he said, taunting her. "Your father still lives." Maybe.

She blinked, taken aback, but not for long. "I gave him twice the amount of poison needed to slay a man. He'll not survive the day."

He took a short and careful step forward. She thrust the flame toward him, forcing him back.

"What did he do to make you hate him so?" he asked. "Why slay all the others as well?"

"Oh, come now, Lieutenant! You spent all morning questioning Amethu and Simut. Don't try to convince me you don't know Nebmose was my beloved, my betrothed. The one man who touched me as no other will."

The torch, as long as Khawet's arm, could not be easy to hold, thrust out the way it was. She was a strong woman—her use of the sling had proven that—but how long could she continue to grasp the thing at such an ungainly angle?

"I know of your feelings for him, yes, and I know he was one of the many who failed to return from that deadly sandstorm five years ago."

"Do you also know that some men survived at the expense of others? They found a safe haven and turned away all who wished to share their good fortune."

"I heard a tale, yes." Bak spoke with care, refusing to admit a man still lived who had sheltered in that haven. Khawet had followed her pattern slavishly—until today. He had no wish to sacrifice User should she somehow manage to escape and go after the one man she had missed in her reign of vengeance.

"They turned Nebmose away," she said bitterly, "forcing him to go on in the face of the storm."

Bak stepped forward once more. As before, she thrust the torch toward him, forcing him back. If she had been holding him at bay with any ordinary weapon, a spear, for example, he would have grabbed it and twisted it from her hand, but not this fiery standard.

"How do you know this?" he demanded. "Did Sergeant Senmut tell Sergeant Min, who confided in mistress Hatnofer?"

She bowed her head, acknowledging the guess. "Senmut was born a braggart, and Min could keep nothing from Hatnofer."

"Your father found shelter somewhere else," he pointed out, "not with Senmut and the others."

"He and Min did, yes. And they found a donkey laden with food and water." She paused, added with a sneer, "Enough to sustain three men with ease."

"Nebmose came upon them," Bak guessed, "and did they also turn him away?"

"The shelter they'd found was small, an overhanging boulder with a ridge of sand in front, forming an alcove. Min refused to put the donkey out, refused to make space for Nebmose. According to Hatnofer, he laughed, saying a dumb beast was of more value than a lieutenant. They fought. Min, much the stronger of the two, felled Nebmose and . . ." Her voice wavered. "And my father thrust a knife in his back."

Bak was not surprised by the gravity of Djehuty's offense, only by its pointlessness. A man afraid to die, slaying one who was already down. And him a nobleman. No wonder the governor had refused to divulge his secret. The tale showed him up for what he was: a coward and a murderer, unworthy to sit in a seat of power. One who should have been taken before the vizier and been made to account for his crime. Or crimes.

No wonder he had closed Nebmose's house to all but temporary guests. No wonder he had ordered Ineni to move the horses to the estate in Nubt. Both dwelling and animals must have mocked him, reminding him always of his weak and despicable behavior. The house, he had made into a lifeless shell. The horses, long out of sight and deliberately forgotten, he had ordered traded away when Bak began asking questions.

"Min vanished from Abu five years ago," he said. "Hatnofer surely knew all along what he and your father did. Why did you wait until now to seek retribution?"

"She'd vowed not to say a word, and she didn't. Even when Min failed to summon her to his new post, breaking her heart, she kept her word." A humorless smile touched her lips. "Until one day, about two months ago." The smile grew to a soft, cynical laugh. "That's when she and my father quarreled. He burst out with the truth, taunting her, admitting he and Min had argued and the sergeant had fallen into the water gauge, where he cracked his head open and died."

"What really happened? Did Min demand a reward for his silence, and Djehuty could see no end to the levy?"

"So Hatnofer believed." Khawet raised the heavy torch, bending her arm at the elbow for relief. "She was convinced he slew Min to get him out of the way for good, and she was too angry to remain silent. So she came to me with the tale. I could've slain my father then and there—I wanted to—but I wanted more to make him suffer. So I thought of a way, the patterns you were so quick to see."

Bak noted the sign of weariness. He took a quick step forward, forcing her again to thrust out the torch. As she expected him to, he backed off, but less than half the distance he had shifted forward. "What if Djehuty had failed to see your purpose?"

"My father's not a stupid man, Lieutenant. He saw." She sneered. "He pretended he didn't, but he did."

"Why slay Hatnofer?" He inched forward, stopped. "Was she not your ally?"

"Was I to place myself in her hands as my father had put himself in Min's?" Her laugh was sharp, hard. "No. Nor did I initially intend to slay her. She'd served my family well, and I was rather fond of her. But she guessed what I was up to, and she had to die. Fortunately, the timing was good and her death fitted into the pattern."

He took a slow, careful step forward. "If you hadn't slain

her, who would've died in her place? Lieutenant Amonhotep?''

''He did no wrong.'' She spoke as if she could hardly credit Bak with so ridiculous a question. ''He, too, would've been turned away to die in the storm if he'd followed Nebmose's path.'' She formed a cruel smile. ''No, I planned to slay my father next.''

Bak gave her a surprised look. ''You would've taken his life the day I arrived?''

''Why not? You were new to Abu, a frontier policeman. A man praised by the vizier for stumbling upon a smuggling operation. One of limited imagination and skill.'' She gave an ironic laugh. ''Or so I thought.''

''That's why you left those unwanted gifts on my doorstep?''

''By then, you'd spotted the patterns to the slayings and I no longer underestimated you.'' A smile flitted across her face. ''I wasn't sure I could frighten you off, but I thought it worth a try. And I wished also to tease you.''

He thought her arm trembled, but so slightly he could not be sure. He took another slow step forward. ''You must've been disappointed when we moved to Swenet. Or had you delivered all your messages?''

''I thought one more after my father's death, his baton of office perhaps.'' Her voice turned cool, no longer playful. ''Now you've forced my hand a day early, making me act out of necessity, not according to plan.''

''With us so close behind, why did you take the time to come here?''

''I wanted to make one last offering to Sarenput, to seek his aid should I live or die.''

''Why take so great a risk? I see by the inscriptions that he's not the ancestor your father so greatly values, that he lived a generation or so later.''

''During the reign of Nubkaure Amonemhet,'' she said with a nod. ''This man and his wife were Nebmose's ancestors as well as mine. My betrothed and I were of the same blood, you see, destined to be together through eternity.''

Bak realized she did not care if she lived or died. If she could get away free and clear, she would do so, but death was equally acceptable. "You surely don't expect to join your beloved in the Field of Reeds after all you've done to tilt the scales of justice."

Her eyes flashed anger. "I've punished where punishment was due, Lieutenant, balancing the scales, not tilting them."

Seeing her distracted, he leaped forward, swinging his shield, thrusting aside the torch. Her hand struck the pillar to her right, the fiery staff sent sparks racing up the painted figure of Sarenput. Fire licked the cowhide shield, singeing the hair, giving off an odor sharper than the incense. Bak lunged at her, going in low, thinking to shove her into the niche at the back of the chamber, where she would have no space to move. As agile as a cat, she freed the torch, ducked away from the niche, and slipped behind the nearest column.

"Leave me in peace, Lieutenant. I've slain no one who didn't deserve to die. What purpose will it serve to stand me before . . ." She gave him an ironic smile. "Before who? My father metes out justice in this province, and he's a dead man."

Bak had had enough. Her conviction that she had done no wrong was an abomination. "Did the child Nakht deserve death? Or Lieutenant Dedi?" He snorted, making his contempt clear, hoping to goad her into a rash act. "Both were innocent of Nebmose's death, probably had no idea how he died. You slew the boy because he was easy prey, the officer because you didn't have to stand up to him. The horse took his life for you."

Incensed by his disparagement, she leaped out from behind the pillar, raised the torch high, and swung it at his head. Fire spewed. He parried the blow with the shield and lunged at her. She ducked around the next column and darted into the niche-lined corridor. Sparks flew behind her racing figure, tiny stars pricking the swathed images of Osiris. Bak chased after her, dagger in hand. He had never used a weapon to fell a woman and was not sure he could bring himself to do so. A weakness he had no intention of letting her know.

He caught up in the larger columned court. As he was about to grab her, she swung around, the flame traveling with her in an arc. He ducked back, narrowly missed being scorched, the heat so close he felt it pass his face. She stood in the central aisle, her back to the exit, holding the torch toward him as before, keeping him at a distance. Her breathing was quick, harsh, her smile tight. He stood facing her, close enough to pose a threat, far enough to leap away, his body shielded, dagger poised for use. His weapon was the more deadly of the two, but hers allowed a longer reach. If only he had his spear! It would make all the difference.

They stood there for some time, catching their breath, each seeking an edge over the other, neither able to find a breach in the enemy's defense.

Determined to break the stalemate, Bak displayed the dagger, letting the light play on its blade, and took a step toward her. She thrust the flame his way. Teeth clenched tight with determination, he took another step forward. Feinting a thrust at his head, she lunged off to the side, slipped the torch past the shield, and brought it down hard on his hand. He ducked too late. Fire seared his fingers. The dagger flew into the shadows.

Driven by a sudden look of exultation on Khawet's face, Bak leaped at her, swinging the shield to shove the torch aside, and grabbed the arm holding the fiery brand. They struggled for possession. She clung as if her life depended on it—as it did. He squeezed her wrist, felt her fingers give, and jerked the torch away. He swung her around with her back to him, meaning to shove her arm high up between her shoulder blades. She twisted free and ran.

He raced after her, no more than two steps behind. She cleared the last pair of pillars and darted into the entrance passage. He grabbed for her, felt her linen shift beneath his fingers, but she was too far ahead to catch. She darted out onto the sunlit terrace. He followed her through the passage, raced into the light, lost much of his vision. Flinging the shield to his left, the torch to his right, he leaped at her in a flying tackle. His arms went around her waist, his momentum carried them forward. He glimpsed something passing beneath them—the low wall along the terrace. Khawet screamed, and they fell forward.

He released her, giving them both the freedom to save themselves, and tumbled into the sand beyond the wall. He struck with a good solid thump that jarred his shoulder. The steep slope grabbed him; the loose, slippery sand carried him down. Face forward, chest in the sand, he slid out of control toward the base of the hill. *Like a sledge,* he thought, *broken loose and hurtling unrestrained.*

He remembered the boulders below, pictured himself ending his flight against one, bones broken, body battered. Keeping mouth and eyes tightly shut, he flailed out with his arms and legs, trying to slow himself and turn over. The bandages peeled off his torso and arm, the sand dislodged the fresh scab from the wound on his side, his skin burned. Grit collected in his hair and burrowed beneath his kilt. With a mighty heave, he rolled over onto his back and swung his body around, feet formost. He half sat up, saw a boulder not far ahead, dug in his elbows and heels. His speed began to drop.

He smashed into the boulder feetfirst. One knee came up hard under his chin, making his head spin, his world turn dark.

"Lieutenant Bak! Sir! Are you alright?"

He came to his senses flat on his back, his legs buckled up between him and the boulder. Opening scratchy eyes, he looked in the direction from which the voice had come. Kasaya was half running, half sliding diagonally down the slope. The tracks he left behind came from midway up the staircase Bak had climbed, betraying the Medjay's failure to obey orders.

Bak's thoughts flew to the terrace, the plunge over the parapet, the prisoner he had caught and released. Khawet! Where was she? Slowly, carefully, straightening his legs one at a time, checking for breaks and finding none, he pushed himself away from the boulder and hauled himself into a sitting position. She lay a few paces to his right, partly on her side, facing away, unmoving. She must have struck a boulder even harder than he.

"Sir!" With barely a glance at Khawet, Kasaya dropped shield and weapons in the sand and knelt beside Bak. He stared at the bedraggled bandage, the newly reopened and bleeding wound, the burned hand, the skin scraped red and raw. His face clouded over. "Do you think . . . Can you stand up, sir? Can you walk?"

Bak formed a crooked smile. "It's not as bad as it looks, Kasaya. Help me up and let's see to mistress Khawet."

The big Medjay offered an arm and, as gentle as if he held a new-hatched duckling, lifted his superior to his feet. Bak stood quite still, letting a wave of dizziness pass, while Kasaya picked up the shield and two spears.

He offered one of the weapons to Bak. "Your spear, sir."

Bak stared, taken aback. "This is the reason you climbed the stairs?"

"I know you told me not to go up there, sir, but . . ." Kasaya shifted his feet, flushed. "I thought you might need it."

Bak bit back a laugh. Of all the understatements he had heard, that was the best—or worst.

They walked to the woman crumpled on the sand and knelt beside her. Bak knew the instant he saw the pallor of her face that she was badly injured. He took her shoulder, damp from exertion and gritty from the tumble downhill, and rolled her onto her back, taking care not to hurt her further. Her body was limp, her head lying at an impossible angle. He felt for the pulse of life, found none. She was dead, her neck broken.

Chapter Eighteen

What a waste, Bak thought, his eyes on the prone form lying in the bottom of the skiff. The body was covered with a length of rough linen the farmer had given them in exchange for a spear. *Who shoulders more blame?* he wondered. *Djehuty for stealing away all she held dear? Or Khawet because she would not accept Ineni and leave her father's house for a new life, as was right and proper?*

"Do you think the governor still lives?" Psuro asked.

Bak shrugged. "The physician said he stood on the brink of the netherworld." He glanced to the west, where the lord Re was clinging to the day, his golden orb hovering above the row of tawny, sand-draped hills that overlooked Abu, including the hill that had taken Khawet's life. "By now, the gods will surely have decided his fate."

Kasaya adjusted the braces, spilling much of the breeze from the sail, slowing the vessel's approach to the landing-place below the governor's villa. "I'd not like to go home to Buhen thinking we failed in our mission and let him die, but would it not be easier than taking him to Waset to stand before the vizier and seeing him die anyway, accused as a slayer?"

"You echo my thoughts, Kasaya."

Bak's father resided on a small estate across the river from Waset, and he longed to see him again, but the thought of drawing attention to himself so close to the royal house did not appeal. Their sovereign, Maatkare Hatshepsut, had exiled

277

him to the southern frontier and had hopefully forgotten him. He preferred not to revive her memory. Buhen was now his home, where he took pride in standing at the head of his Medjays and enjoyed nothing more than talking with his friends, sharing a jar of beer, a joke. Especially with Imsiba and Nebwa and Nofery and . . .

"It's not unheard of for a man recovering from a serious illness to have a relapse." Psuro sneaked a look at Bak. "If we find him alive, I could stand guard tonight. Make sure he's not disturbed. Who knows? Perhaps when the sun rises, he'll have joined Khawet in the netherworld." He grinned. "A fate they both deserve through eternity."

Bak was sorely tempted, but could in no way justify the very crime he had come to prevent. "The thought appeals, Psuro, but no. And that's an order. No!"

"Yes, sir," the Medjay said, unabashed.

Kasaya whistled. "Look, sir." He pointed upstream toward an imposing warship maneuvering around the southern end of the island, passing with the utmost care among rocky islets and sunken boulders. The sail was lowered and over three dozen oarsmen were controlling the vessel in the treacherous waters. The pilot, a local man, stood at the prow beside the captain, calling out orders, while the helmsman tended the rudder. The drummer, silenced at so crucial a time, stood poised above his instrument, ready to respond the instant a need arose.

Bak recognized the symbol on the prow, the lord Montu, god of war, and the colorful pennants flying on the mast. The vessel was the fastest between Abu and Buhen, cutting two and sometimes three days off the nine- or ten-day voyage. His sense of accomplishment fled like a wary gazelle.

"It's the viceroy's flagship. What's he doing here?" Inebny, viceroy of Wawat and Kush, the most powerful man south of the land of Kemet, second only to the vizier in importance.

Psuro muttered an oath. "And us with the governor dead or dying and his daughter gone as well."

"They must've just come down through the rapids." Kasaya, who loved ships, was too excited to notice their distress. "I've never trod the deck of so grand a vessel. Do you suppose they'll let me aboard?"

"Did Djehuty summon him, I wonder?" Bak asked Psuro. "He threatened often enough to register a complaint, seeking our dismissal from the villa."

Psuro's expression was grim. "Let's hope he didn't paint too black a picture."

In spite of Khawet's many offenses against the lady Maat, Bak did not wish to move her body from the skiff to the governor's villa without due respect. He sent Psuro off to the garrison to report her death to Troop Captain Antef, the highest ranking officer in Abu, and to get a litter on which they could carry her like the lady she once had been. Kasaya he ordered to remain at the skiff with the body. Knowing how fond Antef was of Khawet, Bak regretted not bearing the news himself, but the viceroy's arrival forced him to go first to learn Djehuty's fate.

Bak eyed the ragged bandages Psuro had rewrapped around his torso and arm, the scratches and scrapes on body and arms and legs, his burned hand. He had bathed in the river and cleansed the injuries as best he could before leaving the west bank, but still he looked like a refugee from a battlefield, one whose army had lost the war. The last thing he wanted was to stand before the viceroy—or anyone else, for that matter—in such a disreputable state, but what choice did he have? The official would come to the governor's villa, whether or not Djehuty had summoned him. And he would demand an accounting.

Thinking he might at least have time to change the bandages, Bak hurried up the steps from the landingplace. As he strode past the gatehouse, the sentry on duty shot to attention and gaped. Bak ignored him and walked on, passing the family shrine on his way to the front door. If he had paid more attention to this small structure and to Nebmose's shrine, the tale he had to tell the viceroy would be ending in a different way. Or would it? Had the gods ordained

Khawet's demise, with him as their instrument of death, long before either had ever heard of the other?

Hurrying on to the house, he went inside and hastened across the entry hall. He raised his hands to shove open the double doors to the audience hall. They flew back before he could touch them, opened from the other side. Imsiba stood there facing him, as amazed to see him as he was to see the big Medjay. Beyond the sergeant's shoulder, Bak saw Commandant Thuty standing in front of the empty dais, eyes on the doorway, a smile spreading across his face.

"Imsiba! What are you doing here?"

"My friend!" The Medjay clutched his upper arms in greeting. "We've come to help you snare the slayer you seek."

"How long have you been in Abu?" Bak wiped tears of laughter from his eyes and stifled a new wave that threatened to overwhelm him. Imsiba and Thuty must think him demented.

"We've just arrived." Thuty scanned the empty room and his brows drew together in irritation. "Where is everyone?" he demanded. "I know the day's drawing to a close, but doesn't the governor post guards? Doesn't he have scribes documenting the results of the day's audience? Doesn't he have an aide to see each task done properly?" His eyes settled on Bak. "And what, for the lord Amon's sake, happened to you?"

Bak suddenly remembered the warship. "Is the viceroy here?"

"Not yet. He stayed with his vessel while they brought it down the rapids, as any worthy official would. We came by skiff, thinking a smaller craft faster." Thuty flashed him a sharp look. "Why? What's wrong?"

"The last I saw of Djehuty, he'd been poisoned. A physician was with him, trying to save him."

"So the slayer struck again! Made a victim of the governor himself!" Thuty struck a column with his fist. "I feared we'd get here too late."

"Governor Djehuty lives." Lieutenant Amonhotep stood at the door by the dais. His face was wan and drawn, with dark circles beneath red-rimmed eyes, emphasizing his exhaustion and the strain he had suffered. "He's asleep now, resting. The physician thinks he'll recover."

Bak offered a silent prayer of gratitude to the lord Amon. If nothing else, he had accomplished his goal.

"What of Khawet, Bak?" The aide, who must have learned the truth from Amethu or Simut, hesitated, then his voice dropped to a near whisper. "He was asking for her."

Bak laid a hand on the young man's shoulder and urged him to sit on the edge of the dais. He dropped down beside him, lowered his face into his hands, and rubbed his forehead. He felt as worn out as Amonhotep looked, as weighted down by circumstances. Aware the telling would get no easier with the passage of time, he looked up at Thuty and Imsiba. "You'd best sit, both of you. I've a tale to tell."

The sun had vanished behind the western hills, leaving the sky bright with afterglow. Bak, finished with his recital, sat on a stool outside the rear door of Nebmose's villa, where the light was better than indoors. The physician, a stern man in his late thirties, who wore a linen headcloth to cover his baldness, occupied a second stool, facing the reopened cut on Bak's side. A jar of oil, a bowl containing a greenish salve that smelled strongly of fleabane, and a roll of linen lay within arm's reach, sharing the bench with Commandant Thuty and Imsiba.

"Now tell me how you happen to be here," Bak said.

Thuty, disgruntled at learning how tardy his arrival had been, gave a cynical snort. "The day after you left, Inebny sailed into Buhen. He'd been summoned to Waset to report to our sovereign, Maatkare Hatshepsut, on trade and tribute passing north through Wawat. As I'm responsible for all traffic through the Belly of Stones, he wanted my thoughts before he left. When we finished with that, we discussed your mission. I told him what Lieutenant Amonhotep had said, and Nebwa repeated all Nofery had recalled about the governor as a youth."

"She didn't say much." Bak wove his fingers together on top of his head, keeping his arms high so the physician could place a fresh poultice on his side. "Only that he was headstrong and foolish, as are many youths born into noble families."

The physician tut-tutted. Whether he disapproved of so irreverent an attitude toward the nobility or Bak's failure to sit still was impossible to know.

"Troubled by what we told him, he asked to see Nofery. We summoned her, and they talked. One recollection led to another, and together they remembered Djehuty losing a company of men in a desert tempest."

"Nofery said nothing to me of the storm." Bak scowled. "If she had, my task would've been easier."

Imsiba hastened to her defense. "She'd heard the tale, as you yourself had, but, like you, was never told the name of the man responsible."

"I didn't like anything they had to say about Djehuty. He sounded a first-class swine." Thuty glared at the physician, daring him to register an objection. "Inebny agreed. As he had to go to Waset anyway, I thought to sail as far as Abu with him—and bring Imsiba along." His voice turned wry. "I thought you might need the weight of my authority."

"Where's Lieutenant Amonhotep?" Thuty asked, glancing into the governor's private reception room.

"The physician ordered him to sleep." Bak walked on down the poorly lit hall toward Djehuty's bedchamber. "I suspect he gave him a potion, thinking only a drug could keep him away from what he considers his duty."

The viceroy Inebny, a slender man of medium height with a prominent nose and large ears, smiled. "The aide sounds a man conscientious to a fault."

Ineni burst through the door ahead. Looking neither right or left, he strode swiftly past, giving no indication he saw them. He reached the stairs and raced down, vanishing from sight. Bak could not imagine what Djehuty had said to his adopted son, but whatever it was, it had to have been unpleasant.

Leading the way through the door, mouth tight, chin jutting, Bak was prepared for anything—or so he believed.

The bedchamber seemed a different place since last he had seen it. The soiled bedding had been taken away and replaced with a fresh sleeping pallet and sheets that smelled of sunlight and fresh air. The wilting lilies were gone, along with their heavy, sweet scent. In their place, a bowl of dried flowers gave off a more subtle and pleasing odor. The morning light was soft and delicate, filtered through thin linen hangings a servant had placed over the high windows.

"Khawet, my Khawet." Djehuty's voice was feeble, querulous. "Such a nice, agreeable child. Where is she?"

The viceroy exchanged a glance with Thuty and stepped forward. After hearing Bak's tale, he had decided that he should face the governor, presenting the news of Khawet's death and the accusation of murder.

The physician reached out a hand to halt his approach and shook his head, signaling for silence.

"Where has she gone?" Djehuty, his shoulders propped high on spotless white pillows, patted the sleeping pallet next to his thigh. "I want her here beside me."

Bak stared at the governor, startled by the change in him. He had been thin before but now was skeletal, and his pallor had a grayish cast. His eyes, black and glittering, looked as if they had sunk into his skull. He had aged twenty years. No wonder Ineni had rushed from the room, giving no word of greeting. Whether or not he loved his father, the shock must have been great.

"Where is she?" Djehuty peered around the room. His eyes seemed unable to stay in one place for long, as if he had trouble focusing. "Why is she always somewhere else when I need her at my side?"

Tut-tutting in place of words, the physician took the governor's hand in his and patted the long, bony fingers.

Djehuty jerked his hand away and glared at the man, like

a child offended by a touch. "Did she go out to play?" he asked, his eyes darting around, alighting on nothing. "Or did Hatnofer take her to the market? I hope she's holding her hand. Little girls should never wander around alone. It's unseemly."

Inebny sucked in his breath, startled. Thuty muttered a few words Bak could barely hear, possibly a spell to ward off the demon that had invaded the governor's heart.

Recognizing a second, more dire reason for Ineni's distress, Bak moved up behind the physician. "Is he always like this?" he whispered.

"What was that?" Djehuty demanded, turning waspish. "What'd you say? Don't whisper in front of me, young man. I don't like it."

"I asked if you're well, sir."

"I'm hungry, that's all. Haven't eaten in . . ." Djehuty's voice tailed off and he tilted his head to peer at Bak. "Who are you? What are you doing in my bedchamber?"

Bak found himself at a loss for words. How does one respond to a grown man whose thoughts have carried him into another realm? He queried the physician with a glance, got a shrug in return. The man was no help at all.

"Well?" Djehuty snapped. "Who are you? Answer my question, young man, or I'll have my father send you to the desert mines. He's governor of this province, you know."

"I'm a servant, sir, new to your household." The less important he made himself out to be, he hoped, the sooner Djehuty would accept him. Or, better yet, forget him.

"Go away." Djehuty flicked his long fingers, signaling Bak out the door. "Go find Khawet. I need her. Now!" He glanced toward the viceroy and the commandant. "You go with him. Both of you." His eyes began to wander. "Servants! Bah! Useless creatures, all of them." He looked down at the sheet covering him and frowned. He pulled the crumpled fabric one way and another, stretched it, patted it, trying to smooth out the wrinkles. He seemed unaware of their departure.

*   *   *

"How long has he been like this?" Bak asked.

"I wasn't certain when first he awakened from the poison-induced sleep." The physician rubbed his eyes, as if wearied by a failure he could in no way have prevented. "I thought I might cure him. I hoped to, but . . . Well, as you can see, no potions I could give him, no spells to frighten away the demons, no prayers to the gods would reorder his wits and allow him to think as he should. In the end, I accomplished nothing."

"Will he ever again be right?" Inebny demanded.

The physician hesitated, obviously impressed by so mighty a man and desirous of saying what he wanted to hear. But the truth could not be avoided. His eyes fell away from the viceroy, skipped over the commandant, and landed on Bak, a man more easily spoken to. "I've seen this before. Long ago, when first I began to learn my profession in the house of life at the mansion of the lord Amon in Waset. A man was brought in for us all to see. One who had been thrown into a pit of scorpions by a vile trader from the land of Retenu. As punishment for dishonesty, we were told."

His eyes flitted toward Inebny and Thuty, returned to Bak. "When we saw him, ten or so years after the occurrence, he behaved like Governor Djehuty. A child yet not a child, one who confused the passage of time and his place in it." He bit his lip. "The poison. The pain. The shock. I don't know. Maybe in the governor's case, the realization of how much his only child hated him."

He looked at the viceroy at last, his gaze level, his admission frank. "Whatever it was, his wits are addled now and likely always to remain so."

"You are your father's son," Inebny said. "His family, and therefore yours, has held the seat of power in this province for many generations."

"Sir." Ineni stood stiff and straight in front of the dais, his eyes on the viceroy. "I've never wished to be governor, nor do I now. I want only to return to the family estate in Nubt. If, that is, you deem I have the right."

Inebny, seated in Djehuty's armchair, glanced at Bak, who was standing nearby with Imsiba and Thuty. Behind them, crowding the audience hall, was a multitude of people from Abu, Swenet, and farms and villages throughout the province. These men and women from all walks of life had heard their governor was ill. Too ill to ever again occupy the seat of authority. They had come to see for themselves this lofty officer from afar, seeking reassurance that chaos would be averted, justice and order would be maintained, and life would go on as before.

During the two days that had passed since Khawet's death and Djehuty's escape from reality, the viceroy and the officers from Buhen had discussed at length all Bak had learned during his search for the slayer. Now Inebny had to decide how best to use the information, how much he should take to heart, in trying to resolve both provincial and personal affairs. Though outside his realm of responsibility, his rank placed him in charge. The decisions he made would most likely be approved by the vizier.

"Djehuty adopted you as his son, and that you remain." Inebny sat at ease, comfortable with his task. "As his sole heir, the estate is yours by right, and so is the governorship. The latter includes, as you well know, the two villas in Abu and the cultivable land at the north end of this island. You're also entitled to a percentage of the provincial taxes and a share of the tolls paid by passing traders."

The viceroy wore a simple white kilt, a short wig with tight curls, a broad collar of gold and carnelian and turquoise beads, with equally elegant bracelets, armlets, anklets, and rings. A large and muscular Kushite servant stood behind him, stirring the air with a magnificent ostrich-feather fan. The onlookers were suitably impressed, Bak felt sure.

Ineni would not be swayed. "I'm a farmer, sir. I have neither the patience nor the knowledge to sit on that dais and make lawful and wise decisions. Why should I be given a task I'd do poorly when I'd much prefer the task I do well?"

Inebny's mouth twitched as he held back a smile. "Your honesty alone recommends you for the position."

"But, sir . . ."

The viceroy raised a hand, silencing him. "The province will suffer from your abdication, I've no doubt, but I wish you a long and happy life on the estate in Nubt, and many children to succeed you."

Ineni stood still and quiet, slow to comprehend. Then relief wiped away the confusion, the surprise, and set his face alight. "Thank you, sir. Thank you!"

Flashing a brilliant smile at Bak, he swung away and strode in among the crowd, whose startled silence grew to a clamor. Men reached out to clap him on the shoulder, women to squeeze his wrist or hand. They voiced disappointment at the defection of a man whose family they had served for many generations, yet at the same time they showed their delight that this man they liked had been allowed the life he preferred. Inebny looked on, his face expressionless, his eyes aglitter with satisfaction.

As the tumult died down, the scribe responsible for the smooth functioning of the proceedings called the next man on the viceroy's list. "Troop Captain Antef!"

The officer, who had been shocked to hear Khawet was the slayer and appalled by her death, had begun to grow accustomed to the idea that she would never again smile upon him. He stood as straight as Ineni had, as much in command as always. Helping him along, Bak suspected, was the thought that Djehuty would no longer order his troops to inappropriate or degrading tasks.

"This province needs a governor, Troop Captain." Inebny studied the man standing before him with interest. "Is it a position you've ever coveted? Or do you, like Ineni, prefer a task more suited to your talents and training?"

If Antef noticed the viceroy's gentle teasing, he gave no hint. "Sir, may I be bold enough to make a suggestion?"

Inebny leaned forward, eyes narrowing. "Go on, Troop Captain."

"Lieutenant Amonhotep has served as Governor Djehuty's right hand for almost five years. He knows far better than . . . Forgive me, sir, but I must speak with candor." Antef paused, waited for the viceroy's nod. "He knows the laws of our land better than Djehuty ever did, better than I do, better than anyone in this province. And he has the wisdom to uphold those laws in a true and just manner. He, not I, should be appointed governor."

The recommendation silenced the onlookers and took Bak's breath away. He, too, had told Inebny he believed the aide would be a superior governor, much better than Djehuty. But to hear the words uttered by a man such as Antef, who far outranked the young lieutenant, was startling. And refreshing.

"He's very young for so demanding a position," Inebny pointed out, as he had to Bak.

"I'd do all I could to smooth his path, as would the chief steward and chief scribe." Both Amethu and Simut, standing to the right of the dais, voiced enthusiastic agreement. "Of equal importance, he has the respect of the people of this province, that I know for a fact."

A murmur swept through the crowd, grew to a din equaling that for Ineni.

Inebny threw Bak a wry smile. "Can we compromise?"

Antef was slow to answer, suspicious of the viceroy's intent. "Yes, sir?"

"In addition to your present position as commander of this garrison, Troop Captain Antef, I'm appointing you acting provincial governor." Inebny raised both hands, palms forward, staving off the many objections he saw on the faces before him. "Lieutenant Amonhotep will serve as your aide. If you choose to seat him in this chair while you're otherwise occupied at the garrison, so be it."

All who heard understood. The viceroy believed Amonhotep should serve as their governor, and he would take the belief to the vizier in Waset. In the meantime, an older and wiser man must sit on the dais, guiding the younger until the appointment was blessed in the capital. The onlookers cheered outright, not solely for Amonhotep's good fortune and theirs, but for the viceroy as well.

Bak was well satisfied with Inebny's decisions, but he had

mixed feelings about the fate the gods had chosen for
Khawet and Djehuty. Somehow the punishment seemed not
to fit the scale of their crimes. Khawet had slain five people,
yet the gods had taken her life in a single, swift moment.
Djehuty had slain not only Min and Nebmose, but his nonsensical order to his men to hold their places in the caravan's
line of march had led to the death of over one hundred soldiers. Now here he was, returned to childhood, with no
greater care than passing the remainder of his days in ease
and comfort.

Inebny's warship, its mast and yards stripped, sails stowed
belowdeck for the long voyage downstream, rocked gently
on the swells, bumping the landingplace. Mat-like fenders
hung along the hull, preventing the wood from rubbing the
stone. Fittings creaked, pennants fluttered in the chill breeze
of daybreak. A caged leopard, the viceroy's gift for the
queen, snarled at its confinement. The captain stood at the
head of the gangplank, counting the oarsmen filing aboard.
At the stern, the helmsman knelt to examine lashings that
held rudder and tiller in place. The drummer tapped a soft,
nonsensical rhythm on his instrument.

The viceroy, standing at the foot of the gangplank, smiled
at Bak. "You've done a fine job, Lieutenant. The outcome
isn't all I'd hoped for, but you can't be held responsible for
the whims of man and the gods."

"Thank you, sir."

"You've long been due the gold of honor. I'll see that
word reaches the proper ears."

Bak sneaked a wink at Imsiba. He had earned the coveted
golden flies three times before for laying hands on men who
had upset the balance of justice, offending the lady Maat. He
had never been given the reward. For him, more than duty
above and beyond the norm would be necessary. He would
some day have to appease a sovereign he had inadvertently
angered. A woman who quickly forgot, but rarely forgave.

The viceroy raised his baton of office, saluting Commandant Thuty, smiled at Bak and Imsiba, and marched up the

gangplank. A sailor pulled the ramp onto the ship, others released the hawsers attached to the mooring posts and leaped aboard. The drummer settled down to serious rhythm, and the oarsmen rowed the vessel away from the landing-place.

Bak looked at Djehuty's traveling ship, tethered to mooring posts driven into the riverbank a short distance downstream, the same vessel on which he had sailed to Abu, loaned to Thuty for the journey upriver.

"May we now go home to Buhen, sir?" he asked.

"Why the hurry, Lieutenant?" Thuty eyed the close-packed structures across the river. "I've not set foot in a civilized city for close on a year. Didn't you say the trader Pahared, who once plied the waters of the Belly of Stones, has opened a thriving place of business in Swenet? A house of pleasure?"